Anthya's
World

To Julie,
Nice saying hi on the phone.
Hope to meet you one day.
Happy reading!

Anthya's
World

An adventure of mystery
and intrigue spanning the galaxy

Cil Gregoire

Cil Gregoire

PO Box 221974 Anchorage, Alaska 99522-1974
books@publicationconsultants.com—www.publicationconsultants.com

ISBN 978-1-59433-300-2
eBook ISBN 978-1-59433-301-9
Library of Congress Catalog Card Number: 2012942363

Manufactured in the United States of America.

Books by Cil Gregoire

Oracle of Light series:

Crystalline Aura
Anthya's World

THE DEVASTATED CONTINENT

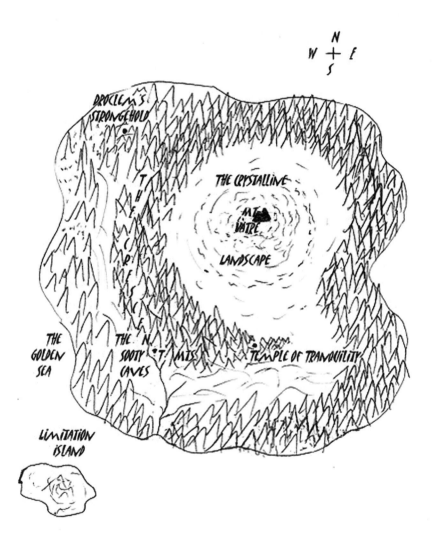

Dedication

To my loving husband
Of forty years,
Who cooked many meals,
So I could
Write.

Contents

Acknowledgments

I express heart-felt thanks to all my reader mentors; Renamary Rauchenstein, John Connolly, Lisa Caldwell, Joseph Gregoire, Samual Gregoire, and Dawn Rinehart who read the manuscript, all or in part, and offered such wonderful advice.

Special thanks to the Red Hot Ravens, Talkeetna's Red Hat Society, for all their wonderful support and encouragement. If it weren't for all the Red Hat skits I was driven to write, Rahlys may never have been born.

Special thanks to Linda Gordon for arranging a memorable road trip up the Dalton Hwy. to Prudhoe Bay and back. The experience served as a major source of inspiration for much of this novel.

And finally, I express my gratitude to all my fans who asked repeatedly for the next book. Here it is; I hope you enjoy it.

Chapter 1
Around the Bonfire

Raven soared above the mighty Susitna River and forest-covered ridges that stretched into rolling hills backed by mountains; he was surveying his domain. The land lay respectfully quiet as Sun dropped low over the western edge, blazing the sky with iridescent pink, orange, and violet behind him. Gradually, the radiant colors faded and the late summer underbrush under towering birch and spruce forest darkened in the diminishing light. The return of night after the long daylight of summer was heralded in by the appearance of First Star.

Raven flew toward the east, following the creek to the bears' favorite fishing spot. Here, the creek bed widened and the shallow waters rippled over the rocky stream bed. His favorite perch, an old birch with a broken top, conveniently overlooked the bounty of tasty tidbits of spawned-out salmon left by the gluttonous bears. Soon, the salmon run would be over and the bears would move into the hills to hibernate, but Raven did not stop to feast. He knew where even more tantalizing tidbits could be found.

Rahlys stepped back from the painting she had been working on, pushing long strands of darkening honey brown hair that used to be blond, now starting to gray, behind her shoulder. With stoic seriousness, she studied her work critically and smiled with satisfaction at the surprised expressions on the black bear and young girl's faces as the two painted figures spot one another across a bountiful crop of berries.

Around the room, rich-with-life paintings depicting scenes of rustic living covered the walls of her log home. Sturdy, stout, home-made counters, cabinets, tables, chairs, and a day bed made from local birch comfortably furnished the large single room downstairs. A stairway, nearly blocked by an overflow of boxes filled with canned goods and painting supplies, led to the bedroom upstairs.

"Aaaaarrrk!"

Images of the sunset flittered through Rahlys' mind as Raven attempted to remind her of the gathering. Maggie and Vince had invited everyone over for a celebration, because today marked the third anniversary of Droclum's defeat and the formation of the Order of the Oracle.

Donning a jacket against the chill of approaching night, Rahlys grabbed some vegetable scraps, leftovers from the salad she made from her own garden to take to the party, and rushed out to greet her familiar. Raven paced about impatiently.

"Yes, I remember about the party," she said, tossing him part of a lettuce stalk. "Ilene is bringing her flute, so there will be music, too. She has been teaching Melinda to play the flute, and tonight they're going to perform a duet they've been practicing." Raven pecked at the lettuce with lackadaisical interest; there would be better pickings at the gathering. *I need to wash out my paintbrushes and change my clothes*, Rahlys thought to herself. *I'll be there shortly*, she reassured Raven as he flew off toward Vince and Maggie's place.

When Rahlys bought Trapper Bean's cabin deep in the woods of the northern Susitna valley, Raven sort of came with it. The lonely trapper had often fed the large black-feathered scavenger meat scraps and the two old-timers had formed a friendly bond. Long after Trapper Bean left the cabin and the woods for the last time, the raven continued to return regularly looking for his lost friend. The raven had visited when Rahlys and Maggie came up on the flag stop train and hiked through the woods to look at the cabin on the market for the first time. Of course, they couldn't resist feeding the curious bird.

Several weeks later, when Rahlys returned as the cabin's new owner, it was Raven who had been there to greet her. And on that same highly eventful day...she also had to chase a bear out of the cabin...the raven snatched up a strange crystal off the river bank, changing their lives forever.

By the time Rahlys teleported over to Vince and Maggie's backyard, the others were already gathered around the bonfire, including Raven, perched in a nearby tree waiting for any tidbits that were forthcoming. The distinct scents of burning wood from a large fire pit and roasting chicken coming from the grill added richness to the fruity smell of the forest.

"I've got you!" Maggie jumped up from the bench and grabbed Leaf, already nearly three, into her arms. Leaf laughed heartily. Sharing the same reddish orange hair and green eyes, there could be no mistaking mother and son. She hugged the little toddler, kissing him on the top of his head, but couldn't confine him for long. Soon, he wanted down so he could join the others gathered around the bonfire. Then Maggie noticed Rahlys.

"Oh, good, you're here! Let me take that," she said, relieving Rahlys of the salad she carried, placing it on the food table.

Friends since college, Maggie came to Alaska when Rahlys returned here after living for many years in Seattle. Rahlys had been raised on her parents' homestead in the Matanuska River Valley. She later left Alaska at the tender age of seventeen to go to art school in Seattle.

Maggie, born and raised in Seattle, had taken the urban greenhorn under her wing. Maggie soon dropped out of school, but Rahlys remained dedicated to her studies, and a hard-earned career as a commercial artist followed. Then after many years of urban living, Rahlys chose to return to a rustic lifestyle in Alaska, working as a freelance artist. At first, Maggie, though adventurous in her own way, didn't take to the idea of living a remote lifestyle without stores and plumbing. But then she met Vince, Rahlys' closest neighbor to the north.

"Here is a seat," Vince said, setting out a lawn chair for her by the warmth of the fire. "The chicken is still a half hour away," he informed her, his solemn brown eyes and graying brown hair giving him a serious demeanor. A rugged outdoorsman, his robust strength hid a gentle nature.

Vince had been certain his life was set when he retired from the Marines and moved to the bush to be alone. After many years of retirement in the woods; hunting, fishing, and writing action/adventure novels based on his experiences in the Marines, Vince had become resigned to a lone existence. Then Rahlys bought Trapper Bean's place and moved in, and her friend Maggie came to visit. Now Vince and Maggie were married with a family neither thought they would ever have, and there was another baby on the way.

"Where's Melinda?" Rahlys asked, looking around, knowing she had to be here, just out of sight.

"She is in the house practicing her flute piece. She is so nervous about performing tonight," Maggie said.

"Can I get you something to drink?" Theon asked, strolling over, clutching a cup in his gnarled hands. "Would you like to try my own brew?"

"Is that what you are drinking?"

"My best batch yet!"

"Can I taste a sip of yours?"

"Why, of course—here," he said offering the cup to her.

Rahlys sniffed the clear liquid closely and drew her nose back. "Whew, smells strong!" Then tilting the cup against her lips, she took the most miniscule sip she could manage. Her resulting shudders and facial expressions sent Theon into rolling laughter. "Didn't I tell you it was good?"

"I pass," Rahlys said when she was able to speak, and handed the cup back to him.

Theon came from a world across the galaxy. He has been living on Earth since the New Stone Age. By his calculations, he is over twelve thousand Earth-years old, an extended longevity even for his world. Theon cultivated many personas over the centuries and today many in the region know him as Half Ear, a low-wit, backwoods wilderness man, missing the top half of his right ear.

"Here, Rahlys, I brought you a glass of wine. I wouldn't drink that stuff either," Ilene said, handing her the glass.

"Thank you. I'm looking forward to the performance."

"It will take place shortly. We were waiting for you to arrive. I feel we should get it over with so Melinda can relax."

Ilene is Theon's daughter, a fact she learned shortly before Droclum's demise. Although Ilene had known Half Ear all her life, her contact with him had been minimal. Her mother had always refused to give her even a clue to her father's identity. Shy and quiet growing up, Ilene lived a wallflower existence, excelling in school, but failing socially. She wasn't ugly, just sort of colorless with frizzy mossy brown hair and quiet dark gray eyes. That all started to change when she discovered Theon, her real father. Over time, Theon taught her to be far more confident, breathing new life into her. Now, Ilene was fun, animated, her dark gray eyes sparkling with interest in everything around her.

"Here she comes now," Ilene said.

"Well, let me give you an introduction." Maggie grabbed two spoons off the food table and began tapping them. "Everyone listen up! We are in for a real treat. For our listening pleasure, Ilene and Melinda will now perform Johann Pachelbel's 'Canon in D' on flute. Let's give them some warm encouragement." Everyone applauded enthusiastically while Melinda and Ilene positioned themselves together a little away from the bonfire.

Melinda played the first run through of the melody, solo, with unfaltering perfection, and then Ilene joined in playing note for note with her. On the third round, Ilene demonstrated her exquisite skills on the flute, accompanying Ilene's melodic melody with broken chords and sweet trills.

Rahlys watched intently as Melinda played. Her warm brown skin, long straight black hair, and almond-shaped dark eyes glowed in the firelight. Melinda was born in Southeast Alaska, growing up in a small native fishing village. When Melinda was still quite young, her mother died, and she and her father lived on their fishing boat, *The Taku*. They were taking shelter from a storm, as they had many times before, in a tiny secluded bay along the coast north of Ketchikan when they encountered Droclum. The encounter had been tragic. Droclum whisked away their boat before squeezing the life out of Melinda's father as Melinda watched helplessly. The horror of the scene left her mute, but her nightmare wasn't over. Droclum took her to his cave, subjecting her to even more horrors. It was Rahlys who finally rescued her from Droclum's evil clutches.

Melinda remains mute even today, but during her captivity, she had somehow acquired telepathic abilities. In the three intervening years, she has grown from an awkward teenager into a graceful young woman, Rahlys realized as the musical piece came to an end.

"Bravo! Bravo!" Theon roared over the applause.

"Tooo…tooo…tooo…tooo," Leaf sang in imitation of the flutes when the performance was over. Theon placed more logs on the fire and Vince turned the chicken on the grill as Rahlys rushed over to praise the musicians.

Anthya approaches.

The Oracle's message took Rahlys by surprise. Reflexively, she touched the colorful beaded pouch hanging from her belt containing the crystal, the Oracle of Light, which had given Rahlys her extraordinary powers. Maggie had beaded the pouch with loving care and much secrecy to replace the leather one that had been destroyed along with Droclum.

"Anthya is coming!" she blurted out to the group. Her announcement brought a quiet lull to the merry chatter.

Anthya! Now, what? The councilor's visits were never inconsequential. Named after the great sorceress and present when the oracle was formed, Anthya was forever linked to Rahlys and the crystal.

"We haven't heard from the councilor since she assured us Quaylyn was recovering. She must want something," Theon said. Though a bit grizzled, he seemed quite robust in the early evening firelight. His mind was always sharply alert and agile, ready to spring into action.

Suddenly, Anthya appeared in the glow of the bonfire.

"Pretty 'ady," Leaf gasped, pointing at the presence with smooth ivory white skin, light gray-blue eyes, and long white-gold hair that had formed out of thin air. Anthya stood before them with a soft smile and a peacefully intelligent gleam in her eyes, her tall slender frame draped in a shimmering lilac gown.

"Greetings, Sorcerer Rahlys, Guardian of the Light," she said, bowing her head slightly, "members of the Order of the Oracle…and Master Leaf," she added, turning toward him.

Anthya rolled her hands in the air and a ball of light appeared before her. She gently blew it toward Leaf, and then turned her attention back to Rahlys. "I bring you greetings from the High Council."

"Greetings, Councilor Anthya," Rahlys said. "It's good to see you again. And what does the High Council want from me now? Is there another evil sorcerer from your world threatening Earth for me to subdue?" She hoped she was being facetious and the High Council of the Crystal Table on Anthya's world had no intention of putting her and her friends in such danger again.

Anthya smiled warmly at Rahlys' candidness and Leaf's delight as he caught the ball of light that drifted into his hands.

"The High Council of the Crystal Table invites you on a mission to the Devastated Continent."

"What? Invites? You mean I have a choice?"

"Of course, but we hope you will accept our invitation." Leaf laughed with glee as he repeatedly threw the ball and watched as it floated back to him.

"How? When? What kind of mission? Humans from Earth do not, as a norm, visit other worlds." Rahlys wanted to get as much information as she could as fast as possible. When appearing in *non-permanent physical time,* as Anthya did, communications tended to be brief. But Anthya's speech was unhurried.

"Not long after Quaylyn came to Earth to help you defeat Droclum, an expedition was sent into the broken lands from the time of the Dark Devastation on our world. That expedition has not been heard from since. With Droclum's destruction, the taint left behind on the land should have dissolved, but we are still unable to communicate or teleport even to the outer limits of that realm. The closest point to the devastated region where the elemental forces are still operative is on an island in the Golden Sea still some distance from the mainland. From there, another expedition is being outfitted to go in search of the seven members of the missing team. You have been invited to join that mission. It is believed that the Oracle of Light, which you possess, may be the key to unlocking the mystery that still grips the continent."

Rahlys struggled to grasp the scope of what Anthya was proposing. "But how…? Travel across the galaxy…?" Her concerns were so monumental she couldn't even put them into words.

"You may choose three of your warriors to accompany you," Anthya offered in lieu of explanations. Rahlys realized that by doing so, she would once again be putting her friends' safety at risk.

"What about Quaylyn? How is he doing?" Rahlys asked. Quaylyn, the son of Droclum and Sorceress Anthya, had been unconscious when Councilor Anthya took him home after Droclum's defeat. Since then, all she had informed the Order was that Quaylyn lived and was recovering slowly.

"He will also be going on the journey to the wastelands. You and the warriors you choose to accompany you must be ready to leave in three Earth-days."

And with that, Anthya and Leaf's glowing ball were gone.

"Wait! What if I choose not to go?" Rahlys cried out.

"Gone." Leaf showed Rahlys his empty hands.

"Yes, Anthya left and took her ball with her."

Rahlys' head was spinning. A journey to another world...how was that possible? She would see Quaylyn again, and he was recovered enough to go on an expedition. Choose three warriors to go with her. Who should she pick to accompany her, assuming she actually went on such a mission?

"Wow! That's incredible. Are you really going to go?" Ilene asked, breaking into her rampaging thoughts.

"Are you?" Vince asked.

"Who are you going to take with you if you do?" Maggie asked.

"Aaaarrrk!" Raven cried in concern.

"You need not worry about the mode of travel," Theon assured them. "It's as safe as driving a car."

"You are going, aren't you?" Ilene asked.

"Yes, well, Anthya didn't leave me much opportunity to say 'No.'"

I'll go with you, Melinda volunteered. Melinda had been listening quietly and Rahlys could sense her desire to go, but she was a child yet.

"So, who *are* you going to take with you?" Maggie asked again.

Rahlys paused before answering. Who *should* she choose to go with her? It didn't take a lot of reasoning. By process of elimination, she ended up with the only possible answer. Maggie was out of the question, she was a busy mother expecting another baby; and she certainly couldn't take Vince away, even though she was certain he would go to protect her if she asked him to. Leaf, of course, is too young to even be considered. Melinda is willing to go, but she's only sixteen, still too young to expose to that kind of danger. That left only Raven, Theon, and Ilene.

Raven was an easy choice to make. He was only a bird, if one could refer to Raven as only a bird, but he could also prove to be quite useful as her familiar. Theon was also a logical choice. He would be going home. His knowledge of the devastated continent would certainly be invaluable, and his often-expressed wish to see his world again before the end of his longevity, which had to be near, would be fulfilled. But Theon would not go without his daughter, Ilene, which would necessarily make her the third companion choice. Ilene was of both worlds, and her developing skills as a healer would also be an asset. But how would she explain her departure to her mother? Elaine was either unaware of Theon's true background, or she simply refused to acknowledge it.

"Well, I strongly feel that Vince and Maggie's responsibility is to their young family, and Maggie will need Melinda's help, especially when the new baby comes." Melinda used to live with Rahlys, but after Leaf was born, she spent so much time at Maggie and Vince's she eventually ended up just staying with them. In anticipation of the expected new arrival, Vince and Maggie had added a large new addition onto the side of the cabin that they now called the children's room, which Melinda and Leaf now shared. "That leaves Theon, Ilene, and Raven."

"Aaaark!" Raven cried in reply.

There was an audible gasp from the assembled group. Of course, Theon would be going home and Ilene was his daughter, but Ilene was from Earth with a human mother. And how would the High Council react to Raven being chosen? He was just a bird, albeit a magically enhanced one, not a person.

"Theon's background knowledge of the area and events leading up to the destruction make him a valuable asset," Rahlys explained. "Plus Ilene should get to know the other world she is descended from. And as Vince has often said, Raven is a hell of a reconnaissance unit." She hoped her reasoning met their approval.

Vince was first to respond. "Of course, Melinda is already a member of the family, and with the new addition, there will be plenty of room for all of us, but are you sure you want to travel across the galaxy by means we can't even fathom?" Rahlys seemed to detect a slight sigh of relief that he would not be pulled away from Maggie and his growing family.

"Rahlys and Ilene can make the journey without undue apprehension, I can assure you. As for me, I will gladly return to my native world if Ilene will accompany me. We just need to figure out what to tell her mother. What do you say, Ilene?" Theon asked his daughter.

Ilene sat speechlessly, her curly, unruly grayish-brown hair tied tightly back in a ponytail. Despite her growing self-confidence, she was hesitant to respond. Travel to another world? She wasn't sure she was hearing right. Of course, she could never let her father go without her. Deprived of a father/daughter relationship most of her life, she was not willing to be separated from him now. If only her mother could accept Theon for who he really is instead of clinging to the false image of the uncultured oaf she envisioned him to be.

"I don't know," Ilene said quietly to stares all around, "I guess so."

Chapter 2
Saying Goodbye

Ilene's mother, Elaine, was busy in her gift shop on Main Street when she heard the train whistle in the near distance. The little railroad-stop town served as the closest source of supplies by train or riverboat for the vast remote region beyond the end-of-the-road community. She looked up from her task of dusting and rearranging her stock of mostly locally made items.

Ilene will be home shortly from her trip up the tracks, she sighed with relief. Her daughter seemed changed from just a couple of years ago. Although the change had been somewhat gradual, it was undeniably profound. What had become of the quiet, withdrawn, self-doubting young woman she once knew? The change was for the better, but what had been the catalyst, she couldn't help wondering. She gazed at the paintings on display by the artist Ilene so frequently went by train to visit. Somehow, there was a connection.

Her daughter had never been especially pretty. Her grayish brown eyes and frizzy hair had always seemed a bit lifeless, but now, her eyes sparkled. Elaine looked at her own tired, worn face and graying hair in the mirror by a display of knitted hats and scarves. She hadn't had much in the line of beauty to offer a daughter, and as for Ilene's father...she couldn't go there...it was best to pretend he didn't exist.

Surprisingly, just a few years ago, her daughter had been romantically involved with an exceedingly handsome young man. Although he was a bit cold...she could see it in his eyes. Tragically, he had been mauled to death by a bear, which was one reason why she worried when her daughter was up in the woods. Elaine was jarred from her thoughts at the sound of the shop door opening. She expected to see Ilene, but instead it was an out-of-town customer coming in to browse.

Ilene stepped off the train, pack in hand, and glanced around unseeing, deep in contemplation. She was about to leave on an unimaginable journey to a distant world, and somehow she had to explain what was about to happen to her mother. This was not going to be easy.

Shouldering her pack, Ilene passed a fleeting glance over the quaint little town as she ambled across the nearly deserted park, a sadness settling in her heart. The park was usually a hub of activity during the fast-paced summer months, but the cool rainy season and the appearance of the first golden leaves of autumn had heralded a retreat of tourists to warmer climates, and the locals to the warm coziness of indoors. She walked unhurriedly by an inn, a tavern, and the general store, buildings as old as the town itself, and then onto Main Street, thankful that she hadn't run into anyone that would require her to stop and socialize.

"There you are," her mother greeted warmly as she held the door open for a graying middle-aged couple leaving with bags of purchased goods in hand.

"Thanks," the gentleman nodded in passing, the lady merely nodding her head.

"How was your weekend?" Elaine asked as Ilene closed the door and dropped her pack to the floor.

"It was great, and yours? I see you've done a little business."

"A few customers are still drifting in. That'll change as soon as the snow flies. So what did you do?"

"Huh?" Ilene absentmindedly straightened the lace on a homemade doll, lost in her own train of thought. Elaine couldn't help noticing her daughter seemed a bit distracted for some reason.

"Up in the woods, this weekend, what did you do?"

"Oh, well, we had a barbecue at Maggie and Vince's place, and Melinda and I performed together on the flute. Our duet was a smashing success."

Elaine knew that Maggie and Vince were Rahlys' neighbors, and Melinda was Rahlys' mute niece, but where she came from and why she lived with Rahlys was not clear.

"Mom, I would like to invite Theon to dinner tomorrow night."

"Who?"

"Theon...Half Ear, you know who I'm talking about."

Elaine gasped audibly. "Why,...whatever for?"

"You won't have to do anything," Ilene quickly jumped in. "I will plan and prepare the meal, and clean up afterwards." Her stomach tied up in knots at the look of horror on her mother's face, but now that she had broached the subject, she wasn't letting go. "Please, it is very important to me."

"If you are concerned about Half Ear being fed, you can always take leftovers to him. You don't have to invite him here. Are you sure he is even in town? He may be up the tracks."

"He'll be here tomorrow night."

"How do you know?"

"Because he was at the barbecue."

For reasons Elaine could not begin to comprehend, Half Ear was also part of the group Ilene was hanging out with. Ilene's friendship with Half Ear made Elaine feel very uneasy.

Before Elaine could think of what to say next, Ilene spoke up, "Thanks so much, Mom," kissed her on the cheek, grabbed her pack, and ran out the door and up the stairs to their apartment above the shop.

"I don't like this," she heard her mother call after her, but Ilene did not stop.

Upon reaching her bedroom, Ilene shut the door, dropped her pack, flung herself on her bed, and breathed a deep sigh of somewhat relief. At least she had made it across the first hurdle.

Her eyes roamed about her tidy room, surveying the curtains, walls, and the matching furniture. It was too girlishly decorated, she realized as she glared at lacy pink curtains and flower print wallpaper. *This room is not me, but what my mother wants me to be. I will give the room a bold makeover when I return.* If she returned, of course, was a distinct possibility. A journey as unheard of as the one she was about to embark on offered no guarantees of a safe return. *Am I really looking at my room for the last time?...and saying goodbye to my mother forever?* Tears welled up blurring her vision, but she quickly wiped them away.

She jumped up and reached under her bed, pulling out the painting she kept there, not so much hidden as out of sight. For better viewing, she propped it up against her pillows. The painted image of a crystal left its position on a snow-covered spruce bough in snowy woods on a dusky night, and floated out as a hologram image glowing softly with multi-colored light. Some of the oracle's magic must have seeped into the canvas when Rahlys painted it, for the holographic crystal was no ordinary hologram.

What do you know about Anthya's World? Ilene asked her crystalline mentor telepathically. The crystal blazed a trail of light through the air, forming letters.

LOTS.

The word sparkled and glittered for a few moments then faded away. Asking such broad questions did not elicit useful, specific information. She tried again.

Can a human from Earth such as myself go there and live to tell about it? Without hesitation, the crystal scribed its answer in a sizzling, fiery display.

YES.

Once again, the letters momentarily glowed before her before slowly dissipating. Ilene could hear her mother entering the apartment, and to her surprise, her mother's footsteps continued without pause to her bedroom door. At the sound of her mother's knock, the crystal reentered the painting. For the first time ever, Ilene did not attempt to stash the painting back under her bed.

"Come on in," Ilene said unhurriedly.

Elaine entered. Ilene could see she was still agitated over the impending dinner guest tomorrow night. "Ilene, we really should discuss this more…" her speech trailed off as her gaze moved to the painting.

Elaine recognized the work; it hung on the gallery wall for a time. She remembered experiencing a vague uneasiness whenever she looked at it, and a feeling of relief when it was finally sold. The handsome boyfriend, later mauled to death by a bear, had purchased it and eventually gave it to Ilene. She figured her daughter kept it under her bed because it was a painful reminder of him. Perhaps enough time had finally passed for her heartbreak to have healed and she was ready to place it on her wall.

"Can I hang this up in the living room?" Ilene asked.

"In the living room? Why not over your bed?"

"I don't want to hide it anymore. In the living room we can both enjoy it."

"Sure, I guess so," Elaine agreed reluctantly. "Let's go find a place for it."

Ilene didn't know what had possessed her to make such a suggestion as she followed her mother into the living room, carrying the painting. Several fine paintings by local artists hung on the walls, but so far, none by Rahlys. They both did a visual sweep around the room looking for a suitable spot, when Elaine walked over to the wall by the front door that led to the entrance into the kitchen.

"How about over here? We could move the clock somewhere else," she said, lifting the clock off its nail, producing sufficient space for the painting. Ilene stepped up and placed the wire hanger over the existing nail, straightened the frame until it looked level, then stepped back to get a better view. "It needs to drop down just a tad on that end," Elaine said, pointing to the right corner. Ilene made the minute adjustment. "There, that's perfect."

Mother and daughter stared in mutual admiration at the iridescent glow of the crystal's light on the sparkling snow. The painting had a three-dimensional look about it and the glow of the crystal seemed to admit a little light into the room. Elaine resisted an urge to reach out and touch it.

With mounting fear, Ilene speculated on her mother's reaction to seeing the crystal actually leave the painting, but for now, the crystal remained in place. Would it eventually reveal its true nature to her mother? That would be minor compared to the revelations she and Theon were prepared to make.

Leafy! Where are you? Melinda called mentally, casually searching through the tall brush for her young charge as she absentmindedly brushed away tiny annoying black flies that gathered around her almond brown eyes and small oval face.

Here.

Here, where?

Melinda felt his response in her mind, but couldn't see him. With berry bucket in hand, she waded through the late summer growth of heavily laden high bush cranberry bushes, fireweed stalks mottled red, green, and brown, its once bright red flowers bloomed out and turned to seed fluff drifting on the air currents, and tall grass with purplish seed heads waving in the breeze. Plump ripe rosehips and juicy high-bush cranberries gleamed red in the warm late-August sunshine, their fruity aroma permeating the air of the forest.

Unable to locate the toddler, Melinda felt for his familiar signature, searching through the brush around her, but Leaf was not there. With growing concern, she mentally widened her search…still not finding him. Panic flooded over her. Dashing about frantically looking for him, she tripped and dropped her pail of huckleberries.

Where?

A mile away as the raven flies, Rahlys put the final touches on the painting of the bear and the girl. Sensing a presence behind her, she turned quickly.

"Leaf Bradley, how did you get here?"

"Rah…ess!" the carrot-topped toddler beamed, his arms stretched out in gleeful greeting. Purplish blueberry juice and pulp stained his hands, face, denim overalls and plaid shirt.

"Beerr…eees!" Leaf exclaimed, offering Rahlys a handful of squished berry pulp and juice oozing between his fingers. Before Rahlys could respond to Leaf's generous offering, she picked up on Melinda's urgent message.

Rahlys, is Leaf with you?

Yes, he's right here. He brought me some berries. Rahlys felt Melinda's sigh of relief.

He just disappeared on me. Wow! Leaf can teleport!

That does seem to be the case.

Can you bring him back before Maggie and Vince find out?

I'll bring him back as soon as I get the berry juice off his hands.

But what do I tell Maggie and Vince? Rahlys could feel Melinda's concern, and rightly so. A ward of the Order of the Oracle, Melinda was a big sister to Leaf. Unable to speak vocally, she had spoken with him mentally from the time he was born. Maggie herself had often communicated with her infant son this way, for she could better sense his needs through thought impressions than from his crying.

Try telling them the truth...without scaring them too much. Toddlers were by reputation hard to keep track of, but Leaf's parents were going to be doubly challenged keeping tabs on a toddler who could teleport.

I'll do what I can.

Turning her attention to Leaf, Rahlys grabbed a clean sheet of watercolor paper, "Oh, thank you so much for the berries. Let's try making a picture with them."

"Picture," he said in all eagerness, for Rahlys had painted with him before.

Placing the paper on the floor, she bent over, him holding his little arms out to prevent the further spread of berry juice as she gently lowered his bottom to the floor. "We'll make a picture of Leaf's hands."

"Picture," he piped again in agreement. Rahlys rubbed his little chubby hands together to evenly spread the berry juice, and then placed his hands on the paper.

"Press hard," she directed, and Leaf put his bodyweight into it as Rahlys helped him press his hands onto the paper. When she let go, he lifted them up, revealing two bluish purple handprints.

"Good job!" Rahlys reassured him.

"Pretty!" Leaf exclaimed, pointing to the impression with purple-stained fingers.

"Yes, very pretty," Rahlys had to agree. "Now, let's see about getting you cleaned up."

She poured warm water into a pan from the recently refilled kettle on the woodstove, grabbed soap, a clean washcloth, and a towel, and set the items on a chair so Leaf could reach them.

"Hot," Leaf said, pointing to the pan with serious concern.

"No, it's not hot, just warm." Leaf edged over to the pan on the chair and with dramatic caution, touched the water with one finger, jerking it back quickly. Then deciding the water temperature was tolerable, he politely submitted to the wash up.

Rahlys, is Leaf all right? Rahlys detected a bit of dismay and panic in Maggie's telepathed message. *Melinda said he teleported himself to you!*

Yes, Maggie, he's fine. You have a talented little lad here.

How am I ever going to keep track of him if he can just teleport himself anywhere he wants to go?

We are going to have to get across to him that he can't just go off somewhere without telling anyone. Fortunately, he can only go to places he can picture in his mind.

Are you certain?

Rahlys was fairly certain, but let it go.

We'll be there shortly. I'm washing berry juice off his hands. "Your mommy and Melinda are worried about you, Leaf," Rahlys explained to the toddler as she dried his hands. "You should never just leave whoever is looking after you without permission. If something were to happen to you, it would break our hearts."

"Break heart?" Leaf asked, puzzled.

"Yes, because we love you so very, very much, our hearts would break from sadness if anything bad happened to you."

"What bad happen?"

"Well, someone could steal you away from us...or something could come along like a big mean bear or a big bad wolf and eat you up. Or you could fall and hurt yourself and we wouldn't know how or where to find you."

"Oh...."

Rahlys couldn't help but smile when his usually merry green eyes reflected serious concern. *I'm going to miss so much by leaving,* she realized as she disposed of the huckleberry-tainted wash water.

"Paint," Leaf broke into her thoughts. By now, he was climbing up on the table to get to her paints.

"Wait, I'll set you up on the floor."

Averting a watercolor disaster just in time, Rahlys lifted the youth off the table and lowered him to the floor where she provided him with paper and watercolor pencils, then sat down beside him to keep him focused. Adding an occasional stroke to hold his interest, she thought about the journey ahead of her. How long would she be gone, and what would she encounter there? She tried to recall the descriptions Quaylyn had provided them of his world, while trying to suppress the fear and uncertainty gnawing at the pit of her stomach. Leaf quickly lost interest in drawing and Rahlys teleported them to Maggie and Vince's yard.

"We're here," Rahlys announced, opening the door. An inviting comfort-food aroma assailed her nose. The wood-burning cook stove burned hot with pies in the oven and a moose pot roast simmering on top of the stove. Steam seeped out from under the lid of the pot, gathering as moisture on the windows, screening out the approaching nightfall.

"Oh, Leaf!" Maggie cried, giving her little son a thankful hug. "You gave us such a scare. Even Mommy and Daddy let someone know where they are going before leaving."

"Sorry."

"Don't ever just leave like that again," Maggie said, giving him another hug.

"I won't," Leaf said, his voice full of contrition.

"What do you have here?" she asked, pointing to the painting he clutched in his hand. Leaf handed it to her.

"Picture...hands," he said, showing her his still slightly blue hands in explanation.

"How pretty! Good job! We'll tack it up in our art gallery," Maggie said, indicating a wall already overburdened with children's art.

Vince stuck his head in at the door. "Melinda! Leaf! Chores!"

Leaf ran circles around Melinda, playing airplane as she came out of the children's room. Melinda greeted Rahlys, and then helped Leaf into his jacket, handed him a water pitcher, and ushered him out the door.

"Thank you, Sweetie," Maggie called out to Melinda in heartfelt appreciation as she closed the door behind them.

"What am I going to do about Leaf?" Maggie moaned when the house was quiet again.

"He can only go to places that he can clearly picture in his mind," Rahlys reassured her again, "and in his short lifetime, that isn't very many places."

"Let's hope you're right. We're going to have to watch him extra closely... and hope nothing happens to him before we can find him, should he try something like that again," Maggie said, stirring the steaming pot and adding water. Then she filled two coffee cups and they sat at the table in her toasty warm kitchen.

"I can't believe you are leaving? Are you sure you really want to do this? There could be a lot of risk involved here. Forget 'could be,' there will almost certainly be a lot of risk involved."

"I have to go. I know it may be dangerous, but I can't let Anthya and the Council of the Crystal Table down. We thought events ended with Droclum's destruction, but there are some loose ends still. Besides, I haven't done much with my talents. I feel guilty about that. I have all these powers; I should be doing more to right the wrongs in the world. Instead, all I do is hide out in the woods and paint."

"Now, don't be hard on yourself. When did all the problems in the world become yours to solve? What do you want to do, hang out at airports and intercept terrorists? You saved the world once. I was counting on you being here when the baby comes."

"Maybe I'll be back by then."

"In two months? I doubt it." There was a quiet lull as the close friends contemplated a long separation.

"You will see Quaylyn again," Maggie said, her frown turning into a smile.

Rahlys often thought of Quaylyn over the years. Quaylyn had been sweetly boyish, but lionhearted too, a little irritating at times, yet an endearing soul. Sent to Earth by the High Council of the Crystal Table, his mission had been to train Rahlys in the use of her powers and help her to defeat Droclum. What Quaylyn didn't know at the time was that he was also Sorceress Anthya and Droclum's son. Droclum had defiled his mother, and while Quaylyn was still an infant, stole him from his mother in the Temple of Tranquility. Centuries later, the child was found by the first expedition to the Devastated Continent, encapsulated in suspended animation.

"We have a favor to ask," Maggie said, reaching for something on the table. "Vince and I have written Quaylyn a letter and would like for you to deliver it for us."

Quaylyn had spent a lot of time visiting with Maggie and Vince, eating Maggie's good cooking and debating political philosophy with Vince. Sometimes, he visited them to give Rahlys much needed space.

"By all means; of course, I will," Rahlys said, taking the sealed envelope.

Vince entered the cabin carrying in a blue five-gallon plastic container of water followed closely by his young helpers, Leaf and Melinda. Almost immediately, Leaf placed his quart size pitcher of water down on the floor.

"Heavy," he said dramatically, pointing to the pitcher of water.

Wimp, Melinda telepathed teasingly as she passed by him with an armload of wood for the cook stove.

"Good job, everyone!" Maggie praised them heartily. She went over and picked up the water pitcher, placing it on the table, and then helped Leaf out of his jacket.

Rahlys noted that Maggie was the picture of contentment, thriving on family life. Despite the fulfillment she derived from painting, she sometimes felt her own life lacked some hard core purpose in comparison. It hadn't always been that way. There had been a time when she viewed herself as being the one full of purposeful drive while Maggie lived the life of a free spirit. How things had changed!

"Dinner is still a half hour away," Maggie announced to expectant faces.

Can we watch a movie while the generator is on?

"You can start a movie, but I don't want any arguments about putting it on pause when dinner is ready." Leaf took off at a run into the next room to pick out his favorite DVD, Melinda following to help him put it in the player. Vince looked over at the computer, debating whether or not to get right to work on his fifth novel, but joined Rahlys and Maggie at the table instead.

"So, you are still going?" he asked Rahlys, settling into a chair.

"Yes."

Vince could hear the decisiveness in her voice and knew her mind was made up. "I wish you luck. I can't say we won't worry about you. A very strong part of me wants to go with you and protect you on this journey, but my love needs me." He reached over to Maggie and touched her hand. "My family is the most important thing in my life now."

"Yes, it is, and it is important to me that you stay here with Maggie, since I won't be here to help her."

"I need to take the pies out the oven and put the bread in," Maggie said, rising from her chair.

"I'll do it, you take a break," Vince said getting up.

"Well, at least I know you are in good hands."

———————

The next day, Melinda and Theon were working together on a science project of their own making, a machine that would generate electricity using cold air as fuel. The cold generator was set up on the rustic ax-hewn table Theon had made for the little guest cabin in the woods behind Rahlys' house. The cabin, originally constructed to house Quaylyn when he was here, was now used as a schoolhouse for Melinda and a place for Theon or Ilene to stay when they spent the night.

I don't want you to leave.

"I will miss you, too," Theon reassured her.

You don't understand. There won't be anyone left here once you and Rahlys and Ilene are gone. Who will be my teachers? Even Raven is leaving! It's going to be so boring around here.

She looked up at him with mournful eyes. "Melinda, one thing in life is certain: There will always be change. You learn to live with it, grow with it, and find new focuses."

I want to go with you.

"But you can't leave now. Maggie and Vince and Leaf need you. If you are having feelings of abandonment by our leaving, then imagine how Leaf will feel with you gone...especially after the new babies arrive."

Babies?

"Yes, well, I didn't want to say anything, but I seem to detect two signatures developing in Maggie's womb. I don't recommend you say anything to Maggie, though; it's not our place to do so...and I could be wrong. We wouldn't want to alarm her unnecessarily." Theon gave Melinda their secret-sharing wink and turned back to setting the power crystal in place.

Melinda struggled to turn her attention back to the cold generator they were working on. According to Theon, it was almost complete. It looked nothing like the diesel generators Vince and Rahlys used. For one thing, it was so light and small she could carry it around herself. What looked like an ordinary crystal sat in an elaborate metal wire frame set on a wooden base large enough to house a plug-in receptacle. The inner support frame that held the crystal was mounted on swivels.

But how does it work?

"There is molecular energy stored in all forms of matter, but the energy stored in crystals is the most efficient to harness. I've programmed the molecular structure of the crystal to release a minuscule amount of stored energy when fueled by cold. The crystal will convert energy released by contraction in severe cold to electrical energy we can use. I believe we are ready to test it," he said, making sure everything was in place.

But it isn't winter yet.

"We will create winter. Here, plug that end of this extension cord into that lamp by the bed and I will plug this end into the generator. Don't forget to turn the lamp on."

Melinda plugged in the lamp and turned it on, and then watched as Theon concentrated on the air around the generator, steadily lowering its temperature. Soon, frost crystals began to form on the window, the table, and the metal framework around the crystal as the super cooled air lost its ability to hold moisture. The metal frame around the crystal snapped and popped as it contracted, and the crystal began to spin and glow softly. Then, suddenly, the lamp across the room came on.

It works! Melinda clapped her hands gleefully.

"Of course it works. Didn't you expect it to?"

Melinda was sure there was not another teacher like Theon in the entire world. While scientists may be pondering ways to harvest energy from cold in a lab somewhere, she doubted there were many teachers building working cold generators in the classroom.

"Now, this winter when it drops below zero, put this outside and plug the cabin into it, and you will have electricity. The colder it gets, the more energy it will produce, but the crystal can store any excess power, sort of like a car battery. So you may still draw electricity for a while after it warms up."

Theon ceased lowering the air temperature around the generator, and began warming it back up to the ambient temperature in the room. Gradually, the crystal slowed down its spinning and became less bright. The frost around the generator melted, and the lamp went out.

How long will you be gone? Melinda asked, returning to the topic uppermost in her mind.

Theon gazed down at Melinda's youthful, inquisitive countenance with painful regret. "I don't know. It could be a long time…maybe forever. I have outlived my expected longevity by centuries. I can't have too much time left."

Melinda knew that Theon was old. Not as old as the stars and the mountains, but older than the pyramids and Stonehenge. Her eyes welled up with tears and she fought back the urge to cry. She could not imagine never seeing Theon again.

"Now, now, cheer up." He could sense Melinda's stress. "I'm not gone yet. And I do believe Rahlys has cooked up a fine pot of spruce grouse stew for our dinner. Why, I can smell it from here. Um, um! What do you say we go and check on its progress?"

A gray cloud sheet brought in by a freshening breeze blanketed the sky as they made their way through the little stretch of woods leading to Rahlys' cabin. The breeze darted and dashed through the tops of the trees, making the yellowing birch leaves jiggle. It smelled of rain, not spruce grouse dinner, Melinda reflected. Then Raven flew overhead cawing loudly, projecting images to their minds of the forested hills and valleys tinged with fall, the underbrush tall, but spent, with the waning of summer.

"Aaaarrrk! Aaaaaa!"

He landed on the branch of a nearby birch tree. "What's gotten you so riled up, my fine-feathered friend?" Theon asked, scanning the surrounding woods and finding nothing alarming.

"Klaaawock!" Raven gurgled deep in his throat.

Melinda and Theon understood. Raven was also leaving soon; leaving Melinda, Leaf, Maggie, and Vince; leaving the mighty river, the familiar forests, mountains, and streams. Leaving, maybe forever, this place he called home.

After dinner, Melinda, still in a melancholy mood, strolled down to the rocky edge of the creek that flowed below Rahlys' cabin. Raven soon joined her, his powerful wings swooshing air as he sped by. Circling around, he landed in a nearby tree.

I don't want you to leave, Melinda telepathed to him, the message burdened with her sadness.

"Aaaaaa...," Raven gurgled in return, his sentiments equally sad.

Disheartened, Melinda strolled over the rocks along the edge of the stream, staring down at them with little interest. *It's going to be so boring around here with everyone gone. Why did Anthya have to ruin everything? She should have stayed away,* Melinda pouted.

"Aaaaarrrk!" Raven called, breaking into her thoughts. From his perch above the creek, he sent Melinda an image of a perfectly round golden stone he spotted under the water. Melinda's line of sight from the rocks on shore made finding the stone a bit harder, but finally she located it in shallow water, a couple of feet out. With little thought to the icy cold water, Melinda stripped off her shoes and socks, rolled up her pants legs to her knees, and waded in, stepping cautiously over the slippery rocks, the intense cold of the water numbing her feet. Two steps in, after pushing up her sleeve to prevent it from getting wet, she quickly reached into the babbling creek, grabbed the stone, and hurried back to shore. Sitting on the dry rocks away from the stream bed, she dried off her feet with her jacket, and put on her socks and shoes. They felt wonderful on her cold feet!

I wonder where it came from, Melinda pondered, rolling the smooth stone between her fingers. She gazed into the luminously translucent golden stone, searching its depths for hidden worlds...clues to its origin...but the orb revealed no secrets. Dropping it into a pocket of her jeans, she climbed back up the hill to Rahlys' cabin.

———

The train whistle finally blew around the bend, signaling its approach. Ilene, dressed in jeans and a brown cotton flannel shirt, huddled against the wall of the train-stop shelter, shivering from the cold drizzle and chilly breeze.

She should have worn a jacket, but refusing to let summer go, convinced herself she didn't need it. Now she regretted her decision, for the train ended up being late as usual and she was damp from the rain.

The train lights appeared around the bend and the engineer blew the whistle again. It squealed to a stop with the passenger exit and baggage car door aligned with the unloading platform, and hunters and weekenders, all dressed for the rugged outdoors, disembarked. Ilene spotted Theon in the baggage compartment, in the guise of Half Ear, conversing with the plump jolly conductor.

"I'm telling you, that dried moose there is the best you will ever have," Half Ear said, pushing a package into the hands of the surprised conductor. "I guarantee it."

"Well, thanks. You're in a good mood today," the conductor said, graciously accepting the gift. "What's the occasion?"

"Just expressing my gratitude." Half Ear paused as though carefully choosing his next words. But "Take care," was all he said, in a rare contemplative moment for the persona he was portraying. He patted the conductor on the shoulder and climbed out of the boxcar. Ilene noticed he descended with less agility than she'd seen in the past.

"Hello, my pretty!" he greeted Ilene jovially. "Where's your jacket?"

"Poor judgment on my part; I didn't think I needed it." Ilene felt the air around her warming and knew Theon was expending energy, energy he shouldn't have to expend, to keep her warm, which made her regret even more leaving her jacket behind.

"How's your mother doing? Have you told her anything?"

"Not yet. I know she is dreading dinner tonight. So am I," Ilene added as an afterthought.

"What? Don't like my company?"

"You know that's not true." She hooked her arm into his, not caring who may be watching, and leaned against him fondly.

Elaine heard them coming up the stairs and met them at the door. "Good evening, John," she greeted him as she held the door open.

"Good evening, Elaine. But you know my name is not John. And it's not Half Ear either," he added quickly before she could speak.

"All right," she said, barely over a whisper, waving them inside before anyone could overhear. "And what should I call you?" she asked, closing the door behind them."

"Call me Theon. My name is Theon."

What followed started out as an awkward moment, but soon ended with a startled shriek from Elaine as the crystal drifted out of the painting. Elaine stared in wide-eyed shock at the hologram glowing softly, suspended in the air.

"Now, now, it's all right," Theon said, embracing Elaine gently. "It's just a harmless spell. Rahlys imbued a tiny bit of her magic into the painting when she painted it; she didn't even realize it was happening at the time."

"Rahlys...? Magic...?"

"Oh, yes, Rahlys is a powerful sorceress." Theon said, leading Elaine to the sofa and sat down beside her....Ilene took her cue and exited to the kitchen to finish up dinner.

"What does all this have to do with my daughter?" Elaine asked, fighting to calm herself.

"Our daughter," Theon corrected her, raising her anxiety level again. "Our daughter and a fine daughter she is, too."

"You really expect me to believe that my daughter is half alien? I know something is going on between you and Ilene, and I want to know what you are keeping secret," Elaine stated bravely.

"Let me give you a little more background information first. Then Ilene and I can announce our surprise over dinner." Theon patted her hand reassuringly. She did not try to move it away.

"As I was saying, Rahlys is a sorceress, and the real crystal, that's just a portrait of it," he said, pointing to the floating image, "brought the Oracle of Light which gave Rahlys her powers so she could defeat Droclum, a truly foul sorcerer." Elaine stared at Theon with startled incredulity.

"Droclum used to be my boss," he said as an afterthought. Alarm joined the startled incredulous look on Elaine's face.

"No, no, don't worry! I'm one of the good guys now. I helped Rahlys destroy Droclum."

"What about that thing there?" Elaine asked, pointing to the floating image of the crystal.

"That thing? Little more than a child's toy. Watch, I'll ask it a question. What is my name?" he asked the crystal. The crystal blazed into action, burning letters into the air.

THEON.

The answer sparkled before them, and then slowly dissipated. Elaine could only gasp.

"You try it. Ask the crystal something simple like, what are we having for dinner?"

Elaine hesitated, but then cooperated by mumbling, "What are we having for dinner?" She looked toward the glowing, spinning apparition with expectation, but nothing happened.

"No, no, not like that. Put your mind into it. In fact, you don't even need to use spoken words. Relax, focus on the crystal, connect with it, and then ask the question in your mind. Elaine took a deep breath and focused on the hologram as best she could, trying to connect.

What are we having for dinner? she asked in her mind, and felt a slight tingling sensation in her brain. The crystal twirled into action, blazing letters across the room.

CHICKEN CACCIATORE.

"Um! Smells good, too. You see, the crystal can tell what is known, but it has no ability to predict the future. For example, now, ask the crystal when you will die, and see what kind of answer you get."

"Huh?" Elaine gasped and jumped back, out of Theon's grasp. "I'll do no such thing!"

"Okay, okay. Then ask it when *I* will die, if you are worried about the answer, and see what it says.

Still reluctant, Elaine struggled to concentrate on the spinning light. *When will Theon die?* she asked, again feeling the unusual brain sensation, unaware that Theon was helping her communicate. The crystal responded immediately, giving its sparkling answer.

UNKNOWN.

The word melted away as Ilene entered the room. "Dinner is ready!" she announced cheerfully.

Cozily seated at the little table by the kitchen window with Theon in the middle looking out at the darkening night and her mother at one end, Ilene sat opposite from her. Lacking a separate dining room, Ilene had done all she could to achieve elegance in the tiny space available. The table was covered with a delicate white tatted tablecloth, and had been set with fine china, silver salt, pepper shakers, and linen napkins in silver napkin holders her mother kept stored away at the back of the cabinets and never used. Two silver candlesticks with lighted candles supplemented the light across the room to provide subdued lighting.

The meal was exquisite, the conversation safe, and they were enjoying a second glass of fine red wine before the real topic at hand was finally broached.

"So what is this surprise you were going to tell me about?" Elaine asked, bursting the bubble of contentment that surrounded them.

After a pregnant moment of silence, Theon started to speak, "Elaine…"

"No...it's my responsibility from here," Ilene said, surprising even herself. Theon graciously bowed out, giving Ilene the floor. "Mother...Father and I are going on a trip...to a place far, far away, to another world across the galaxy...Father's homeland."

Elaine gripped her chest, unable to breathe. Then, finally, she took air into her lungs. "I'll never see you again," she gasped to her daughter.

"Now, Elaine, that isn't true," Theon spoke up. "Ilene will be gone a year maybe, two at the most." Elaine did not look consoled. Ilene hated to see her mother suffer so, but she had suffered, too, and there was no turning back now.

"I have learned a lot about who I am since discovering Theon is my father, the father you denied I had and kept secret from me all these years."

"I was only trying to protect you."

"Protect me from what? A father's love and protection?"

"I just wanted you to have a normal life. I was protecting you from ridicule and harassment."

"You denied half my existence!"

"I only wanted what was best for you! I love you."

"I love you, too, Mom, but now it is time for me to find out who I really am."

"By trekking across the universe? How? How will you do this?"

"We will travel in *permanent physical time*," Theon explained. "It will take about three Earth days."

"What...? When...?"

"We leave tomorrow," he said.

"Tomorrow...? Just like that?"

"Just like that."

"What will you tell people? How will you explain your absence?"

"Actually, since we will be gone, *you* will have to explain our absence," Theon rationalized. "You could claim Ilene has gone off to school somewhere. As for me, I'll hardly be missed. If anyone should ask, you could tell them you don't really know...which would be true enough. Since I will teleport Ilene and myself to our rendezvous tomorrow, the train conductor will report, if questioned, that I was last seen coming into town, so there shouldn't be much of a search for me in the woods."

"You're leaving me?" Elaine moaned, turning toward her daughter. "Tomorrow...?" She had taken in little of Theon's speech, lost as she was in the struggle to comprehend and accept.

"Only for a while, I'll be back, I promise." Overcome with emotion, Ilene hurried over to her mother, put her arms around her, and cried on her shoulder. They held each other tightly and cried deeply as they forgave each other for past transgressions both real and imagined.

Theon sat quietly, and patiently waited. When they were cried out, he refilled their glasses with the remaining wine.

"So let us celebrate the undertaking of a grand adventure, and I will tell you all about home. Of course, I haven't been there for a while, but surely some things haven't changed."

Putting on a brave smile, Elaine lifted her wine glass, joining Theon and Ilene in a toast. "To a grand adventure!" Theon proposed.

"To a grand adventure!"

Chapter 3
Anthya's World

Across the great bulging center of the Milky Way galaxy, safely nestled between two of its spiraling radial arms of stars and star-making materials, a yellow sun, half again the mass of Sol, provides a wide habitable zone for its one orbiting planet. Basking in the heat of its glorious sun, the golden planet, slightly more massive than Earth, boasts of oceans, land masses, and life.

Over hundreds of thousands of Earth-years, the intelligent life-forms evolved mentally, learning to use the neurons and processing power of their brains to do work by drawing molecular energy from the elemental forces around them. Of course, ability varied, and eventually power turned to greed...until nearly twelve thousand Earth-years ago, greed led to the near destruction of their world. Like a dog scratching at unwanted fleas, the entire planet shuddered with Mt. Vatre's violent eruptions, nearly eradicating life altogether, totally transforming one land mass now known as the Devastated Continent.

Unreachable by teleportation, the new virgin territory remained vastly unexplored for thousands of Earth-years. Descendant from the handful of human survivors of the Dark Devastation, Sarus, had the honor of leading the second expedition from the now known world to the vastly unknown on the other side of the globe. The first expedition launched by the Academy to the Devastated Continent hundreds of Earth-years earlier reached inland only as far as the Crescent Mountains, sharp, unassailable peaks that curved protectively around the interior of the continent. But the goals of Sarus' expedition had been far more aggressive. Its targeted destination had been Mt. Vatre itself, or what was left of it, far beyond the Crescent Mountains.

A dull throbbing in his head brought Sarus slowly back to awareness. He wanted to reach up and touch the spot that ached, but had not yet regained enough consciousness to make the mental connection to the muscles in his hands and arms. Increasing awareness brought increasing physical pain...followed by immense emotional sorrow and despair.

They had been seven in the expedition he led to the Devastated Continent starting out, all highly accomplished, strong, and eager to explore, but one mysterious disappearance followed another until they were only two. For rotations, he and Caleeza had struggled on, hiking, climbing, and sometimes crawling on hands and knees through a rambling landscape of jumbled crystal rocks, columns, and boulders, some the size of houses, in an attempt to reach the slopes of Mt. Vatre. And they were so close; the dark jagged peaks of Mt. Vatre had been visible before becoming shrouded in storm clouds.

Sarus opened dark, midnight blue eyes haunted by failure, and looked around. Cloudy skies above grew ominously darker, storm-threatening. He lifted his head to search for Caleeza, but a sharp stab of pain behind his eyes blinded him momentarily. When the pain subsided, he tried again, managing to sit up. Looking around, he searched for her, but she was not in sight. She had been standing right beside him before the ground quaked. So where was she now?

"Caleeza!"

Shouting made his head hurt more. Gingerly, Sarus struggled to his feet, straightening his badly bruised and somewhat gaunt body; he and Caleeza had been surviving on food tablets for far too long. "Caleeza!" he called again.

The wind picked up, blowing his words away. "Caleeza, where are you? Answer me!" Sarus could not stifle the rising anger and fear in his voice. There was no answer. He was alone.

He had seen Caleeza fall forward, vanishing into oblivion when the sharp, rugged, crystalline landscape jolted him off his feet. Was her disappearance tied in with the ground quake, or was the simultaneous occurrence of the two events merely happenstance? She hadn't vanished into an opening in the ground, or over the edge of a drop. Like Selyzar and Caponya before her, she had suddenly winked out of existence. He knew they had not simply teleported to another location because unexplained forces on the devastated continent prevented anyone from drawing on the elemental forces.

Sarus stood defiantly against the rising wind that whipped his long burnished brown hair thrashing his face and coal gray cloak entangling his legs. The whole expedition was lost. One by one, the members of his team had either lost their mind or inexplicably vanished altogether. They had been seven in number when they started out, and now he was all that was left.

Sarus took a step forward and stopped, his determination shattered. *Why go on?* The expedition had ventured deeply into the continent. He had been determined to reach the base of the shattered mountain, but now with the loss of Caleeza, he felt no incentive to go on. What was the point of going on...alone? Sudden pelting rain dampened the last of his forward drive, and he scrambled to find shelter.

Wrapped in his cloak for warmth and squeezed onto a crystal ledge under a crystal overhang for shelter, Sarus stared out into the pouring rain, drowning in the expedition's long string of failures. His mission had been to explore and commune with the devastated continent and then return to the High Council and report his findings and results. There was much to report, but none of it was good. Mysterious, unknown forces were at work in the lands of the Dark Devastation, forces that prevented the members of his expedition from tapping into the elemental energy that made telepathy and telekinesis possible, forces that had taken the mind of one member of his team, and may have been responsible for the disappearance of the others. Painful grief clutched his heart; he fought to recover.

I must turn back. If he turned back now, would he make it out alive? Perhaps, on the return trip, he could find some of those who had vanished. The return of the expedition was long overdue. *What if the High Council sent out another expedition to search for us? I should return and warn about the dangers.*

Sarus stared listlessly out over the desolate crystalline landscape, the storm expressing his rage. Eventually, exhaustion overcame grief and despair, and the rain lulled him into a deep sleep. While Sarus slept, the storm's energy flowed through the crystal quarry, connecting to neurons in Sarus' brain, and he began to dream.

The storm raged on for several rotations before it spent itself out. Finally, the sky lightened and the sun broke through, sending the fragmented clouds away. Catching the sunlight, the crystals, large and small, lost their dull grayish pall to the sparkling sunshine, and they began to glow softly in ever-changing colors. The colors grew in intensity and the crystals began to hum. Sarus continued to dream in a deep sleep on the crystal ledge.

———•———

The Order of the Oracle assembled in Rahlys' yard, prepared for departure, or there to say good-bye. The cold drizzle had stopped, and a cool breeze skittered away the last remnants of clouds. Gleaming sunshine brought out the increasing encroachment of fall color, giving the woods a festive aura. A flock of geese honked their way south in a brilliantly blue sky as the group stood around in quiet anticipation, having said their goodbyes a hundred times over.

Ilene gently wrapped her arms around Theon in an attempt to quell her feelings of sadness. Her mother had refused their invitation to see them off in the woods, but she had made peace with them and reluctantly gave them her blessings. It had been difficult to see her mother cry as they said their goodbyes. To ease the heartache, Ilene tried to picture a scene of joy upon her return, but a realization of the actual likelihood of that ever happening brought on renewed heartache.

"Are you all right?" Theon asked, patting her hand. She knew he could read her anxiety, but she nodded to him reassuringly.

For good luck, Melinda said, handing Rahlys the smooth translucently golden stone she and Raven had found in the creek. Rahlys gave her a hug.

"Thank you. What a strangely beautiful stone!" she exclaimed, looking at it closely. "Where did you find it?"

Raven spotted it in the creek; I fished it out.

"Aaaarrrk!" Raven confirmed from the woodshed roof.

"It will be a wonderful reminder of you, and of home," Rahlys reassured her, dropping the stone into a pouch of her pack containing a lighter and a small pocket knife, habit from living in the woods, and Vince and Maggie's letter to Quaylyn. Theon had instructed them to pack light, so like the others, Rahlys carried only a small pack with a change of clothes, toiletries, and a few personal items. The beaded pouch containing the Oracle of Light she wore from her belt.

Anthya approaches!

The oracle's message was received by all.

Waiting for Anthya's appearance, Vince, Maggie, Melinda, and Leaf were grouped together, the picture-perfect family, until Leaf dashed after a fluttering moth in the warming sunshine. Raven paced back and forth on the woodshed roof, nearly dancing a two-step, while Rahlys paced the few steps between Maggie and Vince, and Ilene and Theon.

Then Anthya appeared standing before them, her slate blue gown shimmering in the diminishing breeze and glimmering sunlight. "Greetings Sorceress Rahlys, Guardian of the Light, and members of the Order of the Oracle. I see you are ready to travel."

"Greetings, Councilor Anthya. Yes, we are ready. The three warriors I have chosen to accompany me are Theon, his daughter Ilene, and Raven."

"Very good choices," Anthya said, giving her approval. "Are there any questions before we set out?"

"I have one," Ilene spoke up. All eyes turned toward her, but she spoke boldly, "What will it be like traveling in *permanent physical time*? What does it feel like? What will we see?"

"It is somewhat different for everyone," Anthya responded carefully. "To some, arriving at their destination is like waking up from a short nap. Others experience wakefulness and see kaleidoscopic colors and zooming stars. While traveling, one's sense of time becomes distorted. The journey may seem to last for a brief moment...or an eternity."

"I'm ready," Rahlys said after a quiet moment. Theon and Ilene agreed.

"Aaaaaark!" Raven cawed in sync.

"Then, it is time for us to leave. Just relax, and we will be on our way." Rahlys took a deep breath to calm her, and with that, Anthya, Rahlys, Theon, Ilene, and Raven disappeared.

They're gone. Maggie could feel Melinda's sadness and placed a comforting arm around her, giving her a little hug.

"That *was* sort of sudden, wasn't it? But imagine all the great stories we will have to tell when we are reunited."

They will have great stories to tell, not us.

Maggie lifted Melinda's chin and gazed into her tear-moist eyes. "We will have great stories to tell, too. You will see."

Melinda gave Maggie a weak smile and dried her eyes on her sleeves.

"Who wants to ride?" Vince called out. He started up the four-wheeler and Melinda and Leaf piled on.

"I'll walk," Maggie volunteered with a playfully conniving smile, "especially if you have the kids." She wanted some time alone, to adjust to the idea of Rahlys being away.

"I drive," Leaf announced, perched up on the front edge of the seat, his arms extended to reach the handlebars. Vince climbed on, maneuvering himself between Leaf in front and Melinda seated behind him.

"I'll meet you half way. After I drop the kids off at the house, I'll turn around and come back for you."

Maggie smiled lovingly at her husband's back as he headed down the trail.

Rahlys felt disembodied, void of physical substance, removed from time and space, speeding across the universe. She could see no one, only stars streaking by. She experienced no fear, no joy, no wonderment, only a state of unsubstantiated existence. She was in between nowhere and everywhere. Then she heard a voice speaking to her.

"Greetings, Sorceress Rahlys, Guardian of the Light."

Rahlys squinted in bright hot sunshine radiating from a large golden sun that seemed to fill more sky than it should. She felt sluggish and heavy like she had put on ten pounds from holiday eating and unfamiliar perfumed scents assailed her senses. She fought a moment of lightheadedness as her eyes focused on the elegant lady of stunning presence greeting her. The lady was dressed in a light, shimmering silvery white gown of dignified beauty and stood in an unearthly exotic garden. Strongly lean and imbued with quiet aged wisdom, she appeared capable of competing victoriously in both mental and physical combat.

"I am Councilor Zayla. Welcome to our world."

Shielding her eyes from the sun, Rahlys looked around for the others. She found Ilene, Theon, and Anthya standing close by in the vast flower garden of incredible splendor. Then, to her relief, she finally spotted Raven perched on what looked like the back of a crystal park bench.

"Greetings, Councilor Zayla. Thank you for inviting us to your world. May I introduce my warriors?"

Zayla smiled warmly, "Please do. I wish greatly to meet them."

"This is Warrior Theon," Rahlys said, pointing to Theon standing next to her.

"Greetings, Warrior Theon. We have a lot of catching up to do."

"My lady," Theon bowed graciously. "I'm surprised you remember me. It has been a long time. You couldn't have been much older than my daughter Ilene here, last we met."

"What happened to your ear?" Zayla asked.

"My ear...oh, yes, I had an encounter with a bear, big burly beast...bit my ear right off." Anthya and Zayla exchanged a knowing smile. There had been no bear. Anthya had singed that ear in a carefully placed shot of energy hurled at him back when he was still a follower of Droclum.

"May I introduce my daughter, Ilene?" Theon nudged Ilene to approach the councilor, but she was immobilized by awe. The daunting presence of the dark lady with long flowing graying hair left Ilene speechless. She gazed enthralled into Zayla's dark eyes brimming with calm wisdom.

"Greetings, Ilene, daughter of Theon." Ilene felt a gentle mental touch, almost a caress. "You have a talent for healing. We will provide you with some training. A healer will be a valuable asset on our expedition."

"Thank you," Ilene whispered. That, with a little curtsy, was all she could manage. She said 'our expedition' Rahlys noted. *Does that mean Councilor Zayla will be accompanying us?*

"Aaaaaark!"

Everyone's attention turned toward Raven growing increasingly uncomfortable in the hot sun and strange garden. Taking a step on the back of the crystal bench, he crouched into a launch, spreading his wings in flight, with a bit of uncertainty at first, but soon gaining altitude.

"Oh, how beautiful!" Zayla exclaimed, her eyes following Raven in wonderment and delight. "It's been so long since I've seen a creature in flight."

"Is there anything out there that can hurt him?" Rahlys asked with concern.

"There is nothing for Raven to fear," Anthya said. "He has the sky to himself."

As Raven flew over the unfamiliar landscape, he sent images telepathically back to Rahlys of a bright, colorful landscape of yellow, orange, rose, blue-green, and lavender foliage, stone, and crystal. The flower garden was one of many large courtyards of parks, meadows, orchards, and fields, surrounded by stone and crystal dwellings that melded into the surrounding terrain of hills and forests.

"Life forms that had the ability to fly became extinct on our world during the period of the Dark Devastation. The skies have been empty for a span of time equal to about 12,000 of your Earth-years."

Rahlys stared at Councilor Zayla in astonishment. A life-sustaining world without birds was unimaginable. She searched the skies looking for movement to prove her wrong, but nothing stirred except for Raven. Raven circled back from his excursion, seeking shade close to Rahlys, and landed in a nearby tree with long curvy branches and large blue-green leaves with silvery serrated edges.

Wonderful! What a magnificent creature you are! Zayla praised him. Raven strutted with pride along the branch. "If you are ready, it is time to enjoy some cool shade, and meet the other members of the expedition."

Rahlys and Ilene breathed an audible sigh of relief as they followed the rest of the group through a vine-covered arbor to a peaceful setting of crystal benches by quiet pools in dappled shade.

Rahlys spotted Quaylyn seated with another gentleman. They were both dressed in loose, lightweight pants and short-sleeved white tunics v-necked in front, and sandals on their feet. Rahlys and her warriors looked out of place in their cotton flannel shirts and denim jeans and were becoming increasingly uncomfortable in the heat.

Quaylyn stood and took a step toward her as she approached. With eyes locked on each other, she walked right up to him. She wanted to throw her arms around him in greeting, but dared not do so because of his austere demeanor.

"Greetings, Sorceress Rahlys, Guardian of the Light. I am here to serve you."

Rahlys, stunned by the formality of his salutation with hardly a smile, took a step back. The solemn man standing before her looked like the Quaylyn she remembered, but hardly resembled the boldly optimistic, boyishly endearing adventurer warrior she once knew.

"I am very pleased to see you again, Rahlys," Quaylyn added gently when she failed to speak.

"It is so good to see you again, Quaylyn. Are you all right?" she asked with real concern.

"Yes, of course. So you let the council talk you into this mission. Why?"

"What do you mean, why? Why are you going on this mission?" Rahlys asked with some indignation.

"It is my responsibility to right my father's wrongs as best I can. Allow me to introduce you to another member of the expedition." Stunned by the change in him, Rahlys did not protest when he lead her toward a stern-looking seasoned warrior.

"Sorceress Rahlys, this is Councilor Brakalar, head master of the Academy. He is also the leader of our expedition."

"Greetings, Sorceress Rahlys. Thank you for joining us." Rahlys glanced at hard, cold, restless eyes in a harsh, unemotional face, until a brief smile brought welcomed warm relief.

"Greetings, Councilor Brakalar. Thank you for having me."

"Brakalar and Zayla were on the first mission to the Devastated Continent," Quaylyn informed her, "…and found me." Rahlys didn't miss the emotional turmoil in Quaylyn's tone.

Rahlys stared at Brakalar with interest. Every member of the expedition was connected in some intricate way, she mused. All of their lives were entwined. Theon had been Droclum's closest companion, and Ilene was Theon's daughter. Quaylyn was Droclum's son. Anthya had been present when Quaylyn's mother created the Oracle of Light, the crystal in Rahlys' pouch. Raven, her familiar, found the crystal in Alaska, along the Susitna River, and brought it to her. Brakalar and Zayla found the infant Quaylyn encapsulated in suspended animation during the first expedition into the bad lands. And they were all joined together here today because Droclum had, for a time, defied death.

"Sarus, the leader of the lost expedition, was Brakalar's student and colleague," Quaylyn said, tightening the connection.

"Won't it be hard on the High Council and the Academy if so many of you leave to go on this expedition?" Rahlys asked.

"It will only open opportunities for others," Brakalar said, surprised by her question. "There are always new opportunities. I am where I am meant to be, same as you. We have been chosen by the power of the Runes of the Crystal Table; our destiny is set."

But Rahlys had chosen her three warriors. Had the Runes of the Crystal Table foreseen her choices?

"Quaylyn, my buddy," Theon greeted with robust informality, joining them with Ilene in tow. "Good to see you again. How has life been treating you?" Theon's animated salutations hardly sparked a response from Quaylyn's cool demeanor.

"Greetings, Warrior Theon! May I present Councilor Brakalar?" If Quaylyn's greeting was cool, Brakalar's was downright cold.

"Warrior Theon," Brakalar barely nodded in greeting. "Might I add I'm a bit surprised you decided to show your face here again?"

"Brakalar, good to see you, too!"

Chapter 4
Musk-oxen and a Wolf

Suddenly, Caleeza was standing in a cold landscape of swirling white, with bitterly cold wind biting into her exposed flesh. *Where am I? How did I get here?* The urgency of her situation left little time for speculation; already, she was shaking violently from the cold. She had to do something quickly, or she would freeze to death. Attempting to draw energy from the elemental forces, and relieved at her success, she created an aura of warmth around her body by heating the air molecules surrounding her. Success meant survival for the moment, but she had to find shelter. She was ill dressed for an expedition to such a cold region with only a cloak to keep her warm. Her thin garments were designed for protection against the sun, not freezing temperatures; consequently, she was expending a lot of her strength and energy maintaining warmth.

Where am I? she asked the vast emptiness, but the cold, roaring wind offered few clues. One thing was certain: She was no longer on the Devastated Continent.

Caleeza stumbled across frozen snow-covered terrain, her silvery-blue cloak pulled snugly around her, the hood covering her head and shadowing her face, concealing shortly-cropped dark red hair, creamy white skin, and violet eyes. The cold, white terrain looked deceptively level and smooth, but mats of short crispy frozen foliage mixed with jagged jumbles of rocks and ice crystals hidden beneath a covering of snow challenged each step. She didn't know where she was going, but she could not stay here. Maintaining body heat expended a lot of energy, an energy expenditure she couldn't maintain for long.

Caleeza tried to recall her last moments in the Crystalline Landscape. In an effort to reach the shattered volcano, ground zero of the Dark Devastation, she and Sarus had struggled for rotations to cross the landscape of monolithic crystals...when the ground began to tremble. She remembered losing her balance and falling forward, bracing herself for violent contact with the sharp crystals. Somehow, she never made contact. *But how did I get here?*

In a fluttering instant, she had been transported to this astonishingly brutal frozen landscape of blowing snow, with Sarus nowhere in sight. *Am I on another planet? Or was she in another dimension, maybe a parallel universe?* There were no frozen wastelands on her world, and instead of the warm golden sky of home, the sky above her was a bitterly cold blue streaked with gray. Clearly, she was no longer in the land of the Dark Devastation, so where? Cold wind whispered ominously of a cold death as she struggled forward toward a weak sun, blurred by the haze low on the horizon. Desolate, frozen landscape stretched in every direction as far as she could see.

Caleeza's heart moaned in chorus with the wind. To speed up her forward progress, hopefully, to somewhere more hospitable, she teleported herself to a relatively high spot on the horizon and looked about. The high spot turned out to be a mound of rock and ice erupting from the frozen ground. As she surveyed the vast frozen desert around her, the diminutive weak sun sank from view with a diffused splash of color reminiscent of home.

Her thoughts turned to Sarus as she scanned her bleak surroundings. What had happened to him? Was he still in the Crystalline Landscape...alone? Preparing to draw once again on her drained reserves of strength for another leap toward the next horizon, Caleeza spotted several dark forms lying low against the leeward side of the rock mound. At first, she thought they were part of the terrain, but one snow-dusted dark form in a long thick shaggy coat moved. He stood up on four short legs, or maybe they just seemed short, for the creature's thick, shaggy coat was so long it nearly dragged the ground. Across his forehead, ran short, wide, curved horns that came to a point at each end. Her heart pounding with the excitement of discovery, she gently probed the mind of the life form, seeking clues on how to proceed in making her presence known.

The thoughts she detected were slow and ponderous, collective memories through unfathomable time. The mental connection took her on a journey over endless distance through countless seasons, through continuous unending cycles of life and death. Detecting her presence, the short shaggy life form turned toward her with primordial alert and concern. Caleeza soothed the creature's uneasiness, telepathically reassuring him that she posed no threat. Darkness was closing in and she needed shelter for the night. Then, with his acceptance, she gingerly made her way down the wind-blown rock mound. The herd offered her shelter and protection. Needing rest, she nestled down close to the dominate male, seeking warmth. The smell of his musk filled the darkness. How long the darkness would last, she could not guess.

The sky cleared, revealing a spattering of distant stars with one thick band of stars cutting through it. There was no evidence of a moon. Her stomach growled with hunger, but she forced herself to ignore it. Her supply of food tablets was running low. She would eat whatever the native life forms ate when it was light again, which she hoped would be soon.

When Caleeza opened her eyes at dawn, two members of the herd were already grazing, rooting and exposing a frozen mat of dead-looking foliage from under the snow. She rose off the ground, stiff and cold, depleting most of her energy reserves to prevent further loss of body heat. Walking several yards from the sleeping herd to where the others were cropping and munching, she kicked away the snow from the frozen foliage below. Then grabbing a handful of small, elongated reddish-brown leaves and short twigs, she brought the food to her mouth and took a crunchy bite. It was not easy to chew, or as palatable as she had hoped, and after a couple of mouthfuls, she decided to consume one of her few remaining food tablets.

She also needed to hydrate, but all the sources of water were frozen. Her companions seemed to get what they needed directly from the snow. Her efforts to transform frozen water to liquid or maintain her body's core temperature eating snow also expended lots of energy. She obviously couldn't survive here for long; it was time to move on. Leaving the life forms with a mental thanks and farewell, Caleeza teleported to a visible point before the foggy distance. A cold sun burned feebly through the patchy fog.

Many physical short hikes and teleported long jumps later, she was still alone in a vast, white, frozen wilderness. Only the contour of the land had altered some, from undulating flatness to long gently rolling hills with blue peaks on the far horizon.

Caleeza came across tracks in the snow that suggested great numbers. Following the tracks, she eventually came across what made them. Cresting a hill, she spotted innumerable life forms stretching out before her in a broad valley below. These four-legged creatures were smaller and thinner than the first, or maybe it was the lack of thick, bushy, long-haired coats that made them appear so. They wore long curved antlers on top their heads, and were lithe and light of feet, able to cover ground with quick ease.

Caleeza didn't know which life form to focus her thoughts toward, there were so many. She noticed some agitation and movement along the edge of the herd directly across from her. Upon closer examination, she spotted the cause. Two humanoid shapes dressed in white, to blend in with the landscape she assumed, were sneaking up on the gathered creatures. They carried long curved objects that could be a weapon of some sort. Were the humanoids meat eaters hunting for food? She crouched down to conceal her presence and watched. With a soft mental touch, she picked up on the two signatures and connected. A lust to kill, so intense it made her shudder, flooded her mind.

Caleeza watched with intense interest as the men snuck up on one of the hoofed life forms they had separated from the herd. Occasionally, the hunters dropped to the ground, remaining motionless for a time to elude detection by their target. Then, one of the hunters stood ever so slowly raising his arms up level with his chest. Taking aim with the strange instrument he carried, he released a missile that struck the target in the neck. The creature dropped. Quickly, another missile was released and the four-legged creature did not move again.

Caleeza stayed hidden as she stealthily watched the hunters disembowel and dismember the body into several parts using a handheld cutting tool. Since they had not noticed her mental touch, she probed a little deeper while they worked and saw images of family and community. Their lives were not just about killing. Would it be safe to ask for help? The men packed the meat onto a small sled they had carried in with them. She thought about revealing herself, but the lust to kill she had read earlier made her cautious. She let them go. They would leave a trail that she could follow.

Once the hunters were safely out of sight, Caleeza inspected the kill site. The snow was red with blood, the pile of internal organs still steaming slightly in the frigid air. Hunger reigned. Immediately, she began digging through the remains, stuffing bits and pieces that looked edible into her mouth. The tidbits were warm and moist and chewy. On her world, food from animals only came from the sea. The practice of using land animals for food died out long before she was born, when most land animals became extinct during the Dark Devastation.

The sun was already setting again. She needed to start moving; the men had enough of a head start. Caleeza cleaned her hands with snow. The herd had moved off quite a distance, but the tracks she intended to follow went in the opposite direction.

Following the distinctive markings two men dragging a sled left in the snow was not a problem, as long as there was light. Where were the men unknowingly leading her? Hopefully, there was a village nearby with food and a warm place to sleep. She was contemplating comfort when she spotted the two men in the near distance. Having nearly caught up with them, Caleeza dropped down into a shallow depression in the snow, counting on the contours of the land, increasing darkness, and the hunters' determined forward momentum to conceal her.

As darkness cloaked the landscape, the hunters turned on lights they wore on their heads. No longer able to see depth and contrast in the gathering darkness, Caleeza stumbled on, following the light. She fell repeatedly; tripping over unexpected rises and dips in the tortuous landscape. Then, after a time, the lights ahead of her climbed a short rise and stopped.

There was a pause of movement; perhaps, they needed a moment to catch their breath. Then the beams of light jiggled around as the hunters moved their heads in various directions, talking to one another, and intent upon some task. Caleeza crept in closer under cloak of darkness to get a better look. There was something else standing there, silhouetted in the dim starlight, something big, dark, and unmoving, as though it had been patiently waiting for the men to arrive.

Suddenly, a humming noise and bright light spilled out from the large dark form. It seemed to be mechanical rather than biological in nature, Caleeza decided, as she watched the men load the sled and its contents into a large cavity they opened up at one end. With the meat and sled loaded and the open cavity closed, the two men climbed into the mechanical device from opposite sides and closed themselves within. A little disheartened, Caleeza watched the conveyance as it moved away, its lights quickly diminishing in the distance. *Maybe I should have revealed my presence,* she admitted to herself as she climbed up onto the deserted rise, the wind blowing cold in the loneliness that surrounded her.

Not knowing what else to do, Caleeza started walking in the direction the mechanical transport had taken. It was easy going compared to the terrain she had been crossing. The surface was flat, hard-packed, and for the most part, cleared of snow, except for what the wind blew across it. The trail had obviously been constructed expressly for mechanical transports like the one she had already seen. It was likely that, eventually, more vehicles would pass this way. With this thought in mind, her spirits lifted. *The path leads to somewhere; all I have to do is follow it.*

Laughing gleefully, Maggie and Leaf romped around the yard and on the nearby trails, brightly covered with golden leaves, in an effort to wear off some of Leaf's youthful energy. They ventured into the woods while Vince and Melinda hauled firewood and water to the porch and house. Already, the trees were nearly bare, the red and gold of the underbrush fading in color. Clouds obscured the sun low on the horizon; the air felt cool and damp.

"Come!" Leaf called, running ahead a little, luring Maggie ever deeper into the woods.

"Leaf, wait for me!" Maggie hurried to catch up with him. "Look," Leaf said, running up to a pile of autumn leaves on a moss-covered stump.

"Oh, yes, isn't it amazing how high the pile of leaves has grown," Maggie said a little breathless. She inspected the leaf pile with exaggerated interest while her son gathered more leaves to add to the pile. It did seem like the leaf tower had gained some unexpected height since she and Leaf were last here. Did he and Melinda come this far into the woods without telling her? She made a mental note to ask Melinda about it, when Leaf stopped his leaf-gathering effort suddenly and pointed to something directly in front of him.

"Mommy, look!"

A short distance away stood a rangy gray wolf, low growls rolling from its throat, its tongue dripping frothy saliva between bared fanged teeth.

"Leaf, don't move," Maggie gasped in horror, suppressing icy fear as she took steps toward placing herself between her son and the growling wolf.

Wolf, Leaf picked up from his mother's mind. Leaf didn't move, but he read his mother's fear. He would protect her from the big bad wolf.

"Bad wolf," he reprimanded the feral animal, his right arm stretched out before him.

"Leaf, no," Maggie coaxed, nearly closing the gap between them. The wolf crept threateningly closer and crouched, ready to leap.

Leaf would not let anything hurt his mother. He pointed his chubby little forefinger at the beast that glared back at him with wild staring eyes.

"Bad wolf!" Leaf cried with strange intensity as the wolf sprang forward, yelped loudly in midair, and fell to the ground stone dead.

Vince heard the sharp yelp, the sound traveling easily in the thinned out autumn woods. He reached out mentally for Maggie's signature. She was crying. Dropping the firewood, he rushed to the scene, teleporting across most of the distance, a feat he hadn't accomplished in some time,...and found Maggie clutching their little son as though she would never let him go.

"Maggie! Leaf! What's wrong?" Vince asked, arriving on the scene. "Anyone hurt?"

"No," Maggie said, trying to say more.

"I killed the big bad wolf," Leaf said, mimicking a favorite story. Vince spotted the dead wolf a short distance away.

"What happened here?"

Maggie, still in shock, didn't know how to answer. Had she really witnessed her little boy, not yet three, kill a wolf...how? Rahlys and Anthya may have such powers, but Leaf was just a small child.

"I killed the big bad wolf, Daddy."

"You…" Vince walked toward the dead wolf.

"Don't touch it!" Maggie cried. "It's sure to be rabid." Leaf struggled for release, and she let him down, holding on to his hand.

"It's dead," Vince said after brief inspection.

"It wasn't dead a moment ago," Maggie said, in almost a whisper. She looked like she was about to collapse. Vince ran up to her, offering her support.

"Let's get you two back to the cabin. I'll come back and take care of this," he said, giving the dead wolf a quick glance. *Then you can tell me all about what happened here.* Vince hoped that only Maggie could pick up his mental message.

While Leaf and Melinda played Candy Land, Leaf's favorite board game, on the living room floor, Maggie and Vince were seated at the kitchen table, discussing quietly what had transpired in the woods. They leaned toward each other for support and comfort, their faces drawn, even grim, from the gravity of the discussion.

"Wolves generally avoid people, unless they're starving, or sick," Vince said.

"It appeared so suddenly, seemingly out of nowhere, and it was so close to Leaf...." Vince took her hands into his own.

"Are you sure that Leaf actually killed that wolf? If it was sick, and it probably was, it may have been time for it to drop dead.

"I'm certain Leaf killed it. I know what I saw," Maggie said emphatically. The image of her tiny son taking control blazed fresh in her mind.

Leaf's ability to kill using powers they didn't understand was a hard concept for Vince and Maggie to accept. They didn't question the fact that their son was an exceptional child, but this was phenomenal.

"You know, it's not like he did anything evil. Leaf is not a vicious killer; he was only protecting his mother."

"For which I am grateful, but Vince, he's just a toddler. What might he kill next? Can we really expect a toddler to act with discretion based on moral judgment? He shouldn't be killing at all."

"Where and how did he get these powers?" Vince couldn't help wondering. "And what about our unborn child? Are we in for more surprises?"

Maggie instinctively placed a protective hand over her protruding belly. "I don't know. I guess time will tell. We are going to have to take life's challenges one day at a time. Meanwhile, what are we going to do about Leaf?"

"We are going to give him lots of love, teach him right from wrong, and like all parents, and hope for the best for him." The noise level from the other room rose, and Vince leaned back in his chair. "What's going on over there?"

Both Leaf and Melinda jumped up and rushed over to Vince to try their case. Melinda, being older, held more power and spoke first.

We accidentally knocked our pieces off their spots on the board. Now Leafy wants to put his man way ahead of where it was.

"It there," said Leaf.

No, it wasn't there. Melinda's attitude was one of sophisticated impatience.

"How did the pieces get knocked off their spots in the first place?" Vince asked, searching for more evidence...and time to work a solution.

We were laughing and giggling and horsing around, and I accidentally kicked the board, Melinda admitted.

"With her foot," Leaf said, kicking the air and laughing in delight at the memory of how the pieces had tumbled.

You're silly, Melinda told him telepathically and smiled. There was no malice in her thoughts.

"Well, I think you should start the game over and try not to upset the board this time," Vince suggested.

"Okay," Leaf said, and ran off in youthful exuberance to set up the board for a new game.

"Is that okay with you?" he asked Melinda.

Of course, Melinda said, giving him a reassuring smile.

"Come, Melinda!" Leaf called eagerly from the other room.

You're a sweetheart, Maggie praised her. Melinda sensed that they were having a private discussion about something. Leaf told her he killed a wolf, but Melinda doubted that. Giving Maggie a little hug, she left them to join Leaf in the other room.

"See, our kids are perfectly normal," Vince reassured his wife tenderly.

"Yes, perfectly normal," Maggie agreed. She felt fortunate to have Vince as a partner in this daunting task of parenting. His cool logic, fair reasoning, and loving support comforted her.

But she wished Rahlys were here.

This thought she did not share with Vince.

Chapter 5
The Community of the High Council

Zayla guided the members of the expedition out of the garden through a stone arch of lavender and rose that led them onto a wide, cool, crystal-domed avenue. Raven flew over to join them, strutting along uneasily at a comfortable distance behind the rest of the group.

Stone and glass mosaics depicting pastoral scenes covered sections of wall spanning between more lavender and rose stone archways that opened to parks, pools, gardens, orchards, and outdoor sport arenas. High overhead, the crystal ceiling fractured the sunlight into brilliant colors that spilled across the stone avenue, wide enough for ten people to walk abreast.

"This walkway we are on is called *The Way* and runs the entire length of our community," Anthya said for the benefit of the visitors. "At this end, The Way leads up to the Council Hall of the High Council."

"What's at the other end?" Ilene asked, finding wonderment at every turn and brimming with excitement over the whole adventure.

"The Academy," Theon said, his thoughts transported back to another time. Her father had said little since arriving on this world, but his eyes told volumes. He was home.

Rahlys purposely lagged behind the others to join Quaylyn who stayed pretty much to himself off to one side. She still hadn't gotten over her cool reception in the garden.

"I have something for you," Rahlys said, reaching into the pouch of the small pack she carried. "It's a letter from Vince and Maggie."

Quaylyn took the envelope from her hand without any emotional response, and tucked it away into a pocket without comment.

"You *do* remember Vince and Maggie?" Rahlys asked, stunned by his reaction, or rather his lack of one. She had imagined Quaylyn joyfully animated over receiving the letter and had expected him to ask numerous questions in regards to their health and happiness.

"How *are* Vince and Maggie doing?" he asked with belated spark after picking up on Rahlys' deep concern, but too late to sound convincing.

"They're fine. Their son, Leaf, is almost three. Melinda is sixteen, and they are expecting another baby in a couple of months."

"They're going to have another baby! That's great!" Quaylyn exclaimed, suddenly animated, drawing the surprised attention of those in the back of the group who heard him. Then, he quickly composed himself. "I *will* read the letter later," he assured her, nearly smiling. "I can easily envision Vince and Maggie with a house full of children."

For a brief moment Rahlys had caught a glimpse of the Quaylyn she knew and loved emerging from where he was buried, hidden beneath self-blame and sorrow...and then he was gone. By "loved," she meant loved as a friend, of course.

"Vince and Maggie's family is growing so rapidly Vince had to add another room onto the cabin to accommodate them all. They sure do miss you," Rahlys said softly.

So do I, she added quietly to herself, keeping a tight rein on her thoughts and emotions.

Quaylyn didn't respond, and they walked on in silence.

She had been so excited over the prospect of seeing Quaylyn again, and now he was walking beside her. She couldn't express her disappointment over the condition she found him in, but could she help him recover from his emotional turmoil?

The Way ended at two massive doors set in a stonewall, one of which stood wide open. Zayla ushered them in following close behind, but Raven, unable to tolerate closed spaces, lingered outside.

The Council Hall was vast and airy, covered with a high crystal dome. Rahlys circled around, mesmerized by its beauty. In the center of the hall stood the massive oval crystal table of legend, the eight silver etchings of the Runes of the elemental forces adorning it, just as Quaylyn had described it to them years ago. Eight crystal armchairs with silver cushions encircled the table; a ninth crystal throne sat on a raised crystal dais, set back from the table at one end. Aqua stone support arches opened invitingly onto botanical gardens enclosed by the stone wall and crystal dome.

"Please, everyone choose a seat," Zayla said. "Brakalar will join us shortly." Brakalar left the rest of the group earlier while they were being served refreshments and hadn't returned by the time they left the garden.

Rahlys took a step forward and gazed in awe at the legendary Runes of Power etched into the table, one before each seat. Even from as far away as across the galaxy, these Runes had managed to impact her life. She was to sit at the Crystal Table, Rahlys realized, a table endowed with great power! Admittedly, her heart constricted a little in apprehension. Were they to go through some kind of ritual or test? She randomly chose a seat. Since she couldn't decipher the runes, she didn't know which elemental force she had chosen.

By the time they were all seated, Brakalar arrived accompanied by another man, as warmly appealing as Brakalar was coldly intimidating. The stranger, to Rahlys and apparently to most of the rest of the group judging from their reactions, stood tall in his lean muscular frame, his deeply tanned, strongly sculpted face warmed by smiling blue green eyes streaked with gold. His mane of curvy, dark brown hair fell in thick locks to below his shoulders. The two men nodded a greeting to those already seated at the table and slipped into the remaining seats.

Who is he? Rahlys wondered. *Will he also be going on the expedition? If so, why hadn't he joined them earlier in the garden?* All eyes turned to the entrance way again as a stunning lithe woman with dark brown skin and long black hair braided with jewels entered the hall and took a position on the raised dais. The doors to the Council Hall closed behind her with a soft swoosh.

"Welcome Councilors, friends, and visitors. I am Clova, High Councilor of the Crystal Table. You have been summoned here before the Eight Runes of Power: Crystal, Water, Fire, Air, Soil, Sun, Moon, and Void because you are embarking on a long and perhaps dangerous mission. The Crystal Table does not only serve councilors by helping them make wise decisions, but can also be utilized to help launch any endeavor of great importance. Together, we seek purpose and direction for the greater good of all. If you are ready, this meeting will begin."

There were no objections; no one spoke. Before Rahlys could gather her thoughts, the crystal dome above them darkened suddenly, and the eight Runes etched into the table before them...began to glow!

"When the Rune in front of you moves above the center of the table, it is your turn to speak. If you are chosen to speak, it is because the Power of the

Rune wants us to hear what you have to say. While your symbol is in place, no one else, besides me, is allowed to speak. You must speak truthfully. A spoken falsehood would be instantly recognized and would disqualify you from the expedition. If you are ready, we will begin." Everyone nodded an affirmative.

With a wave of her hand, Clova opened the proceedings and the glowing Sun Rune in front of Brakalar floated up, glimmering over the center of the table. "Councilor Brakalar, as leader of the mission, you have been chosen to speak first." Clova took her seat, and Brakalar rose to speak.

"Thank you, High Councilor." Brakalar surveyed the expectant faces of the chosen members of the expedition. "I wish to thank you...all of you...for undertaking this important mission. I want you to know that whenever you have a problem or a concern, you can come to me at any time. I will do all that I can to help."

Brakalar took a step closer to the man he had brought in with him. "I would like to introduce to you Rojaire, whom I doubt any of you have met. Rojaire is a lone independent explorer who has spent more time on the devastated continent than anyone else on the planet."

Independent explorer? Likely just a cover for "renegade," Zayla thought silently to herself. There were still those few who acted, lawlessly or otherwise, independently from society, without regard to the common good of all. *How did Brakalar find this independent explorer?*

"The safety of the expedition is of paramount importance. The more we know about some of the dangers we may face, the better prepared we will be. Rojaire has agreed to share his knowledge and accompany us on this expedition."

But why has Rojaire agreed to this? Zayla couldn't help but wonder. His type always had an ulterior motive.

That moment, the Sun Rune returned to its place in front of Brakalar and the Soil Rune before Zayla rose with an earthy glow and moved to the center of the table. Brakalar sat down; it was her turn to speak. She stood to address the group. There was a brief pause as she guided her thoughts back to positive civility.

"I am Councilor Zayla, second in command of the expedition. May I be the first to welcome you to the team, Rojaire, on behalf of myself and the rest of the group? Knowledge and experience such as yours will indeed be very valuable." *But I wonder at your generosity. What do you hope to gain by joining us?* These sentiments she didn't voice out loud.

"I'm looking forward to working with all of you," Zayla continued. "An expedition has been lost, seven bright dedicated individuals, never heard from again. Part of our mission is to find out what happened to them. Brakalar and I have mapped out the route of our first expedition, taking off from the beach, then going inland to the Crescent Mountains and the Sooty Caves where we found the capsule that contained Baby Quaylyn," she smiled softly in Quaylyn's direction as he struggled to conceal his embarrassment, "and returning by a slightly different route on the way back to avoid certain pitfalls we had encountered on the way in. Perhaps Rojaire can help us plan a better, safer route based on his experiences." Then to Zayla's relief, the Soil Rune returned to its original position in front of her.

To Rahlys' surprise, the glittering Crystal Rune directly in front of her rose to the center of the table. At first, she just stared at it in admiring disbelief. After too long a pause, High Councilor Clova spoke.

"Sorceress Rahlys, Guardian of the Light, the Runes of the Crystal Table wish for you to speak." All eyes were upon her. Rahlys rose, intimidated by the proceedings, and with great effort, collected her thoughts.

"I am Rahlys, from the planet Earth. It is an honor to be here and a pleasure to meet all of you." The group nodded in acknowledgement, then looked to her for more. "As you know, I possess Sorceress Anthya's powers through the Oracle of Light. I am here because I want to help this world heal its devastating wounds." She couldn't help a quick glance at Quaylyn seated almost directly across from her. Could Quaylyn's emotional wounds be healed? The Crystal Rune still held the center of the table. "I want to learn to use my powers...Sorceress Anthya's powers...to help others."

"Perhaps you could show us the crystal," Clova suggested.

"Oh, of course." Rahlys put out her hand, palm up, and conjured the crystal to it. Immediately, it appeared hovering before her, twirling slowly, emitting its soft light of ever-changing colors. She removed her hand and the crystal began to circle around the table. "It was Raven who found the crystal originally," she said, searching for something to say. The crystal paused only once in its circuit...recognizing Councilor Anthya...then completed the tour to hover in front of Rahlys. She conjured the crystal back into her pouch and sat down before realizing the Crystal Rune was still in the center of the table. "Oh," she said out loud, not meaning to, as she jumped back up. There were amused smiles all around.

"And where *is* your familiar?" Clova asked.

"Outside the doors to the Council Hall. Raven is a creature of flight, at home only in wide open spaces. He doesn't go into buildings," Rahlys explained. Finally, the Crystal Rune returned to its place, and Rahlys' turn to speak was over. Gratefully, she sat back down.

Quaylyn was chosen next as the Void Rune glowed hollowly in the center of the table. He stood without hesitation and began immediately to speak with a vengeance.

"I am Quaylyn, son of Droclum, the scourge of the universe. I go on this expedition to help right my father's wrongs, and to visit the site where I was found encapsulated," Quaylyn gave Zayla a scornful look, "and to locate the site where I was born. I carry my father's ashes, to dispose of them, for I believe only when my father's ashes are returned to the bowels of Mt. Vatre will his curse on the land be removed." Rahlys could barely stand to hear the pain and hatred in his heart.

Stone silence followed Quaylyn's speech as the Void Rune left the center spot, and the Rune for fire took its place, burning brightly in the center of the table. Theon was being called upon to speak. He rose slowly, almost painfully, to address the gathering.

"I am Theon, once Droclum's closest friend, but I am not the same man today that I was then. Since the Dark Devastation, I have lived on Earth. A lifetime on that world...a long lifetime I might add... has taught me much. I wish to revisit the lands of my youth, assuming they are even recognizable, and I am willing to answer any questions you may have about Droclum and my past, especially if it will help with the success of the mission."

Seemingly satisfied, the Fire Rune burned out, and the Moon Rune, shining brightly, took its place. It was Ilene's turn to speak. Timidly, Ilene stood up and looked at the expectant faces turned toward her.

"I am Ilene, daughter of Theon. I was born on Earth. It is only recently that I learned that Theon is my father. Realizing my father's desire to return to his world, I decided to come with him...to be with him. When he was hurt in the battle that destroyed Droclum, I discovered I had a talent for healing. I wish to learn more about healing while I am here."

"We welcome you, Ilene, daughter of Theon," Clova said reassuringly. Then, the Rune signs changed once again. Now, the Water Rune wavered phosphorescently in the center of the table and Rojaire boldly stood before those assembled.

"As Brakalar said, I am Rojaire, a lone, independent explorer. I would like to emphasize the word 'lone,' for I am affiliated with no one and break no bonds of loyalty by joining this group." There was a dramatic pause. Rojaire's mannerisms and expressions were ideal for the stage. "I explore for the excitement of discovery. I have seen things you can hardly imagine. Every venture into the devastated lands brings new discoveries. It will be my pleasure to work with Councilor Zayla on mapping the region." His smile was warm and looked genuine, and his independent self-assured air made him charmingly irresistible...almost.

If he's not a renegade, he's surely a rogue, Zayla decided to herself. *I will keep a close eye on this one.*

The Water Rune retreated and Rojaire sat down with a gracious bow. Only Anthya was yet to speak. The ethereal Air Rune rose into position at the center of the table. It shimmered luminously like an aurora in the darkness, beckoning Anthya to speak.

"Councilor Anthya." Clova spoke softly, urging her on.

Anthya stood, by all outer appearances, calm and serene.

"Greetings...all of you...," she paused, choosing her words carefully. "I want to see, as much as anyone, a successful conclusion to our mission. I was born during the Dark Devastation. The great Sorceress Anthya delivered me from my mother's womb into a shattered world. With my mother's last breath, she named me Anthya, in her honor. Orphaned and homeless, Sorceress Anthya took me with her as the world fell apart around her. She and her community raised me through the hardest of times. I was a young woman when I assisted her in the forging of the Oracle of Light. Anthya wove a spell into the Oracle that gives me a communication link to the crystal and my First Mission, assigned by the High Council, was to take the crystal to Earth and hide it until it was needed to help defeat Droclum. At long last, Droclum has been defeated, but the taint of his evil remains on the Devastated Continent. I am here because I would like to see Droclum's curse lifted and access to the power of the elemental forces restored on the continent." Anthya waited calmly for the Air Rune to return to its place before her, and quietly sat down. Then the crystal dome above became transparent again and the great hall was flooded with daylight.

High Councilor Clova rose from her seat on the crystal dais to address the group. The High Councilor had the power of final decree. "Each of you has much to offer toward the success of this mission. May you use your resources wisely. When the star Seaa rises, making conditions prime for teleporting, you will go to Limitation Island, a short distance off the coast of the Devastated Continent. It is the closest you can travel to the continent by teleportation. From there, a ship has been outfitted to take you to the mainland. I wish you a safe and successful journey." And with that, Clova departed, rather quickly, Rahlys thought, as though she had a pressing agenda. The meeting was adjourned.

"How long before Seaa rises in the sky?" Rahlys asked, fighting off weariness. It seemed the day had no end. Was it only this morning they had arrived?

"Not for another rotation, giving you time to rest," Anthya said, picking up on her weariness. Upon leaving the Council Hall, she teleported them to a residential area sculpted out of the mountains surrounding the fertile valley. Veins of crystal running through colorful foliage-draped stones of aqua and rose were cleared free of vegetation to let in natural light. Wide steps, cut into the side of the mountain, led up to the entrance way.

"A day has already passed on Earth since your arrival," Anthya explained, leading Rahlys, Ilene, and Theon through a maze of light airy crystal and stone corridors, chambers, steps, and opened-air balconies to what would be their quarters for the duration of their stay. It was refreshingly cooler in the mountain catacombs than out on the surface. "Earth completes a single rotation on its axis in roughly twenty-four Earth hours, but one complete rotation of our world takes about six Earth days."

"You mean when the sun finally sets, it's going to be night for three days?" Ilene asked, doing the math.

"You'll get used to it," Theon reassured her. "Besides it doesn't get all that dark, most of the time, because of Seaa."

"You may also be interested in knowing," Anthya continued, "that a month has already passed on Earth due to the time distortion created when traveling in *permanent physical time.*"

"What?" Rahlys couldn't help exclaiming. She tried to picture Maggie, already a month further advanced in her pregnancy, and Vince a month more anxious over the outcome.

"These are your rooms." Anthya entered a sky-lit chamber and paused, indicating three archways that led into separate living spaces. "Food, water, bedding, and basic comforts have been provided. I will come for you again when you have rested. May your stay prove to be comfortable," and without further ado, Anthya was gone.

"Let's take our chances and pick blindly," Rahlys suggested, too exhausted to compare or care. Was she experiencing some kind of jet lag? "I'll take this one. See you later," she said, and stepped through the first arch and around a short privacy wall, without waiting to see which archways Ilene and Theon chose.

Rahlys expected the room to be small and simple, but the deep, spacious chamber she walked into was simply elegant. The polished stone furnishings built into the walls and ceiling and floor were carved into utilitarian and artistic shapes right where nature had planted them. Some of the niches and surfaces were covered with padded cushions and fluffy pillows to serve as seats and beds. Crystal sky lights and a large opening looking out over the valley let in ample light.

Drawn by the view, Rahlys strolled to the wide, waist-high stone railing that guarded the cliff end, and peered out of the window onto the cultivated valley below. The opening was protected by a rock overhang, but there was nothing to keep out the wind and the rain and the bugs, although none of these things seemed to be a problem at the moment. Beyond the stone railing ran a small unprotected ledge that led to a dizzying drop below. From her high vantage point, she could see fields, orchards, forests, and open spaces bisected by The Way, with the crystal dome roof of the Council Hall at one end and the massive stone structure of the Academy at the other. Beyond the valley, the Golden Sea stretched to the horizon, glimmering softly golden in the sunlight, mirroring a softly glowing golden sky. Standing at the railing, she could feel the encroaching tendrils of outside heat seeping into the coolness of the mountain. *Where is Raven?* she wondered suddenly.

Rahlys closed her eyes and searched for him, mentally calling him to her. Soon, through the eyes of the raven, she was flying over a frolicking stream cleaving through a cut in the crystal mountain. She could see the stream glistening in the sunlight as it meandered along the base of the foothills and out into the Golden Sea. Then she spotted him flying toward her, across fields and orchards, a lone figure in an empty sky where nothing else moved, not even a cloud.

"Aaaarrrk!" Raven cried as he landed on the ledge. A couple of hops, and he was up on the stone rail strutting to and fro a bit indignantly. He had been searching for her everywhere. "Aaaaaaa!" he whined again, nearly in her ear.

I'm sorry...but look at these nice quarters, she telepathed, indicating the mountain ledge and stone rail so perfect for him and the chamber with its elegant furnishings for her. She offered him something to eat from the sculpted wooden platter she spotted on a table, but he had already helped himself to an all-you-can-eat smorgasbord from the fields and orchards below. *Hopefully, that won't be a problem.*

Thanks for coming with me, she told him, stroking the top of his head with a finger. Rahlys could feel his homesickness; she was feeling a little of the same. *I just need some rest,* she reassured herself. *Try to stay out of trouble while I get some sleep,* and leaving Raven, she turned away from the ledge, seeking her bed.

"What do you say?" Theon asked. "Shall we tour the other two chambers together?" Theon sensed his daughter was still too hyped to sleep, but that would change soon when euphoria allowed exhaustion to take over.

"Yes, I would like that." The second archway led them down a curving hallway, up a short staircase, and into living quarters similar to Rahlys', but facing more toward the river. At first, Ilene could only gasp and exclaim over their findings. "Oh, it is so beautiful, all of it, the room, the scenery! Is this how you remembered it?" she asked her father.

"Well, sort of," he tried to explain. "I lived more on the outskirts of society... but it's the same planet."

Ilene gave him a bemused smile. He looked tired; she probably should let him get some rest, she decided, and was about to suggest they take a quick look at the other apartment, when she spotted Raven flying toward the mountain. "Look, there's Raven!" she cried out in excitement as she ran to the railing along the edge of the ledge overlooking the valley.

"Rahlys has probably summoned him," Theon speculated, and they watched Raven's approach until he disappeared around a contour of the mountain to their right.

"I want these living quarters," Ilene said.

"Now, don't jump to a decision too fast. You might like the other one better."

"Nothing could be better than this." Ilene tried to take in all the strange beauty around her. "You can stay here with me; it's plenty big enough for the two of us."

"Oh, no, you need your space, and I'm not such an old fart, I can take care of myself." Although he was home, he spoke more like an Alaskan woodsman. "Let's go see what the other archway has to offer?"

They descended the stairs and wove their way through the curved hallway back to the sky-lit chamber. The third archway was across the room from the first two and opened onto a long corridor that ramped gently down to the left before leveling off into spacious living quarters level with a high rocky valley, secluded and untamed, on the opposite side of the mountain from the Academy and Council Hall community.

"This is the place for me!" Theon smiled broadly as he gazed out at smooth, large-leafed foliage of yellow, red, blue-green, and orange growing over out-croppings of crystal and rose and lavender stone. "You can have your cliff dwelling,"...and your view of the establishment, but he kept that part to himself. "I'll be fine here. Why don't you go and get some rest."

That was just what Ilene wanted to do, she realized suddenly, and since her father seemed happy and content, she kissed him on the cheek and left for her own quarters.

It was what Theon wanted also; he needed to be alone so he could think. He walked through the chamber, hardly looking at it, to the open-aired window and door, and stepped out into the valley. Finding a natural stone bench, he sat down in the hot sun to a view of the forested valley below. *If I were younger and I didn't have Ilene to watch over, I would take off walking here and now... never to be seen or heard from again...*but it couldn't be.

While feasting his eyes, he thought about the chosen members of the expedition. Rahlys, Raven, and Ilene he was sure about and knew he could trust, at least for now. Anthya and Quaylyn were probably okay, although Quaylyn's emotional state left something to be desired. The only reservation he had concerning Anthya was Zayla's possible influence over her. But Brakalar, Rojaire, and Zayla were all red flags of concern in his opinion.

The Zayla he once knew so long ago had been bold and determined, and highly intelligent, but now she seemed dangerously intelligent. He wasn't sure why he felt that way. Zayla and Brakalar found Quaylyn long after the Dark Devastation on a previous expedition...still an infant, encapsulated in suspended animation. Now that was an unlikely miracle!

That same Quaylyn, the son of Droclum, had been sent to Earth for his First Mission to destroy his father. Now, Quaylyn was here today as a member of the expedition. What else might they have found besides Quaylyn? For Theon knew of objects wrought with Droclum's evil power that must never be found. Where they were hidden he did not know specifically. Droclum had kept this kind of information to himself, but based on where Brakalar and Zayla found Quaylyn, he had a good idea where to look.

Brakalar was hiding something for sure...but what? And this Rojaire fellow, his cocksure attitude reminded Theon of Droclum in their younger days.

But Quaylyn, despite being Droclum's spawn, was not evil. *He's just afraid he's going to be evil, and needs some sense knocked into him. I would have thought seeing Rahlys would have cheered him right up.*

Chapter 6
TRUCKER STANLEY

To Leaf's playful delight, the first flurry of snowflakes danced and twirled on the breeze, swirling up, crackling brown leaves. Bundled up in snow pants, coat, winter boots, hat, and mittens against the cold, he danced about, "Snow! Snow! I want to go sledding!" Running to the porch, he grabbed the plastic sled used to haul wood to the house, and dragged it over the hard, bare, frozen ground to a spot near a short, gentle slope at the edge of the yard. With a padded thump, he plopped down into the sled, wiggling his body in an effort to make the sled move forward.

Watching him from the porch, Maggie chuckled at his antics, and then called out to him. "There isn't enough snow yet for sledding."

"Not enough snow?" Leaf turned to face his mother.

"Not enough snow, Leafy. Maybe tomorrow, if it snows all night, you'll be able to go sledding in the morning," which didn't seem at all likely as the weak flurry of snowflakes was already petering out.

"I want to go sledding now. I make snow."

Maggie didn't know how to respond to such a vivid imagination, and watched as her little son climbed out of the sled and stood with his head leaned back looking up into the sky, his arms spread wide as though he were heralding in a snowstorm. Maggie felt uneasy just watching him; she didn't like him playing wizard; it struck too close to home. Her apprehension grew as the cloudy day darkened unnaturally and it began to snow in earnest. Big fluffy snowflakes filled the sky as the darkly gray clouds descended and the snowstorm gained in intensity. Accumulating rapidly, the snow fell in increasingly thicker and thicker clumps until it totally obscured her view of Leaf still standing out in the yard.

"Leaf!" Maggie ran toward where she had seen him last, trudging through snow that deepened with every step she took. "Leaf!" she screamed again, the thick snowfall muffling the sound.

"Here, Mommy!" Leaf called out cheerfully from just a couple of feet away, buried to his chest in snow and exhibiting no fear of the snow event whatsoever. "Can I go sledding now, Mommy?"

Maggie reached his side panting and pulled him to her. "Leaf, make it stop now, please." She couldn't believe what she was saying. Asking him to stop was actually confirming that she believed he caused the snowstorm in the first place.

"Okay," and as quickly as it had started, the snowfall ended. The sky lightened back up to the dull cloudy gray it was before with small intermittent snowflakes swirling on the breeze.

Upon seeing the heavy snowfall from their respective windows...Melinda in her room doing schoolwork and Vince at the living room table typing away on another novel...they stopped what they were doing and rushed out onto the porch for a better view. The snow stopped soon after they poured out the door, but what they saw was an unusual sight indeed. Snow, two and a half feet deep where Maggie and Leaf stood, tapered off to frozen bare ground again just a hundred feet away from them in every direction.

"I'm almost afraid to ask what happened here," Vince muttered as Maggie made her way back to the porch with Leaf in tow. There could be no doubt that this had been another Leaf-generated phenomenon.

Leaf made a sled hill, Melinda thought, astonished.

"It's hot chocolate time," Maggie said in passing, and lead them all back inside.

Walking instead of teleporting to reserve the energy she needed to maintain the aura of warmth that kept her alive, Caleeza pushed on mindlessly, placing one foot in front the other. The wide, flat, level trail was easy walking, but the cold was biting and the wind blew fiercely, pelting her with blowing snow. A sliver of a moon shining like a jewel-studded crescent glistened coldly above the frozen landscape. The wind picked up until one gust nearly blew her off the path, forcing her to climb down the leeward side of the embankment to seek shelter. Finding a spot out of the punishing wind amongst snow-covered rocks piled against the base of the trail above her, she settled in to rest.

Caleeza struggled to stay hydrated. Getting water out of the dry frozen air and snow crystals was very difficult, requiring a lot of energy for little in return. Cupping snow in her hands, she melted it down to water, producing a bit of moisture which she licked off of her fingers. To keep her dwindling energy supply up, she swallowed another food tablet.... "Only two left," she moaned to herself...then snuggled into a ball wrapped in her cloak. Exhaustion overrode discomforts and she fell asleep instantly.

A rumble on the trail above her woke Caleeza with a start. Unfurling from her nest, she looked about quickly and saw the lights of another mechanical beast retreating into the distance. How many opportunities for rescue had she missed while she was sleeping, she wondered? It was still dark, but she knew time had passed because the sliver of a moon had moved across the sky. Somewhat rested, Caleeza climbed back up to the trail and started walking again, following the retreating lights.

Benevolently, the wind had died down, and after some time, the sky began to lighten. In the early dawn light, Caleeza could see a long low serpentine structure on legs that ran roughly parallel to the trail off to the left, and like the trail, continued on as far as the eye could see. She thought about teleporting to it for a closer look, when she spotted another mechanical beast with shining lights bearing down on her from behind.

This time, Caleeza was determined to make contact. Reaching out mentally, she touched the mind of a male life form similar to the ones she had encountered before, but with a different signature. The mental images she read did not seem threatening, and to her relief, he was alone. Should the encounter prove dangerous, she would have a better chance of fighting off one adversary instead of two.

Assuming a warrior's stance in the middle of the trail, Caleeza waited with calm alertness for the conveyance to reach her. As it drew closer, it loomed larger, larger than any mechanical beast she had seen so far. It made all kinds of loud blaring noises as it approached until finally coming to a stop. The enormous monster, boxy in the front, long and cylindrical in the back, the outer surface uniformly crusted in dark gray, rumbled an arm's length away. Eventually, one side of the boxy part opened up and the life form she had detected inside appeared at the opening.

"What the hell are you doing in the middle of the road?" Stanley yelled at the top of his lungs.

The strange lady, dressed in some sort of superhero costume with no coat... and apparently no sense...failed to respond. Stanley scanned the vast empty landscape and deserted road. *Where in the hell did she come from? There isn't a vehicle in sight.* Although the lady hadn't spoken, Stanley experienced a gentle plea for help, and he softened his tone.

"Are you all right? Do you need help?" The lady still didn't answer, maybe she didn't speak English.

Encouraged by his softer kinder tone, Caleeza approached the cab of his truck.

What am I going to do with this broad? Stanley moaned silently. They were nearly 90 miles from Deadhorse and he had another 400 miles to go before reaching Fairbanks. He didn't want to just leave her out here to freeze to death. He couldn't understand why she wasn't frozen already!

"Damn!" Reluctantly, Stanley climbed down. This was not turning into a good day; already, he had a late start this morning and now this. Didn't anyone understand he had a schedule to keep?

"Listen here, lady! You can't stand out here in the middle of the road, and I'm not supposed to pick up hitchhikers. Who are you? How did you get here?" he asked, coming face to face with her.

Caleeza didn't understand what the man was shouting, but introducing herself seemed the polite thing to do, so she pointed to herself and said, "Caleeza."

"Caleeza, is that your name?"

"Caleeza," she repeated.

"I'm Stanley," he said, none too happy with the situation. He was getting cold jabbering out here without a coat on, plus he was letting all the heat out of the cab of his truck. Besides, he had to get moving; he had a long way left to go before this day was done. "Get in," he barked. It was the only solution he could come up with.

Caleeza wasn't trained to speak the tongue of this unknown place, but it didn't sound too difficult. All students at the Academy were trained in language acquisition. With a little effort on her part, she should be able to pick up this one fairly quickly. Stanley's hand movements and mental images indicated to Caleeza what he wanted her to do, and she climbed up, with his assistance, onto a tiny ledge only part way up to the opening into the huge mechanical beast; and then, at his urging, she climbed in the rest of the way onto a cushiony seat. Warm air blew pleasantly on her from somewhere.

"Scoot over," Stanley said, appearing in the opening and making motions with his hands. Caleeza climbed over to a second cushiony seat beyond and Stanley climbed in closing the opening. Soon warmth enveloped her all around.

"Brrrr…..cold!" Stanley rubbed his hands to warm them, and then opened his thermos, looking up and down the long stretch of road. He could see a long ways. Fortunately, there were no trucks approaching. Using the plastic lid from the thermos for a cup, he poured some coffee into it and handed it to her. "Would you like a cup of coffee?" She took it gratefully, searching for words of gratitude in his head.

Impulsively, Stanley said 'thank you' out loud...then wondered why.

"Thank you," Caleeza said.

"You're welcome," Stanley said, pouring coffee into his ceramic mug.

Caleeza studied the slightly steaming dark liquid, sniffing it first, and then brought the cup to her lips and sipped with caution. The taste was strong and slightly bitter, but it was warm and fluid and she drank it all down.

"You're probably dehydrated," Stanley said, watching her. He dug into a storage compartment and pulled out a bottle of water. "Here," he said, handing it to her.

Caleeza examined the strange bottle made of a substance she couldn't identify. The clear container appeared to contain water, and with thirsty eagerness, she searched for a way into it.

"Twist the top off," Stanley said, inadvertently providing her with a how-to mental picture as he did so.

Caleeza twisted the cap off and took one cautious sip, establishing it was drinkable water, before gulping down most of the bottle's contents.

"Thank you," she said.

"I guess you're hungry, too." He located the boxed lunch with the extra sandwiches he had requested, and tossed her one. "I need to get this rig moving; I'm not supposed to stop in the middle of the road."

While Stanley concentrated on directing the mechanical beast, Caleeza watched him in action, touching controls and moving levers to force the enormous mechanical conveyance into forward motion. This was her first opportunity to study one of these humanoid life forms up close.

Her benefactor had thinning light brown hair with a hint of gray, and a beard to match. He wasn't very muscular; although he wasn't fat either, except for a bit of a paunch that stuck out in front of him. His highly animated face and light brown eyes with golden highlights riveted her attention, his expressions constantly altering with his frequently changing thoughts and moods... none of which seemed to be dangerously threatening at the moment.

"How in the world did a pretty little thing like you end up out here all alone?" Stanley asked, once he had them going again.

"How...?" Caleeza didn't understand, but she was sure the inflection had been interrogative.

"Yes, how...?"

"Yes, how...?" Caleeza repeated. She didn't know. With her stomach growling angrily, she turned her attention to the strange food package Stanley had tossed to her. The contents were enclosed in a clear pouch made of a material similar to the water container, but more pliable. She found a way to pull it open, and took out one of the two pieces of what looked like animal and plant products between two pieces of some kind of leavened bread. Nibbling on it cautiously, she found it palatable enough and gratefully consumed it.

Settling into the straight stretch of road, the radio quiet and no other truckers in sight, Stanley made a quick study of his unexpected passenger. In the seven years he'd driven the Dalton Highway, he'd never encountered anyone lost on the tundra before. Actually, she wasn't bad looking, just a little weird. Her bright red hair, ivory skin, and violet flower-petal eyes were certainly eye-catching. But the way she studied that sandwich, you would think she'd never seen a sandwich before in her life, Stanley thought with an amused smile.

"Where are you from?" he asked, his eyes back on the road.

"Where...?" Inflection suggested this was another question.

Warm and no longer hungry and thirsty, Caleeza allowed herself to relax from urgent basic needs and focus on language acquisition. She did not understand what he said, but she could sense he wanted to know more about her. Using telepathy, she sent him mental images of the expedition she had been on and her sudden transference from there to this cold frozen treeless landscape. She showed him how she had spent the night with the first life forms she had encountered.

"Musk-oxen," Stanley filled in. He shook his head. Where were all these images coming from? Of course, he recognized the pictures from the North Slope, but the images that had preceded those didn't look like any place he knew of on Earth.

Then Caleeza showed him images of the large herd of life forms with thin legs and long curving antlers...but held back from revealing information about the hunters.

"Caribou." Stanley saw the images in his mind, and shook himself out of what felt like a daydream. If he didn't know better, he would say this broad was messing with his mind.

Caleeza continued to stimulate speech acquisition by sending Stanley mental pictures which he impulsively named. Soon, she learned that the trail they traveled on was called a road, sometimes he referred to it as the 'haul road,' and the mechanical beast they rode in was a truck. He called the long serpentine structure on legs that continued to follow, sometimes close to the road, sometimes off in the near distance, a pipeline, and for some reason that she could not discern, that pipeline was deemed very important. Then, suddenly, she spotted a scar on the terrain, a settlement of some sort, and Caleeza tensed with quizzical anticipation. How would she be received here?

"Pump Station No. 3," Stanley said, identifying the collection of box and round shaped structures and mechanical devices off to the right; but to her amazement, he made no effort to slow down, driving right past the connecting road. Caleeza couldn't believe it; the first sign of a village in this vast land that she had seen and he just passed it by.

I sure hope we are headed for a warmer place, Caleeza ruminated.

They rode in silence for a while, gazing at the approaching mountains, deep blue shadows on white reaching into a clear blue sky. Occasionally, other trucks passed them headed in the opposite direction, toward Deadhorse according to Stanley, and he talked to the life forms in the trucks using a device he called a radio.

Needing to relieve himself, Stanley pulled the truck over onto a turnout. Caleeza, unaware that she had drifted off, jolted awake as the big rig came to a stop. The warmth and comfort inside the cab and the monotonous noise of the road had lulled her into restful sleep. Stanley suggested she take the opportunity to stretch a bit and he opened the cab door, reviving her with a cold rush of fresh air, but the wind seemed to have stopped completely.

When they were back in the warmth of the truck, Stanley reached for the food box and pulled out lunch. There were more of the food conglomerates he called sandwiches, which he ate quickly with a ravenous appetite. Caleeza still had half a sandwich left. He offered her a bag of chips, which she declined, pointing to what he identified as an apple instead. He gladly offered it to her, having little interest in fruit himself. In no time at all, Stanley was finished eating, and with the ease of experience, he pulled back out onto the road again.

Settled back in the comfort of her seat, munching on the apple, Caleeza became overwhelmed by the beauty of the landscape. Now that she was not struggling moment by moment to stay alive, she could appreciate the raw brutal majestic beauty of the land. Finely sculpted glistening white mountains with faceted shadows of deep blue rose from the frozen expanse of white, embracing them closely as they drove deeper into the tranquility of the Brooks Range.

For the next few miles, Stanley did a lot of squawking on the radio, and from the mental images she could pick up, the concern was for a certain spot where the road crossed over the mountain.

And then she saw it.

"Atigun Pass, 4,800 feet," Stanley said as they watched a truck with a wide load crawl down the steep embankment, coming toward them. Stanley pulled his rig over onto another turnout, giving the other truck plenty of room to pass. The driver of the other rig waved as he went by, and then Stanley started the long, steep climb up the mountain.

The truck climbed and climbed, unbelievably higher and higher up the side of the mountain, eventually moving so slowly, Caleeza wondered if it would even make it. The view from this perspective was so incredibly beautiful, it took her breath away. And still they climbed some more before finally cresting over the top. As they leveled out somewhat, she spotted a group of four-legged life forms with fluffy white coats, long pointy snouts, and brown curling horns on the peak across from them, and pointed them out to Stanley.

"Oh, yeah, I see them, Dall sheep, nice ram there," he said, unable to take his eyes off the road for long.

Already, they were crawling down the steep grade on the other side of the pass, when they heard a whooping noise growing steadily louder. After some searching, Caleeza found the source of the strange sound and couldn't believe her eyes. A blue and white mechanical beast appeared high in the clear blue sky. The noisy flying machine was longer than it was wide; its head a transparent bubble tapering down to a whirling blur at the end of its tail. There were two parallel bars suspended from its belly, and a pole rising from its back ended in another circular blur of motion, much larger than the one on its tail, the mechanism which apparently held the flying machine aloft. Reaching up mentally, Caleeza detected two signatures inside, and saw images of the spectacular view of the mountain range from their perspective high above it.

"The big wheels are taking advantage of a clear calm day in the pass," Stanley said, indicating the helicopter. "Imagine what the view must be like from up there!" Soon, the helicopter passed over the mountain peak and was out of sight.

Slowly, the truck rolled down the steep curved grade. What kept it from losing control and plummeting off the side of the mountain was beyond Caleeza, but she picked up on Stanley's tension, and was relieved when the road finally curved out onto a level stretch, the crossing complete.

As they came around the base of the mountain into a wide valley, Caleeza was astonished at the change in the landscape. There were trees! Thin scrawny patches of struggling trees with dull grayish-green pin-like leaves dotted valleys, ridges, and mountain slopes covered with withered brown dead foliage and only a light dusting of snow.

"So what do you like to do?" Stanley asked, relaxing some now that Atigun Pass was behind him. Of course, the entire haul road was dangerous, depending on conditions, but there were some distinguished points of ill repute that always put him on edge, the pass through the Brooks Range being only one of them.

"Do?" Caleeza asked puzzled, looking for clues.

"Do you like to go out? Have a few drinks? Get romantic?" *It doesn't matter what I say, she can't understand me anyway,* Stanley decided.

Caleeza picked up images from Stanley's mind of gatherings of people merrily drinking liquids and laughing and talking loudly while watching moving pictures in picture frames...perhaps the first sign of the use of magic on this world that she'd seen. But then she caught images that disturbed her, for Caleeza detected a desire in Stanley that ran unfettered in his imagination.

Caleeza didn't attempt to answer him and looked out the window with increasing interest. As they drove on, the terrain beckoned invitingly. The dusting of snow disappeared, and trees became a little stouter and fuller and more numerous as the elevation dropped. They even passed a stream of flowing water with ice-laced edges.

It was time to thank Stanley for all his help, and leave him with his thoughts of passion, Caleeza decided. She studied the grassy forested ridge outside her window and prepared to make a move.

"Thank you," Caleeza said sincerely to Stanley, and picking a woodsy spot on the nearby ridge, she teleported herself there.

"You're welcome...." Stanley swerved, nearly running off the road as he stared in shock at the empty passenger seat. Just like that, the strange lady was gone.

Chapter 7
The Band of Rogues

"Perhaps we could strike a deal with the High Council, a trade-off of some sort...like their lost expedition member for some decent food," Tassyn said in disgust, tossing his half eaten zan fruit into a cluster of zan fruit bushes. The knee-high spiky bushes with round golden leaves dotted the lavender and blue dry dust of the otherwise barren landscape as he and Stram made their way to their guarded captive. Zan fruit, a tasteless yellow sponge in an orange shell, was about the only thing that grew in abundance in this region of the devastated lands. It's highly nutritional crunchy outer skin and water-rich inner pulp were essential to survival, but failed miserably as a palate pleaser.

Of course Tassyn didn't expect his suggestion to be taken seriously. He wrinkled dark bushy eyebrows under straggly dirty orange-brown hair, contorting his face in distaste as he wiped zan fruit drippings from his fingers onto his already soiled gray, or perhaps they had once been white, breeches and tunic.

"That might not be a bad idea eventually...but for now, the prisoner can serve our purpose," Stram said. Stram's features were blunt; squished in nose, flat face, short muscular arms, and barrel chest. A ragged turban of sorts, matching his worn beige breeches and tunic, protected his bald pate from the sun.

"What if he doesn't want to serve us?" Tassyn asked under his breath, not quite sure what purpose Stram was referring to. Stram didn't confer with him like he used to. When they first formed the Band of Rogues...a name they gave themselves, that probably hasn't made anyone quiver in their sandals in the inhabited world yet...he and Stram had been equal partners. But more and more lately, Stram told Tassyn what they were going to do without including him in the decision making process.

Tassyn longed for the good old days when he, Stram, Edty, and Rojaire arrived together on a mission of their own making, to explore the unknown continent. Of course Rojaire had been the driving force behind the adventure, but he and Stram had gladly joined him, and Edty went wherever Tassyn went. They had fun back then, watching each other's backs, exploring the continent in jolly camaraderie, but Rojaire took his work far too seriously, and the rest of them were just out for a good time. Eventually, Rojaire left the group to work on his own. He said he could better devote his time to his research with fewer distractions working alone. Tassyn blamed Stram's erratic behavior for Rojaire separating from the group. Things have gotten a lot worse since.

Not long ago, Tassyn and Edty learned that Stram could actually draw energy from the elemental forces...how was that possible? What bothered Tassyn the most was how the power seemed to be going to his head! And now, they've taken a prisoner, a member of an exploratory expedition sent by the Community of the High Council. Tassyn didn't have any reverence for the High Council, but kidnapping was taking a grudge too far.

They arrived at the prison cell, a protected enclosure of randomly tumbled massive stone slabs several layers deep, in shades of green and blue. Open spaces in the jumble of monolithic stones formed a maze of pathways toward the outside, but all paths taken ended at openings too small for a man to pass through. Stram had drawn on the elemental forces that no one else seemed able to do in the devastated lands to teleport the prisoner inside his prison cell.

Edty, the guard, not that he was actually expected to guard anything, spotted them coming. He jumped up from where he had been resting in the shade, trying to look alert as they approached.

His short gaunt frame supported a weathered stubble-covered face under shortly cropped gray hair. His beady dark eyes stared fixedly on Tassyn.

"So have you decided what we're going to do with him?" he asked, eagerly. Whatever they had decided would be all right with him. He didn't have any use for a captive, and didn't understand why they had taken one in the first place.

Edty didn't like making decisions. With decision making came responsibility, and he hated responsibility, so he left all the important decision making stuff to Tassyn and Stram. True, he did much of the mindless dirty work, but he didn't care as long as they treated him like a full member of the band. Well, he really didn't like the way Stram had been treating him lately, but Tassyn assured him things would get better.

Traevus heard movement outside his prison and crawled gingerly through tight spaces, holding bruised ribs, to a portal that gave him a clear view of the three men. The one they called Stram seemed to be in charge. *And he can draw on the elemental forces!* Traevus reminded himself as he listened.

"He's going to be our servant," Tassyn blurted out.

"I don't think a member of the Academic Community is going to be willing to work for us." Edty was as wise as he was short.

I have fools for partners, Stram moaned to himself. "We won't give him a choice," Stram said out loud, and he teleported the prisoner before them.

Suddenly, Traevus lay prone on the ground, out in the open at the feet of the three men. Spirals of disheveled gold-highlighted dark brown hair framed the delicate features in his uplifted face. Thin and lithe, he quickly jumped to his feet, bringing himself on a level with them. Maybe he would finally get some answers as to why they had waylaid him and taken him captive. He wasted no time.

"Who are you?" Traevus asked, "Ump...!" He doubled over; something had punched him in the gut.

"You do not get to ask questions," Stram said, obviously the source of the punch, although Traevus hadn't been physically touched.

"How is it that you can draw energy from the elemental forces?" Traevus asked boldly, not heeding Stram's warning.

What felt like a battering ram slammed into the side of his head, sending him sprawling to the ground. This time, Traevus wasn't in a hurry to rise. He had received beatings for asking the same questions rotations ago, and he still suffered from a couple of bruised ribs.

Edty watched the brutality with increasing unease. He had wanted to ask the same question the prisoner had for some time now, but didn't dare. He gave Tassyn a questioning glance, but understandably, Tassyn made no attempt to restrain Stram.

"You are to obey orders only," Stram reiterated. "Now, get up and find us something to eat," he ordered, tossing a gathering bag toward him.

Glad to be free of the cave and hungry besides, Traevus decided to bide his time and play along for now; there wasn't much else he could do at the moment. Painfully, he pushed himself back upright. Perhaps he could drift far enough away from the group while foraging to make a run for it. Then he could warn the others about Stram and his followers. But he should have grabbed the food sack with one hand on his way up; now he had to bend over again…a painful proposition. Retrieving the bag without a grimace, Traevus headed north away from the camp in search of food.

"Keep an eye on him," Stram ordered the other two.

Who was he kidding, Traevus thought? There was no way he would be able to run; just walking was painful enough. By Seaa's light, how had he allowed himself to be taken in the first place? He was a trained warrior; had he let his guard down that much? They had thought the continent was uninhabited, but that was no excuse. Traevus had simply been teleported away, out of sight of the other members of the expedition, bound and gagged immediately, and then teleported, in several short hops, far from his colleagues, leaving no trail for them to follow.

How long had it taken the rest of the group to notice his disappearance, he wondered? What effort did they make to try and find him? Traevus paused at the edge of a shallow moist ravine, followed closely by his two guards. Hopefully, the abundance of growth in the moist depression would offer something more appetizing to eat than zan fruit.

"Edty, is that what they call you?" Traevus asked the featherweight standing beside him, bracing himself for what promised to be an excruciating climb down to the floor of the long narrow hollow.

"Yes, Edty."

"Don't tell him anything," Tassyn warned.

"Sorry, Tassyn." Then Edty realized his mistake in using Tassyn's name. "Sorry."

"I'm Traevus," he said, finishing the introductions. "So what are you fellows doing out here?" he asked nonchalantly.

"Never you mind what we are doing," Tassyn spoke up. "You heard the boss; gather us some food."

Traevus made his way down, holding his breath against the pain with each step, while Tassyn and Edty settled themselves comfortably to watch. Obviously, they had no intention of helping. Reaching the bottom of the ravine, he paused in relief, and then surveyed the offerings. Large patches of the blue-green leafy plant, *tisse*, a good cooking vegetable, grew along the center of the moist depression. He carefully lowered himself down next to a large patch and proceeded to pluck large handfuls of it, stuffing the gathering bag. Then he spotted something else: shade-loving, low-growing, *yuyta*, hidden under the foliage of pinkberry bushes growing along the edge of the bottom of the rise. He would have missed them if he weren't sitting down. Crawling over to them…easier than getting back up…he picked handfuls of the spicy little above-ground nodules, which would add excellent flavor to the *tisse*. With hands occupied, his mind wandered to thoughts of the expedition. Rotations had passed since his capture. *Where is the expedition now?* he wondered. *Hopefully, they didn't waste too much time looking for me. Better they move on than risk falling to this group of renegades.*

The expedition had been plagued by misfortunes, with accidents, illnesses, and mysterious disappearances all along the way. They should have been headed back to the coast by now, but they had yet to reach Mt. Vatre.

"How are things going down there?" Tassyn shouted, mostly as a reminder that he was being watched.

"Fine," Traevus said, standing back up. Now, for some pinkberries. He ambled around the waist-high pink and orange spiky-leafed bushes, plucking the juicy thumb-size pink teardrop fruit. At first, they all went into his mouth, but after having his fill, he topped off the harvesting bag, adding sweetness to the mix.

Closing off the bag, he glanced over at the steep rise, dreading the climb back up. Standing in the shadow of the cliff, Traevus gazed at the relaxed figures of Tassyn and Edty above, silhouetted by the dropping sun at their backs, when a third silhouette joined the group.

"What's taking you so long?" Stram demanded.

"I'm done," Traevus said, pointing to the full bag.

"Good, because you have other work to do. We need water, and you will prepare the meal."

The next thing Traevus knew, he was standing at the top of the rise with the others. Looking around, he suppressed a tremendous sigh of relief over not having to climb back up out of the ravine after all. Unintentionally, Stram had done him a tremendous favor.

———————

Rahlys woke to the sound of splattering rain, so pleasant a sound she was sure she was back in her bed in the northern Susitna Valley. Then she opened her eyes, bewildered by the unfamiliar surroundings, until the sequence of events that had brought her here rushed through her psyche. Relieved to reach recognition, she sat up, inhaling deeply the coolly refreshing moist air, and stretched theatrically, feeling well rested and eager to carry on. Swinging her feet to the polished stone floor, she slipped on her shirt and jeans, and made her way to the balcony to look out into the sheeting rain. Rain splattered almost to the top of the railing as it bounced on the exposed edge of the rock ledge. She searched for Raven, but he was nowhere in sight; she had to assume he had found shelter elsewhere.

Her stomach growled. *How long did I sleep?* It was still light out, although that light was greatly subdued. Whether it was dusk, dawn, or just heavy cloud cover, she couldn't be sure.

Leaving the balcony, she turned her attention to a polished greenish-blue stone table that curved gracefully from the cavern wall. Upon it, an unusual platter, carved from wood into a multi-level array of nooks and depressions and offering a variety of fruit and roasted grains, beckoned invitingly. Rahlys reached for a cluster of the red teardrop fruit she had seen growing in the garden when she first arrived. Bunched like grapes in one area of the oddly contoured tray, she picked one off the stem and popped it into her mouth. An explosion of sweet nectar flooded her mouth and throat, making it necessary to swallow quickly to prevent the overflow from oozing out of her nostrils.

"Rahlys?" It was Ilene, calling her from the chamber outside her entrance.

"Come on in, Ilene," she called out to her while munching a handful of silvery nuts.

"Good morning," Ilene greeted jubilantly, waltzing in through the privacy corridor. "Father says it will be dark soon so I guess it's not really morning. Regardless, it's about time you woke up."

"Really, I slept that long?" Rahlys threw water upon her face from a stone basin carved out of the cavern wall through which water flowed. Then, reaching into her pack, she pulled out a small brush which she passed quickly through her long darkly blond hair before braiding it.

"I just got back from my first training session on healing at the Academy," Ilene told her, controlling her excitement with only a modicum of dignity, "and Anthya is going to continue my training while we are on the expedition."

I should have been up hours ago, Rahlys reprimanded herself. "So what's next on our schedule? Do you know?"

"We are to meet at the Academy after everyone has awakened and eaten. I think Anthya meant after you have awakened and eaten, because everyone else is up. We're going to discuss the expedition while waiting for Seaa to rise...no Crystal Table involved this time."

"Good, perhaps then, we can ask questions." Rahlys reached for another red teardrop, when Ilene intercepted.

"Try this one!" she exclaimed, choosing a fist-sized dark purple acorn-shaped fruit from the bottom tier of the serving dish.

"Why, what is it like?" Rahlys asked, taking the fruit from her.

"Just try it," Ilene giggled.

Rahlys took a cautious bite, and her eyes shot wide open! A barrage of fruity, fizzling, purple crystals tickled her tongue and palate before dissolving away in her mouth. Ilene laughed delightedly at Rahlys' sequence of facial expressions.

"Wow! That was different!" Rahlys said after swallowing, and took another bite of the teasingly delicious fruit. Then they heard Theon outside her door.

"Hello, girls, mind if I come in?"

"Come on in," Rahlys invited. Theon strutted in, looking spryer than she'd seen him in a long time. To her surprise, he wore cool loose-fitting native clothing, adding to his air of comfort.

"If you ladies are ready, Brakalar has requested that I escort you to the meeting, already in progress."

"I'm ready," Rahlys announced, donning the beaded pouch without delay. "Let's go."

Instantly, they arrived under the sheltering crystal dome of the Way, standing in front of the outside entrance to the Academy, a massive lavender stone structure slowly being swallowed by crimson and orange creeping vines. The first monument built devoted to the survival of humanity after the Dark Devastation, the Academy embodied the hopes and dreams of the new order.

They entered through a stone archway that led them into an enormous cut stone chamber lit by floating glow globes. Rahlys paused, gazing in wonder at the display of relics from an era that had been destroyed, remnants of objects she couldn't identity. Theon led them across the octagon stone floor to the eastern corridor, up curving stone stairs lit by more glow globes, and down a long hall hung with colorful tapestries to a large airy dimly lit room. Three arches in the eastern wall led to a balcony looking out toward the Golden Sea, now nearly obscured by darkness. In the center of the room, silvery cushions on raised stone daises, many already occupied by Quaylyn, Anthya, Zayla, Brakalar, and Rojaire, were arranged around a low polished white stone table. A three-dimensional topographical map of the Devastated Continent glowed upon the table.

"Have a seat anywhere," Brakalar invited them. Theon returned to his seat between Brakalar and Rojaire, so Ilene chose a place beside Anthya. Rahlys was about to take the seat next to her when she sensed Raven's approach.

"Aaaaaaark!"

Raven's loud squawk drew Rahlys toward the balcony. The rain had stopped and several bright stars were already visible in the darkening sky. *Are any of them the star Seaa?* she wondered. Then she spotted Raven as he came in for a landing, perching on the outer railing.

There you are, she greeted him telepathically. *Still gluttonously feasting in the orchards?*

"Aaaaaaark!"

I can take that as a...yes?

"Aaaaaaark!"

"The Raven is welcomed to join us, or he can just watch and listen from the balcony if he wants," Brakalar said.

Rahlys made sure Raven understood Brakalar's offer, but Raven remained on the balcony. Leaving him there, she made her way to a vacant seat next to Rojaire, who gave her a welcoming nod.

"What you see here," Brakalar explained to the new arrivals, "is a map of the Devastated Continent, most of the details of which have been provided by Rojaire."

Brakalar picked up a small, thin wand and pointed an even thinner blue beam of light to a location on the map, "When Seaa rises, we will teleport to Limitation Island, where Captain Setas will take us by boat to this beach, where we will disembark," he said, moving his pointer accordingly. Rahlys noted that Limitation Island lay some distance off shore to the southwest, facing what appeared to be the most assessable approach onto the continent. "These are the Crescent Mountains and here is Mt. Vatre," Brakalar continued, naming off and pointing out major landmarks.

Rahlys stared at the glowing three-dimensional topographical rendition of their proposed destination. The Devastated Land was an ameba-shaped island continent with mountains, hills, lowlands, and rivers. In the center of the continent rose the dark blown out caldera of Mt. Vatre, encircled by a broad band of glowing...were those crystals? A crescent of tall, pointed, sword-blade mountain peaks embraced the interior of the continent, opening to the southeast. Another broken crescent of mountains barred most of the coastline from entry, the foothills of both mountain ranges crushed in between. She studied the map intently, doing her best to commit it to memory.

"On the first expedition, you may recall, we only made it in as far as the Sooty Caves, and then we came back out again after finding the capsule containing Quaylyn." Brakalar highlighted an elliptical loop from the landing beach to the Sooty Caves, located on the western edge of the Crescent Mountains, and back to the beach.

"The lost expedition planned on following the route we took out, and then veering to the southeast in search of a way around the mountain range. We now know, thanks to Rojaire, that the crescent of mountains does eventually end in a point to the southeast. Of course, we can't be certain the missing expedition stuck to their plan, but we must assume that they did until we can find evidence otherwise. Therefore, they should have found their way into the interior of the continent. Once in the interior, the land flattens out but it's sliced by ravines. The biggest obstacle to reaching Mt. Vatre, though, is the Crystalline Landscape," he said, pointing to the glowing wreath of crystals Rahlys had noticed earlier. "According to Rojaire, a broad area of the land around the still smoldering relics of the mountain has actually crystallized, forming huge crystals that produce dangerous energy fields." Brakalar swept a glance over his listeners, welcoming comment, but no one spoke so he continued.

"As an independent explorer who has traversed most of the continent, Rojaire proposes we follow a different route if we want to reach the interior of the continent." The thin blue beam of light guided by Brakalar's hand headed northeast instead of southeast from the shore and eventually wove its way right through the seemingly impassable mountain range.

"Across the mountains?" Anthya asked in surprise.

"No, through them. I know the way," Rojaire assured her.

"This doesn't look anything like the land I remember," Theon said, "but aren't we looking for the missing expedition? We aren't likely to find them if we go in the opposite direction." It seemed like an obvious point to Rahlys, and she was glad he brought it up.

"For the most part, we will attempt to follow the route of the lost expedition...with a couple of detours," Brakalar explained, "but it doesn't hurt to know of an alternate escape route if things do not work out as planned." He paused, but no one else spoke, then he stood and began to pace.

"Our goals are many. We are to explore and map out the territory. As Theon said, it has changed. Only a few, like Rojaire, have explored it extensively. We seek to learn what it is in the devastated land that prevents the drawing of energy from the elemental forces. If we discover the problem, we may be able to come up with a solution. And we are looking for any clues we can find that may lead us to the whereabouts of the lost expedition. We also want to further explore the Sooty Caves and what remains of the Temple of Tranquility.

Therefore, the route I propose is this. From the beach, we head in northeast to the Sooty Caves where the capsule containing Quaylyn was found. Then, from there, we can follow the contour of the Crescent Mountains southeast, hopefully intercepting the trail of the lost expedition on the way to the Temple of Tranquility, located near the southeast tip of the crescent of mountains, and finally head north to Mt. Vatre. If, for some reason, our retreat is cut off, or we are looking for a shortcut on the return trip, we can follow Rojaire's suggested route back."

"What kind of equipment and supplies will we carry with us?" Rahlys asked. "Won't we need protection from wild animals and insects?" For some reason, her second question awarded her unwarranted stares.

A reverent silence followed as Zayla, Anthya, and Brakalar bowed their heads solemnly. She and Ilene exchanged puzzled looks, while Theon fidgeted uncomfortably in his seat. *Did I say something wrong?* Rahlys wondered. Then Rahlys' gaze met Quaylyn's, his painfully contorted face and cold glacial blue eyes twisting a dagger in her heart. Only Rojaire's haughty smirk remained unchanged. Finally, Anthya broke the silence.

"There are no insects or wild animals," Anthya explained quietly. "Most life forms, especially land animals, were snuffed out of existence during the Dark Devastation. Only a few fishes in the sea remain."

Rahlys could only gape in response. It had been hard enough accepting the extinction of birds...but all animals...even insects! How had people survived? As though reading her mind, Zayla began to speak.

"Less than a thousand people survived the destruction of our world, and even today, we number less than ten thousand. When the land and sea settled down again and the ash finally cleared enough for the sun to burn through, the few scattered pockets of survivors sought each other out and began to form communities. The largest group settled here, and the Community of the High Council was founded."

"But why haven't you repopulated?" Ilene asked. "It is my understanding that the Dark Devastation occurred thousands of Earth-years ago."

"For what purpose?" Zayla asked. "The world does not need to be filled to capacity. People are more destructive to a planet than helpful. The wisest, most powerful among us forged the Crystal Table, imbuing it with the powers of the elemental forces, to help guide us. The Dark Devastation took place only a couple of generations ago. We have not forgotten."

"To answer your first question," Brakalar said, sitting back down. "You will be provided with suitable clothing and footwear to protect you from the elements and the rugged terrain, a cloak to shield you from the sun or keep you warm when it is cooler, a light pack, pouches of dried foods, a printed copy of this map, basic survival tools, gathering bags, water containers, and for extreme circumstances, food tablets to sustain you when nutrition is otherwise unavailable. Also, everyone is expected to keep a written journal of their experiences and observations. These will also be provided."

"Aaaaaark!" Raven's cry pierced the night. Ilene lifted her head at Raven's cry.

"What is that?" she exclaimed pointing toward the balcony. All heads lifted or turned to look in the direction she pointed.

"Seaa has risen," Brakalar said quietly. "With her help, we will be able to reach Limitation Island."

Theon rose casually from his seat and walked out to the balcony. Ilene jumped up to follow him, triggering a general movement by all assembled to do the same. "Twinkle, twinkle little star," certainly would not apply here, Rahlys mused, for Seaa looked more like her true nature, a distant sun, smoothly round and golden, rather than a twinkling star. The night sky, which had been so richly spangled with stars a short while ago, was now washed out by Seaa's light, and the Golden Sea shimmered distantly in the ghostly illumination.

Chapter 8
A Log Cabin in the Woods

Leaf's glorious miniature sled hill, preserved by temperatures just below freezing, supplied him with hours of delight. But after numerous joyous sled runs stretched over days, the snow hill became hard-packed and looked all the worse from wear. Leaf wanted to make more snow, but his mother wanted him to wait for it to snow naturally. Bored, he abandoned the sled and walked over to Melinda.

Melinda had been taking pictures of Leaf playing as a possible subject for her next painting, using the new digital camera she had received as a gift for her sixteenth birthday from Vince and Maggie. When she found a photo she wanted to express artistically, Vince printed it off for her on the computer. Rahlys had been an inspiring art teacher, and Melinda a patient, diligent student, making great strides in developing her own style. She used acrylics for color, combined with preserved bits of nature—sand, seeds, spruce needles, tiny twigs, curled slivers of birch bark, gravel, leaves, flower petals, etc., for creating texture. She wanted to do a piece using Leaf as a subject for Maggie and Vince.

"Let's go to school," Leaf suggested, tugging at her sleeve.

We can't go to the schoolhouse now. It's too far away, Melinda explained. She knew that by, 'Let's go to school,' Leaf meant the log guest cabin near Rahlys' home that served as a schoolhouse when Rahlys, Theon, and Ilene were there. Now Vince and Maggie were the only teachers she had left.

"It's not too far," Leaf said.

Before Melinda could debate the issue, the two of them were standing in the cold, lifeless schoolhouse with walls covered layers deep in art work, charts and graphs, posters, and compositions from lessons past. *Wow, Leaf!* Melinda cried silently, startled. *You did it!* She poked around. How she missed going to school here! How she missed Rahlys, Theon, Ilene...and Raven!

"Read to me," Leaf said, holding up a favorite book he had almost forgotten about.

Leaf, we have to go back before Mom and Dad start looking for us. You remember how upset Mom was when you made it snow. Take us back now.

Leaf ignored the urgency in her appeal. "What's that?" he asked, running up to the rustic birch slab table, pointing to the cold generator she and Theon had built. Seemingly knowledgeable about everything, Theon had been the greatest teacher of all, inspiring in her an interest in geology, astronomy, botany, and physics.

It's a generator that runs on cold temperatures.

Leaf knew what a generator looked like because he had watched his dad change the oil once, but this didn't look anything like his dad's generator. He stepped up to take a closer look, his eyes about level with it, sitting there on the table.

When it gets cold, the moving parts contract, causing the crystal to spin and generate electricity.

"It's cold," Leaf said, and he hugged himself, shaking for dramatic effect.

Not cold enough. Come on, Leaf, let's go back, she begged telepathically, gently grabbing him by the coat. She knelt down beside him, bringing her eyes to his level to better reason with him. *If we go back before anyone discovers we left, this could be our secret place. Won't that be fun, having a secret place?* If she didn't convince him to teleport them back home, she would have to walk the mile back by trail, dragging Leaf along. A flawed Plan B at best.

"Okay," Leaf agreed, intrigued by her suggestion of a secret place. And in a blink of an eye, they were back home in the yard again.

———————

Caleeza shivered, acclimating to the outdoor cold after the warmth of Stanley's truck. It wasn't as cold here as it had been on the other side of the mountain, probably just around freezing, but still too cold to be comfortable without drawing on the elemental forces to generate a little warmth. Traveling in what she assumed was a southerly direction based on the movements of the weak sun, she decided to stay away from the road, though she continued to use it as a landmark, and the pipeline too, spotting it from various vantage points along the way. It was best to refrain from further contact with the dominate life forms until she learned more about them, or was in desperate need, whichever came first. Her concern now was locating some kind of shelter for the night. Night and day rotated very quickly here and night seemed to be getting the upper hand with each rotation.

As darkness encroached, Caleeza found herself in a scenic valley with a flowing ice-edged stream, denser forest growth, most of which appeared to be either dormant or dead, and a stony mountain backdrop topped with snow. The forest was a mix of bare skeletons of trees with long thin leafless branches, and thicker taller trees with dark green pin-like foliage. The stouter trees with pointy foliage offered some protection from the wind, and she hunkered down to rest, sheltered by the aromatic branches. *I'll use some of these thick dark green branches to make a bed and cover for the night,* she decided, *and there are enough dry brittle branches to build a fire.*

Anxiously, Caleeza looked up at the darkening sky, a blanket of low gray clouds hiding the setting sun. It was getting dark quickly; she needed to get to work.

While scouting out the best location with the most resources to set up camp, Caleeza spotted something that stopped her in her tracks. A low, dark unnatural structure nearly camouflaged in the surrounding trees...and seemingly constructed of trees itself...stood sentinel in the darkening forest. She darted back under cover, hoping her presence hadn't been detected. Biding her time, she waited quietly, listening and watching; there was no sound or movement. Carefully, she reached out mentally, probing for life form signatures. She found none; the structure and its surroundings were completely deserted.

Stepping out from her cover, Caleeza proceeded with caution, approaching the structure with wonder. Although rectangular in shape, it didn't really resemble any of the structures she had seen from Stanley's truck. For one thing, the walls were composed entirely of dark gray trees stacked horizontally, one on top of another. A sagging triangular roof, extending over the top of the structure, sheltered it against the elements. A tall black cylinder, reaching skyward, perched on the slope of the roof.

Upon reaching the shelter, she tried to open what looked like it could be the way in, but her entrance was barred. Walking around the perimeter of the structure, she brought her face up close to a small transparent square on one wall and peered inside.

The light was dim, but she could see strange furnishings and objects that filled much of the interior space, leading her to surmise that the building had served as living quarters once, though she doubted it had been lived in for some time. Caleeza focused on an empty area in the center of the room and teleported herself inside.

It was murkily dark inside the structure, the tiny window letting in far too little of the dwindling daylight. Drawing on the abundant molecular energy around her, Caleeza created a glow globe to light the dim room, sending it hovering high enough overhead to light the whole area...and looked around.

On one side of the room, wooden frames covered with dusty cushions, no doubt intended for sitting and sleeping, lined the walls, along with shelves and a small corner table burdened with dusty piles of clutter. On the opposite end, dark metallic vessels and utensils she assumed were used for cooking hung on the wall over a rough wooden counter. Another table, larger than the first, but with little on it, was wedged into one corner next to what still looked like it could be a door leading out.

But the dominate feature of the room...and nearly centrally located...was a large dark metallic box. A long black cylinder, also metal Caleeza discovered by tapping it, rose out of the back of the heavy black box. She followed the black cylinder with her eyes upward to where it went through the triangular roof above her head.

Caleeza examined the massive black box with interest and found a lever that unhooked the heavy hinged door, inadvertently releasing a sprinkling of ash that drifted down onto the ash-stained wooden floor. Opening the door wide, she found ash and charred bits of wood inside. The heavy metal box had obviously been used to contain a fire, a fire that could be used for heating and cooking. That wasn't the greatest discovery though, for on the counter, large tightly sealed see-through jars containing what looked like dried grains stood in a row against the wall. Food...Caleeza's spirits soared. Grains could be cooked in water to soften them enough to eat!

She had shelter and, with fire and water, she would have food. Recalling a stack of short lengths of chopped up trees against the outside wall of the dwelling, she conjured a few pieces into the box, sprinkling the floor again with a dusting of ash, and proceeded to light a fire. Drawing deeply on the elemental forces, she superheated the outer molecules of the pieces of wood inside the box, along with the air around it, until the wood began to smoke, and then burst into crackling flames. Quickly, Caleeza closed the heavy metal door to the black box.

But there was a problem. Smoke seeped into the room from numerous seams instead of up the dark, rusty cylinder as she had expected. She examined the apparatus closer looking for a solution to the smoke problem and found two controls with movable parts, one on the cylinder leading up to the sky and the other on the door to the box of fire. She adjusted them until she could hear a flow of air feeding the fire and sending the smoke up the cylinder.

Needing air, Caleeza turned her attention to the door-like structure in the tree-wall opposite the fire box, and with some fumbling, found a latch release. Leaving the door wide open to let out the smoke, she rushed out into the fresh air...and falling snow!

Caleeza's mouth opened wide in astonishment as soft white flakes dusted her hair and eyelashes. So this was how the snow fell and covered the ground! Fascinated, she put out her hands to catch the fluttering flakes that melted upon contact with her warm skin; then she tried catching them with her tongue. Tilting her head back, she gazed up into the dark gray sky filled with white snowflakes racing down toward her until her neck began to ache. Then easing the muscles in her neck, she looked all around at the thin dusting of white that was already transforming the landscape as darkness descended.

Regaining her focus, Caleeza reentered the dwelling, brightly lit by the light of the glow globe, and closed the door behind her. Warm heat radiated from the firebox, holding her attention for a moment as she basked in its comfort. But her work was not done. She still needed to collect water from the stream. Taking a large cooking vessel and the glow globe with her, she headed back out into the night.

It was still snowing as she carried the large metal container to the bank of the flowing stream not far from the dwelling. A jumble of ice along the edge of the stream made access to the water treacherous. The glow globe illuminated a thin downward sloping shelf of ice that hung over flowing water, slushy with ice crystals. Caleeza couldn't safely reach the water to physically dip it out, but she did have a solution.

Placing the container she wanted to fill down on the bank above the sloping ice sheet, Caleeza drew the energy needed to pull a thin spout of water from the stream to the vessel, which she maintained until the container was full. She then teleported the full container from where she stood to the large table inside the dwelling.

The snow continued to fall, but Caleeza was not overly concerned. She had water, shelter, heat, light, and if she was right about the contents of the glass jars, she also had food. By the light of the glow globe, she harvested a bristly branch from one of the stout trees on her way back to the shelter that she would try boiling for tea. When she reentered the tree-walled dwelling, she found it pleasantly warm.

Without urgency, Caleeza returned the glow globe to its place under the peak, conjured more wood to the fire without even opening the door to the fire box, and dipped smaller amounts of water from the larger container on the table into what looked like smaller cooking pots. These she set them on the flat surface of the now hot metal box containing fire.

While the water was heating, Caleeza reached for the fullest jar of grain on the counter and studied it carefully. Remembering the lesson on opening the bottle of water Stanley had given her, she grabbed the lid, much wider than the one on the water bottle, and tried to turn it. Meeting resistance, she gradually applied more force, until somewhat reluctantly, the lid gave up its resistance and turned. With the lid off, she reached inside for a handful of the small hard white pellets, and after examining them closely, dropped them into the pot of not yet boiling water, followed by a couple more handfuls. Using one of the utensils stored upright in a blue stone urn on the far end of the counter, she stirred the grains in the water. Hungrily impatient for it to start cooking, she drew energy from the elemental forces, hastening the movement of the water molecules in the cooking pot until the water boiled rapidly.

Then Caleeza tore off short sections of tree foliage from the branch she had harvested and dropped them into the second cooking pot, which by now was also starting to simmer. Soon the dwelling's old musty scent was replaced by the life-sustaining aroma of cooking grain and the aromatic fragrance of brewing tea.

The boiling grain absorbed water quickly and expanded. Using her stirring utensil, Caleeza spooned some out, bringing the plump moist steaming white morsels to her lips. She blew on them softly to cool them off, and then scraped the still steaming grain off the flat wooden stirring implement with her teeth.

It was wonderful! It tasted a little bland, but it was wonderful, and there was plenty; she could feast. Quickly, Caleeza removed the pot of grain, now boiled dry, from the heat to the counter, and spooned cooked grain into a small bowl she found sitting on a shelf above the counter. Then she poured green tree tea into a small cup-like vessel with a handle and took a sip. It was delicious! Taking her delectable dinner to the little corner table across the room, she plopped herself down onto the dusty cushioned seat beside it.

Caleeza ate ravishingly, refilling her bowl and cup repeatedly until all was consumed. She couldn't remember the last time she had been so pleasingly full. After a few moments of languid contentment, she roused herself enough to further explore the contents of the dwelling.

First, she examined the pile of dusty clutter within easy reach from where she sat. Still too full to move, she picked up a volume of bound paper sheets off the top of the stack on the little table. Opening it, she found it was filled with writing and pictures. Settled comfortably in her chair, Caleeza grabbed an armload of these, and one by one, she leafed through them. She couldn't decipher the writing, but there were pictures of oceans and forests, deserts and grasslands, mountains and swamps, and frozen lands of ice and snow like the one she was currently experiencing. According to the pictures, all these environments supported a wondrous variety of life forms, large and small, even birds and insects, things that can fly. There were pictures of places that looked warm and tropical with people wearing skimpy clothing. Other pictures showed tall structures built close together with lines of mechanical conveyances and throngs of people filling in all the spaces in between.

After some time, Caleeza got up, stretched, and walked to the counter. Stored underneath the counter were two boxes made of a thick brown paper-like material. She pulled one out and opened it. The box was nearly full of items of clothing that released a musty odor into the room as she rummaged through them. Checking the contents of the second box, she found more of the same. Searching through the boxes, she looked for clothing to wear over her own to blend in with the natives and keep her warm outdoors. Most of the stuff was way too large, or too worn, but she found a long-sleeved top garment of blue and brown crisscrossing stripes and breeches made from a tough dark blue cloth with long legs she had to roll up to prevent walking on them. She even found a heavy black outer garment with a hood that crackled when she unfolded it, but would help keep her warm outdoors.

Her feet did not fare quite as well. On the floor behind the boxes, she found an old pair of heavy footwear, sort of like what Stanley had been wearing, but so crushed and bent over she feared they would tear apart as she worked at straightening them out. Still she tried them on and discovered that if she wore her own footwear inside, she could make them fit. Of course, she didn't intend stealing all these items, but the laws of survival allowed her to borrow them for a time. When it was possible, she would teleport them back to their rightful owner.

Donning these clothes over her own, she stepped outside, summoning the glow globe to follow. It was still snowing steadily, a thick layer of snow already covering the ground, but Caleeza wasn't concerned. Breathing in the fresh snow-scented air, comfortable in her warm clothing, Caleeza smiled. Let it snow! She had food, water, warmth, and shelter, everything necessary for survival; she could wait out the storm, at least for a while. Filled with contentment, she gazed with fascination at the falling snow. Gradually, her thoughts turned to the expedition, her life before falling snow. What had become of Sarus? She and Sarus had gone through so much together, the misfortunes, the disappearances, the hardships...until they were the last two standing. She ached to tell him what happened to her, to relieve his pain of wondering. And what about the other members of the team, Selyzar, Caponya, and Traevus who had disappeared before her? Where were they now? Had they also been whisked off to another world?

Finding no answers in the falling snow, Caleeza eventually stepped back inside the shelter, the glow globe following her, and shut the door against the storm.

"Bye, thanks, come again," Elaine called out to the retreating back of the last customer. Desolate, Elaine turned to the task of closing up. She hated this time of day when the shop closed and she was left alone with her thoughts.

It used to be her favorite time of day. She and Ilene would lock up the shop, tally the sales, and close the register, then climb up the stairs together to rest and relaxation. They would enjoy a cool drink, a simple dinner prepared and eaten together, followed by a movie or a good book. Now there was only loneliness to go home to, and anxiety over Ilene's safety and well being.

Locking the shop door securely behind her, Elaine trudged up the stairs and unlocked her deserted apartment. Even when she was home, the apartment remained deserted, she thought to herself, for her lonely soul no longer filled it. Dropping the keys onto the coffee table, she plopped down onto the sofa, took off her shoes, and wiggled her toes. Then she listened to the silence. She could hear voices passing by down on the street below, a dog barking halfheartedly in the distance, laughter nearby, but none of this was part of her world; her world was empty.

Darkness was already creeping in through the windows when Elaine finally stirred. Slowly, she strolled hesitantly to Ilene's bedroom door, kept closed since her departure...and opened it. Walking in, she stared at Ilene's untouched bed, seeing through it in her mind to the floor underneath where she had fearfully re-stashed the frightful painting.

Getting down on her hands and knees, she tremulously reached for the portrait of the crystal and pulled it out. Immediately, the crystalline image began to glow in the fading daylight. Elaine jumped up and back as though she had been burned.

Don't be afraid, she told herself. *It can't hurt you.* Gathering her courage, Elaine stooped, picked up the painting...and holding it as far away from her body as she could...rushed it back to its rightful place on the living room wall by the door. As she stepped back, the crystal emerged from the painting as a hologram and floated toward her like a giant glowing insect. Reflexively, she emitted a short scream, batting it away with her hands. Then a sudden unexpected knock on the door startled her further, eliciting yet another yelp as her heart jumped into her throat.

"Elaine, are you all right?" she heard through the door.

The crystal returned instantly to the painting, appearing totally free of any thaumaturgic powers. *And you better stay there,* Elaine glared at the painting as she cautiously opened the door.

"Hi, Elsie, nice to see you," Elaine greeted her, trying to sound relaxed and causal.

"I was on my way to the store and I heard you scream. Is something wrong?" Elsie's plump, round face looked up at her with genuine concern, her gray curls bobbing. Elaine and Elsie had known each other most of their lives, but never visited, even though Elsie's daughter Angela and Ilene were best friends, or had been until Angela moved to Anchorage, and Ilene took up with that bunch living up the tracks.

"Oh! Everything's fine," Elaine even managed to chuckle. "I was just mad at myself for forgetting something I shouldn't have." It was the best she could come up with at the spur of the moment. "Come in."

"Oh, no, I don't really have the time right now. I was cooking dinner when I realized I didn't have any eggs for the cornbread. So I need to get back quickly. Have you heard from Ilene?"

"Yes, she's doing fine," Elaine knew she didn't sound convincing, but Elsie didn't press her; she had exciting news of her own to tell.

"I'm not supposed to let the cat out the bag just yet," Elsie's plump round body shook with unconcealed joy, "but Angela and Steve are going to have a baby!" she announced, shrieking the word 'baby' at the end.

Elaine couldn't help being jealous of Elsie. Her daughter Angela had married a nice hardworking young man last spring, and now Elsie was going to be a grandmother.

"Congratulations," she managed to say calmly, even sweetly, with a smile.

"Well, if you are sure you are all right, I'd best be going. It must be lonely for you with Ilene away at college. You should come by and visit some time."

"I will," Elaine said, knowing in her heart she never would. "And thanks for stopping by."

"Of course, no problem," Elsie turned from the door to leave. "Take care of yourself now," she added jovially, holding on tightly to the hand railings as she carefully double footed the stairs on the way down in an effort to spare her chubby knees. Elaine watched her descend to the street, and then quietly closed the door. Taking a deep breath, she went into the kitchen and poured herself a glass of wine.

After taking a couple of sips to calm her nerves, Elaine went back into the living room and confronted the crystal. In response to her glare, the crystal drifted out of the painting, glowing and spinning in the air before her. At least it had remained dormant while Elsie was here.

I have a question to ask, Elaine said silently, directing her thoughts to the holographic crystal while bracing herself for the answer.

Is Ilene all right?

The crystal zoomed across the room.

YES!

Elaine almost passed out with relief. The answer blazed in burning light, sizzling and sparkling, before winking out. Elaine wanted to jump for joy over the glitteringly positive response.

Is she happy? Is she well?

YES!

Well, maybe more than just one question, she corrected herself. 'Yes' or 'no' questions went by fast.

Is she safe? Elaine decided to ask.

FOR NOW.

How do you know?

The room blazed with light as the crystal wrote.

THE ORACLE OF LIGHT.

Elaine wasn't sure what that meant, but she could feel some of the tension she had been storing leave her body. Ilene was safe; well, alive anyway. Theon said she could trust the crystal's answers. One more question then.

Where is Ilene?

Again, the room lit up as the crystal blazed out a response.

ON ANTHYA'S WORLD.

So far away! With wobbly legs, Elaine stumbled to the sofa and collapsed in tears of both relief and longing.

Chapter 9
Captain Setas

Captain Setas gazed up at Seaa, already high in the sky, from the large oval deck of her ship moored in the sheltered cove. *They will be here soon*, she muttered to herself, for tonight the expedition was scheduled to arrive. She didn't exactly look forward to their arrival, but ferrying expeditions across to the mainland and doing surveillance toward their return was her service, making it possible for her to live the solitary life she clung to on Limitation Island. *I am too far along in longevity to change course now.*

Setas remembered life before the Dark Devastation; she had been one of the few survivors. For the longest, she had been the oldest living person on the planet...but the news that Theon had returned changed that. *How could he still be alive?* She had been a young woman seeking a shortcut to wealth when she first met Theon, already in middle longevity...so very long ago. As it turned out, the world hadn't lasted long enough for her to become involved in Theon's enterprises...and then wealth suddenly had no value at all.

The captain's thin-to-gaunt silhouette moved with grace, a stick figure come to life in the mystical starlight as she readied her craft for the journey. The vessel, built by Setas herself, was the only one of its kind. Each polished board of deck and rail, the forward beam shaped into a long pointed prow, and the sleek steering pedestal built into it, all had been crafted by her own hands.

Setas had never imagined that one day she would become a boat captain. It wasn't until after many spans of the seasons had passed and the new order had become firmly established that she learned the island of her birth, to some extent, had survived the maelstrom. Of course, it hadn't been called Limitation

Island when she lived there; no one could have conceived back then of a limit to their ability to draw on the elemental forces. When the Academy first considered an eventual expedition to the Devastated Continent, Setas had been given the opportunity to return to the island, a decision she has never regretted. She cherished her solitude and resented the interruption...at least that's what she repeatedly told herself.

Opening a panel in the pedestal built into the long pointed prow of the vessel, Setas stored the last of the spare solar-charged crystals she used for power. When she turned from her completed task, the expedition stood before her, eight signatures in traveling cloaks carrying pouches and packs. She had been told there would be nine. She spotted Raven as he flew up, circled around the bay, and then landed on the protective wooden railings enclosing the deck.

"Aaaaaaark!" Raven cried, mesmerizing the ferry lady's attention. Setas had thought she was long beyond surprises.

"Why, in all my days, I never thought I'd see another winged creature," her voice rattled deep in her throat.

"Greetings, Captain Setas, Lady of the Ferry," Brakalar bowed respectfully.

Yes, yes, let's get on with it, she wanted to say, but instead, she bowed her head politely in return, "Greetings, Councilor Brakalar," she croaked. "I'm very pleased to serve. Welcome aboard my ship."

Ship? Rahlys looked around with dismay; she hoped they weren't venturing too far out to sea. The floating deck with railings on which they stood was no ship; it hardly passed as a seaworthy vessel at all. And the skeletal old lady with thin grayish white hair and sunken face didn't look capable of being the captain of a toy boat in a bathtub.

"You know Zayla and Anthya," Brakalar continued.

"Yes, welcome councilors. I'm pleased to serve."

"Thank you, Captain," Zayla said, speaking for both. "If I may introduce the others; this is Quaylyn, Rojaire, and Theon. Theon and Setas did remarkably well at not showing any signs of recognition...as did Rojaire. She welcomed them aboard, one by one.

"And from Earth, we have Theon's daughter Ilene, Sorceress Rahlys, and her familiar, Raven." Captain Setas surveyed her off-world passengers with some interest.

"How is it you speak English?" Rahlys asked after the formal introductions were over.

How is it you are a sorceress? was at the tip of Setas' tongue, when Councilor Zayla came to her rescue and explained.

"In a way, Captain Setas is also a member of the expedition, although she will stay with her ship. Therefore, she was also required to learn English."

"If everyone is ready, we will shake into action," Setas said, gliding to the control pedestal.

"We're going in the dark?" Rahlys asked in surprise.

Afraid, Earth Girl? was Setas' initial unspoken response. "We must take advantage of calm seas," she explained to Rahlys gently.

Feeling put in her place, Rahlys looked away. Seaa illuminated a tropical looking island off the stern of the ferry. *That must be Limitation Island,* she surmised, but apparently they would not be going ashore.

Setas engaged a few buttons, and the craft shuddered, causing Raven to take to the air in protest. Watching him fly off, Rahlys wished she could do the same. Raven consoled her with images of the island and the outer sea as he flew a wide circle overhead.

Using levers to steer, Setas carefully jogged the boat around obstacles only she could see, reaching the open channel. Gradually, the ferry picked up speed, its bow quartering the gently rolling surf, aimed at a distant landmass looming darkly on the dim horizon. "You might as well make yourselves comfortable," Setas shouted hoarsely over the low hum of the engine and the even louder gushing of water beneath the deck and out the back of the boat as the vessel propelled itself forward. "It's a long time till landfall."

The speed of the craft was steady, although not great. Most of the members of the expedition readily took her advice and rolling themselves up in their cloaks, stretched out in the center of the wooden deck. A few, still wide awake, leaned against the port and starboard railings and gazed out to sea wondering what they will find when they reached their destination.

Rahlys stood near the stern watching the water gushing out from under the boat. *Amazing,* Rahlys thought quietly as the craft glided smoothly forward. The breeze created by the boat's momentum felt pleasingly refreshing in the sultrily warm night air. To her surprise, Quaylyn joined her, staring quietly out at Seaa's dim light glimmering softly on the gentle surf of the Golden Sea.

"I read the letter," he said after a while. Rahlys turned to look at his face, his glacial blue eyes no longer so cold. "I would love to visit with Vince and Maggie again someday. It must have been hard for you to leave them." Rahlys smiled, relieved by his softening.

"Maggie has often said she enjoyed cooking for you more than anyone because you always relished every morsel. And Vince claims the political and sociological discussions he had with you were the most stimulating he has ever enjoyed." It was Quaylyn's turn to smile.

"Thank you for sharing that with me. Well, I guess we should get some rest," he said soon after. "Brakalar will want us to start hiking as soon as we reach the shore."

The 'ship' didn't offer any amenities of any kind; no cabin, no below deck, not even a bench or a chair. When they became weary of standing, they sat or slept on the open deck. Eventually, even Raven returned to perch on a railing, finding nothing but water all around.

Seaa arched slowly across the night sky while Captain Setas stood unfailingly at the controls in the bow, her hawkish eyes scanning the sea. Long after the members of the expedition finally allowed the monotony of the journey to lull them to sleep, Theon quietly rose to his feet and joined Setas in her surveillance.

"Seek heart, not soul," Theon said in quiet earnest, reverting to their native tongue.

Setas did not respond right away. When she did, she didn't turn to look at him. "You could be disintegrated for treason for uttering those words, Earth Traveler," she cautioned softly.

"Yes, I'm sure. I heed your warning, Accepted One, and the heart is grateful, but I have little longevity left to risk." The address of acceptance swelled Setas' heart, but acceptance into an organization that no longer existed had little meaning.

"You take my warning lightly, Earth Traveler," she said, turning her head and looking directly at him. "I wouldn't, if I were you."

"I'll be careful."

"It's your longevity at risk, not mine," she said, sotto voce, her eyes back on the velvety smooth rolling sea.

"Who else is on the mainland that you know of?" Theon asked conspiratorially. The long quiet that followed made Theon uneasy. Perhaps she would not join with him after all.

"I only ferry for the Academy and the High Council, if you are implying otherwise, Earth Traveler. And my island is warded against intruders."

"I'm certain that is true," Theon cleared his throat, "but my heart tells me you do not seek soul." At first Theon thought she would offer nothing, the span of silence that followed stretched for so long. Without turning toward Theon to speak, Setas shared telepathically an image of three men.

"You will not be alone in the devastated lands," she said for his ears only.

"Three men?"

"There were four, one you already have with you."

Rojaire! Theon shouted to himself. "Anything else?"

"Look for the stone as round and smooth and golden as Seaa herself."

"A stone? What is its purpose?" Theon asked.

But Setas would give no more.

"Seek heart, not soul, Earth Traveler," she said dismissively.

Theon turned away, deep in troubled thought. Were Rojaire's thugs waiting in ambush? And if so, was Brakalar in on it? Or Zayla? Or even Anthya? And what was so important about a stone as round and smooth and golden as the star Seaa? Theon glanced at Ilene, sleeping peacefully, and then leaned against the port railing gazing out to sea. Would he find the answers to these questions before it was too late?

"I can't wait to get off this boat," Ilene moaned, huddled against Theon for added warmth. The air had become increasingly cooler as the long night progressed.

"We're almost there," he reassured her.

Will I be able to keep Father safe? Ilene wondered. She knew he wouldn't be around forever. Then her thoughts drifted to her mother so far away back on Earth, a tweak of guilt for leaving her clawing at her stomach.

Everyone was up by now, gathered at the railings in anticipation of landfall. Raven had flown off toward the continent some time ago. Rahlys felt a sense of uneasiness as she studied the dark mysterious landscape. *What will we find here?* she wondered.

The ferryboat began to slow down; the reduced speed of the craft lowered the wind chill factor, making the air feel warmer. A few details of the shoreline, looming ever closer, emerged in the dim light of Seaa, now low on the western horizon. For the most part, the continent remained shrouded in darkness. Seaa would set soon and true darkness would descend until sunrise lightened things up again.

Theon studied the rugged coastline, looking for suspicious movement as the ferryboat approached the shore of the Devastated Continent. Setas cut the craft's speed even further as she nosed her ship toward the beach, its long shadow leading the way across the glassy calm water of the bay.

"I'm going to pull in over there," Captain Setas croaked, pointing to a spot on the beach, "Hold on to a railing!" Without looking back to see if anyone obeyed her command, Setas gunned the long pointed prow into the sandy beach and shut off the power. They had arrived.

The night darkened as Seaa inched her way below the horizon. They had arrived, but it was now too dark to see. Without thinking about where she was and how her abilities might be affected, Rahlys conjured the crystal from her pouch. Immediately, it appeared before her. *Light!* she commanded, and the softly glowing crystal brightened as it rose above the party...lighting a circle of astonished faces.

"The Earth girl is extremely powerful," Setas announced profoundly. Rahlys wasn't sure what they were making such a fuss over.

"How did you do that?" Brakalar asked.

"What do you mean? I just summoned..." then Rahlys remembered the warning that they would not be able to draw on the elemental forces in the devastated lands. "It must be the oracle's power at work." The stares of her companions intensified under the clear light of the crystal. Rahlys could see some of them straining to draw energy...but apparently to no avail...because nothing happened.

Ilene expected everyone to immediately disembark, but instead they watched as Captain Setas opened a compartment built into the bow next to the control pedestal. Using her cloak for hot pads, she pulled out a large covered pot. *I hope that's food,* she thought to herself. Suddenly, she felt extremely hungry.

"You might as well wait till daylight to go ashore," the captain said. "While waiting, we will eat." The steaming hot aroma that wafted through the air when she removed the lid sent everyone scrambling to their packs to fetch bowls and eating utensils. Then, to everyone's delight, Setas opened a second compartment on the opposite side of the control pedestal and pulled out another covered pot, this one containing steaming hot roasted fish and roots. The meal had been cooking, crock pot style, while the ferry crossed the channel.

"Oh...this is delicious!" Rahlys exclaimed after the first hurried bites to appease the hungry void in her belly. "What is it?"

"*Ahsyki,*" Setas said, "made with fruit, vegetables, nuts, and grains, all from Limitation Island." There were seconds available for everyone, and soon, Rahlys was headed for a refill.

"Wait a moment, Rahlys," Brakalar called out to her. "Let's explore the extent of your abilities without using the crystal...since the rest of us have none." Rahlys had noticed Brakalar's frequent hard stares since she had provided them with light. Now, she noted some bitterness in his tone. "Why don't you try replenishing your bowl from where you are...and let's not spill any of this good food," Brakalar challenged her.

Rahlys also wanted to test the full extent of her abilities, but in private, away from the others. She would then decide how much to reveal...assuming she had any abilities at all...but she didn't like Brakalar's condescending tone, or the way he stared at her bowl waiting for more *ahsyki* and fish to instantly appear.

Taking a deep breath, Rahlys relaxed her grip on her bowl and, focusing energy on it, gently moved it from her hand, sending it hovering across the open deck to the covered pots of food. Directing mental energy from where she stood, Rahlys carefully removed the lids and ladled more *ahsyki* and roasted fish with tubers to her hovering dish. Finally, replacing the lids on the pots, she drew her bowl back to her hands and resumed eating.

"This is really delicious," she praised Setas again, and took another bite of the roasted fish, ignoring the appreciative stares from the other members of the group.

"You are a clue to the answer to the puzzle," Zayla told Rahlys thoughtfully, "...and a valuable asset to the expedition." While her comment had been sincere, Rahlys couldn't help detecting a tiny spark of envy.

By the time all the food was gone, leaving filled bellies and empty pots in its place, a faint glow awakened in the eastern sky, its source still hidden by the distant Crescent Mountains. The expedition members gathered their belongings, packing them away. Some rinsed out their bowls and eating utensils with a dab of drinking water, others waited to wash them in the little stream that emptied into the bay.

"Aaaaaark! Aaaaaark!" Raven cried in the near distance, returning from his inland excursion. He flew over them, and then circled down, landing on the beach.

"It's time for you to depart," Captain Setas announced suddenly. "I must leave on the falling tide." She opened a hinged section of rail near the bow, dropping it down to form steps to the beach.

Grabbing her pack, Rahlys disembarked via the steps to join Raven, who had nothing alarming to report. The crystal followed her, leaving the rest of the team in relative darkness. Rahlys sent it higher up to cast its light over a broader area, illuminating broad-leafed red, orange, and blue-green foliage blazing out of the lavender earth.

"Did Raven see anything?" Theon asked Rahlys in a whisper when he reached her on the beach. He had tried using telepathy, but couldn't even detect her signature...and she was standing right in front of him!

No, and I'm not picking up any other signatures in the area besides our own, she informed him. Theon nodded, indicating that he had received the information. But why was it possible for Rahlys to send a message to him telepathically, when he couldn't send one in return?"

"I will check the beach every three rotations," Captain Setas promised, locking up the gate railing after they had all descended. Rahlys did the math; three rotations at approximately six Earth-days per rotation. That meant that Setas would check the beach about every eighteen days in case she was needed. *Has she been doing this the entire time the lost expedition has been on the continent?*

With mixed feelings, the group watched as Captain Setas jogged the ferry's prow back out of the sand. "Good luck," the captain added unexpectedly, then made a wide looping turn, heading out of the bay.

Chapter 10
The Devastated Continent

The sky was getting lighter, so Rahlys conjured the crystal back to its pouch, letting their eyes adjust to the strengthening daylight. The expedition stood on a lavender sandy beach that funneled inland, squeezed between sparsely forested, brush-covered hills pushed up against razor sharp dark blue coastal mountains.

"We might as well start hiking," Brakalar said when Captain Setas disappeared in the morning mist. "If you feel as I do, it will be a relief to stretch stiff muscles after the long boat ride. Has anyone tested the water in the stream?" A small stream, narrow enough to jump across, gurgled invitingly over lavender and rose colored rocks a few steps away.

"It's good; we can fill our water containers," Anthya informed them.

"We will hike in pairs," Brakalar said, reigning in their attention. "Rojaire and I will go first so we can scout ahead some. Theon and Zayla will lead the rest of the group, when everyone is ready. Let's have Rahlys and Ilene in the middle watching the flanks, and Anthya and Quaylyn watching our rear. Of course, Raven will be flying reconnaissance overhead."

"What are we looking for?" Ilene didn't hesitate to ask.

"The unexpected," Brakalar answered, in all seriousness. "Don't hesitate to sound the alarm if you see anything questionable. And that goes for everyone." There was a nod of consent from the entire team, then Brakalar and Rojaire, their conical packs slung over their shoulders and across their backs, headed up the sloped beach of lavender sand and disappeared into the tall brush. Raven flew off into a golden dawn, circling wide overhead, surveying the strangely quiet landscape surrounding them.

As the rest of the expedition finished rinsing out bowls, filling water containers, and adjusting packs, the sun rose, painting the sky golden and transforming the land that had looked so menacing, when veiled in dim light, into a colorfully serene storybook landscape. Soon, everyone was ready to go, and with Theon and Zayla leading the way, the rest of the expedition quickly fell into step.

It was easy going at first; the land rose so gently, the rise was hardly noticeable. The swath of land they followed was flatter than the terrain to either side, as though they were following an old washout, or perhaps an ancient lava flow. Except for some tall bushes and the scattered clumps of willowy trees that dotted the landscape, their long streaming leaves of blue-green and gold touching the ground, most of the dew-laden foliage was low enough to see over and sparse enough to weave through without any difficulty.

Theon and Zayla caught occasional glimpses of Brakalar and Rojaire up ahead as they hiked in silence. The torrent of thought that crushed Theon's heart left no room for conversation. He didn't blame Brakalar for not forgiving him. He had helped destroy his world. Not directly...but he had enabled Droclum by going along with his madness.

"Rahlys, look at this place. Isn't it beautiful?" Ilene gasped after some time. "I can hardly believe I'm really here,"

"Certainly colorful," Rahlys added. Back home, the most colorful mushroom was the deadliest.

The sun was already hot, and Anthya paused to remove her lightweight, light gray cloak from one of the many storage compartments of her pack, and donned it for protection against the sun. Following her example, Quaylyn stopped and did the same. To Anthya, Quaylyn seemed more focused today than she had seen him in a long time, fueling her hope that he would regain his sense of positive achievement during the course of the expedition.

"After you, my Lady," Quaylyn bowed his head graciously, when they were ready to move again.

Anthya smiled at his touching sentiment, and to her warm surprise, Quaylyn smiled hesitantly in return. Subtly, she returned his bow and stepped out ahead with Quaylyn following.

The playful exchange reminded Anthya of another time long ago, when she had challenged Quaylyn to a game of *traw*, an athletically strenuous game played on a triangular playing field. On that day she had informed a more innocent Quaylyn that he had been assigned his First Mission to the distant planet called Earth.

Slowly, the landscape changed. The wide swath of relatively flat land eventually bottle-necked into overlapping hills, and the trickle of a stream they followed meandered through increasingly inaccessible narrow dark blue rock chasms. By now, the overlarge sun dazzled high above the peaks of the distant Crescent Mountains to the east.

"We'll take a break here," Brakalar announced as the rest of the group caught up. "From here, we will be forced to traverse the long rolling hills, up one side and down the other, in the way of forward progress."

Rahlys and Ilene welcomed the pause. They splashed cool refreshing water over their faces and refilled their water containers. Grateful for the chance to relax for a while, they leaned back against dark blue boulders covered with plush iridescent orange and pink mosses...but they weren't given a chance to rest for long. At Brakalar's signal, somewhat reluctantly, Ilene and Rahlys rose from their resting places to resume the hike.

"We'll shuffle partners," Brakalar announced. "This time, let's have Quaylyn scout ahead with me, Anthya and Zayla leading the rest of the group, with Ilene and Rojaire watching our flanks and Theon and Rahlys guarding our backs." Rahlys noticed that the pairing with Rojaire seemed to add new pep into Ilene's step as she headed toward him.

The expedition continued east northeast toward the Crescent Mountains and the Sooty Caves, their progress now dampened by the arduous task of traversing hills. As time progressed, ever wider gaps separated the pairs. Rojaire, with Ilene in tow, could not maintain the pace of the leaders, and Rahlys didn't mind lagging behind with Theon at the back of the pack. Ahead of them, they could see Rojaire and Ilene carrying on a brisk conversation.

"Why did you start exploring the Devastated Continent?" Ilene asked Rojaire as they marched steadily forward. Remembering that she was watching their southern flank, she returned her eyes to the terrain, letting her ears await his answer. Rojaire was so ruggedly handsome; it made her uncomfortable being with him. Aaron had also been ruggedly handsome and a bit of a rogue. It had been a long time since she had thought of Aaron, she realized, with a twinge in her heart.

"I had an issue with the academic community," Rojaire said matter-of-factly.

"You mean you broke the law? You're a criminal?" Ilene couldn't help turning to look his way.

"I didn't say that. I said I had an issue with the academic community."

"But is it so?" Their eyes met, and they came to a stop.

"Only if being an individual thinker is a criminal act," Rojaire said defiantly, and walked on.

"So you ran away to the Devastated Continent!" Ilene surmised as she struggled to keep pace with his long strides. "How did you get here?"

"You ask a lot of questions. What about you? What are you running away from? Aren't you a long way from home?"

"I'm not running from anything; I came here with my father. I'm part of this land, too." Theon and Rahlys caught snatches in the breeze of Rojaire and Ilene's discussion as they followed, guarding the rear.

Theon touched Rahlys' arm, indicating he wanted them to drop back. "I think Brakalar is hiding something," Theon said as the distance between them and the other two widened.

"What makes you think that?" Rahlys asked.

"I don't like his style," he said, filling his mouth with purple berries he plucked from a short woody bush nearby.

"That's not a valid reason to suspect him of anything."

"Still, I would like for you to help me keep an eye on him."

"Sure." She tried one of the berries, expecting it to be sweet, but it had a peppery taste instead. "I don't really like Brakalar's style either."

When they finally came to another stop for recharging, Rojaire shared his knowledge of the native foods. "The plant life that abounds is not of wondrous variety, but most of it is edible."

There were pinkberries, zan fruit, pepper berries that looked like purple grapes growing on stubby pinkish green bushes, and large green and orange striped cantaloupe sized melons growing on short stubby plants with thick pointed red and green leaves. Tall gold and orange stalks with cascades of edible lavender blossoms grew in abundance, the stalks' crunchy inner cores a good source of energy. The long willowy leaves of the zaota tree could be woven into mats, and the bark, when boiled, made an invigorating tea. Tufts of greenish-blue grass grew in clomps, producing a seed head that could be ground into flour or cooked as a hot cereal. Rojaire pulled up a small unassuming plant with dull gray and silver leaves and shook lavender soil off lavender roots, revealing a bountiful crop of crunchy orange nuts in soft blue shells.

"Of course not all the plants are friendly," Rojaire warned. "That pink and blue ground cover with white flowers irritates the skin. The bluish-black berries growing on this sprawling bush are poisonous. And there is a tall spiky plant that I don't see here," Rojaire said, looking around, "that will nick you if you get anywhere close to it...but its tubular roots are great roasted," he added with a roguish smile.

Brakalar rose from the protruding blue stone on which he sat. "One more push, and we will make camp to get some rest during the hottest part of the day," Brakalar said, by way of encouragement. "Let's have Rahlys and Theon scout ahead, followed by Zayla and myself, with the rest of you holding the rear. Be on the lookout for a good stopping place."

Stretching to warm muscles gone cold over the lengthy break, the expedition eased back into forward motion. Raven took off first, and Theon and Rahlys started hiking uphill through the tall brush, keeping to an easterly direction. As soon as they were out of sight of the others, Rahlys teleported herself and Theon, in two short hops, to the crest of the next hill, and after a quick glance about, pulled him down the slope on the other side.

"What are you doing?" Theon asked, breaking loose from her, puzzled by her inexplicable jumpy behavior. "Why did you drag me down the hill like we were under attack?"

"I want to be sure we are far enough away from the others, we can't be overheard. You were right. Brakalar is hiding something," Rahlys whispered conspiratorially.

She had his interest.

"How do you know?" Theon asked. "Let's keep moving so we stay ahead." Now, he was pulling *her* down the hill. To assure their lead, Rahlys made a couple more jumps, taking them to the bottom of the long hill and into the thicker foliage of the moist valley.

"Enough of that!" Theon said, surveying their surroundings. "How do you know that Brakalar is hiding something?" he asked her again.

"Because I can feel it...it's in his pouch...I can feel it when I'm near him."

"Feel what? What do you feel?"

"I'm not sure what it is, but something he carries in his pouch emits prevailing tendrils of seeking energy?"

"Seeking...seeking what...?"

"I don't know," Rahlys said, but Theon didn't seem to expect her to.

"That's all right," he reassured her. "You've done well. Let me know if you learn anything else." Theon turned away deep in his own thoughts, as he considered the possibilities in his head. The conclusions he came to were frightening. *I better find whatever that thing is seeking before Brakalar does.*

"Can you teleport the two of us to the top of that distant peak so we can take a look around?" Theon asked Rahlys.

In an effort to comply, Rahlys focused on the taller ridge far to the east. Drawing on the molecular energy around her, she reached for it...but an obstruction blocked her way.

"I...I...can't," Rahlys shuddered, a bit shaken. "There is some kind of obstacle preventing it."

117

"It must be a question of distance; you moved the two of us up and down that hill. Theon searched for a middle range destination. How about to that tree over there, can you make it that far?" The tree Theon indicated, a good five hundred feet away, was a zaota tree, Rahlys had learned, the only tree species on the continent.

"I'll try," Rahlys said, no longer quite sure. She forced herself to relax, then concentrating like it was her first time, she drew deeply from within, mentally placing herself by the tree. And she was there! Rahlys was pleased to find herself standing next to the towering zaota tree, its thick branches hidden under a dense umbrella-shaped canopy of long thin blue-green and gold leaves waving like a giant hula dancer's grass skirt, chiming softly in the breeze. Raven came in for a landing on the mass of budding tips at the top of the tree's canopy.

"So, it seems to be a matter of range," Theon said, upon reaching her. "That's still better than nothing." Rahlys couldn't help but agree.

To further test that range, Rahlys teleported herself short distances up nearby rises to survey the surroundings. Each hilltop revealed a wide vista of more hills and empty valleys. There was no life except for the foliage that evenly blanketed the landscape. Not a single insect buzzed by her ear or got in her face. Not a single bug crawled over the coarse lavender soil or smooth colorful plants. There were no tracks, large or small, in the moist loam of the valleys. And not a single bird, except Raven, flittered through the trees or soared across the sky. The Alaska wilderness was quiet, but even in winter there were the occasional bird calls or squirrel chirps to accent the quiet. In summer, insects and the arrival of more birds created a continuous soft underlay of sound that was noticeably missing here.

Rahlys returned to Theon's side and they hiked on, with Rahlys scanning the terrain around them and Theon quietly formulating a plan, until Rahlys jarred him from his thoughts.

"What's that?" she asked, pointing at something that moved in the near distance.

Theon pulled a spyglass out of his pouch and focused on a red, black, and white flag mounted on a branch supported by stacked rocks.

"It looks like an expedition marker," Theon said, after studying it for a while. "Probably left by the lost expedition." The Academy had provided them with an assortment of coded flags to mark locations, as needed, along the way. Rahlys took the spyglass Theon offered and focused on the small tricolor flag on a stick moving in the breeze supported by a constructed rock pyramid. Handing the spyglass back to Theon, she pulled out her journal and looked up the meaning of this particular flag.

"It says it's a warning of danger, advising others to stay away," Rahlys said. "We better inform the others." Rahlys looked around and as a precaution, reached out mentally in search of unfamiliar signatures, at least within her limited range, but found no one...even the rest of the group were still too far off to detect...which made her feel uneasy.

"Wait, we should check it out first. It could be just a hoax to keep us away, or a decoy to divert our direction toward a trap," Theon said.

"We aren't supposed to investigate things on our own. Besides, there isn't anyone here to play a hoax," Rahlys pointed out, still preferring to report back to the others.

"Rojaire's buddies are here somewhere."

"Who...?"

"I happen to know, from a reliable source, that Rojaire didn't explore this continent completely alone, and his three buddies are still roaming around here...somewhere."

"A reliable source! What, you have twelve thousand-year-old contacts?" Then Rahlys made the connection. "Captain Setas!" Theon and the captain had to be the oldest entities on the planet! Theon didn't confirm or deny. "All right, I'll take us to the site."

She teleported them to the site of the marker, searching again for unfamiliar signatures, but there was no one around. Together, they explored the general area, but found nothing threatening, or even significantly different from the rest of the terrain they had crossed. Raven circled overhead, but raised no alarm.

"There's nothing here." Rahlys fanned herself with her notebook, wishing for shelter from the hot sun. "Are you ready to head back?" she asked.

"Our footprints will make it obvious someone has been here," Theon pointed out.

"No, they won't," she assured him. After transporting them back to the rise where they had first spotted the flag signal, Rahlys wove a spell that smoothed over their tracks like a wave sweeping clean the sands on a beach...then she focused on locating the rest of the group.

"The others are about to catch up," she informed Theon. "We can wait for them here. It will look like we did what we were supposed to do...wait for the rest of the team instead of investigating something suspicious on our own." Soon, Brakalar and Zayla broke over the crest of the hill a hundred feet away; Rahlys and Theon called them over. The rest of the group followed. Without saying anything, Rahlys pointed in the direction of the marker, and Theon handed Brakalar the spyglass.

"What is it?" Zayla asked, spotting something in the distance.

"It's an expedition flag warning of some danger," Rahlys said. Brakalar studied the marker through the spy glass, and then scanned the area for anything that might be connected to the warning.

"Shall we investigate...or heed the warning?" Zayla asked, as Brakalar handed her the spyglass.

"We investigate," Brakalar answered firmly. The rest of the group arrived and a discussion ensued. All agreed it was part of their mission to investigate.

Rahlys felt the searching reach of the filaments of energy exuding from Brakalar as he approached her. "Can you sense anything, any anomaly?" he asked her.

Rahlys wanted to say, "Yes, coming from you," but instead she just said, "No."

"Any signatures indicating others are present?" Zayla asked.

"No."

Brakalar addressed the whole group. "We advance slowly. Everyone will stay together and watch each other's back. It you see so much as an eyelash twitch, holler."

Once again, Brakalar and Zayla took the lead, proceeding with extreme caution. Not a word was spoken as they made their way diagonally across the sloping hillside to the marker at the edge of the valley below. Before long, the expedition reached the site without incidence.

"Well...?" Zayla asked no one in particular after the team had scoured the area finding nothing disconcerting, except for the flag itself.

"The lost expedition wouldn't have placed a marker for no reason," Anthya offered.

"Maybe someone else found or took the flag from a member of the lost expedition and placed it here for reasons of their own," Quaylyn speculated, surprising everyone by saying anything at all.

"That is a possibility we need to consider," Zayla agreed.

"Who else is on the continent, Rojaire?" Theon asked. "Have you run into others in your travels?" Rojaire could read from the tone of Theon's voice he knew something.

"There is one group that I know of, but I don't think they're a threat to us. They aren't very smart, or very well organized...and we outnumber them three to one."

"So what are they doing here?" Anthya asked.

"Escaping the shackles of society," Rojaire stated boldly. That incited such scathing stares from Brakalar, Zayla, and Anthya; he trimmed his rebellious tone before continuing. "They are harmless do-nothings, calling themselves the Band of Rogues, and would rather laze their days here than contribute to society. I really doubt they had anything to do with this. They're not that energetic...or that creative." Theon didn't respond. To reveal Rojaire's association with the Band of Rogues would mean betraying Setas.

"We move on!" Brakalar said quietly. "Anthya and I will lead, followed by Ilene and Theon, then Rojaire and Zayla. Rahlys and Quaylyn will bring up the rear. We'll stop at the first shade we find."

"Who do you really believe put that marker there?" Ilene asked her father as they hiked side by side.

"I don't know; I'm not quite ready to make accusations."

"I believe it was left by the lost expedition," Ilene decided. "It may just be that the danger that was present then is no longer present now."

"Maybe," Theon agreed...anything was possible.

"Oh, look at those beautiful flowers!" Ilene exclaimed, taking three strides in their direction before disappearing completely...right through the foliage covering the ground.

"I think we should take the hidden pass back to the western side of the mountain range where there is more to eat," Tassyn said, looking cleaner since Traevus washed their clothing.

"Yes," Edty agreed, "it's a lot nicer out west." Confronting Stram was risky business, but he seemed to take it in stride for once.

"I'm thinking we could use a little larger labor force to build our community out west," Traevus overhead Stram say as he approached the camp carrying fresh water. He quietly set the water containers down and listened.

The Band of Rogues had been camped for rotations, hidden in a deep clef in the rocky eastern foothills of the Crescent Mountains. Their water source, a cool spring conveniently located in the cave behind them, offered no opportunity for escape, which meant Traevus could fetch water without a guard.

"What are you suggesting?" Tassyn asked.

"I propose we return to where we intercepted the expedition, follow their tracks, and convince them to join us.

"What? Have you lost your mind?" Tassyn was surprised by his outburst, but couldn't take it back. Fortunately, Stram decided to use the art of persuasion instead of force.

"Do you want to live in a hovel...or a palace? How hard do you want to work? How well do you want to live? Every visionary who has ever lived has been called crazy at some time."

"I don't know, Stram, enslaving people...?" Tassyn wasn't sure how to continue, but Stram jumped up from his seat on a large boulder that served as a crude throne and paced before them.

"Consider this: We would have women. And any woman who bears our offspring will no longer be a slave. Our community will have a chance to thrive and grow, free from the stranglehold of the Academy and the High Council. Think about it," Stram added after a dramatic pause. The camp grew quiet as Tassyn and Edty tried to wrap their minds around Stram's vision. When enough time had passed, Traevus returned with the water.

"You will lead us to the other members of your expedition," Stram told him without preamble. "I'm assuming they are headed for the slopes of Mt. Vatre. Do you want to tell us why?"

"I'm not leading you anywhere," Traevus answered defiantly after setting the water containers down on a rock ledge. Stram swung out a powerful arm and fist that made contact with Traevus' jaw, knocking him painfully to the ground.

Traevus forced his way back up. Had the Band of Rogues been responsible for any of the expedition's other misfortunes? he wondered. It didn't seem likely since the incidences had been widely spread out over time and distance.

"What do you want with the expedition?" Traevus asked when his head cleared of stars and the pain in his jaw eased enough to speak.

"What did I tell you about asking questions?"

"Oooo...." A hard blow to his left side, this time without physical contact, bent Traevus over; a second blow sent him curling back down to the rocky ground.

"We will leave when Seaa rises," Stram announced as the band gathered around Traevus, curled in a fetus position, moaning pitifully. "Meanwhile, get some rest," he directed to Tassyn and Edty. "I'll guard the prisoner." There was little guarding needed. Traevus didn't move...and didn't intend to for some time.

"Your little band will be my first slave laborers," Stram said quietly, as much to himself as to Traevus, after the other two had gone to sleep. "I will build a great empire in which men will be truly free, and the Devastated Continent will be under my control to rule as I wish." Somehow, Stram was able to rationalize the two conflicting concepts in his own mind.

Chapter 11
Railroad Tracks

The snowstorm relinquished its power to dull gray skies with a hint of sun to the southeast like a faint glow globe obscured by swirls of gray. It was time to move on. Caleeza locked the door to the shelter made of trees, and resumed her journey south. The hand span depth of snow and the extra layers of clothing she wore, along with the awkward additional foot coverings, made walking over the rough terrain more difficult, but at least she was warmer. To alleviate the difficulty, she frequently teleported herself ahead, as far as forest and terrain allowed her to see. From time to time, she caught glimpses of the great road and the all important pipeline and thought of Stanley. *What would have happened if I had chosen to satisfy his fantasies?* She smiled at the absurdity of the idea.

As the land rose, the forest disappeared for a time, leaving only a rocky, snow-blown landscape at the mercy of the wind. Then the land dropped again and the forest returned, offering some shelter, but obstructing her view. Eventually, she came to a mighty river, cold and swift, flowing between steep snow-covered banks. A flying creature as black as darkness startled her as it flew overhead, swooshing powerful black-feathered wings. It emitted a loud piercing cry and spread its wings wide, gliding down over the river, eventually landing in a tree on the opposite bank. Nothing else moved. Caleeza teleported herself to the opposite ridge, far from the flying creature, and left the river behind.

Snowflakes danced around on the breeze, hazing the distance, forcing her to shorten her jumps forward. Twice, she stumbled across small fur-covered creatures with long ears that quickly loped away under cover, blending into the landscape. Caleeza located the life forms mentally and felt their fear of her. Her stomach growling, she pulled out a cloth-wrapped ball of cooked grain, unwrapped it, and began munching. *In these conditions, I would make better progress following the great road,* she decided after some thought. Saving half of the ball of cooked grain for another meal, she headed east to reconnect with the road.

It took a couple of jumps for Caleeza to find the road again; it had taken a more southeasterly direction, putting some distance between them. Once she was on the road again where the snow had been cleared away and she could see a lot farther, covering great distances became a lot easier. She made sure no mechanical beasts were in sight before teleporting herself forward, and when one approached, she teleported herself away from the road altogether. Advancing in this fashion, she eventually came to a junction with another road as deserted as the one she had been following. Now, she had to make a decision. *Should I continue in the same direction or turn to the west?* she debated with herself. In the end, she decided to continue in the direction she had been going.

At first, there was no change, but gradually, she started encountering more and more mechanical conveyances of various shapes and sizes, some filled to capacity with people. The increase in traffic and the attention she drew made it necessary to leave the road and travel through the woods. More and more people-made structures dotted the landscape along the road corridor, many of them guarded by short, four-legged creatures that made loud explosive noises, baring sharp teeth.

As darkness descended, Caleeza came to a brightly lit structure with several mechanical conveyances parked out front. Some of them were pulled up to tall thin stands and connected to them by long hoses. Veiled by the increasing darkness, she placed herself where she could watch without being seen. A young man with drawings on his exposed forearms came out of the building eating something he carried in his hand. He climbed into one of the conveyances parked out front and drove away. *Is this a place for acquiring food,* she wondered?

Soon, another man with a paunch like Stanley's, accompanied by a short chubby female, exited the building and walked up to a mechanical beast connected to one of the upright fixtures. The woman, carrying a bulging white sack, climbed into the conveyance while the man disconnected the hose from their mechanical beast and placed it back into the stand before driving away.

Soon after the man and woman pulled away, another conveyance, smaller and more aerodynamic, turned off the road and stopped in front of the building. A rotund man with sagging jowls and long black and gray facial hair climbed out of the conveyance, with some difficulty, and headed for the entrance. Caleeza watched him carefully as he waddled slowly up to the transparent door, peered inside, then pulled the door open, and went in.

Cautiously, Caleeza approached the entrance. Having observed all this activity, she decided to study the situation closer. Following the man's example, Caleeza walked up to the front door, peered in briefly through its transparency, and walked in, setting off a jingle of bells overhead. A flood of strong unfamiliar scents...some pleasant, some repelling...permeated the warm air. The grizzled broad-shouldered man standing behind a counter, and seemingly in charge of the place, hardly gave her a glance, allowing her a chance to look around. Rows of shelves filled with unfamiliar items crowded the entire room, except for the area between the doorway and the counter. The man with the long facial hair stood in line behind a tall thin woman in a large puffy coat. The woman was receiving some flat round discs that the broad-shouldered man behind the counter dropped into her outstretched hand. Soon, after she left carrying a bag of items, and the man she had followed in stepped up to the counter. Caleeza got in line behind him.

"Well, hi, Jim," Russ greeted his neighbor from behind the counter. "What can I do for you?"

"A hotdog, please."

"A hotdog? Is that the best you could come up with? That will be four dollars." Caleeza watched as the man behind the counter moved away, apparently to fulfill Jim's request.

"So, Russ, how's Grace?" Jim asked, fishing in his wallet for the money and placing it on the counter.

"She's doing great!" Caleeza watched intently as Russ constructed Jim's hotdog. "The grandkids are coming up next summer."

When Russ was finished, he returned to the counter, picked up the green slips of paper Jim had placed there, and handed him a paper dish containing leavened bread cut in half, with a tube of something nested inside. Jim took the hotdog and turned to a table next to the counter, where he added a squirt of something yellow from a yellow container and a squirt of something red from a red container. He then spooned on a green substance with red specks from a square box and some chopped up whitish chunks from another before taking a mighty bite.

"What can I do for you," Russ asked Caleeza, after returning from putting the green paper slips away. Caleeza froze for a moment, and then gathered her courage.

"A hotdog, please," she stated clearly.

"Anything to drink with that?" Caleeza didn't understand, and shook her head 'no.'

"Four dollars," Russ said, eyeing her skeptically.

Caleeza didn't have any of the green slips of paper, but she spotted a flat disc on the floor similar to the ones she saw him give to the woman in the fluffy coat. Stooping down, she picked it up and placed it on the counter.

"You need another $3.75," Russ said, starting to lose his patience. Jim, enjoying his hotdog, studied the girl dressed in old oversized clothing.

"The girl looks hungry," he said. "Give her one of your over-priced tube steaks. I'll pay for it." Jim threw a fiver on the counter. "And throw in a bag of chips." It wasn't clear to Caleeza what they were saying, but from the images she gleaned from their minds, she determined that Russ was helping her acquire a hotdog.

"Thank you," she said.

"You're welcome." By the time Russ handed Caleeza her hotdog and a small light-weight yellow bag like the one she had seem in trucker Stanley's food box, Jim was finished eating. "Catch you later," he said, and walked out.

"Yes, later," Russ waved him out. "Condiments are over there," Russ said pointing to the table.

"Thank you." Following Jim's example, Caleeza turned to the condiment table and attempted to squeeze some yellow stuff out of the yellow container. It sputtered spattering yellow spots propelled by air on her food and hand. When she tried the red bottle, the red stuff oozed out thickly, forming a red puddle the length of her hotdog. Foregoing the rest of the additives, she brought the hotdog to her mouth and took a large bite, screwing up her face in reaction to the bittersweet assault on her taste buds.

A chatty couple of similar build and height walked in and started searching through the rows of items, apparently looking for something in particular. As Russ went to their aid, Caleeza exited the building carrying the strange yellow bag that crunched if she squeezed it too hard and the rest of her hotdog. Outside, cold air dominated once again, making her shiver momentarily as she re-acclimated. She finished off her hotdog, licking red and yellow stuff off her fingers, and then stashed the crunchy yellow bag in her coat pocket with the half-eaten ball of cooked grain.

While she stared out into the snowy darkness beyond the island of light considering what to do next, the chatty couple who had entered the building after her walked out. She watched as they climbed into the seat of a much smaller version of Stanley's truck with another compartment attached behind it. As they turned onto the road going south, she scanned the large square compartment they were pulling for life forms. It was empty.

Before carefully thinking it through, Caleeza teleported herself into the compartment, and found herself standing in a tiny moving room with a table, seats, and a bed. The moving room was cold, but she could keep herself warm. She could hardly believe her good luck.

Caleeza sat at the little table, looking out into the night. Occasionally, they passed lights that lit up spots marking people structures. As they continued on, a soft glow appeared above the trees in the distance. She knew it wasn't sunrise, not according to the pattern of day and night she had experienced thus far. So what was lighting up the sky? Eventually, there were lights spaced at even intervals along the road, more roads crossing one another, and more mechanical monsters. People structures, lit from within and without, dotted the landscape. It looked like she had finally reached a sizable settlement.

The couple drove on through the glow of lights until darkness closed in again, except for a few weak lights marking more residences. Then the moving room slowed down, turned in at one of the structures, and came to a stop. Caleeza went on tight alert; they must have reached their destination. Would the chatty couple want their moving room now that it was no longer moving? The couple climbed down out of the truck. She could hear them talking, and although she couldn't understand what they were saying, she detected great weariness.

"You want to unload the camper tonight?" the male voice asked.

"No, I'm tired. I'll get it tomorrow. There isn't much left in there anyway," the woman yawned. Then there was a horrendous noise as a part of the outside wall of the structure rose, opening a portal into a dimly lit enclosed area. The couple entered and just as quickly, the wall came back down, closing Caleeza out.

Caleeza breathed a sigh of relief; she was safe for the moment, also tired. Drawing an aura of warmth around her, she removed her outer garments and crawled into the bed. Exhausted from the day's journey, sleep came quickly. But in the wee hours of the morning, she started to dream.

Caleeza stood alone among giant hexagonal crystal columns and crystal boulders tumbled topsy-turvy across the landscape. Mt. Vatre, a broken remnant of a mountain, loomed darkly in the distance, partly obscured by a blanket of dark orangey gray clouds that hid the sun and cast a dull sheen on the chaotic array of softly glowing transparent crystal pillars.

"Sarus, where are you?" she called out, time and time again, but there was no answer. She tried to search for him, but moving around in the jumble of monolithic crystals was slow and difficult. Suddenly, the clouds departed and the sky cleared to a brilliantly clear white gold. Bright sunlight struck the crystalline landscape, fracturing the light into glowing colors. The crystals began to hum. "Sarus, where are you?" she called again.

"I am here," Sarus said.

She looked everywhere, but still she couldn't find him.

"Where?" she asked again.

"I am all around you. Do not be concerned for me. I am learning the answer."

"What answer? I don't understand."

"You will," Sarus' voice said, and for some reason, she believed him.

"Sarus, where are you? Show yourself. Let me see that you are all right."

"You must not concern yourself over my wellbeing; I have gained so much." Why did he sound emotionally distant?

"What about us? Sarus, I love you. Please, help me. Help me find a way home." But there was no answer. The Crystalline Landscape faded from her dreams, and Caleeza continued to sleep.

Optimistically well rested, she woke to a gray dawn. Dressing quickly, Caleeza teleported herself outside the movable room and hurried down the road. A life form protested loudly as she passed in front of another living structure. She needed to get away from the residences and the roads. Fortunately, the woods were nearby and soon, she was heading south again across uninhabited terrain. The snow was not as deep here, making walking a lot easier. There was little wind to speak of, and the grayness dissolved into a mosaic of blue sky, white clouds, and sunshine. For breakfast, she nibbled away the rest of the cooked grain and drank snow she melted in a little cup.

It was mid-morning when she came across a different kind of trail altogether. Two raised metal bars ran parallel to one another, mounted little more than an arm length apart on thick black slabs embedded in a raised bed of rock not much wider than the trail itself. The trail, for the most part, was snow-free and ran uninterrupted as far as she could see, curving to the contour of the land. Caleeza had no idea what the trail was for, but submitted to the natural inclination to follow it, staying alert to anything that might be approaching from either direction. She noticed quickly that the spacing of the black slabs were off sync with a comfortable stride and walked along the edge of the woods by the side of the raised trail, teleporting ahead along long straight stretches, whenever possible. While hiking the short distances in between hops, she stopped frequently to listen and watch for danger.

Then to Caleeza's surprise, the metal, wood and rock trail crossed a road; whether it was the same road she had followed before or a different one, she didn't know. For a moment, she considered following the road instead, but after a few vehicles passed by, she decided to continue down the quieter narrower trail.

When hunger struck, Caleeza pulled out the little packet of thin golden wafers from inside her coat. The sealed bag was flatter now and the wafers smaller, albeit more numerous, than before. She managed to pull the bag open, and then placed one of the thin yellow wafers in her mouth. It was tantalizingly salty. Quickly, she ate another, and another...feeling almost compelled to eat more, until the bag was empty...leaving her licking greasy salty fingers. Almost reverently, she carefully folded the empty yellow sack and tucked it away in her coat.

Caleeza was off the trail of wood and rails, seeking cleaner deeper snow to melt for drinking water when she detected a low deep rumble, which quickly grew in intensity, coming up from behind. Bends in the pathway winding around hills hid whatever approached. Finally, she saw lights breaking around the curve. To her astonishment, it kept on coming...and coming...and coming...a long serpentine monster, on rolling wheels that fitted perfectly on the metal rails. She reached out mentally, searching for a signature, and found two. The serpentine monster was driven by people! Spotting her at the edge of the woods, one of the men signaled with a loud piercing whistle as the head of the monster slithered by...but the monster's long cylindrical segmented body kept coming for some time, clacking rhythmically, seemingly without end, until finally the tail end came into view and passed her by. Caleeza watched as it eventually disappeared around another bend. Now she knew what the trail was for and why there was so little snow on it.

The trail of rails crossed a river and intersected the road again. This time, there was a community off to the side. *Should I stop at this community or move on?* she asked herself, looking around. Some of the structures were made from trees laid horizontally like the shelter she had stayed in up north during the snowstorm. Here, she caught her first sight of a new person since her arrival on this world, two of them, individuals not yet grown, walking the side road leading into the village.

Caleeza strolled around, not knowing what she was searching for, but soon the answer seemed clear. *I must move on. There is nothing for me here.*

As the day progressed, Caleeza continued to follow the trail of wood and rails, taking the opportunity to leap ahead when she felt she could do so safely. She passed places where the terrain had been eaten away by large skeletal mechanical giants; she could see one grazing in the distance. A few isolated structures dotted the area, but all were apparently deserted.

The terrain changed as the trail rose gaining altitude, hugging a mountain on one side and overlooking a terrifyingly long vertical drop into a narrow rocky chasm below on the other. Mountains pressed in on all around, filling the sky and shadowing the valley. The forest dwindled away with the increase in altitude, and eventually she was in a broad treeless mountain pass.

From there, the route started to descend again. The forest returned bigger and thicker than before, the covering of snow diminishing the further south she reached. Soon, only a dusting of white covered the ground, and then there was none at all.

Have I finally outdistanced winter?

It was warmer here, barely freezing, and she even opened her heavy outer garment to let excessive body heat, accumulated by physical exertion, escape. The trail of rails followed a wide forested valley dominated by a mighty river framed in by hills and distant mountains. Many smaller tributaries emptied into the dominate river, cutting their way through a dense forest of leafless trees with grayish white trunks, leafless bushes, and tall conical shaped trees with dark green pin like leaves. Everywhere, golden brown underbrush lay limp and lifeless, bent over the hard cold ground. Occasionally along the way, a path broke out of the woods where the foliage had been worn down to soil, forming a trough through the otherwise undisturbed landscape. She scanned the surrounding forest for what might have made the marks, but found nothing threatening.

And then she felt it.

For the first time since she landed on this world, Caleeza felt the use of magic!

Maggie tried to get comfortable on the sofa as a twinge of a contraction passed over her, the second one today. She and Vince and the kids were going out on the passenger train tomorrow, staying in town until after the baby was born. *Wait till tomorrow night*, Maggie spoke silently to her unborn child, *you're not due for another week.* Vince heard Maggie sigh softly as she changed positions.

"Are you all right?" he asked apprehensively, prying his attention away from the manuscript he feverishly edited to glance her way. He hoped to finish editing the manuscript before catching tomorrow's train.

"Relax, I'm fine," Maggie reassured him...and she was. "Listen to them," she said with a jerk of her head toward the kitchen where Melinda and Leaf were noisily doing the dishes. "Leaf chatters on and on, and even though you can't hear Melinda, you know the two of them are in constant communication."

"Meaningless chatter. I suspect it is only when Leaf speaks silently that they say anything worth hearing." Nevertheless, some quiet time for Maggie, not to mention himself, was in order. "How are you two doing in there?" Vince asked loud enough to be heard over their noise.

"We're almost done," Leaf called back. Then Vince and Maggie heard a fit of laughter. When and how had Leaf become so vocal, Maggie wondered? It seemed like he was still speaking baby talk just a few weeks ago. Now he was stringing sentences together.

"I want you two to put on your hats and coats and go outdoors for some fresh air...before it gets dark," Vince told them. Melinda and Leaf came bounding into the room.

"We're done," Leaf laughed. Vince glanced at Melinda for confirmation, and she nodded her head.

"Very good, put your coat on...here, I'll help you." Vince got up from the computer and dressed Leaf warmly while Melinda readied herself.

"Don't go too far," Maggie reminded them.

We won't, Melinda replied automatically. The two children burst through the door, which Vince closed after them, breathing in the silent relief.

"You know the noise level will increase with a new baby," Maggie reminded him.

"We may have to add on yet another addition," he smiled at her lovingly.

Leaf, a spring being unwound, ran circles around the yard before stopping at a sloping mound of ice, what little remained of his once great snowstorm. Watching Leaf run around, Melinda recalled when she and Raven used to explore the woods together. Raven, Rahlys, Theon, and Ilene...what was happening to them now?

Melinda's attention was drawn back to Leaf when before her eyes she saw the hard-packed, snow-turned-to-ice mound steam into slush, and then water, spreading out across the slightly frozen ground. The warm water melted the still thin layer of icy soil crust enough for the water to seep in, leaving only a wet spot that would now refreeze.

What did you do? Melinda asked in obvious awe.

"I made the snow go away. I didn't want it anymore."

Remember, Leaf, what I said about not letting Mom and Dad see you do magic, she warned him for the zillionth time. Knowing how preoccupied they were,

Melinda doubted that they had seen anything, but they were sure to notice later that the ice mound was gone.

"I remember," Leaf said. "Let's go to our secret place. I'll show you what I can do."

Before Melinda could respond, she and Leaf were standing in the little log schoolhouse near Rahlys' log home.

Leaf, I told you to let me know when you are taking us somewhere before you teleport us away, she reminded him again.

"Okay, I'm sorry. I forgot."

I doubt anyone will notice if we are gone for a little while.

"It's cold. Let's make a fire."

We can't stay that long. Besides I don't have a lighter.

"I can light it," Leaf said with certainty. In light of the recent ice mound meltdown, Melinda had no doubt that he could. She opened the stove door, crumpled pages of old school work, stuffing them into the stove, and stacked the little pile of kindling conveniently left for the next fire on top of the paper.

It would help if we had a couple of larger pieces of firewood, too, she said. No sooner than she said it, first one and then a second chunk of firewood appeared in the firebox. *Where did those come from?*

"The woodshed."

Rahlys' woodshed?

"Our woodshed."

Leaf focused on the stack of paper, kindling, and wood, raising its temperature. Tendrils of smoke appeared, charring the edge of the crumpled paper at the bottom of the stack. Then, Leaf screeched with delight as the paper burst into flames. Soon, the merry crackle of burning kindling greeted their ears. Melinda closed the door and checked the draft. Immediately, Leaf took off his coat.

It's not warm in here yet, she told him. Leaf ignored that.

"Want to see what I can do?" Without waiting for the expected affirmative, Leaf went into action. His youthful little face squished up with effort, and soon a floating ball of light appeared before them. Leaf danced about with delight over his success. Melinda remembered the floating ball of light that Anthya had produced for Leaf to play with. It was during her visit when Anthya had announced to Rahlys that she and three of her warriors were invited on a mission to the Devastated Continent. Leaf must have been trying to make one himself ever since. Then, suddenly, Leaf froze in place and the floating ball of light winked out.

"There is someone here, hiding in the woods," Leaf said.

Are you sure? Who?

"Someone. Let's go see."

No... Melinda tried to say, but they were already there, Leaf without his coat, standing in the woods outside the schoolhouse. A woman with orange hair, violet eyes, and dressed in old clothes stared at them in startled shock over their sudden appearance. Melinda was a little startled, too.

Who are you? Melinda asked.

The girl could communicate telepathically, Caleeza realized. By doing the same, she could relate more with thought and feeling.

I'm Caleeza.

"I'm Leaf Bradley," Leaf piped in quickly. Caleeza smiled at the little youth. She hadn't really directed her thoughts to him; he was so young.

What are you doing here lurking in the woods by our schoolhouse? Where did you come from? Melinda asked, suddenly realizing that they were communicating telepathically.

Caleeza couldn't understand the words, but the thought images aided in the exchange. *I have traveled a long way across frozen landscape,* Caleeza related, showing them images of her journey, which suggested to Melinda that she must have come from up north. *Somehow I was transported from my own world to yours,* and she shared images of a world that looked a lot like the one Theon had often described to them.

Anthya's world?

You know of my world? Caleeza asked, surprised by a mental glimpse of Councilor Anthya she picked up from the young girl's thoughts.

Are you from Anthya and Theon's world? Melinda asked.

Caleeza stared back incredulously. She wasn't sure who Theon was, but there was no mistaking the images of Councilor Anthya that flittered through Melinda's mind...and there was something else, something that the girl thought she had successfully shielded...the feel of Droclum's evil. How was that possible, Caleeza couldn't help but wonder?

I am from Anthya's world, and I need your help to return.

It was at this inconvenient moment that Leaf jerked his head toward home and announced, "I think Dad is calling us?"

Wait! Not yet! Melinda said quickly, before he could take them away. *We need to decide what to do about Caleeza.*

"She can stay in our secret place," Leaf said.

You're right; she can stay in the schoolhouse, at least for now. Caleeza, follow us, Melinda said and she and Leaf led her into the little building, now pleasantly warm.

Stay here. We'll bring you food. There's firewood in the woodshed on the other side of these trees, she said pointing toward Rahlys' cabin. *We have to go now, but we will try to sneak back some time tonight. Do you understand?*

Yes, Caleeza said, for Melinda had provided her with ample visual clues.

And, Leaf, when you take us back home, place us just a little into the woods so no one will know we were here, okay?

"Okay. Now, Melinda?" Leaf asked cautiously.

Yes, now.

The children vanished, leaving Caleeza standing alone in another shelter made of trees.

Melinda and Leaf returned that night to the schoolhouse as promised. They brought bags of unfamiliar food with them, for which Caleeza was very grateful. As they emptied the bags out onto the table, proudly displaying their loot, Leaf named off the items and Melinda explained telepathically how to consume them. Starving, Caleeza grabbed the only food she recognized among the offerings, an apple, and bit into it hungrily. Realizing how hungry she must be, Melinda opened a can of meaty pasta...demonstrating the use of a can opener...and spooned out the contents into a pan, placing it on the stove to heat. Caleeza compared the picture on the outside of the can to the contents in the pan. The picture looked similar to the food Melinda was heating. Not to be outdone, Leaf demonstrated how to make peanut butter cracker sandwiches, making a mess in the process.

Caleeza studied the new persons intently while they ate. Melinda, so quietly mysterious, was meticulous in her efforts to help. When she communicated information, she was thorough, projecting precise mental pictures for clearer understanding. But she didn't exhibit any significant abilities to tap into the elemental forces, other than telepathic communication. In fact, she never spoke verbally, not even to the little one. Unlike the other sentient life forms Caleeza had thus far encountered, Melinda's mind was the first not totally open for her to read. She had learned to some extent to shelter her thoughts and lock them up...but she was not always successful.

Droclum had nearly destroyed her own world long before Caleeza was born...yet this new person on another world knew of Droclum! She wanted to ask questions, but knew she would have to wait until she had gained the girl's trust, as well as a better understanding of the language, before she could broach the topic.

The little one, Leaf, exuded untrained unstructured ability. Things he reached for nearly jumped into his hand, or worked without him actually touching them as he cheerfully laughed and played...never still for a moment. It was fortunate the child was so good natured; otherwise, he would be dangerous. Leaf was the one who actually teleported the two of them back and forth...and it was his use of the elemental forces that she had detected from the trail.

Caleeza learned that the structure she now occupied was actually a mini academy and all the written papers and paintings on the walls were lessons that had been successfully completed. Leaf brought her a round, light-weight learning machine with colored pictures on the surface. The youngling moved a pointer to a green image. "Leaf. That's me," he said, pointing to it while laughing boisterously. Then he pulled the handle. "Leaf," said a recorded voice in the machine, and he laughed even harder.

Caleeza picked up a large ball in a stand that sat on a shelf. The areas of brown, green, pink, and blue looked like they might represent the continents and oceans of a planet. She presented it to Melinda.

Earth, Melinda said taking the globe. *This is our world. Do you want me to show you where we live?*

"Yes," Caleeza said, and Melinda pointed to a spot near the top of the globe.

We are here, in Alaska.

"Alaska," Leaf chirped merrily.

"Alaska," Caleeza repeated after him.

Then Caleeza learned that the new persons were about to leave the woods with their chosen mother and chosen father for the birth of another new person. Melinda was uncertain when they would return. How could a community of so few Accepted Ones nurture so many new persons, Caleeza wondered? Besides the younglings, Caleeza had found only three other human signatures in the whole immediate area.

We will bring you more food when we return from Wasilla. Is there anything you want from town?

"I want candy," Leaf said, "What do you want?" he asked Caleeza.

"Want...?" Caleeza tried to understand, and Melinda telepathed feelings of longing, want, and desire, accompanied by images...that meant little to Caleeza...of the things she wished for most.

Thinking she understood, Caleeza dug into a pouch of the heavy outer garment she had worn for warmth, now hanging by the door, and pulled out the carefully folded yellow bag.

"Want," she said, handing the empty potato chip bag to Melinda.

Chapter 12
The Sooty Caves

"Ilene!" Theon cried out for all to hear. In desperate haste, he dropped down on hands and knees, tearing back foliage that spanned across a narrow chasm. "Ilene! Where are you?"

Theon's shouts brought the rest of the group rushing over to help. Even Raven flew in to investigate.

"I'm down here," Ilene cried back.

"Make sure you have solid ground underfoot before you take a step," Brakalar cautioned.

"Are you all right?" Theon asked as his efforts revealed Ilene wedged in a crevice of blue violet stone ten feet below him.

"I think so, but I'm wedged in; I can't move."

As the others cleared more brush, it turned out the split in the ground extended for nearly twenty feet. The crevice gaped about three feet across at its widest, narrowing down to mere inches where Ilene's feet were wedged in stone.

"Now we know why the marker was there," Zayla said, assessing the situation.

"I can get you out," Rahlys told Ilene calmly. "Be ready to catch her," she instructed the others. Rahlys focused on drawing energy, pulling Ilene out of the crevice and teleporting her to the surface. When Ilene appeared beside them, Quaylyn and Rojaire stepped in quickly, catching her before she dropped...and gently lowered her to the ground.

"You have a bump on the back of your head and a scratch on one arm," Anthya said, checking her for injuries. "Can you move your feet?" she asked with great concern. Ilene moved first her left foot, then her right...flinching a little.

"It's my right ankle. It feels like I strained it," Ilene said, "but I think I can walk." Anthya removed Ilene's protective expedition issued boot and examined her ankle carefully.

"I can't feel any broken bones. Right now I'm more concerned about the bump on the back of your head," she said. "Unfortunately, I don't seem to be able to draw and transmit healing energy."

"Let me try," Rahlys volunteered. "I'm not a healer, but I might be able to help." Rahlys knelt down behind Ilene and stared at the angry bump. "How does your head feel?"

"It still smarts some where I banged it, but the pain is diminishing."

"You do have quite a bump there," Rahlys said upon examination. The scratch on her arm was minor. She moved down to Ilene's sprained ankle, holding it carefully as she drew on what renewable healing energy she could reach from deep within her, directing it caressingly to Ilene's injuries. After some time, Ilene insisted she felt much better and was ready to stand up and try to walk. The bump on her head did look much better, so Rahlys and Anthya gave Ilene a hand getting to her feet. Once upright, Ilene took a couple of cautious steps, and then assured everyone she was fine.

To avoid any further accidents, the men had set to work cutting walking sticks from the straight sky-reaching branches of a zaota tree, towering above all the other foliage. Soon, there were enough poles, stripped of their leaves and cut to length, to provide everyone with a walking stick.

"These staffs are to be used as probes," Brakalar said holding his up as they each chose one from the pile, checking its feel in their hands. "Use them before each step you take, even if you are following in someone else's footsteps."

Brakalar walked over to Ilene, who was engaged in choosing the smallest staff she could find. "How are you feeling? Do you think you can go on?" he asked Ilene.

"Yes, I'm okay."

"We'll see," he said nodding to her, and then continued louder for all to hear. "This valley could be full of crevices, or maybe that's the only one. This pink and silver ground cover seems to grow extensively in this region," he said, waving his hand over the valley; they could see several large patches of it from where they stood. "There's no telling what it may be covering."

The group continued forward, tapping the ground before them like mountaineers traversing a glacier, probing for hidden crevasses under the snow. They crossed the riddled valley without further incidents, although four more narrow crevices were found. All were safely stepped across or circumvented. There was no evidence of cracks in the ground as they crossed the next valley over.

The team's weariness was starting to show in earnest as they trudged up yet another hill, still searching for a suitable place to camp. Reaching the top of the rise, Rahlys thought she was seeing a mirage, when the landscape before them dropped gently into a secluded oasis. A sizable stream, murmuring invitingly, tumbled over dark blue, orange, and lavender rocks and sand, with an abundance of edible and fruit-laden plants growing along its banks and on the surrounding hillside. Tall, tilted slabs of dark blue stone covered with flowering vines rose majestically out of smooth lavender sand, offering shelter from sun or rain.

"We'll camp here," Brakalar announced.

Rahlys sighed with relief. It had been a long hot day, the sun already high in the sky. The oasis offered food, water, and shade; all highly welcomed. Everyone drank, filled their water containers, and then splashed refreshingly cool water on their hands and faces. Further downstream, they found a deep bathing pool, and ample firewood to brew tea and cook vegetables and grains.

"Isn't this a beautiful spot," Ilene sighed in near ecstasy, floating on her back in the pool. "We needn't go any further."

For now, Ilene and Rahlys had the pool to themselves.

"Don't you want to complete our mission?" Rahlys asked.

"Of course. It's just it's so nice here."

"How's your head...and your foot and your arm?"

"Great! The bump on my head is gone," Ilene said, rubbing the remembered spot. "My foot is fine, and my arm is as good as new...see?" she said, showing Rahlys her blemish-free arm. "You did a great job!"

For that, Rahlys was grateful, but why she was still able to draw energy using the elemental forces when the rest of the group couldn't remained a mystery. "I'm going to sleep like one of those stone slabs," Rahlys said, pointing to a group of them on the stream bank. She sounded tired even to herself.

"How long in Earth-hours do you think we hiked?" Ilene asked.

"By my calculations, a day and a half." Of course, there had been breaks, but still, it had been a long stretch.

When Rahlys and Ilene returned to the campsite, preparations for a feast were underway. The abundance of fresh fruits and vegetables, cooking fires, and flowering vines created a festive atmosphere.

"If I didn't know better, I would say it's a Hawaiian luau. All we need is music and leis. I can provide the music," Ilene said.

True to her word, after the feast had been consumed and everyone lay about contentedly full, Ilene pulled her flute from her pack and began to play; the hauntingly melodious notes so alien to this world drifted over the quiet landscape. Clean, fed, and exhausted, Rahlys lay wrapped in her cloak on smooth lavender sand shaded by two vine-covered stone monoliths. There she slept oblivious to the sun's long slow arch across the cloudless golden sky.

"Aaaaaark! Aaaaaark!" Raven squawked close to Rahlys' ear.

Rahlys jolted awake. The sun was starting to descend toward the west. She turned on her side to scan the whereabouts and activities of the others. Everyone was milling about preparing for departure. Everyone but her. Rahlys eased herself up, shook the sand out of her cloak, stuffed it into her pack, and joined the others as they gathered around Brakalar.

"Hopefully everyone is well rested and ready to move on," Brakalar said, smiling and nodding at Rahlys.

Climbing out of the oasis, most of them still carrying their walking sticks, the landscape returned to what it had been before, rolling hills sparsely covered with low to shoulder-high brush, rock outcroppings, and zaota trees. Gradually, the hills became steeper, the valleys narrower and deeper, and vegetation became increasingly sparse with rock formations sprouting through the thinning soil.

What did grow looked like it could use some water, but not a cloud marred the brilliant yellow white sky. On and on they hiked, up and down hills and across valleys, their progress steady and uneventful...the land eerily quiet. There were no more expedition markers, no sign of the Band of Rogues or the members of the lost expedition; no sign of life...whatsoever...other than the vegetation. Cresting another hill, Rahlys could spot the others, here and there, weaving through brush as they descended the long slope into the next valley...another valley that looked exactly like the one before...and the one before that.

As darkness approached, they came to a sheltered cove with an underground spring that trickled out from the hillside. An abundance of woody shrubs and zaota trees provided firewood.

"We'll camp here until Seaa rises," Brakalar announced. "That will give everyone plenty of time to get some rest."

Rahlys joined Rojaire, Ilene, and Quaylyn in gathering fruits, grains, nuts, and vegetables. There wasn't as much variety here as at the oasis, but enough to satisfy everyone's hunger. Since Ilene seemed to be enjoying Rojaire's attention, Rahlys followed Quaylyn, who had wandered some distance from the camp to a small grassy meadow that yielded a bountiful crop of ground nuts. The two of them filled their gathering bags in silence. While harvesting, Rahlys worked on a suitable opening remark to draw Quaylyn into conversation. When she looked up, he was standing right beside her.

"I'm sorry," Quaylyn said, gazing into her eyes with grave sincerity.

"What for?" Rahlys asked, stunned.

"I'm sorry I failed you. I should have fought beside you, protected you. Instead, I fell apart."

"Quaylyn, stop it! You didn't fail me! You taught me everything! Without you, I could never have faced Droclum! And as far as the battle goes, events transpired as they were meant to. We were both pawns in the greater scheme of things."

Quaylyn said nothing, his face darkly distorted with pain and confusion. Rahlys gazed back at him with tender concern. She fought to keep her voice from quivering.

"When Anthya took you home, you were unconscious...close to death. Maggie and Vince, Theon...we all worried about you for the longest, before Anthya finally sent us word that you were recovering slowly. And still we were concerned."

Quaylyn looked away. "I wanted to contact you, but I couldn't bring myself to do so. I hurt too much inside."

"You didn't fail me, Quaylyn!" she reiterated. How could she make him see that? "When you handed me the necklace your mother had made to protect you, you provided me with what I needed to defeat Droclum."

Quaylyn laughed bitterly. "That's what the High Council of the Crystal Table said, 'Your First Mission was a success. You successfully helped Rahlys to destroy Droclum.'"

"We both know that your mother, Sorceress Anthya, defeated Droclum. Does it really matter? He's gone. It's time to put it behind us and move on."

"It's what I hope to accomplish on this mission," Quaylyn said, and without another word, he turned away from her and headed back to camp. Rahlys could only watch him go.

As rotations passed, Rahlys discerned a pattern emerging, as once again, they stopped to camp during the hottest part of the day. They ate, rested, and slept until the sun reached toward the western horizon; then they hiked until just before dark, camping until Seaa rose. In this fashion, the expedition covered considerable ground, closing in on the Crescent Mountains. "If we continue to make the progress we have so far, we could reach the Sooty Caves by next sunrise," Brakalar announced as they prepared to head out again.

In about four Earth-days, Rahlys calculated silently. She glanced quickly at Quaylyn, looking for a reaction to Brakalar's mention of the Sooty Caves as he shouldered his pack...but there was none. In fact, Quaylyn seemed far less sullen now than he did when she first arrived. The challenge of the journey invigorated him, despite his dark heritage and bleak state of mind...but still he remained non-communicative with her.

Seaa was shining brightly, washing out the night sky, when the expedition set out once again. In her ghostly light, the landscape opened onto a broad expanse of flat grassland that stretched to the very base of the mountains rising before them. From where they were, the mountains looked close, but Rahlys knew the distance across the grassland was great. Brakalar had paired Rahlys with Rojaire at the back of the pack for this leg of the journey. As they walked across the flat terrain, so easy to navigate, Rahlys gazed frequently up at Seaa, a small golden globe burning brightly high in the night sky.

"Two suns, one for day and one for night," Rahlys mused. "And no moon, I guess you don't need a moon with Seaa."

"Actually, only one sun and we do have a moon," Rojaire said, pointing out a tiny crescent low on the southern horizon. "Our planet doesn't revolve around Seaa, at least not in a celestial sense. However...half a revolution from now...we will be on the opposite side of the sun from Seaa. Then night will be dark, lit only by the distant stars."

"What season is this? Or do you even have seasons?"

"It's late winter."

"This is winter?" Rahlys asked incredulously. "This is nothing like winter where I live."

Rojaire laughed heartily. "Ilene has told me about your Alaska. In the summer the land is green and in the winter the land is white. Here summer and winter are not determined by the tilt of our planet on its axis, but by its distance from the sun."

"What do you mean?" Rahlys asked.

"When Seaa rises, her gravitational pull tugs on our planet, nudging it into a slightly elliptical orbit, away from the sun, but still within the habitable zone of space, giving us winter...which is what we are experiencing now. Then as our planet orbits away from Seaa, the gravitational pull of our sun draws us back, bringing us closer to the inner edge of the habitable zone, giving us summer, until Seaa rises, pulling us away again." Rahlys tried to picture this in her mind as she scanned the terrain for anything out of the ordinary.

"Isn't the ground a little dry?" she asked. "The landscape looks like it could use some rain."

"Winter tends to be dry. The rains will come," Rojaire said matter-of-factly. Then he paused, watching Raven circling languidly overhead.

"That's quite a friend you have there," he said, indicating Raven. Like the others, Rojaire looked upon Raven's flying abilities with near reverence.

"Yes, he's wonderful," Rahlys agreed, also pausing momentarily to watch Raven's graceful flight.

"Tell me more about the Band of Rogues," she said when they started walking again. She hoped she sounded like an innocent schoolgirl full of curiosity. "Did you spend much time in their company?"

"I spent some time with them," Rojaire said, no longer turning his head to glance at her. "We came to the Devastated Continent together. I didn't know they were going to become such nuisances then. When I could no longer tolerate their lack of desire to do anything worthwhile, I ventured off on my own to do what I had set out to do. I guess I'm just a loner at heart." Rojaire ventured an endearing smile her way.

"What did you set out to do?"

"I have spent much of my longevity exploring this continent, mapping it, studying the topography and vegetation, searching for anything left from the old world."

"And have you found anything?" The question came out smoothly enough... but Rojaire would say no more, and a long silence ensued. She must have gotten on his bad side for being too nosy.

"Guardian of the Light, is that what they call you?" Rojaire said with a hint of sarcasm, not expecting her to answer. "That's a pretty hefty title! But then you did stand up to Droclum, I'm told." He eyed her up and down as though to ascertain if that were even plausible. "It must have taken a lot of courage; I have to give you credit," he conceded.

"Yes, well, I did have some help," Rahlys said, without elaborating.

They hiked most of the night over the open prairie without reaching the mountains, until finally Brakalar called a halt as Seaa started to set in the west. Making camp with the crystal providing them light, Rahlys heated water for their tea, focusing energy to speed up the molecules in the water in lieu of firewood. Then she sat next to Theon and informed him telepathically, on a tight beam, what little she had learned about Rojaire. Theon wanted to tell her that he had seen what Brakalar was hiding, but didn't dare even whisper with the others so near.

The expedition started out again at daybreak in high spirits, their first targeted destination within reach. By sheer luck, Rahlys and Theon were paired together to bring up the rear on the last leg of the trek to the caves. Brakalar had placed himself and Rojaire in the lead. It was only after Theon was certain they had lagged far enough away from the others to avoid the risk of being overheard that he gave her the news.

"I know what Brakalar is hiding," he revealed.

"You do? What?"

"He has the key to the chest containing the Rod of Destruction. I saw it in his hand as he was fumbling through the contents in his pouch. It was just an accidental glimpse...I don't think Brakalar even knows I caught a glance...but I recognized it all right."

"What is the Rod of Destruction?" Rahlys asked, knowing she wouldn't like the answer.

"It's a Dark Oracle, a rod of formidable destructive power...forged by Droclum. We must find it before anyone else does. In the wrong hands, it could be the end of what is left of this world."

Rahlys gasped. "And you think it's in the Sooty Caves?"

"I think the key was found there, unless Rojaire found it somewhere else and gave it to Brakalar." It wasn't wise to lag behind long out in the open like this. Someone might wonder what they were up to. "One other thing, something Setas said." Theon glanced around as though looking for spies.

"Setas, the ferry lady?"

"She said to look for a stone as round and smooth and golden as Seaa herself."

"What does that mean?"

"I'm not sure, but keep your eyes out for anything fitting that description."

The Crescent Mountains loomed ever closer, long, narrow, jagged, dark blue-violet peaks...the chipped, cracked, discarded, broken sword blades of celestial giants, rising point up from the prairie floor. For the longest, the mountains had seemed to Rahlys unreachable and impassable. Now, as they made their final approach, they seemed only impassable, until they got even closer and she saw what looked like a pathway, a narrow, dark, sunless sand and rock passageway curving around the bases of two monolithic mountain peaks standing before them. The leading members of the expedition paused in the shade of the mountain by the passage opening, waiting for the others to gather.

"When we found this opening on the first expedition, we had hoped it would take us all the way through to the other side," Brakalar recapped for the group. "Instead, it leads to the Sooty Caves."

After a brief rest and feed, Brakalar led the group, single file, into the narrow mountain passage. The dry sandy trail, mixed with rocks, was bare of plant life, but their harvest bags and water canisters were full and would hold them over during their stay at the caves.

Walking through the passageway was not always easy. Often, their way was blocked by debris from crumbling mountain peaks, forcing them to climb over piles of sharp rock shards. Newly exposed rock, high up the steep slopes, gleamed red violet in the morning light.

"Heads up for falling rocks," Brakalar cautioned.

As the day progressed with the sun mounting ever higher in a cloudless golden white sky, the band of direct sunshine that at first only kissed the uppermost peaks descended the steep slopes, eventually nearly reaching them in the narrow passage as the sun gained altitude. Then, suddenly, without warning, they were in a wide sunny arena in front of the Sooty Caves.

Upon seeing the caves, it became immediately obvious how they had gotten their name. The rock walls within and around the mouth of the cave were burned sooty black, flamed by dragon fire, or balefire, or worse...or so it appeared. Rahlys walked up to the velvety black stone and rubbed her fingers across it, expecting to find black soot on her fingers when she turned them over...but they came away clean. It was the flat black sheen of the stone that gave it its sooty appearance.

"There is enough space for us to set up camp here," Brakalar said. "And if the weather should change, we can take shelter in the cave. The cave system is not very extensive, but we were able to find openings to three large chambers the last time we were here. After you have rested a bit, Zayla and I will take you to the location where we found Quaylyn encapsulated in suspended animation so long ago. Remember the crystal powered lights you carry have only so much stored energy, so use them wisely."

"We can also use the crystal for light," Rahlys reminded them. She glanced at Quaylyn to see how he was holding up. He seemed to be taking things well. An eagerness to explore the caves soon had the expedition back on its feet, and Brakalar and Zayla led them into the first chamber, with the crystal lighting the way.

The low angular ceiling of velvety black rock and darkly faceted walls did little toward reflecting back light. There were no mineral and water deposited formations such as stalactites and stalagmites, but the floor of the cavern was oddly irregular. Rahlys wanted to throw more light at her feet, but the crystal was up ahead, lighting the way for the others.

Should I draw enough energy to form a glow globe? To do so would further reveal the extent of her abilities unnecessarily. She opted to use the little hand-held solar-charged light she carried instead. Lighting the cave floor at her feet, Rahlys stooped down to investigate. To her astonishment, she discovered they were walking on an undulating carpet made of layer upon layer of tiny blossoming roses of smoky black crystal.

Catching up to the others, she extinguished her light as she entered a second chamber through a roughly triangular portal. This cavern was a little larger than the first, the ceiling high enough for the crystal to shine from above, casting light all around them. Here, the layers of tiny black crystal roses covering the floor formed an enchanted landscape of hills and valleys and bushy mounds, which they were forced to circumnavigate.

"The chamber where the capsule was found is this way," Zayla said as they approached a slit of an opening in the chamber wall. "You will have to duck going through the passageway leading to it; the ceiling is awfully low." Brakalar led the group through the low tunnel, while Zayla stood to the side of the opening, ushering the others through ahead of her.

"This stiff old body doesn't stoop like it used to," Theon complained as he bent to the task. Ilene and Rahlys followed him with Zayla bringing up the rear. The third chamber, except for its blackness, was nothing like the other two.

"It's a shrine!" Ilene said softly as the group spread out around a block of stone dominating the center of the chamber. *More like a mausoleum*, Rahlys thought to herself.

"The chamber has deteriorated since our last visit," Zayla observed, "probably due to seismic activity."

At one time, the room must have been a perfect cube, the walls, floor, and ceiling smooth and unbroken. But great forces, perhaps the Dark Devastation itself, had tweaked and distorted the cube-shaped room, cracking the walls and opening a break in the floor. Only the massive block of stone in the center seemed unblemished...but something was obviously missing. A deep depression in the top of the stone that no doubt matched the shape of Quaylyn's capsule lay empty and bare.

"So this is where you found me," Quaylyn said quietly, trying to keep his voice flat and unemotional...but Rahlys could not help detecting a hint of pain.

"How you were kept alive in this state for so long is beyond our understanding...but you are the living proof of it," Brakalar said, still shaking his head over the incredibility of it all.

"I would like to spend a little time here alone, if I may...to meditate," Quaylyn said softly.

"Of course," Zayla said; no one else spoke. The others turned to go. "We'll see you back at camp." She turned on her handheld light and exited the chamber. Rahlys sent the crystal after Zayla to light the way and slowly the others followed, leaving them in darkness.

When everyone was gone, Rahlys drew energy, forming a small glow globe for subdued lighting and walked over to Quaylyn's side, gently placing a comforting arm around him. To her relief, he didn't shake her off. Together, they stared into the depression in the stone, pondering its significance. From the lines in his face, she could see him visualizing himself as an infant lying there entombed for millennia...by an evil father...a heartbreaking loss for a loving mother.

GROUNDSHAKE EMINENT.

The oracle's warning startled Rahlys into action. "Come on, we have to get out of here!" she cried, tugging on Quaylyn so urgently, he unthinkingly followed...at first.

"What's wrong?" he asked, starting to resist, but before she could explain, the chamber began to shake.

"Come on!" Rahlys crawled into the exit tunnel first, the shaking intensifying around her. She had gone only a couple of feet when sharp pain, followed by nothingness, swept over her.

Rahlys didn't hear Quaylyn crying out her name as the tunnel collapsed into a jumble of dusty rock.

Chapter 13
Under a Zaota Tree

"Rahlys! By Seaa's light, no…Rahlys!" Quaylyn could face anything…but losing Rahlys. Upon reaching the tunnel opening, a cloud of dust choked him back, and then the glow globe went out, leaving him in darkness. Finally, the shaking subsided. Quaylyn groped his way blindly into the tunnel, frantically tossing stones that barred his way.

"Rahlys, can you hear me?" He paused briefly, listening over his wildly beating heart for a response. There was none. Then, suddenly, the crystal appeared, lighting up the chamber and tunnel behind him, giving him renewed hope. She was alive. The crystal's presence was assurance of that.

"Rahlys!" he cried again, tossing more rocks. His hand found a leg. "Rahlys," he whispered softly as he cleared rocks from around her. He knelt beside her, a tight fit in the narrow tunnel.

"Rahlys, wake up," he cried. "I'll get you out of here. Please, just stay with me." To Quaylyn's relief, she moaned softly. "Rahlys, can you hear me?" He was afraid to move her, not knowing the extent of her injuries.

"Quaylyn?" Rahlys opened her eyes. There was someone next to her, but he was hardly recognizable with all the dirt and grime on his face. Was that blood on his cheek? "What happened?" She made a move to sit up, but rejected the idea for a moment.

"The tunnel is blocked. I need to get you out of here. Where do you hurt?"

"A bit all over. Just give me a minute and I'll be all right. Where is all the light coming from? Is that the crystal?"

"It just appeared on its own," Quaylyn said.

Rahlys dimmed the light and conjured the crystal to her hand. In its glow, she gazed thankfully into Quaylyn's face. There was so much she wished she could tell him, so much she wanted to confide in him. She remembered fondly a time when she had trusted Quaylyn...a time when they had been allies. How she wished it could be that way now.

"Thanks for coming to my rescue," she said, smiling up at him sweetly. Carefully, she rolled onto her side to see for herself that the tunnel ahead was indeed blocked. Then she sat up cautiously. "The crystal can take us out of here," she reminded Quaylyn. The chest containing the Rod of Destruction would have to wait. She knew where it was...and so did Brakalar... but he would have to clear the tunnel to get to it.

Take us out to the clearing in front of the caves, Rahlys commanded the crystal...and sunshine licked their faces in the open arena. Raven cawed raucously in joyful celebration at their appearance, and the rest of the team quickly surrounded them as Quaylyn helped Rahlys up on her feet.

"We were just about to start digging you out," Zayla said, with obvious relief that they were safe and alive. "Are you all right?"

"We're fine," Rahlys assured her. There was excited chatter about the quake for a while, and then the group dispersed to explore, or nap, or pass their free time as they pleased. Rahlys wanted to clean up, but there was little water to spare. She needed to talk to Theon...alone. Finding a way to do so privately would be difficult in such a confined area.

"Come sit down with me here in the shade for a while and have a cup of tea," Zayla coaxed, pressing a small vessel of hot liquid into her hands and leading her to a sliver of shade along the western edge of the arena. Rahlys sat...gratefully she realized after she sat down...and cradled her tea, sipping it thoughtfully.

"The Devastated Continent has changed greatly in the short span of time since the first expedition," Zayla said, contemplating what she'd observed. "There are more plants in both variety and density covering the continent now, but the shape of the land keeps changing. Looking out upon the land-scape, it looks stable, but it is in constant flux, changing rapidly."

"What was it like on the first expedition when you found Quaylyn?" Rahlys asked, gazing groggily at Zayla. She needed to get some rest too, Rahlys realized.

"Bleak and barren," Zayla said. "Very little grew on the land back then, and what did grow grew mostly near the coast. It is heartening to see the transi-tion...." Rahlys heard no more.

When Rahlys opened her eyes again, the sliver of shadow had swallowed up the arena and was climbing up the unassailable peaks to the east above the caves.

The Rod of Destruction! Rahlys jumped up, despite still feeling groggy. She had to find Theon. Reaching out mentally, she located him in the second chamber of the Sooty Caves. To her dismay, Brakalar and Rojaire were there, too. The rest of the group was slumbering in the open arena. She telepathed Theon a message on a tight beam.

We need to talk. It's urgent! Meet me in the first chamber. Rahlys had no way of knowing if he received the message since Theon was unable to telepath back, but by the time she reached the first chamber, Theon was there.

"What's so urgent?" he asked immediately.

"What are Brakalar and Rojaire doing?" Rahlys asked, her expression weighted down with concern.

"They're trying to clear the collapsed tunnel so they can further explore the third chamber. Why?"

"The Rod of Destruction is in the third chamber. It's in the stone block in the center of the room."

"That would explain this madness."

"We need to go to the third chamber and find the Rod of Destruction before Brakalar and Rojaire clear the tunnel."

"How do you know it's there?"

"When we were in the chamber together, I detected the key Brakalar is carrying pointing to it. Brakalar knows it's there, too; that's why he's clearing the tunnel."

"Why did you wait so long to tell me this?"

"Zayla gave me some tea to drink; it put me to sleep. I thought she was just trying to be helpful. Do you think she drugged me to keep me from finding the Rod of Destruction before Brakalar can reach the third chamber?"

"I don't know," Theon scratched his head. "Take us to the third chamber. We'll have a look around."

"Take me with you," said a voice in the dark. Both Theon and Rahlys jumped as Quaylyn revealed his presence. "Please, I'm on your side. I know you two are up to something. I just want to help." Rahlys and Theon exchanged glances in the miniscule amount of light reaching them from the cave entrance. *It's safer to take him with us, before he talks to others,* Theon's nod seemed to say, so Rahlys teleported the three of them into the sealed off third chamber.

The room felt stuffy, closed. Rahlys released the crystal; fine unsettled dust drifted in the light. Was it just her unease playing tricks with her mind, or had the room become smaller? She hoped it was still stable after the last groundshake.

Rahlys and Theon fell to searching for a way into the stone block that had once cradled Quaylyn. This chamber had been Droclum's idea of a nursery... the stone block Quaylyn's crib. Rahlys shuddered at the realizations.

"What are we looking for?" Quaylyn asked, studying the stone block along with them. Theon motioned for Quaylyn to speak softly. They could faintly hear the cave-in removal team working on the other side of the rock barrier.

"We're looking for a way into this block of stone," Theon said quietly.

"Is the block of stone the chest?" Rahlys asked softly.

"No, the chest is only about this big." Theon defined a space with his hands about the size of a loaf of homemade bread. "It must be inside the stone."

"What chest?" Quaylyn asked in a whisper.

"Open the stone and you will find out," Theon offered.

"All right, stand back." Theon and Rahlys obediently moved away as Quaylyn lifted the largest section of broken floor he could lift and heaved it with a vengeance against the stone block...but the stone block remained intact.

"They must have heard that," Rahlys said, indicating the miners.

"Rock against rock isn't suspicious. It's your turn," Theon told Rahlys. "Why don't you try using the elemental forces?"

Rahlys sighed deeply. Could she find a way into the block of stone and remove the chest? The sound of scraping rock was getting closer; there was no time to waste. Rahlys dimmed the light, calling the crystal to her hand.

Help me find a way to the chest, she commanded gently, holding the crystal in her hand as she drew energy from air and stone...energy from her very being...uniting it with the power of the oracle. The crystal glowed iridescently, the light seeping out between her fingers as the building force began to flow from Rahlys...through the crystal...and into the stone.

While her solid form remained behind, Rahlys *journeyed* into the block of stone, its interior lit by the glow of energy. There sat the chest, dark and foreboding. As she neared the chest, the many runes etched on its seamless surface became charged by the power flow, and sparked into brightness. She reached for it and the glow of the runes intensified. Squinting her eyes against the blinding brightness, Rahlys picked up the chest. She cradled it securely in her arms and worked her way back out of the stone. Somehow, the distance seemed great. Outside the stone, Quaylyn and Theon waited anxiously as they watched over Rahlys standing emptily beside them, the sound of the miners beyond the collapsed tunnel getting ever closer.

Then, suddenly Rahlys moved, a chest covered with glowing runes clutched tightly in her arms. Rahlys released the energy she held and opened her hand, releasing the crystal. Immediately, the runes on the chest went dark.

"Are you all right?" Quaylyn asked, his face distorted with concern.

"Yes, we need to get out of here." They could hear Brakalar and Rojaire getting closer. Summoning the crystal back to its pouch, Rahlys teleported the three of them to the mountain passage they had hiked in on, placing them a safe distance from the camp.

"Good job, Rahlys!" Theon squealed, nearly dancing a jig when he saw where they were. "Now, all we need is the key."

"What for? You are never to open this chest, do you hear me?' Rahlys lashed out. "We need to destroy this...and the key, too!" she added for emphasis.

"I was just going to look at it," Theon said, his feelings hurt.

"Look at what?" Quaylyn asked impatiently. "What's in the chest?"

"A weapon of mass destruction, my boy. Probably was meant to be your scepter," Theon said. Quaylyn paled visibly.

"So that's what Brakalar and Rojaire are looking for, and they have the key," Quaylyn said. "Rahlys, quick, you must cast a spell to block the key from detecting the lock again."

"Good idea," Theon agreed. With input from both Theon and Quaylyn, Rahlys wove an invisible screen around the chest, protecting it from detection. She examined the darkly tarnished ancient relic covered with etched runes, noticing, as she turned in her hands, that there were no visible seams indicating a lid.

"This stays between the three of us," Theon said, staring intently at Quaylyn.

"You can trust me," Quaylyn said solemnly, and Rahlys felt in her heart that she could. She hoped she was right.

"I'll carry the chest until we can dispose of it," Theon offered. "That is, if you don't think I harbor plans to establish an evil regime."

Rahlys really didn't want to guard the chest herself; she handed it to Theon. After stashing the chest away in his cloak until he could transfer it to his pack, they casually strolled back toward the campsite.

Ambling into the arena nonchalantly, they found nothing had changed during their absence except for the mountain's shadow climbing higher up the eastern peaks. Ilene, Anthya, and Zayla were sleeping; Rojaire and Brakalar were still in the tunnel. Raven alone watched their arrival from his perch on a rock ledge. The three of them settled comfortably around Theon's pack, watching as he secured the chest away...then they sealed their alliance in a shared meal, Raven dropping in for tidbits.

When Brakalar emerged from the caves with Rojaire, his demeanor was dark and foreboding. Rojaire appeared as indifferent as always. The newly formed alliance of three knew Brakalar hadn't found what he was looking for. They struggled to look like they didn't know anything. Rahlys was sure Brakalar's face and arms were twice as dirty as her own.

As darkness descended, the rest turned in after an exhausting day until only Quaylyn and Rahlys were still up. Having slept most of the day, Rahlys was wide awake.

"Want to do some spelunking?" Rahlys asked Quaylyn seductively.

"Sure. What did you have in mind?" Quaylyn asked, smiling back at her. And not just any old smile either, but a real, endearing, Quaylyn smile, complete with dimples.

"Follow me," Rahlys said, and she led Quaylyn into the caves. Once they were out of sight of the sleeping expedition, she conjured the crystal from her pouch.

Find us a hidden chamber with a clean pool of water, Rahlys requested, caressing the crystal with her thoughts. In moments, she and Quaylyn stood in a broad cavern of lavender stone with an invitingly clear pool of water, suitable for bathing, with a skylight above, opening to a star spangled sky.

Seaa rose and set while the expedition continued to camp in front of the Sooty Caves. Brakalar spent most of that time stewing over the disappearance of the object the key sought. He had found it once. The key had clearly indicated the object of its search was in the stone block the capsule had rested on. Then just as he and Rojaire were about to reach the chamber, the key pulled in the opposite direction...before going off alert altogether! Now it had returned to search mode.

From Seaa rise to Seaa set, Brakalar combed the block and the chamber for a lock the key would fit, but found nothing. Having exhausted all his options, Brakalar finally announced, with obvious reluctance, that the expedition would move on at sunrise.

"Let's go hunt for something to eat besides zan fruit," Tassyn suggested, "maybe over by that next ridge; it's on our way." Without further discussion, the group headed northeast, the sun to their backs already starting to set. The Band of Rogues had made it back to the location where they had abducted Traevus and were now tracking the last four members of the expedition in an effort to catch up with them.

Traevus had been cooperative on the return trip, hoping to escape in time to warn the others when they got closer. *Sarus, Caleeza, Selyzar, and Caponya have probably made it to the slopes of Mt. Vatre by now, if they didn't waste too much time looking for me.* He thought of Cremyn, mentally an empty shell after disappearing for a time in the temple ruins, and Ollen's good-heartedness in volunteering to take her to the beach to intercept Captain Setas.

It was getting dark when the band reached a nearly dry river bed with loaded pinkberry bushes growing in wild profusion along its moist banks. As the men loaded their mouths with the succulent sweet teardrop fruit, Traevus, without raising his head or ceasing to eat, eased away from the group in the growing darkness.

Out of the corner of his eye, Traevus spied a rock outcrop to his left that might afford him some cover to slip away. He slowly made his way toward it while continuing to harvest. When he was only a pace away from the rocks, he made a dash for them, breaking into a run as soon as he was out of sight. Pushing and breathing hard, Traevus thought he had escaped, when abruptly without warning, he found himself running along the stream bed, back toward Stram and his men! Realizing he had been caught and turned around, Traevus tried in vain to change direction in mid-stride, when a zap of energy directed from Stram's uplifted hand hit him full force, sending him spiraling to the ground in shuddering pain.

The grasslands were a welcome sight as the expedition emerged from the mountain passage the next morning. Feathery clouds, the first seen since they arrived on the continent, crept in from the west as they turned toward the south, following the contour of the Crescent Mountains. Everyone's spirits, except maybe Brakalar's, were uplifted by the long rest and promise of new adventures. Brakalar and Rojaire walked abreast far ahead of the rest of the group. Rahlys and Ilene were content taking up the rear, and Raven flew wide circles over the landscape, happy to be on the move again.

Rahlys listened to Ilene's chatter about Rojaire's amiable qualities...and the wonders the Devastated Continent had to offer...also mostly from Rojaire. Rahlys wasn't sure Theon would agree with his daughter's assessment of the lone adventurer, but she didn't say anything; the passage of time would bring out Rojaire's true colors...whatever they were.

When Ilene was quiet, Rahlys walked along lost in thoughts of her own. How could the Rod of Destruction be destroyed? What had been Brakalar's plans for the rod? Could they keep it safely out of his reach? What was Rojaire's involvement? Were Zayla and Anthya involved too? Did she and Theon do the right thing trusting Quaylyn? Within her heart, she certainly hoped so.

As the miles passed under their feet, the prairie gradually narrowed and the brush-covered hills closed in again. By mid-morning, a westerly wind ushered in heavy clouds, blocking the sun. Rahlys felt the first big raindrops, one on her arm...then one on her head. Rahlys and Ilene had lagged some behind the others when Raven flew toward them, squawking alarmingly. He could no longer telepath images, but he could certainly express alarm.

"Aaaaarrrrk! Aaaaaarrrrk!"

"What is it?" Ilene asked. "Has he seen something?"

"I think so. Let's check it out."

"Without telling the others?"

"We'll get back to them."

Show us the way, Rahlys directed Raven, and he flew off in the direction he wanted them to follow, a south-westerly course into the hills that veered away from the rest of the expedition. Rahlys teleported them ahead from one visible point to another, trying to keep up with Raven, until they saw what he wanted them to see. There on the hillside an expedition flag fluttered in the storm driven breeze.

"Looks like we've found the lost expedition's trail again."

By the time Rahlys and Ilene led the rest of the group to the marker, the storm was raging around them in earnest, rain pounding the thirsty ground.

"It's a grave marker," Zayla said solemnly, stating a fact they all knew. "Cremyn," she read off the flag. Cremyn had been one of her favorite students, a bright young woman with a promising future. "That still leaves six unaccounted for."

"What do you suppose ended her longevity?" Anthya asked. They looked around, but if clues had been left, there were none to be found.

"What do we do now?" Ilene asked.

"We move on," Brakalar said disinterestedly. "I see nothing to gain by stopping here."

"It's time we look for a place to camp and get out of the storm," Zayla said, gently taking charge. "There's a group of trees below where we can take shelter. I suggest we head for them." Brakalar didn't protest, and Zayla led her soggy troops to the nearby grove.

Zaota trees turned out to be surprisingly good shelters, living grass huts offering dry circles of ground around their trunks. The space under a mature zaota tree is large enough to shelter a half dozen people...two or three comfortably! And there was more head room under the sky reaching branches than Rahlys had expected after passing through its thick grass skirt canopy.

Ilene and Rahlys, having decided to keep each other company during the storm, set to work making the tree they shared more comfortable. Releasing the crystal to light the dimness, they pulled the long dry withered under growth of leaves from overhead to make soft fluffy beds. Rahlys speeded up the drying of their hair and clothing, already designed to dry quickly, by drawing energy to heat the air around them. Once dry, they spread their cloaks over the beds of leaves to make a soft bed to lounge on. The rain continued to come down, the sound muffled by the thick cocoon of foliage around them, adding to the feel of cozy security.

"Comfortable in here," Rojaire said, slipping in uninvited. Ilene was glad to see him, and she moved over offering him a place to sit. Almost immediately, a second body popped in, filling the shelter. It was a soggy Quaylyn carrying a harvest bag full of fresh food.

"I just wanted to check and make sure you…everyone…is all right," he said to Rahlys, correcting himself to include Ilene…if not Rojaire.

"We're fine, thank you," Rahlys said as Theon's head popped in, sending everyone shuffling over in one direction or the other to make enough room for him to bring his back in out of the rain. There were enough trees for everyone to have one, including Raven, therefore no need to crowd in with her and Ilene…unless they wanted to socialize.

"It's a party!" Ilene said.

"Shall we invite Anthya, Zayla, and Brakalar over too?" Rahlys asked sarcastically.

"Let's not," Rojaire said, without hesitation, pulling a dark canister out of his cloak. "I brought some of my brew to share, something I ferment out of zan fruit. There's only enough for five."

"Did you come here to get my daughter drunk?" Theon asked.

"Not at all; I merely intended to lift sodden spirits."

"Then I don't mind if I do," Theon said, jovially. "I have some moose jerky," he said, digging in the pack he was reluctant to leave unattended. "Best moose jerky you've ever eaten. Well, in your case, Rojaire, the best *thing* you've ever eaten."

"Is that so?" Rojaire said, taking a piece of jerky. "Plant or animal?" he asked, scrutinizing it, and tore off a piece with his teeth.

"Animal. Big, ungainly brute, but very tasty."

Uncapping the canister, Rojaire passed it to Ilene, who took a cautious sniff, followed by an even more cautious sip. Screwing up her face, she handed it back to him. Then Rojaire took a large gulp before handing it to Theon, who did likewise.

"Not bad," Theon said critically, offering it to Rahlys. "Almost as good as mine used to be." Rahlys declined, so he handed the canister to Quaylyn, who tasted its contents before handing it back to Rojaire.

"Does anyone know what it is Brakalar is looking for?" Rojaire asked casually. Startled by Rojaire's question, Rahlys quickly scanned for eavesdroppers, but found none. Raven nestled in the branches of the nearest tree. Zayla and Anthya were camped together two trees down, and Brakalar had isolated himself under another tree some distance away.

"Brakalar is looking for something?" Ilene asked in all her innocence.

"Don't you know what he's looking for?" Quaylyn asked, his accusing stare making Rojaire feel uneasy. "You were helping him dig." Tension charged the air.

"Brakalar said the chamber hid something of tremendous importance," Rojaire said.

"Did he find it...the thing of tremendous importance?" Ilene asked in the silence that followed.

There was no response. Theon had been adamant about keeping Ilene in the dark...and Rahlys was starting to understand why.

"Does he *look* like he found anything?" Rojaire boomed in a low roar. "The man can be fanatical sometimes. His mood is as dark and steamy as a summer night!"

With comments like that, Rahlys wasn't sure she was looking forward to summer. Slowly, the tension subsided as the canister made the rounds again.

"Have you ever run into any members of the lost expedition?" Rahlys asked Rojaire, broaching a different topic.

"No, I haven't, but it's a big continent and I returned to the Academy for a time to present my findings. It is my hope that joining this expedition will help legitimize my work." Rojaire took another swig from the canister and offered it around. Only Theon took him up on his offer.

"Weren't you once a member of the Band of Rogues?" Theon asked, looking for facts.

"I was with them for only a short time; they weren't the Band of Rogues then! I am not a criminal!" Rojaire was getting tired of constantly having to defend his virtue. He took the canister Theon handed back and drained the contents down his throat.

"What about you, Theon? We all know your background. Reformed or not, you can't take back the past. From what Ilene tells me about your life in Alaska, you're something of a free spirit yourself," Rojaire continued, still in his own defense. "Well, I, too, am a free man. I don't believe the Runes of the Crystal Table and the High Council have the right to dictate how I live out my longevity, what services I will perform for others, or where I will go."

"But surely, it's not like that!" Ilene gasped.

"Isn't it?" Rojaire retorted.

From there, no one really knew what to say, and eventually the group dispersed to shelters of their own. After Ilene settled in, Rahlys dug into a pouch of her pack for her journal and pen, when her hand inadvertently cupped the golden marble Melinda had given to her for a good luck charm. Pulling it out, she moved it about in her hand, caressing it with her fingers, smiling as she thought of Melinda and the others back home. Sentimentally, she continued to hold the stone as she wrote in her journal. Even after she put the journal away and conjured the crystal back to the beaded pouch, Rahlys still clung to the unusual orb. She lay on her bed of leaves gazing into it; it seemed to almost glow in the subdued lighting. The golden stone...so perfectly round... so perfectly smooth...reflected back what little light there was available, sheltered from a storm under a zaota tree. Golden...and so perfectly round...so perfectly smooth...as round and smooth and golden as Seaa herself!

Chapter 14
It's Twins!

Vince, still overwhelmed by baby times two, returned home alone on Saturday's train. He was here for the weekend only, to pack trails after the big snow. Exhilarated by the freedom and release of tension that only snowmobiling in the great outdoors could bring, Vince made his way on snowmachine, to the only neighbor currently in the area, Grumpy George, who lived on the ridge across the creek from Rahlys' place. With Maggie's heart set on coming home the following weekend, Vince was on a mission to solicit George's help in making that possible. Taking a couple of cigars, one labeled, "It's a girl!" and one, "It's a boy!" Vince hoped to make arrangements with him to start a fire in the stove and warm up the house before they arrived with the babies. Vince knew that the persona 'Grumpy George' was, for the most part anyway, a façade to protect his privacy. George could be counted on when the need was great, of that Vince was certain.

Crossing the creek over a precarious brush and log bridge covered with minimal snow pack was the only real challenge on the trail. Approaching the bridge, Vince slowed down to a near stop, lining up the machine's track and skis precisely with the narrow, sagging bridge. He eased the snowmachine down onto the bridge straddling the seat a couple of feet above the cold, dark flowing creek below. Taking it easy, going slowly, he made it safely across, and with a sigh of relief, zoomed up the bank on the other side.

Soon, he connected to George's trail and found it not only broken, but groomed! It was a joy ride from here. Trails developed a washboard effect with repeated use. It had become a custom in the area to convert old metal bed spring frames into trail drags to groom snowmachine trails. All that was needed for an old discarded metal bed frame to become useful again were a couple of crosspieces bearing some form of extra weight. When pulled behind a snowmachine, a well-constructed trail drag knocks off the high points, dropping the extra snow into the depressions, thus smoothing out the washboard effect. It wasn't long before Vince caught glimpses of the old loner's cabin through the bare trees.

Hearing the snowmachine approach, George met him in the front yard. "Well, hi there, neighbor! What's the news?" he asked as soon as Vince killed the engine.

"Twins! A boy and a girl!"

"Ah, ha! ha! ha!" George roared uproariously, slapping his knee. "Couldn't have happened to a nicer guy." George could read from Vince's radiant smile that all must have gone well. "And how's Maggie doing?"

"Great! She's anxious to come home." Vince partially unzipped his snow-suit to reach the carefully protected cigars in his shirt pocket and handed them to George.

"Twins! Theon was right!"

"Theon?"

"Yes, he predicted two babies months ago."

"He never said anything to me."

"Well, he didn't want to spoil the surprise. So what did she name them?"

"Rock and Crystal."

"Rock and Crystal!" George roared again with laughter. "Rock and Crystal, ha, ha!"

"She thought about naming them Ice and Snow, but decided that was too chilling. Maggie was already in labor when we left in the snowstorm. What a night that was! We dealt with ice and snow from the time we left here, till we arrived at the hospital. The babies were born that night."

"Well, come on in and tell me all about it. I'll put on a pot of coffee."

George's cabin wasn't very large, so every bit of space was tightly utilized. The two small windows, shaded by trees, let in dim light. George moved books, whittling tools, and stacks of papers from the little square table to make room for them to sit. While the coffee perked, Vince gave George details of their horrendous trip to the hospital.

"On the drive down, I had to pull the car over twice to clear the windshield wipers of ice. Every time Maggie had a contraction, I was sure this was it, and I would have to deliver. I don't know what I would have done without Melinda's efforts to keep me calm enough to drive. Of course, Leaf slept through the whole thing. Anyway, we made it. Rock was born twenty minutes after we finally arrived at the entrance to the emergency room...and Crystal less than a minute later."

George poured two cups of steaming ink-black coffee, and then cut them with generous additions of brandy. "So Maggie is anxious to come home? When does she want to return?"

"She would like to come home next weekend, but I hate bringing her and the babies to a cold cabin. With the trains scheduled as they are, there's no way I can heat the place ahead of time, unless I stayed all week, but with four kids, Maggie needs my help in town. Plus, it could snow some more this week, closing the trail again."

"Tell Maggie not to worry about a thing. I will have the house warm and the trail groomed when she arrives next weekend. All you need to worry about is carrying in the babies."

"Thanks, I'll make it up to you somehow."

"No, need for that. It's my pleasure."

———·———

Caleeza sat cozily warm at the little table by the window, gazing out at the falling snow. Melinda and Leaf's last visit was thirteen of this world's quick rotations ago, she noted, adding another mark for the new day. Since then, the forest had changed its cloak from a warm golden brown to a cool lacy white. Winter had followed her south.

Caleeza didn't like depending on the new persons for survival, but she had few options. Here, she had found awareness of her own world; the young ones could be the key to returning home. She didn't want to leave without learning more. Melinda and Leaf had assured her they would be back, but when? She took sparingly from the supply of wood for fire that Melinda had shown her telepathically. Fortunately, because the shelter was small and so well-constructed, it didn't take much fuel to keep it warm.

Food was a far greater concern. She strictly rationed the bags of food the children had brought, and scoured the woods trudging through snow in search of edible foods to supplement her diet, but except for the leaves and barks she brewed into teas, and the little round red fruit she occasionally found frozen on bushes bare of leaves, the white landscape had little to offer.

With time on her hands and a desire to learn to communicate, Caleeza took advantage of the comfortable shelter's scholarly atmosphere. She quickly memorized the names of all the pictures on Leaf's learning machine, useful words like...tree, book, chair, and train...the serpentine monster that rolled on the trail of rails. Sometimes she could hear the train in the distance when it passed by. She also learned names for some of the planet's life forms; girl, boy, and dog...the loud creature she had encountered along the way. But there were others she never heard of...like rooster, cat, and cow. Using what she learned from these words about letter sounds, she started studying a whole book of picture words from one of the shelves of books scattered around.

There were books on many different subjects. She found picture books of Alaska, some depicting landscapes and life forms she had already encountered, books on calculation and natural forces, and books covering events and topics she knew nothing about.

A really exciting find was a chart showing the planet with Alaska on it, orbiting in space around the sun. According to the chart, she was on the third planet of eight revolving around this sun. A band of space debris orbited the sun between the fourth and fifth planet. The last four worlds, probably gaseous in nature, were considerably larger than the first four, and many lesser planets orbited far beyond those. A busy sun system to say the least!

At night, she dreamed of Sarus, alone and abandoned, in the Crystalline Landscape, the dark ragged slope of Mt. Vatre looming threateningly in the distance. In her dream, she woke from her sleep and spoke with him across the expanse of space. His image was hazy, but he seemed greatly changed, more so each time they spoke. In demeanor he had become complacently wise instead of wildly determined. He seemed content, fulfilled...and wished the same for her. Again and again he asked her not to be concerned for him. Once they had been lovers, but now he seemed emotionally unattached. "I am learning the answer," he assured her over and over, never defining the question.

"But how do I return home?" she asked in desperation.

At first, Sarus didn't respond. She knew there wasn't anything he could do to help her, but she couldn't help expressing her despair.

"I will seek a solution," he said to her surprise...or so she thought until she woke up for real.

On the thirteenth rotation, Melinda, Leaf, and their chosen mother and father, returned to the snowy woods with two tiny new persons at the very beginning of their longevity. Caleeza could detect their fresh signatures, after the train, carrying many signatures, pulled away. Melinda reached out mentally seeking Caleeza.

Twins! A boy and a girl! Leaf and I will be over to visit when we can slip out. All right? she telepathed upon locating her.

Boy, girl, all right, Caleeza reassured her telepathically.

Rock and Crystal Bradley were oblivious to the stir they caused in the lives they touched, or the snowy woods bathed in weak sunshine. Wrapped in insulated blankets and nestled snuggly in loving protective arms, Rock in his mother's embrace and Crystal in her father's, they were carried home. The twins slept contentedly, rocked gently by the sway of their parents' unhurried gait. Leaf and Melinda ran up ahead on an immaculately groomed trail that promised they would arrive at a cozily warm house. Maggie lifted the corner of the receiving blanket tent draped over her milk-swollen breast, that shielded her tiny son's face from the cold air, and gazed down at him lovingly, touching his little cheek to reassure herself he was warm...and breathing.

"It's so wonderful to be home," Maggie sighed, reassured.

"You're not home yet," Vince said with a twinkle in his eye.

"Close enough. The woods themselves are also home."

"You don't know how glad I am that you feel that way." Finding a woman willing to live in the woods can be a rare find.

George, Melinda, and Leaf were there to greet them when they finally arrived carrying the bundled infants. "Welcome home!" George shouted out. "I see you've brought something with you."

"Hi, George, good to see you," Maggie greeted warmly.

"Thanks," Vince said simply as George opened the door wide for them to enter the overly warm house after the exertion of the hike. Vince's stomach growled to the aromas of hot bread and savory stew waiting for them on the stove. In one corner of the room stood the crib he had built for Leaf before he was born, just as they had left it, ready and waiting for its new occupant. And right next to it a second almost identical crib stood waiting!

"Oh, it's beautiful!" Maggie gasped when she saw it.

"Where did this come from?" she asked, strolling up to it. "Did you make it, George?" Ever so gently, she placed Rock down in it, removing some of his layers of wrappings.

"Well, I figured you would be in need of another one," George mumbled.

"Thank you so much. This is all so wonderful!" she cried, tears blurring her vision. "And is that fresh bread I smell?"

"I baked it this morning. There's a pot of moose stew on the stove, ready to eat, if you're hungry."

"I'm starved," Maggie said. Breastfeeding seemed to keep her hungry.

"Me, too, I want to eat," Leaf piped up, running to be first in line.

Following Maggie's example, Vince placed Crystal in the crib he originally built for Leaf, removing excess coverings. She slept so soundly he placed a finger near her nose, reassuringly feeling her soft, warm breath against his skin. Contentment swelled his chest as he joined his family for the home-coming celebration.

It wasn't until the third day after returning home, when life seemed to have settled into a new norm, that Melinda and Leaf risked teleporting over to the schoolhouse to visit Caleeza. In the meantime, Melinda and Caleeza communicated telepathically. She had Leaf teleport food to her, especially leftovers when they did the dishes, and some old clothes she might be able to wear. And since Caleeza was working so hard at learning their language, Melinda had Leaf send her some of his books with tapes and a battery-operated tape player, giving her mental instructions on how to use them. By the time the children appeared before her, she had memorized them all...somewhat.

"I am good to see you," Caleeza greeted them.

It's good to see you too, Melinda said, making the correction.

"You can talk," Leaf said with some surprise.

"Yes, talk better. Thank you books."

Thank you for the books. You're welcome.

"Thank you for the eat. You welcome."

Close enough for now, Melinda decided, and to Caleeza's delight, she handed her the specially requested bag of potato chips.

"We have two babies," Leaf told her with mixed emotions.

"Yes, how big they?" Caleeza asked him.

"Little like this," Leaf demonstrated, cradling his own little arms to hold a baby. "Mommy doesn't have time for us anymore," he added in a sigh of resignation. "She loves the new babies now."

Leaf, that's not true! Melinda reassured him. *Mom and Dad love us just the same.* Maggie did look tired...and the babies certainly kept her busy, but she cared for them no less now than before the twins arrived. *If Mom and Dad weren't so busy with Rock and Crystal, we wouldn't be able to sneak off to our secret hideaway,* she offered as consolation.

But Leaf wasn't sure that was a fair tradeoff.

Melinda and Leaf told Caleeza all about their trip to town, the places they went, and the things they did. Caleeza showed them all the materials she had been studying and asked questions about things she didn't understand. When the conversation lagged some time later, Caleeza ventured a question about Droclum.

"How you know Droclum?" she asked, watching Melinda's reaction. The mention of Droclum stirred something dark and deeply repressed within Melinda, something that struggled for release.

Droclum is dead! she spit out with a vengeance.

"Dead? What dead? Dare she believe the impressions she gleaned from Melinda's mind?

He doesn't exist anymore. He was destroyed by Sorceress Rahlys' awesome powers.

Caleeza knew that Sorceress Rahlys was the Guardian of the Light and that Rahlys had acquired Sorceress Anthya's powers through the Oracle of Light. Caleeza remembered Quaylyn had been chosen to go to Earth to help the fledgling sorceress defeat Droclum at the same time Sarus had been chosen to lead their expedition to the Devastated Continent. Now, she was learning that Droclum had been destroyed! If only their mission could have gone as well.

"You know Quaylyn?" Caleeza asked.

Melinda only knew Quaylyn for a short time. When Rahlys rescued her from Droclum's clutches, Quaylyn had just learned that Droclum was his father. It wasn't long after that the final battle took place, ending in Droclum's demise.

Droclum was Quaylyn's father, Melinda said as proof of acquaintance.

Caleeza reeled at the news. Surely, Melinda was mistaken. She and Quaylyn had grown up together in the same community. There was no way he could be Droclum's son!

Caleeza had been left with much to think about when the children returned home. The news of Droclum's destruction was paramount. A serious threat to both worlds had been eliminated. How did this affect the Devastated Continent? Or maybe the real question should be, did Droclum's death change anything? Did it have anything to do with the 'answer' Sarus talked about? There were so many questions.

Caleeza pulled out the sun system chart, laying it out on the table to look at it. Somehow, she had crossed the galaxy to planet Earth...that was how that strange word was pronounced...the same planet Droclum had escaped to after triggering the Dark Devastation. Surely, this was an unlikely coincidence considering the vastness of space.

The issue that perplexed her the most was Melinda's belief that Quaylyn was Droclum's son. Such a thing didn't seem even remotely possible, at least not to her reasoning.

Then Caleeza remembered the bag of potato chips. Smiling with anticipation, she reached for the bag and opened it. *I'll take my time eating them and relish every bite.* At least, that was her intention. She placed the first chip on her tongue, savoring its saltiness. Soon, intentions were forgotten as she started devouring the chips one after another. Actually, there didn't seem to be many chips in the bag...because soon, they were all gone.

When she finally settled into bed, Caleeza wanted to dwell on her memories of a happier time when she and Sarus were nourished by love and aspirations, but the images that came to mind were of Sarus as she had seen him last...confused, angry, yet still determined. These images haunted her mind until she drifted into sleep. Then she saw yet another Sarus, the Sarus that sometimes spoke to her in her dreams...mysteriously calm, quietly self-assured, enormously fulfilled.

"Sarus." Her heart ached for him as he approached her, standing in the crystalline landscape. She knew she couldn't really be here, but it seemed so real.

"Caleeza, you are a treasure to behold."

"Oh, Sarus, just seeing you warms my heart. I love you so much," she said, before she realized she was saying it. Was he still capable of loving her, she wondered?

"I have always loved you, Caleeza. I will always love you, but I am not as I was. I can never leave the Crystalline Landscape, and you must never return to it; it is far too dangerous."

"But what about you, isn't the Crystalline Landscape dangerous for you too?"

"Not without my human form." The statement was so strange she didn't know how to respond, and paused to think.

"But I can see you."

"I am visible only in your mind."

Caleeza let it go; she had far more important information to share with him.

"I have learned that I'm on Earth and Droclum has been destroyed by Sorceress Rahlys, the Guardian of the Light.

"Yes...," he said, seemingly with sudden realization, "I can feel it is so."

"You can feel it?"

"Yes, it is part of the answer."

"Please, Sarus, help me return home," Caleeza pleaded, not wanting to get into the 'answer.'

"I will see what I can learn."

She felt Sarus fade from her mind. Realizing she was still awake, Caleeza opened her eyes to the light of the full moon reflecting off of white snow. Had she really communicated with Sarus? She lay awake pondering this in the moonlight.

Chapter 15
The Temple of Tranquility

"Isn't it beautiful?" Ilene exclaimed, waltzing through one flowering meadow after another. Enchanted with the continent before, she became smitten with it now. The long heavy rain, followed by sunshine, brought new germination and bloom to the land, providing tender leafy vegetables and edible flowers to augment their limited diet. Rahlys had to admit the land had its beauty, but in her own heart the beauty was marred by thoughts of Rojaire's outburst under the zaota tree during the rainstorm.

"Do you ever think about Rojaire's accusation that the High Council and the Academy deny its people free will?" Rahlys asked Ilene casually.

Ilene hesitated just a bit before responding. "I have to admit it has bothered me some. I think Rojaire's gotten a bad reputation just for wanting to make his own decisions in life. And he's right, Father should understand, but instead he seems to suspect him of some sort of foul play...which he won't even talk about."

Rahlys thought she detected a bit of a pout. "Perhaps it would not be wise to get too involved with Rojaire," she advised. "He doesn't seem to be the type who makes a lot of commitments."

"Now you sound just like Father. We're just friends."

Rahlys let the subject drop, but that night as they traveled by Seaa's light, she broached the topic gently with Zayla, who seemed constantly vexed by Rojaire's presence.

"Does the High Council determine everyone's missions in life?"

"Of course," Zayla said without hesitation. "With the council's help, we can all reach our full potential."

"What about the pursuit of happiness?

"At whose expense?" Zayla came to a halt. "Life comes with responsibilities." She was a stern woman when defending her principles. "I am quite knowledgeable of the political and sociological conditions on Earth. Is this chaos what you are offering?"

"That's not exactly what I meant."

"What, exactly, did you mean then?"

"Well, it seems like people here lack the freedom to make choices on how they want to live their lives."

"You've been listening to Rojaire," Zayla concluded instantly, a definite bite in her tone. "Regardless of what Rojaire has been telling you, we all have a choice in how we conduct ourselves, and any mission assigned by the High Council can be declined." She resumed walking.

Rahlys sighed in dismay, staring at Zayla's back, and then hurried her pace to catch up again. She decided to try another tactic. "How is it that Rojaire is so well versed in English?"

"Language training is a simple matter."

"But I had the impression Rojaire was a late addition to the expedition."

"You are very observant," she conceded. "Rojaire was once trained for a mission to Earth, but his appointment was rejected."

"Why?"

"It is not my place to tell you." After walking in silence for some time, Zayla surprised Rahlys with a final note.

"The only time I ever questioned the wisdom of the Runes of the Crystal Table was when Quaylyn was sent to help you destroy his own father." Zayla turned to face Rahlys. "I never should have doubted. The mission was a success."

"What about the impact on Quaylyn?"

"Would you rather have Droclum killing and destroying so Quaylyn could pursue happiness?"

With that, Zayla glided off ahead with all her usual grace, making it clear the conversation had come to an end.

Days and nights began to blur with one another as the expedition traversed trackless hills and valleys searching for a route around the Crescent Mountains. Near the point of the crescent, where the mountains ended, they would find the ruins of the Temple of Tranquility, the site of Quaylyn's birth. Rotation after rotation they continued their journey southeastward, and each night Seaa set a little earlier than the night before. Rahlys knew that eventually, during the long hot summer, Seaa would disappear from the night sky altogether, until the moment of reckoning when once again the sun and Seaa would face off from opposite horizons...delineating winter! *Will I still be here then, so far from home*, Rahlys asked herself. *I sure hope not.*

In her journal, Rahlys tried to keep track of the progression of time in Alaska's Susitna Valley. By her calculations, over two months had passed. That meant it was November, the beginning of the long, cold, period of mostly darkness. She could picture Melinda engrossed in her art and schoolwork, Leaf busy with growing and playing, and immersed in it all, Maggie and Vince...with a new baby! Rahlys felt a pang of regret. She was missing so much.

"Do you miss home?" she asked Theon, hiking beside her, still carrying the chest containing the Rod of Destruction concealed in his pack.

"Of course I do, but when I was there, I missed here."

"Maggie and Vince have a new baby by now!"

"Two new babies."

"What?"

"Maggie was carrying twins. A boy and a girl, I think."

"How would you know that?"

"I could detect their signatures even before they were born."

Thinking of Maggie and Vince and the children reminded her again of the stone. She had logically ruled out the possibility of it being the stone indefatigable Captain Setas of the ferryboat had referred to. After all, Melinda found it in a creek bed back on Earth...a long way from the Devastated Continent. Nevertheless, Rahlys reached into her pouch.

"Before we left home, Melinda gave me this," she said, holding up the smooth, golden stone, reflecting Seaa's light, and "...so it can't be the stone you are looking for," she said, dropping it into his hand, "but I thought I would show it to you anyway." Theon halted and rolled the smooth round marble between his fingers, its reflective glow lighting his studious face.

"And where did Melinda get this?" he asked.

"She found it in the creek by my cabin. I know it can't be the stone you seek, but look at it, it's as round and golden as Seaa herself, a mirror image," she said, pointing to the golden star hanging in the southern sky.

"It certainly is," Theon agreed, turning the stone in his fingers as he gazed upon it with obvious interest. "So what does it do?"

"What? It doesn't do anything. Melinda gave it me so I would have sometime to remind me of home."

"May I hold on to this for a while?" he asked. "I promise I will give it back to you."

"Of course," Rahlys agreed.

Seaa set early, long before the sun was due to rise, leaving a true night sky crowded with stars. Tired and hungry, everyone gathered around the cheerful campfire where a simple meal was cooked and shared. As the embers died down, one by one, they rolled themselves up in their cloaks to sleep the rest of the night away...until only Rahlys and Quaylyn remained.

"Do you have names for constellations of stars?" she asked Quaylyn quietly, gazing up at the unfamiliar celestial dome. She could see his grin in the starlight.

"Actually we do, from antiquity unimaginable. Some even have stories attached to them. You see that large ring of brighter stars containing lots of dimmer ones?" There were so many distinct stars filling the night sky, far more than back home, she had a hard time picking out the formation he indicated. Quaylyn moved closer to her and pointed halfway up the northwest quadrant. Rahlys leaned gently against him sighting along his finger.

"I see it!"

"That's the Great Bowl and all the fainter stars inside are grain, a promise by the goddess Aaia to provide food for her people. And then above the Great Bowl and a little to the right you see that long curved line of stars?"

"Yes." Rahlys continued to lean against him; it felt nice in a surprising way.

"Follow it all the way up to the cluster at the end."

"Okay."

"That's the needle the gods used to sew together the fabric of the world."

"Are you making all this up?" She gave him a playful punch.

Quaylyn pretended to be hurt by her comment. "Are you insinuating my ancestors had less imagination than your own?"

"No, of course not. I didn't mean to imply that."

"Well then, no offense taken," he said with a dimpled smile. Together, they watched the star-studded heavens in silence for a while, pleasantly conscious of each other's closeness. "And, Rahlys," Quaylyn spoke ever so softly, "I'm sorry for how I behaved before."

"All is forgiven," she whispered back just as softly. They watched the night sky, contentedly nestled together. The campfire had long ago gone cold, when Rahlys sat up. "I'm going to get some rest," she whispered. "Good night."

"Good night."

Rahlys moved off away from the fire pit and was comfortably rolled up in her cloak, nearly asleep, when she received Theon's telepathic message.

Your stone is the stone we were looking for! Rahlys picked up on Theon's excitement. *I can draw on the elemental forces!* Then there was a pause. *But that might mean...now you can't.* Rahlys summoned the crystal from her pouch to her hand hidden under her cloak. Immediately she felt its smooth, hard, faceted surface wrapped in her fingers.

Not necessarily. I just summoned the crystal to my hand.

Try something else.

We are communicating telepathically.

Can you still teleport?

I think so.

See the zaota tree silhouetted a few hundred feet south of here?

Rahlys sat up and located the silhouette of a zaota tree against the starlit sky. *I see it.*

Meet me there.

Now?

Yes, of course now...if you don't mind, he added politely.

All right, I'll meet you there. She preferred sleep, but reluctantly teleported to the tree to find Theon already waiting for her.

"Did *you* teleport here?" she asked.

"Yes, and so did you. This means you have your abilities even without the stone."

"But how does it work?"

"I'm not sure. Somehow the stone repels the blocking force...at least to an extent. We need to keep searching; there may be more of these...star stones. And let's keep this to ourselves for a while. It could work to our advantage."

"What do you have in mind?" Rahlys asked, knowing he was scheming something.

"Tomorrow, I'm going to suggest to Brakalar that you, Raven, and I scout ahead of the rest of the expedition to the Temple of Tranquility. There's something I want to try at the site before the rest of the expedition arrives."

"You think Brakalar will go for that?"

"With the star stone in my possession, I may be able to persuade him. He will not suspect me of having any power."

Morning broke clear and warm, and with Brakalar's mentally coerced consent, Theon, Raven, and Rahlys, feeling somewhat rested, headed out while the others were just stirring. As soon as they were out of sight of the camp, Rahlys directed Raven to follow the lavender ridge, covered with red-orange, rose, and blue-green foliage, southeast to the end of the Crescent Mountains. Following the same ridge, Theon located a relatively level area on its eastern slope in his spy glass and pointed it out to Rahlys. Fairly certain the location was safe, they teleported themselves there. In this fashion, they quickly covered great distances, with Raven struggling to keep up with them. Nothing moved. There was no sound except for a gentle wind caressing the thinning zaota trees, grains, and bushes. The dark bluish black peaks of the southernmost reach of the Crescent Mountains gradually diminished in height and ferocity as the ridge they had been following dropped into a broad yellow and purple valley that extended unbroken to the distant end of the mountainous crescent.

"Where are the ruins of the Temple of Tranquility?" Rahlys asked, looking through the spy glass.

"The ruins are on the other side of the peaks. According to Rojaire, a split in the mountain opens up into a passage that leads into the temple ruins. A couple more hops and we should be there." Theon leaned on the zaota tree walking staff he still carried breathing heavily, rivulets of beaded sweat running down his face. Each jump they made seemed to take quite a toll on him, Rahlys noticed. She knew he needed to rest, but he would probably balk at the suggestion.

"Rojaire says he found identifiable ruins, but I doubt there will be much to see," Theon added. "From what I have seen so far, the destruction of the land was too catastrophic to leave many relics. He also said the center of the continent is crystallized. That's another concept I find hard to believe." Theon wobbled a little in his exuberance despite his walking stick.

"Are you all right?" Rahlys asked with some concern.

"As sound as gold," he said, pounding on his chest as proof, knowing she picked up on the lie. He pointed down into the valley. "I'm ready to move on. See where it looks like there's an indention in the side of the mountain? Let's go there. Hopefully, that's the shortcut Rojaire mentioned."

"All right, I'll take us both there," Rahlys said emphatically. Theon wanted to protest, but he knew when to keep silent. She teleported them down into the purple and yellow valley, where an abundance of yellow-orange zan fruit bushes thriving in sandy purple soil gave the valley its vivid colors. The Crescent Mountains, still towering above them in jagged bluish black peaks, dwindled to a point in the distance.

"We can walk from here," Rahlys suggested.

"A little stroll would do me good," Theon agreed.

The warm morning turned into a hot day under a clear golden sky, but a refreshing breeze made it quite tolerable. As they strolled toward the break in the low jagged peaks, Raven's raucous cry hailed them from a distance.

"Aaaaaark! Aaaaaark!" he cried, finally catching up to them.

About time you made it here, Rahlys teased him playfully.

"Aaaaaark!"

Raven landed on a pinnacle of rock above them, watching as they gingerly made their way through the pass. Most of the pass was obstacle free, but in a few places they had to climb over or squeeze through jumbles of small boulders. Finally, they broke out of the Crescent Mountains to the other side.

"Oh…" Rahlys gasped, even while catching her breath, as her eyes discovered the Temple of Tranquility…magnificent even in ruins. She gazed in awe at the immense expanse of crumbling walls, arches, and towers running down into the valley below…partially buried in rubble…and becoming once again a part of the mountain.

"Never in my wildest dreams did I expect to return here," Theon panted softly.

Although he had barely spoken above a whisper, Rahlys heard all the emotion his statement carried. She turned toward him, and gazed into ancient eyes glazed over with sadness…and hard earned wisdom. Suddenly, he looked older than he ever had before, his aged frame slightly bent. Taking his arm, she guided him to a large block of dark blue stone. She urged him to sit, and then sat down beside him. Raven took off into a circuitous flight high above the perimeter of the ruins.

It didn't take long for Rahlys and Theon to realize there was something eerily strange about the place. It had been a bright sunny day before entering the temple, but here, the sunlight didn't seem as bright as it should be, like a haze hung over the ruins, washing out the shadows. The air was unnaturally still, not even a subtle breeze stirred, and the grounds were unnaturally barren, with not a single invasive blade of grass or leafy bush offering to soften the austerity. Even the surrounding rolling purple and yellow orange expanse of sparse grass and zan fruit bushes stretching into the distance kept a wide berth from the disquieting ruins.

Raven's behavior also raised questions. All the while they sat and rested, drank water, and nibbled at zan fruit, Raven never attempted to fly through the ruins or even over the airspace above them to investigate. Usually, he was far more inquisitive than that. Instead, he chortled disconcertingly, urging them to leave. Rahlys tried to communicate with him to find out why he was disturbed, but all she could pick up was a rush of wariness for her efforts. But increasingly, Rahlys could sense the source of Raven's discomfort.

"Aaaarrrk! Aaaarrk!" Raven cried, as thin wisps of fragmented energy, strange invisible tattered forces, drifted all around them. As Rahlys' uneasiness grew, so did Raven's agitation.

"Do you feel them?" Rahlys asked Theon. "There are bands of energy flowing all around us." She stood and walked around, trying to orient on them.

"Yes," Theon agreed, and he also stood to investigate. As they carefully wove their way around piles of rubble, they could feel the changes in the flows of energy.

"What do you think it is?" Rahlys asked.

"The temple was highly fortified with wards forged from elemental forces drawn and worked long ago," Theon began to speculate. "Perhaps we are perceiving remnants of energy from some of the protections that were in place at the time of the Dark Devastation. The spells that guarded the temple had to have been powerful for there to be ruins still left here for us to see."

Brakalar felt once more the tug of the key he carried toward something unknown. There had been nothing since the Sooty Caves. Why all of a sudden now? The pull came from the direction they were headed. Was the lock the key would fit in the temple ruins? If so, why had he gotten a false reading at the caves? His hand reached automatically for the pouch, and then catching himself, he unobtrusively lowered his hand again. Excitement put new spring into his step. There was a treasure to be found, hopefully an artifact wielding great power. He glanced around, locating the rest of the members of the expedition. Zayla was matching him step for step, and Quaylyn and Anthya were following closely, but Ilene and Rojaire trailed far behind, more focused upon animated conversation than hiking.

"What's wrong?" Zayla asked, noticing his agitation.

"Nothing," Brakalar glanced around nervously, "but I would like to pick up the pace." He couldn't completely hide the impatience in his voice. Zayla gave him a suspicious glance, which she quickly veiled over.

"Why don't you just go on ahead," she suggested. "We will meet you at the ruins. Rojaire knows the way." She had long been certain Brakalar was withholding something from her. Despite the day's mounting warmth, she felt a chilling foreboding cold sweat beading down her spine. Giving him some space would be the best way to catch him off guard. It was an offer Brakalar couldn't resist.

"I'll see you at the ruins," he said gravely, relieved she hadn't questioned him further. Soon, his lone figure advanced far ahead of them.

"What was that all about?" Anthya asked as she and Quaylyn approached.

"Brakalar started acting strangely again, like he did at the caves. He became agitated and wanted to hurry. He also reached for his pouch again. I have a bad feeling about this. I fear he could do something that would put Rahlys and Theon in danger. I'm going to push ahead and follow him...just in case."

Quaylyn and Anthya watched her go, taking off at nearly a sprint. Quaylyn realized he needed to keep an eye on both Brakalar and Zayla. If the concealment barrier Rahlys had formed around the chest containing the Rod of Destruction had failed, Theon and Rahlys could indeed be in great danger. But what should he do about Anthya? Whose side was she on? Were there even sides to take? Quaylyn nearly sighed in exasperation, but caught himself. He didn't really want to reveal any information to Anthya, but on the other hand, she *was* a skilled warrior who could help cover his back.

"Let's keep up with them," he said to her. "And stay out of sight."

"What about them?" Anthya asked, indicating Ilene and Rojaire.

"Let's keep them out of it...if they aren't already involved."

"Involved in what?" Anthya asked.

But Quaylyn didn't answer; it was time to get moving. He loped in leaps and bounds higher up the ridge heading southeast. Anthya followed him without hesitation.

Brakalar galloped through the flowering brush growing on the gentle slope. He followed a natural bench of relatively flat land with a single-mindedness that long sustained his forward momentum. Heavy exertion soon had Brakalar gasping for breath and perspiring profusely, but he barely paused in his effort. *I should never have let Rahlys and Theon go on ahead. I can't understand what possessed me to allow it.* The energy from the key grew stronger as he ran, often stumbling, and even tumbling a couple of times, as he hurried along the hillside toward the ruins of the Temple of Tranquility and the distant point of the Crescent Mountains. The longer he pushed forward, the more convinced he became that Rahlys and Theon had what the key was seeking at the temple ruins. But the distance was great. The hot golden sun had already reached halfway to its zenith, and still the mountainous crescent point seemed far away. Exhausted, panting breathlessly, he dropped onto the gritty ground.

As he lay there panting, he pictured in his mind the temple ruins as Rojaire had described them...and Rahlys and Theon...with his treasure in their possession. *The treasure belongs to me...since I have the key,* he panted. *Those two made a fool of me once, I won't let them do so again.* Finding hidden reserves of strength, he struggled to his feet and pushed on.

"What was it you wanted to try at the site before the others arrive?" Rahlys asked as Theon removed the worn leather shoulder sling pack he always wore.

"Let's see how the runes on the chest containing the Rod of Destruction react to this place," Theon said, digging deeply in the pack and pulling out the rune-covered chest. Some of the runes were glowing softly.

"You're not going to try and open it…" Rahlys gasped in a surge of panic.

"No, of course not. Besides, Brakalar has the key."

Rahlys stared hard, her heart pounding, as he held the chest out in front of him and began strolling through the ruins. The lights on the chest changed in color and intensity as the runes reacted to the phantom wisps of energy. To Raven's continuous protest from the sideline, Theon and Rahlys worked their way down to an area of the ruins where larger portions of walls still stood, complete with arches, corners, broken corridors, hints of domed ceilings, and crumbling stairways leading to nowhere.

"Come on. It's all right," he reassured her, when she glanced back toward Raven. Rahlys tried to reassure Raven as well, but he wouldn't give up his protest.

"The runes are just sensing the forces around us," Theon said, moving slowly through a maze of jagged walls, crumbling towers, and rubble strewn courtyards with Rahlys following close behind. As they wove their way through what had once been a magnificent temple, the runes covering the surface of the seamless chest continued to pulsate in glowing colors, and even hummed softly in varying pitches as they covered the grounds. Strung out together, it formed an odd "song" of pulsing light and vibrating notes that haunted the ruins like spectral ghosts.

"What does it all mean?" Rahlys asked.

"I don't know, but the forces are gathering. Maybe we should think of getting out of here."

The change in lighting had been imperceptible at first…deepening grayness on an already cloudy day. Enough time had now passed to discern that the haze was definitely getting darker.

BRAKALAR APPROACHES.

The sudden message on top of everything else made Rahlys' skin prickle. She jerked around to glance quickly at the gap entrance, some distance above them, expecting to see Brakalar already there.

"What is it?"

"The oracle just warned that Brakalar is approaching."

"Already? Gee, the old goat made good time." Rahlys felt Theon was making light of the warning by going into his backwoods vernacular.

"The oracle wouldn't warn us of his approach if it didn't mean danger," she reminded him.

"Come, we will meet him at the pass," Theon said. They hadn't gone very far when Brakalar appeared.

"There you are!" a hoarse voice shouted from above. The bedraggled figure, covered in dust and sweat mixed with his own blood from various cuts and scrapes, was almost unrecognizable from the meticulously groomed man they knew. "Just like I expected, you have what is mine!" Brakalar growled, his eyes fixed on the glowing and humming chest Theon held. Reaching into a pocket, Brakalar pulled out a flat glowing metallic rune...the key to the chest...and held it up as he made his way toward them. "Only I can open the chest."

Both Rahlys and Theon tried drawing on the elemental forces to wrench the key out of his hand, but all their efforts failed. The key, or the chest, or the mysterious forces around them were in control. As Brakalar came closer, all the runes on the sealed chest glowed brightly. But one rune, shaped like the key, sent out a smoky gray beam that guided the key to its lock. Theon tried to pull the chest away, but the beam's pull was too strong. When he was little more than an arm's length away, Brakalar could hold the key no longer, and the key slipped from his grip, melding with the matching rune on the chest. Instantly, the lid sprang open.

What happened next was a blur that resulted in the two men struggling, both with their hands gripping the dark rod, and the chest clattering across the stone paving. Rahlys tried drawing on the flows of energy around her to wedge the rod from Brakalar's hand...without success. Then she picked up a stone to use as a weapon when a voice boomed out from above.

"Brakalar! Theon!"

Zayla rushed down to where the men fought. "Stop this, immediately!" she demanded upon reaching them, but Brakalar and Theon continued to wrestle for control of the rod. Then Brakalar managed to wrench the rod from Theon's grip, hitting him over the head with it. Theon slumped to the ground.

"Brakalar, what have you done?" Zayla demanded. A low moan from Theon assured them he was still alive. Rahlys made a move to go to his aid, but Brakalar's actions stopped her.

"Stay back!" he shouted, brandishing the rod wildly.

"Have you lost your ability to reason?" Zayla continued. "If there is a problem, we can discuss it."

"There's nothing to discuss. It's because of the likes of *him* our world was destroyed." Brakalar emphasized the word "him" by kicking Theon...who was trying to rise...in the back, sending him down again. Zayla and Rahlys each took a step forward in an attempt to come to his rescue, but Brakalar held them back.

"I said stay back!" he repeated, now shaking the rod intensely between them. "I intend making things right again, and with this, I will have the power to do so."

"You don't want to do this," Zayla stressed.

"I'm not listening to you!" Brakalar shouted, his grip on the rod intensifying as he aimed it at her.

Suddenly, a wide beam of smoky darkness shot out of the end of the rod, straight for Zayla...enveloping her in a dark cocoon, muting her brief blood curdling scream. Rahlys watched in horror, not wanting to believe what she was seeing, as the darkness dispersed, leaving only a pile of ash remaining where Zayla had previously stood.

Materializing out of the increasing gloom, Anthya and Quaylyn disarmed and restrained Brakalar in an instant. With Brakalar no longer a threat, Rahlys ran to Theon's side.

"What happened?" he asked, regaining his feet with her help.

"It's Zayla! She's gone," Rahlys cried.

"Gone?" Theon could barely control his sorrow. To Rahlys, that moment he aged even further. Anthya tied Brakalar's hands behind his back with a cord she retrieved from her pack, and then leaving him with Quaylyn, she approached what was left of Zayla and knelt in silent grief.

"I didn't mean to kill her," Brakalar sobbed.

Quaylyn picked up the chest and dropped the rod into it, slamming the lid shut. The key fell out of its side, clattering onto the paving stones, the chest seamless again. Compulsively, Rahlys stooped to pick it up.

"Don't touch it!" Quaylyn cried out, stopping her.

"We can't just leave it here to be found again," Rahlys argued. Then to their astonishment, the key melted into the stone and disappeared.

"Well, that takes care of that. We need to get out of here, quick," Quaylyn reminded them, giving Brakalar a shove toward the exit.

"I didn't mean to kill her," Brakalar moaned again.

Anthya rose from the site of Zayla's demise, her face composed. "Quaylyn is right. Quickly, we must leave the ruins immediately. We will take the chest with us to see that it is destroyed." Her voice didn't quiver; it was the voice of calm but firm authority, velvet on steel.

Quaylyn, the sealed chest cradled in his arms, rushed everyone toward the exit. With Rahlys aiding Theon and Anthya leading Brakalar, they hurried through the descending darkness over stones and rubble toward the gap in the mountain. A cacophony of disturbing notes emitting from the runes on the sealed chest accompanied them as they made their way through the jumbled maze. With great effort, they finally reached the opening, the discordant notes continuing to wail as far reaching tendrils of darkness seeped into the pass, following them. They pressed on, not pausing for breath.

Then, suddenly, they broke out into brilliant sunshine. The rune-covered chest containing the Rod of Destruction fell silent...and at last, Anthya felt free to weep.

Chapter 16
The Cold Generator

As the days grew dimmer, shorter, and colder, the babies plumped out, their weak cries becoming shriller and more demanding. November turned into December, snowy days turned into dry cold dark ones, and the new normal soon felt like the way things had always been. Daylight hours dwindled to so few, darkness was always close at hand.

"Brrrr.....it's cold!" Bundled up and carrying an armload of wood, Vince shut the door quickly to avoid letting out too much heat. "Clear skies, little to no wind...the bottom is going to drop out of the thermometer tonight." He crossed the room and quietly eased the firewood down onto the floor in front of the stove so as not to awaken the babies. In rockers nearly facing each other, Maggie and Melinda each rocked a sleeping baby near the stove's radiant warmth.

"Daddy, Daddy!" Leaf shouted, running up to him from the children's room.

"Shhh...! Not so loud. The babies are sleeping," Maggie reminded him.

The babies were always doing something, Leaf thought, but only Melinda "heard" it. A brief pout crossed his face; then he was over it.

Crystal stretched a little in her blanket on Melinda's lap, but didn't awaken. Rock, cuddled in Maggie's arms, just balled his tiny hands into fists, and then relaxed them again.

"Daddy, can we make popcorn?" Leaf asked, as Vince loaded wood into the stove.

"Certainly. You and I will make the popcorn. Okay?"

"Yeah!" Leaf shouted a bit too loud again as he ran off to get the popcorn kernels from the pantry. Maggie smiled and shook her head. It was a good thing the babies were adjusting to a noisy household.

"I better hurry and get to the kitchen before he has the popcorn already popped," Vince said, closing the stove's door. Indeed, Leaf had out the pot and lid they routinely used for the task, as well as the kernels, oil, and popcorn salt by the time he arrived to see a large bowl appear on the floor with the rest of the items. Vince was as stunned by how completely Leaf had thought out what was needed as he was over how the little fellow had gathered the out-of-reach items so quickly. Swallowing a negative response along with his own discomfort over Leaf's talents, he offered support instead. "Let me help you with that; after all, we *are* partners," he said.

Vince picked up the pot and lid off the floor and Leaf handed him the rest of the items one by one. While the oil heated on the burner, he helped his son measure out a half cup of popcorn kernels, with the inevitable few escapees scattering across the floor. Leaf leapt to collect them as Vince dropped the measured kernels into the hot oil, covered the pot, and gave it a sizzling shake.

Pop!

Vince jumped! What sounded like a kernel of popcorn popping came from behind him. He turned.

"Daddy, watch me make popcorn." Giggling, Leaf threw another kernel into the air.

Pop! The kernel burst into fluff almost as soon as it left his hand, landing on the floor freshly popped.

"How...?" Vince muttered, trying to figure out how to react. Then there was another pop, this time from the pot beside him.

"I want to see!" Leaf cried with excitement. Slowly at first, but quickly picking up momentum, the robust rhythm, followed by the unmistakable whiff of freshly popped popcorn, filled the room. Vince lifted his son up so he could see the action through the heavy glass lid.

"You are an incredible little boy," he told Leaf as they watched the tiny miracle unfold together. Soon, the popping quickly diminished again to only a few individual explosions.

"It's ready!" Leaf exclaimed.

"All right." Vince lowered him down, and grabbing the pot handle and lid, poured the contents into the bowl. He quickly added popcorn salt while Leaf danced about in jubilant anticipation, and then he grabbed some smaller bowls from the cabinet. Filling one, he handed it to Leaf.

"Take this bowlful to Mommy, then come back and get one for Melinda."
Leaf took off, losing a few popped kernels along the way.

"Here, Mommy. I popped popcorn," Vince heard him announce proudly.
Maggie did not know the full truth of the statement.

"Great job! Thank you!"

Where's mine? Melinda asked.

"Coming..." Leaf ran back to the kitchen, quickly returning with a heaping
bowlful for her. Then Vince followed him out of the kitchen with two more
heaping bowlfuls in hand.

"Let's play a game," Maggie said when the popcorn was nearly gone, and
rose to clear space at the living room table. Maggie set Rock gently down
on the sofa, placing a pillow to buffer him from the edge, and then relieved
Melinda of Crystal, setting up a safe zone for her at the opposite end.

"Let's play Chutes and Ladders!" Leaf said excitedly, and ran off to fetch his
new favorite game. He was back in a flash.

I want to play, Melinda said, joining Maggie and Leaf at the table.

"Count me in, too," Vince said. They ate popcorn and played games and
laughed. It was one of those wonderful rare spans of time when both babies
slept. Leaf loved it, until all too soon, one by one the babies woke from their
nap, and all attention reverted back to them.

———·—·———

"Caleeza!" Sarus cried, running toward her, the warm golden sunshine
glinting off his light golden brown hair and tall sun-burnished frame. "We
did it. Brakalar just gave me the news. We are going on a great expedition to
the Devastated Continent," he announced gleefully, lifting Caleeza up in his
warrior-strength arms and twirling her around.

"Oh, Sarus, that is wonderful!" she cried, leaning into him when he finally put
her down. It was their dreams come true; they had worked toward this for so long!

"We will explore a transformed continent and make important discoveries
that will be beneficial to all; I just know we will," he said with youthful confidence and enthusiasm. Their minds raced with expectations and their hearts
soared with love as they harvested vegetables for her family's table.

Caleeza knew she was dreaming, but she didn't want to wake up. She was
happy. She missed being that happy.

Groggily, she opened her eyes to dimming daylight and realized she had
slept most of the short daylight hours away. The planet's quick rotations were

hard to adjust to, and Alaska's position on the planet, being tilted away from the sun, made it even more difficult. The cabin was cold; the fire in the wood-stove had gone out again.

Caleeza found one of the leafless trees lying down in the snow after the last heavy snowfall. She had been reluctant to take down a living tree, but this one had been provided by the forces of nature. Drawing energy from the elemental forces, she proportioned it up to look like the firewood she borrowed from Rahlys' woodshed. She teleported some of the freshly cut up tree to a stack against the outside wall of the little schoolhouse, and sent the rest to the Rahlys' woodshed to replace what she had used.

But this wood was heavier than what she had been using, still wet with the life forces of the tree. Drawing on the elemental forces to dry it out enough so it would burn, took nearly as much energy as drawing energy to warm the air around her. The logical solution was to trade her little pile of wet firewood for some of the abundant seasoned wood in Rahlys' woodshed. The wet firewood would have a chance to dry before Rahlys returned to use it.

Donning the old coat and boots, she teleported herself to the woodshed. The nearly full woodshed of towering neatly stacked rows left little room to stand in. Knee-deep snow walled in the outer perimeter of the large pole structure, sheltered by a sloped roof. The sun had already set and darkness was seeping into the cold, crisp, blue sky. Pulling the badly worn oversized coat tighter around her for closer warmth, Caleeza made quick work of the transfer, teleporting a stack of dry wood to the cabin and replacing it with what she had recently harvested.

Upon returning, she soon had a crackling fire, solving the problem of heat, but not of light. Drawing energy, she produced a small glow globe, and needing a hot drink fast, sped up the molecules in a cup of water to make tea. Caleeza sat back sipping tea as she nibbled sparingly on a rationed cracker, recalling the happy images of her dream. The snapping roar of the fire filled the quiet, but there was nothing to fill the loneliness in her heart. She realized she could leave, find a warmer place where there was more to eat, but instinct told her to stay.

From what she had learned from the children's infrequent visits, her only hope of going home rested on Rahlys returning...unless Sarus found a way first...but she couldn't be certain she had actually connected with Sarus. Rahlys was the Guardian of the Light, possessor of Sorceress Anthya's powers, and destroyer of Droclum. Surely, one so great will be able to help her.

As her mastery of the language improved, Caleeza searched for other references of Droclum's demise from the schoolhouse resources, but could find none. Yet she had been able to pick up thoughts from the children's chosen mother and father that would confirm Melinda's claims.

Rahlys was on an expedition to a distant world...her world! She had joined Councilor Anthya on a mission to the Devastated Continent to find the lost expedition...her expedition! But Melinda had no idea how Caleeza would go about returning home, except wait for Rahlys to return. That was not surprising since the farthest reference she could find of these humans traveling in space/time was to their own moon. Leaf and Melinda were the key to her getting home, of that she was certain. She needed to learn more.

———

Can I have the last piece of blueberry pie? Melinda asked as she and Maggie were finishing up the supper dishes.

"Of course you can." Maggie put the pie on a saucer for her. "Now, we won't have to put it away," she said, handing it to her. The pie came with a thankful little hug. "I don't know what I would do without you," she said in explanation. "You are the greatest daughter a mother could have."

Thank you, Mom.

Well, she wasn't really Maggie and Vince's daughter, but she was glad they loved her and took care of her. It was a wonderful feeling being part of the family. The pie wasn't for her though, it was for Caleeza. Taking it to the children's room, she would stash it with the rest of the food they were taking to her tonight...after everyone went to sleep.

To her surprise, Leaf was already fast asleep, but she would wake him when it was time. It shouldn't be much longer. She placed the pie on her desk, picked up a novel, and began reading by a small lamp attached to the headboard of her bed to pass the time. When the battery bank that served as its power supply ran low, it would be recharged using the diesel generator.

Vince fell asleep twice reading in his recliner...she could hear him snoring in the living room. And the twins were down, for the first part of the night anyway; fortunately, they still slept in their parents' room, so Mom and Dad weren't likely to come into the children's room during the night. Finally, Maggie, tired after another long, hard, but rewarding day of motherhood, made a move to go to bed. Vince would surely follow.

A couple of hours later, the house slumbered into a deep winter's sleep. Now was the time to go. Melinda reached out mentally to Caleeza.

We are coming to visit and bring food. Soon Melinda received a response.

Thank you. I peer ahead for your visit. It was evident Caleeza was still studying English. Melinda nudged Leaf in the silent darkness.

Leaf.

He resisted waking up, and she wished she could let him sleep, but he was the only one who could teleport them. Slowly at first, he rubbed his eyes open, then clicking awake, he scrambled to his feet.

"I'm ready."

Shhhh...

I'm ready.

No, you're not. Get dressed, including a coat and a hat. In rapid succession, pants, shirt, hat, and coat appeared on his little boy frame.

Now I'm ready.

What about your feet? Snow boots instantly appeared over socks nearly halfway off his feet. Melinda, also dressed, reached under her bed for the plastic shopping bags of stashed food, and then picked up the saucer of blueberry pie from her desk. *All right, let's go.*

Focus and concentration crossed Leaf's youthful face. Then in a flutter of a butterfly's wing they were there, standing in the center of the schoolhouse, the room cool and dim. Caleeza rose from her seat by the stove, placing the book she had been studying on the nearby table.

"Good evening, Miss Melinda...and, Master Leaf! Happy you make it."

"Caleeza!" Leaf cried, and ran to her for a hug. Then his attention turned to scouting around the room to locate his favorite games and toys.

It's chilly in here. You are going to have to burn more wood tonight. It's going to get very cold, Melinda said, also giving her a hug after setting the food on the table. She added wood to the stove from the pile on the floor, and opened the draft. *And you need more light than this to read.* The glow globe she had been reading by was barely brighter than a candle.

"I have to save strength. Thank you for taking care of me," she said.

No problem, Melinda assured her.

Caleeza searched through the shopping bags of cans, bags, and boxes for something to eat.

Here, eat this first; it's blueberry pie, Melinda said, handing it to her, and Caleeza promptly obeyed.

As they were putting the food away, Melinda happened to spot the cold generator pushed back against the wall under the table. She quickly retrieved it, blowing off the dust. *Remember this? It's the cold generator Theon built. I think it is cold enough now to put it into service. If this works, you will have all the light you need.*

And you said Theon made this? The same Theon, friend of Droclum?

Yes, but Theon is a good guy now.

Theon is a good guy?

Yes, I'll set this outside and plug the cabin into it, and when the cold charges it up, we should have electricity. Melinda was certain it was cold enough for the generator to work. The little cabin that had served as a schoolhouse had been wired complete with receptacles and light switches. It just needed to be plugged into a generator to make them work.

Caleeza, coatless, and Leaf, still wearing his hat and coat, followed her out into the frigid, star-studded night, the cold dry air searing their throats and nostrils. Their exhaled breaths billowed out in clouds of white smoke and the cold contracted snow underfoot squeaked loudly as they made their way to the side of the house. Melinda could feel the bite of the air on her unprotected head and hands; she would need to complete the task quickly.

Stepping off the packed trail in front of the cabin, she waded through unpacked snow to reach an outside shelf under the eave of the roof. The generator's power crystal, mounted on end in the light intricate metal frame, had already begun to glow and spin as the deep cold caused it to contract. Placing the cold generator on the shelf, she wasted no time locating the end of the electric cord that supplied power to the cabin and plugged it in.

"C...c...cold...d...d.....!" Leaf said, running for the cabin door as soon as she turned to rejoin them, his little body shivering. Caleeza followed close behind him, seeking warmth. Dusting snow off her pants legs, Melinda entered the cabin after them, and flipped on the switch by the door. Light flooded the room from a fixture on the ceiling.

"It worked!" they cried together, enjoying the bright light. Caleeza released the glow globe, dimmed by the new radiance, and relaxed. She was still hungry and offered them something to eat, but they declined, so she quickly ate another cracker while Melinda looked through the books she had laying about.

"Theon went with Rahlys to the Devastated Continent?" Caleeza asked, as though resuming a conversation that had been broken off just moments before.

Yes and Theon's daughter Ilene...and Raven.

"Theon has a daughter from Earth, daughter Ilene," she said, solidifying the fact in her mind. "Who is Raven?"

Raven is a raven, Melinda clarified, sending her mental images.

"Raven is a bird?" Caleeza shuddered, remembering the large dark bird of stealth that flew over her, crossing the big river. The great black bird had instilled in her both wonder and fear. She had since seen one fly over these woods. But why would the Guardian of the Light take a raven with her? Caleeza tried to imagine a raven flying over the Devastated Continent!

Ravens weren't the only flying species that lived in these woods. There were numerous little birds with brown or black heads that cheeped from the branches of the leafless trees, larger gray birds, and black and white birds with long tails, and a larger bird still, majestic and graceful with a white head. All were a wonder to her, coming from a world that had none.

It was Raven who found the crystal.

"The crystal?"

The Oracle of Light, the crystal with Sorceress Anthya's powers; Raven found it originally and took it to Rahlys. That's how Rahlys became the Guardian of the Light.

"Where is the Oracle of Light now?" Caleeza asked, building up hope. The Oracle could be a means of making contact with her world.

It's with Rahlys, of course; she took it with her.

The children left Caleeza with much to think about after their visit. As a young new person, she had learned the history of Droclum's destruction of her world and Sorceress Anthya's efforts to stop him, but the legend of a powerful crystal... the Oracle of Light, ignited with the great sorceress' dying breath...she had always considered to be just that, legend. The existence of such a crystal would explain how Rahlys made contact with her own world. If only Rahlys were here!

An expedition was looking for them on the Devastated Continent! They wouldn't find *her*, of course, but she could always hope that maybe they would find the others. If only she could let Sarus know. Would the new expedition find him and guide him home safely? She could only hope.

The cold outside deepened, causing the logs of the little cabin to pop loudly from contraction. Caleeza kept a warm fire going, using seasoned wood from Rahlys' woodshed, and filled her belly to comfortably full with food the children brought. Then, for long hours, with sufficient light, she studied, learning more about this world from the large collection of books called the *World Book Encyclopedia* until her eyes grew heavy. Finally, she closed the volume she had been perusing and made her way groggily to her narrow bed. Cozily warm, snuggled in her blankets, her head on a soft pillow, she extinguished the lights. Immediately, her thoughts turned to Sarus. She had barely closed her eyes when she heard him speaking to her.

"I have news that may please you," he said, reaching toward her, but never quite reaching her. "I am working on a way to bring you home." Caleeza felt a rush of hope.

"When?"

"Soon. I am learning the answer."

"Oh, Sarus, I miss you so much."

"I will always be with you; I have not gone away."

Caleeza pondered on his statements for a moment, without making sense of them. "There is an expedition headed your way; they are looking for us." A glimmer of concern passed Sarus' projected countenance. "Councilor Anthya is a member of that expedition. Also Sorceress Rahlys, Guardian of the Light, defeater of Droclum, is with them."

"They must not enter the Crystalline Landscape."

"There's more. Theon, self-reformed, is also among them, as well as his daughter of Earth...and a raven."

"They must not enter the Crystalline Landscape," Sarus repeated. "The crystals generate tremendous forces that we are not ready to understand. Collectively, they form energy fields across the landscape. These power reservoirs are like mine fields to humans. When one is triggered, the release of energy can teleport a person through folds in space, across the galaxy, to another world, whether habitable or not...or into the cold depths of the void."

A shiver ran down Caleeza's spine as she imagined such a horrible death. How lucky she was to be alive!

"What are we going to do? We can't let Councilor Anthya and the others come to harm?"

"We must stop them from entering the Crystalline Landscape."

"We...?" Caleeza felt another stab of hope.

But Sarus had already begun to fade.

———————

One long dark night followed another, with fleeting days in between, as Winter Solstice was finally reached, and passed. Tiny seconds of increasing daylight were gained day by day, gradually turning into minutes by the end of January. Vince started thinking of putting in work trails for cutting and hauling firewood. With increasing daylight, he needed to be out doing something after being cooped in with the women and children for so long.

Warmly dressed, Vince stepped out into the cool, crisp air, the sun shining through the leafless tops of the trees, casting long blue shadows in the gleaming white snow. He strolled up to his parked snowmobile, checked the gas and the oil injection, and started her up. The well cared for machine roared into life, beckoning to go. Adjusting his ear plugs, goggles, and hat, Vince climbed on and headed southeast through the woods behind the cabin.

He started off following a winter recreational trail he kept open to the overlook above the big swamp, now a frozen, treeless expanse of white. His plan was to a run a large loop off of the recreational trail to the south and back again, from which he would later make more connecting trails. By the end of wood harvesting season, woodlot trails generally became a confusing maze. He thought he might even make a detour today to check on Rahlys' place.

When Vince turned off onto the unpacked snow, the snowmachine sunk in deeply but continued forward, guided by his steering and body language. The snow could use a little more moisture for packing, he noted, as he steered the machine near stands of trees that could use some thinning out, working to keep the snowmachine level over the soft undulating snow cover. Finally, having gone as far south as he intended, he curved toward the West.

Vince quickly reached the point where he had to make a decision; go on an excursion to Rahlys' place, or swing back north toward home. He wished the snow conditions were better. Stopping the machine but not killing the engine, he paused to take a break and cool off for a couple of minutes. He removed his gloves and opened his jacket to let out some body heat...using body language on a snowmachine can work up a sweat...then geared back up to take off again.

Leaning back in his seat, Vince pressed the throttle and the snowmachine roared to life, but instead of speeding forward when he gave it some gas... the tracks dug into the snow, burying the machine.

A disgruntled Vince got off his snowmachine and pulled it back a foot, packing down the snow. Then he trudged to the front of the machine, stomping the snow down with his boots, and pulled the snowmachine skis up out the snow, for a running start to get back afloat. He decided not to take the detour up the ridge to Rahlys' place until the snow pack set up a little better. *I've had enough exercise for one day.*

Trying again, Vince jumped on his snowmachine and took off, this time with success. Swerving to the north, he headed back toward the recreational trail leading into his backyard.

Chapter 17
Testimony

"Are you crazy? You heard Rojaire's warning!" Tassyn said, close to shouting. "The Crystalline Landscape is dangerous."

"If the expedition can go there, so can we," Stram growled back. "Besides, Rojaire's brain is as pulpy as zan fruit."

"Well, you can go without me. I don't like the looks of this place, and I'm not going," Tassyn said emphatically. Stram had become a mean dictator and it was time someone stood up to him.

"Coward!" Stram's hard cold stare forced Tassyn to take a step back.

"Tassyn is right, we should give this some thought," Edty said tremulously, glancing down at his feet and fidgeting uneasily. "Like, what are we going to do about food? It doesn't look like there is anything to eat among all those crystals." He wanted to sound strongly defiant like Tassyn, but it came out almost apologetic. But Edty spoke up so seldom, Stram actually took pause.

"We'll gather some food to take with us," he grumbled, reluctantly relenting to reason after a moment's thought.

"You know, Stram, the expedition will have to come back out again. Why don't we just wait for them?" Tassyn suggested.

"We're waiting for no one. Fill your gathering bags...and be quick about it," he hissed when no one made an effort to move.

Stram stormed away, fuming. Things just weren't going as he had planned. For several rotations, they had tracked the rest of the expedition without catching up with them, despite his brutal push to do so, and now his men were balking over hiking through a bunch of crystals.

Traevus stood defiantly silent, wrists bound behind his back, gazing across the luminous Crystalline Landscape stretched out before him. The enormous translucent crystals reflected colorfully fractured sunlight and chimed, ever so softly, in deeply mysterious whispery tones. How beautiful! He could easily imagine the place being dangerous. Anything that beautiful had to be deadly! And who was this Rojaire that Tassyn mentioned? he wondered. Dare he ask? What did Rojaire know about the threateningly beautiful crystals?

"I know why Stram can draw energy and the rest of us can't," Traevus said nonchalantly as soon as Stram was a safe distance away.

Both Tassyn and Edty glanced cautiously at Traevus and then in Stram's direction. They could see him a long ways off, back toward the hills where sparse vegetation still offered some sustenance. Stram was well out of hearing range.

"What did you say?" Tassyn asked, inching closer to Traevus. He wanted to hear Traevus say it a second time...just to be sure he heard it right.

"I said I know why Stram can draw energy...some anyway."

"Well then, by Seaa's light, tell us how he does it," Edty whispered with urgency, also moving in closer.

"Untie my wrists," Traevus demanded, turning his back to them in assistance. There was a cautious pause as he waited for them to make a decision.

"I'm going to untie him," Tassyn told Edty.

"Huh? Are you sure we should do that?" Edty frowned with uncertainty. "Maybe we should ask Stram first?"

"He needs to gather food, too. He can't do so with his hands tied behind his back."

"Thank you," Traevus moaned in painful relief as the cut bindings dropped from his wrist. Freed from his bonds, he rubbed sore wrists and stretched cramped arms.

"All right, you're untied," Tassyn said, reminding him of his obligation. A quick glance to the west confirmed Stram still kept his distance.

Traevus had a plan and now was as good a time as any to start putting it into place. "Stram carries a stone on him...a stone as round and golden as Seaa. I've seen it in his hands. He likes to take it out and hold it...caress it... even gaze into it."

Edty twitched with unease at the seductiveness of Traevus' voice.

"The stone somehow blocks or repels whatever prevents us from drawing on the elemental forces; I'm sure of it. Take the stone away from Stram and you will render him powerless," Traevus concluded.

"And how do you expect us to do that?" Tassyn asked.

"Well, I'm sure if the three of us collaborated, we could come up with a plan," Traevus suggested. Stram, still harvesting some distance away, glanced in their direction.

"Better get moving before it looks like a conspiracy," Traevus said. Having planted the seed, he walked away from the group toward the nearest zan fruit bush and started picking. Without agreeing or disagreeing to anything, the others followed his example.

After a cooling off period, Stram approached the rest of the men. "We will set up camp at the last rise near the little stream undercutting the base of the hill. From there, we will work together to formulate a plan of attack." Tassyn, Edty, even Traevus, stared at Stram in stunned puzzlement. Stram did not wait for comments.

I think that sounded magnanimous enough, Stram told himself as he strolled back to the hill. *I'm a good leader; I just need good followers.*

Spotting Rojaire and Ilene in the distance, Rahlys walked out to meet them, with Raven flying overhead, unwilling to let Rahlys out of his sight. Not that it did any good, he fretted, if she didn't heed his warnings.

"What's wrong?" Ilene asked, reading the stress on Rahlys' face.

"Zayla is dead," she announced, calmly.

"What?" Ilene gasped, trying to internalize the news. "But how?"

"What happened?" Rojaire asked.

"She was killed by a dark force at the ruins of the Temple of Tranquility," Rahlys said, circumventing any mention of the Rod of Destruction, especially in front of Rojaire.

"I'm sorry," Rojaire said, sounding genuine. "I know Zayla and I have had our differences, but I've always admired her loyalty to her principles."

"Zayla's gone!" Ilene cried, tears starting to flow.

"I know the temple ruins are definitely darkly disturbed. I didn't spend much time there when I first discovered them because the energy was just too negative. I didn't know it was deadly."

"I thought the temple was supposed to be a place of goodness," Ilene said, struggling for control.

"Not anymore."

"How did she die?" Rojaire asked.

Now he was asking for details; Rahlys didn't know what to say. How much did Rojaire know about the key and what it could unlock? "You will have to ask Anthya for details as to what happened," she said, letting him assume she hadn't seen Zayla die so horribly. With Ilene still shedding tears, they rejoined the rest of the group.

Anthya stood...once again a composed leader. Gathered together, the group watched solemnly as she removed two flags, a warning signal and a grave marker, from her pack, and planted them in the entrance to the ruins. Then with hard-won emotional control, she inscribed Zayla's name on the grave marker. When all was done, Anthya marched sternly up to Brakalar and cut the cords binding his wrists.

"You have been relieved of your duties," Anthya said without ceremony, "and will take orders from me." By a previously designated order of succession, Anthya was now in charge, with Quaylyn as her second. "As long as you do as you are told, you will remain free until you can be handed over to the High Council." Brakalar raised no objection. Sad, haunted eyes stared distantly from his dusty tear-streaked face.

"We need to move on and find a suitable resting place that will shelter us from the sun," Anthya said, gathering them together.

"Councilor, if I may make a suggestion," Rojaire spoke up, "there is a small hidden meadow with a spring near the point of the mountain's crescent. It would provide both shade and water."

"We will check it out. Theon, how's your head? Can you make it a little further?"

"Absolutely, my lady!" he said, mustering strength...from somewhere. "Just a bump on me ol' noggin." Rahlys doubted Anthya picked up on his Old Earth vernacular, but she took it as a yes, and the expedition started moving again.

The day unfurled hot and dry, with no cloud relief in sight. A cool rain shower sure would feel good about now, Rahlys mused, feeling stifled by the heat; at least it would help rinse off the traveling dust. Wordlessly, the bedraggled-looking crew followed the contour of the mountains for what Rahlys was sure was over a mile, before Rojaire paused at an almost imperceptible crack in the dark bluish purple rock face.

"Through here," Rojaire said, sliding into the crevice sideways and quickly disappearing around a curve. Raven flew over the low mountain peak to investigate and quickly circled back.

"Aaaaaark! Aaaaaark!" he cried shrilly in the shimmering heat. It was a cry of joy.

"Raven says, *yes*," Rahlys assured them.

Anthya followed Rojaire, and after a reasonable pause, Quaylyn directed Brakalar to go ahead, slipping through closely behind him. Rahlys motioned for Ilene and Theon to go ahead of her. Bringing up the rear, Rahlys slid into the crevice, the rock warm against her back as she maneuvered around the tight curve that opened into an invitingly cool spacious hollow with shade cast by the mountain. A spring gushed out of a fracture in the rocks, forming a little runoff stream that disappeared again through a rocky hole at the base of the mountain. An uninterrupted carpet of pinkish, sweet-smelling herbs, resembling seaweed, washed up on a beach covered rocks and ground alike.

"Sweetleaf," Theon explained to Ilene and Rahlys as they watched him pluck a handful of the succulent sprawling vegetation and stuffed it into his mouth. Rahlys picked a puffy pinkish-green fork-shaped leaf and took an experimental bite. The tender crunchy leaf gave way easily between her teeth, squirting her tongue with sweet spicy nectar.

"Wow, that's good!" she admitted, "but what I really want, though, is to wash my hands and face." Rahlys followed a path of already trodden sweet-leaf to the spring. There was no avoiding stepping on the stuff; it covered every inch of rocky ground sheltered by the surrounding walls of stone. Reaching the trampled edge of the stream, she dropped to her knees, cupped cool refreshing water in her hands, and drank. Then leaning far forward, she splashed handfuls of water onto her hot dusty face.

Feeling greatly refreshed, Rahlys looked around with interest. The hidden retreat opened only to the sky; the crevice they had passed through the only way in and out, unless one scaled the sheer rock walls. How meticulously Rojaire must have explored to have found this place!

When everyone had drunk their fill of fresh water and cleared rocks of creeping sweetleaf for a place to sit, Raven landed by the stream for a drink. They would wait out the hottest part of the day in this sheltered haven. Anthya stood, taking the opportunity to address the assembled expedition. "I wish to hold at this time a discussion of events leading to Zayla's death." Brakalar's eyes lowered, but he didn't make a sound.

"We have suffered a great lost," she began, "...a tremendous lost...," Anthya paused, then with difficulty continued. "Still, we have a mission to finish, a mission Zayla would want us to complete."

"How did she die?" Rojaire asked, boldly springing the question.

"You will soon find out. Everything will be revealed," Anthya said, moving her gaze to include everyone as she paced before them. "There will be no more secrets. Our lives depend on us working as a unified team. Secrets sever the bond of trust and threaten the success of our mission." There was a general nod of agreement.

"Brakalar, we will begin with you," Anthya said. "How did you gain possession of the key to the chest containing the Rod of Destruction?" Brakalar jerked, as though startled out of his own painful recollections.

"Rojaire gave it to me," he said. To Brakalar's obvious relief, Anthya's piecing gaze riveted instantly toward Rojaire.

"So, Rojaire, same question."

"I found it...at the site of what was once Droclum's stronghold." Rahlys remembered seeing "Droclum's Stronghold," located in the northwest quadrant of the continent, labeled on the map at the Academy. "I didn't know what it was at first, but after I held it in my hand for a while, I began to feel a slight tug of energy. Of course, I followed the key's directional pull, and after many rotations of searching, it led me to the Sooty Caves. The key drew me to the stone block in the center of the innermost cave, but whatever the stone once cradled was gone. I explored the caves high and low...but I didn't find anything there. Later, when I showed the key to Brakalar, he sparked a lot of interest in it, so I offered it to him...as a bargaining chip."

"Brakalar secured a meeting for you with the High Council to petition for recognition for your work on the Devastated Continent," Anthya said, filling in what she already knew.

"Yes."

"So tell me, Rojaire, do you have any more of these artifacts in your possession?"

"No, Councilor, I do not," Rojaire said, indignantly. "Why don't you ask them if they have any more artifacts in their possession?" he said, indicating Rahlys and Theon.

"In due time. Theon," Anthya said, turning her attention to him. "How did you obtain the chest?"

"Well, now, Councilor," Theon said, clearing his throat, "that is a bit of a story."

"Let's hear it."

Theon searched in his mind for a place to begin. "Well, right after we arrived on the continent, Rahlys told me she could detect some kind of seeking energy coming from something Brakalar carried with him. Then, by sheer luck, I later caught a glimpse of the key when Brakalar was rummaging through his pouch. I recognized it immediately and was horrified...because I knew what it was and what it could open."

"But you didn't report it to anyone," Anthya accused. Rahlys and Theon exchanged guilty glances.

"We didn't know who to trust. So Rahlys and I decided we would keep a close eye on Brakalar ourselves. When he gave us a tour of the Sooty Caves,

Rahlys detected the key detecting the chest in the solid block of stone that had cradled baby Quaylyn."

"So it *was* in the cave," Brakalar said, unexpectedly. Everyone waited for him to say more. When he didn't, Theon continued.

"Then the groundshake closed the tunnel. While Brakalar and Rojaire were trying to clear it, Rahlys teleported us back to the inner cave." He didn't mention Zayla giving Rahlys drugged tea to put her to sleep after Quaylyn rescued her from the tunnel. They still didn't know if that was part of a malicious plot, or simply an untimely act of kindness. Zayla was dead now and there was no reason to tarnish her memory. Brakalar's greed for power was his own.

"By 'us' you mean you and Rahlys."

"And Quaylyn."

"Quaylyn?" Anthya's eyebrows lifted with interest.

"Yes, well, apparently, he had been keeping an eye on us keeping an eye on Brakalar, and forced our hand in letting him in on it."

"Quaylyn?" Anthya asked, turning the questioning to him. "How did you know about the Rod of Destruction?

"I didn't. I was clueless as to what was going on, but I could tell Theon and Rahlys were being secretive about something," Quaylyn added. "Anyway, with the help of the crystal, Rahlys was able to enter the stone and retrieve the chest." There was an audible gasp from the listeners. "Then she placed a ward on the chest, preventing the key from detecting it again, and Theon started carrying it around in his pack."

Theon patted the pack beside him. It was still there. "We were planning on finding a way to destroy it, of course."

"Wow! So that's what's been going on!" Ilene exclaimed. Anthya had left Ilene out of the interrogation...and rightly so.

"So, Brakalar, how did you find out Theon had the chest?" Anthya asked, keeping the testimonies flowing. Brakalar hesitated, and then spoke softly.

"The key started working again, only this time it pulled toward the temple ruins."

"The flows of energy at the ruins must have negated the spell," Rahlys said, speaking up for the first time. She wanted to kick herself. *I shouldn't have said anything*, Rahlys chided herself. Of course, Anthya's attention now turned to her.

"Your name has been coming up all through this," she said pointedly to Rahlys, pacing a step closer. "Perhaps you should take up the narrative from here." It was just what Rahlys had been hoping to avoid.

"Well, Theon and I were exploring the ruins and we could feel the confusing tattered flows of drifting energy. In fact, Raven refused to enter, or even fly over the place. We probably should have heeded his warnings, but we didn't. Theon took the chest out of his pack to see how the runes covering its surface reacted to the strange forces moving around us. The result was an eerie light and sound show, as some of you saw. Perhaps the chest actually drew the energy toward us, because the day began to get hazier."

Everyone listened with intense interest as Rahlys told the group how Brakalar arrived on the scene, angrily brandishing the key at them, claiming they had his treasure. She gave details of how when Brakalar drew close, the key sprang from his hand to the chest, and the chest opened. She described the struggle that ensued, Zayla's sudden appearance on the scene, and how Brakalar had threatened them after gaining possession of the rod by knocking Theon over the head.

"Zayla tried to talk to Brakalar, to reason with him, to help him understand what he was doing," Rahlys explained, "but he just kept threatening, waving the rod around, and then a dark beam shot out of the rod, striking Zayla dead on, incinerating her almost instantly." She shuddered, remembering Zayla's one brief cry.

"How horrible!" Ilene cried.

"That's when you and Quaylyn arrived and took the rod away from him," Rahlys finished.

"Theon, do you agree events unfolded as Rahlys described them?"

"I was down on the ground for some of it," Theon said rubbing the tender spot on his head, "but that is what happened."

"Brakalar," Anthya said, placing herself directly in front of him. *How could such a delicate looking woman be so formidable?* Rahlys wondered. "Do you agree with Sorceress Rahlys' testimony?" she asked, her light gray eyes piercing arrows into Brakalar's mind. With difficulty, Brakalar raised his head, facing her directly. "Yes," he whispered in agreement, and then hung his head. "I didn't mean to hurt her," he cried.

"So Theon carries the chest containing the Rod of Destruction, and we are to trust him with it? Where is the key?" Rojaire asked.

"Who *should* we trust to carry it, Rojaire?" Anthya asked in earnest. Rojaire shook his head, declining to comment. "The key has been lost to the ruins of the Temple of Tranquility," Anthya said, starting to pace. "The chest can't be opened without it. The rod and chest must be destroyed."

"How?" Rahlys asked.

"We will find a way," Anthya assured her. "Let's go back to the question about artifacts," she said in all seriousness. "Does anyone here have any more artifacts in their possession that we should know about?" Anthya surveyed each of them in turn, looking for a reaction.

Rahlys didn't know what to do. Should she and Theon declare the star stone? The stone was found on Earth, not here. She felt relief when Theon solved the dilemma for her.

"Well, Councilor," Theon said after a long quiet pause, "I have something in my possession...actually it belongs to Rahlys...that may be of interest." *We better come clean,* he telepathed to Rahlys.

"What is it?"

"It's a stone. A stone that repels whatever it is that is blocking us from drawing on the elemental forces," he said, fishing the smooth round golden rock from his pocket and handing it over to her. "Rahlys has been letting me use it."

"Stram had a stone that looked just like that," Rojaire said, suddenly excited. "If what you say is true, that would explain a few strange incidences that occurred just before I left the band."

"And you've tested it?" Anthya asked Theon, gazing at the stone's golden swirls reflecting light as she twirled it in her hand.

"With the stone, I can teleport short distances and communicate telepathically with Rahlys."

"Where did you find this?" she asked Rahlys, rolling the satiny smooth stone between her fingers.

"I didn't; it was given to me as a keepsake, a sort of good luck charm for my journey."

"And who gave you this...keepsake?" she asked, studying the orb with interest.

"Melinda, a girl from Earth. She found it near my home."

"Can you confirm this?" Anthya asked, turning to Ilene.

"Yes," Ilene gasped under Anthya's hard scrutiny, "Melinda gave it to her before we left."

"Tell us more about this girl from Earth named Melinda," Anthya directed her. "Who is she?" Ilene couldn't believe she was being interrogated. Shaken, she struggled to gather her thoughts.

"Melinda is from Southeast Alaska. She used to live with her father on a fishing boat." Suddenly, Ilene realized...to reveal more would associate Melinda with Droclum.

"Go on," Anthya encouraged. Ilene didn't have the courage, under Anthya's intense scrutiny, to circumvent.

"Melinda's father was killed by Droclum and Melinda was taken captive. Rahlys rescued her shortly before Droclum was destroyed." All was quiet for a while.

Anthya continued to examine the stone with interest. "If these rogues have a stone like this, they could be more dangerous than we thought," Anthya said, breaking the silence. "Armed with this knowledge, we need to be cautious." She tossed the stone back to Theon. "Anything else?" No one responded.

"Our mission here is not over. We still have our agenda. Turning around and going home would accomplish nothing. We are looking for the members of the lost expedition and exploring a vastly changed continent. And now we have a new obligation: We must find a way to destroy the Rod of Destruction."

The team ate and rested, made sweetleaf tea, and filled their water containers; some even took a nap, until Anthya lead them out of the hidden retreat through the crevice in the mountain. Warm dusty wind, blowing from the west, buffeted them as they emerged from the shelter of the low peaks. Turning their backs to the wind, they followed the easterly contour of the diminishing mountains. Before long, the group rounded the low, rocky point of the crescent and veered north toward the center of the continent, the Crescent Mountains cutting off the buffeting west wind.

Now that they had gotten around the mountains, flatter terrain stretched out before them; rolling plains of purples, blues, yellows, and reds, reaching as far as the eye could see. Abundant vegetation covered the primitive blue-violet soil, but there wasn't a zaota tree in sight. Raven flew high above them in ever widening circles, soaring on the warm air currents. To the west, the lowering sun just managed to peek at them over sharp knife-blade mountain peaks. Seaa, a bright spot in the sunlit sky, had already risen in the east.

As they made their way, it quickly became evident that the terrain was not as smooth and level close-up as it appeared to be from a distance. The large-grain sandy ground often placed unexpected rocks, hidden by foliage, underfoot to trip you. Shallow gullies, unseen until you were teetering on the edge, sliced through the gently undulating landscape. Formed by water runoff, some of these gullies were almost deep enough and wide enough to be called little valleys. Nearly all the rocky water courses that ran through these shallow valleys were dry. A light, but constant, breeze of dry air evaporated the sweat from Rahlys' forehead.

The sun had already set behind the mountains when they came across a gully deep enough to shelter them from the wind and wide enough to provide dry ground near a trickle of a stream. Rojaire pointed out an outcrop of porous, pinkish-blue rocks. "We can have a fire. These rocks will burn," he said, tossing a few in a pile. As the sky darkened, Seaa glimmered brighter, providing her distant feeble light. *Another campfire shared...although burning rocks for fuel was certainly different...*Rahlys thought. Another night under the stars; by now she had an inkling of what it must have been like for the pioneers moving across the plains of the American west.

The next few rotations passed without any further incidents as the expedition wove its way deeper and deeper into the continent's interior. With fewer secrets and hidden subterfuges, the team became more united. Only Brakalar remained quietly reticent and aloof on the sidelines. No one tried to engage him, nor did anyone taunt or revile him. Brakalar did what he was told and offered no verbal input. Rahlys felt certain he suffered deeply over what he had done, but Zayla could not be brought back.

As they steadily advanced, the vegetation covering the landscape dwindled in both density and variety. The days grew hotter and drier, the sun's blazing heat forcing them to seek midday shelter, while the nights grew darker with Seaa's increasing absence from the night sky as the planet's orbit around the sun put the sun between them. The nights also grew steadily colder as the increasingly bare terrain allowed more of the day's heat to escape back into the atmosphere. Gradually, a dark smudge to the north became noticeable on the distant horizon.

"What's that?" Rahlys asked, pointing to it, when they crested another low rise.

"That," Anthya said calmly, "is Mt. Vatre."

Chapter 18
Family Life

Over the following weeks, the days gradually began to warm, bringing heavy wet spring snow. After each snowfall, Vince ran his woodlot loop packing the trail with the snowmachine...following with the trail drag. The heavier wetter snow packed down well, and the low night time temperatures froze the trail hard.

Vince felt restless, the hint of spring in the air spurring him into action. Wanting a little adventure, he turned the snowmachine off his packed trail, cutting across the undisturbed snow pack through the center of the loop. He did this a couple of times; forming a giant figure eight trail system. Snow conditions were great. He glanced up into the graying sky, filled with the promise of more snow. *This is probably a good time to try and reach Rahlys' cabin.*

Upon reaching the southwest end of his hard-earned work trail, Vince turned off onto virgin snow and headed up a gentle rise. He leaned forward, out of his seat, as he steered the snowmachine through the trees, seeking the path of least resistance. The terrain nearly leveled out again as he reached the next land shelf. Eventually, he connected with Rahlys' unbroken trail and followed it the rest of the way to her cabin.

As he approached the last rise, the smell of wood smoke triggered alarms in Vince's awareness, warning him to be cautious. Was someone staying at Rahlys' cabin, and if so, who? The scent was even more prominent when he crested over the rise into the untracked yard; so much so, he was surprised to find the cabin undisturbed. But the smell of wood smoke was still strongly evident, and it didn't take long to trace it to the guest cabin schoolhouse.

Whoever was staying there would have heard his snowmachine by now, so there was little point in practicing stealth. They were probably friends of Rahlys, but how did they get here? There were no trails, not even snowshoe or ski tracks. His main concern was the fact that he was unarmed should it prove to be someone dangerous, perhaps hiding out from the law. He decided a direct approach was probably best, and guided his machine through the narrow winding gap that served as a path through the swath of forest between Rahlys' house and the guest cabin.

Upon arriving at the little cabin, it was obvious someone was there. A lazy tail of smoke drifted off the end of the stovepipe and footprints peppered the clearing, but strangely, there was no trail leading on or off the property. Inside, a light shone brightly, although there was no sign of a generator, and outside, on a shelf under the eaves, something bright spun in a wire cage. Then, suddenly, a woman slight of frame with reddish hair and violet gray eyes appeared before him. Although dressed in familiar-looking clothing, her countenance and posture were subtly off-worldly. He shut off the snowmachine, not knowing what to expect.

"Greetings, Vince Bradley, chosen father of Melinda and Leaf. I am Caleeza of the lost expedition from Anthya's World. It is my honor to serve," she said, bowing gracefully.

He certainly hadn't expected that. Vince's tension eased from extreme alert to alert caution. Caleeza didn't seem to present an immediate threat.

"Greetings, Caleeza of the lost expedition. What are you doing here?"

"I seek a way home."

"How did you get here, and how are Melinda and Leaf involved?"

"I walked here following the railroad tracks. Melinda and Leaf helped me. They gave me food and a place to stay."

Vince could hardly believe what he was hearing. Melinda and Leaf had a lot of explaining to do.

"How would you like to take a snowmachine ride?" Vince asked Caleeza. He might as well take her to the house so he and Maggie could find out what was going on.

"That is snowmachine?" Caleeza asked, pointing to it.

"Yes, you can sit behind me, okay?"

"Okay."

"Maggie! Melinda! Leaf!" Vince called upon entering the cabin and seeing no one. Activated by his summons, kids and Maggie poured out of the children's room. Upon seeing Caleeza at his side, Melinda and Leaf held back in realization that they were probably in big trouble. Maggie rushed forward.

"Oh, we have company!" she exclaimed, surprised by the appearance of a stranger in her remote home in the woods. Where could she have possibly come from?

"Maggie, this is Caleeza," Vince said.

"Greetings, Maggie Bradley, chosen mother of new person Melinda, new person Leaf, new person Rock, and new person Crystal. It is my honor to serve." Caleeza's formal salutation gave Maggie a valuable clue to her origin... which startled her even more.

Maggie warmly invited Caleeza into their home while Vince gave Melinda and Leaf a hard stare. "I believe the two of you and Caleeza have already met?" he said, the statement inflected as a question in which the answer was already known. With bowed heads...Leaf following Melinda's example...they both admitted to their guilt. Leaf, quickly deciding the period of contrition appropriately long enough, broke from rank.

"Caleeza!" Leaf exclaimed, running up to her and giving her a hug. She gently reciprocated, acknowledging his affection.

"Please, come have a seat where it's warm," Maggie said. Having helped Caleeza out of a much worn coat that was far too large for her, she guided her guest to the comfortable armchair. "I'll make us some tea," she said, heading for the kitchen.

"Where did you find her?" Maggie whispered to Vince in passing.

"In the schoolhouse," he whispered back. Melinda grabbed on to Leaf when he came into her vicinity and tried to back out of the room with him in tow.

"Hold it!" Vince called out, seeing the move. "I want the two of you over there on the sofa. You have a lot of explaining to do." Reluctantly, they complied, moving baby blankets aside before sitting down. Caleeza spotted the babies in a cushioned enclosed play area filled with baby toys.

"There are the babies!" she exclaimed.

"Would you like to hold one?" Vince asked.

"Oh, yes, may I?"

Vince lifted Rock from the playpen, placing him in Caleeza's arms. She gazed with wonder at the little person gazing back at her. Sensing a tiny bit of alarm on Rock's part over the unfamiliar arms holding him, she sent him happy reassurance. Soon Rock was smiling up at her.

Maggie returned with cups, spoons, sugar, and a selection of teas, placing the loaded tray on the coffee table in front of the sofa and armchair. A full teakettle already simmered on the woodstove. They chose tea flavors and Maggie filled cups with steaming water. Crystal, feeling neglect with Rock's absence from the playpen, began to cry. Maggie went to pick her up. With teacup in hand, Vince sat down in one of the rockers, waiting for Maggie to return to the gathering before asking questions. Crystal stopped crying as soon as she was picked up. Holding her daughter, Maggie took a seat in the other rocker.

"So, Caleeza, where are you from?" Maggie asked casually, although she could guess. Vince sat back and let Maggie do the questioning for now; she had some catching up to do, since he had already gathered some information.

"I am from the world of Theon, Quaylyn, and Councilor Anthya. I think you know them, yes?"

"Yes, of course. Have you brought news of Rahlys? What about Ilene, Theon, and Raven? Are they all right?" Caleeza took a deep breath before answering.

"I'm sorry; I have no news to share. You must miss them greatly," Caleeza said, reading Maggie's disappointment.

"So why *are* you here?"

"I'm not sure how I ended up on your world. One moment I was in the Crystalline Landscape, and the next I was in a land of ice and snow."

"Crystalline Landscape?" Maggie asked.

"Yes, a landscape of giant crystals surrounds Mt. Vatre in the center of the Devastated Continent," Caleeza said, telepathing stunning images. "It might have been energy from the crystals that transported me here."

"But that's where Rahlys and the others were headed," Maggie said.

"I'm a member of the expedition that set out long ago to explore the Devastated Continent. Melinda has informed me that your friends are on an expedition to find us."

"How do you know the kids?" Maggie asked at the mention of them. Maggie and Vince glanced at the kids, and then at each other. Leaf found it increasingly painful to remain still and began to fidget. Melinda kept a hand on his knee, giving him calming strength.

Kids...? Caleeza asked Melinda telepathically, not sure of the meaning.

She means us children, Melinda clarified. Caleeza sensed they were in trouble for harboring her. She had to find a way to make things right.

"I was traveling south along the railroad tracks when I detected someone drawing on the elemental forces. It led me to Leaf and Melinda. The children gave me food and a place to stay. They saved my life." Maggie stared hard at Leaf, unusually quiet, and even harder at Melinda, quieter still, sitting on the sofa.

"How long have you been staying at the schoolhouse?" Vince asked. There was a pause while Caleeza reviewed in her mind the calendar Melinda had taught her to follow.

"Four months," she said finally.

"Four months! Why, that's how old the twins are." Maggie said, turning her attention once again to Leaf and Melinda. "You have known about this for four months and you didn't tell us anything?" Maggie asked Melinda.

We found Caleeza just before we left on the train to have the babies, Melinda tried to explain. *We wanted to tell you, but you had other things on your mind, and she needed our help. When we got back, I didn't know how to broach the subject. Later, keeping her a secret had become a habit.*

"You said you found her. Found her where?" Maggie didn't use telepathy if she didn't have to. Speaking took far less effort.

At the schoolhouse. Melinda realized she shouldn't have said that as soon as she said it.

"You were at the schoolhouse without us knowing about it? When? How?" Maggie grew increasing upset.

Leaf would take us....

"Leaf would take you!" Maggie's heart skipped a beat.

"Leaf is very talented for one so young," Caleeza said in the way of praise.

"See, Mommy," Leaf said, "Caleeza says I'm talented."

Be quiet, Melinda warned. Maggie was speechless.

"I think you two should go to your room for now," Vince said, stepping in. "We will decide what will happen to you later."

Leaf and Melinda gladly departed.

Once in the children's room, Leaf went immediately to playing with books and toys, but Melinda sat in a corner worried. Would Vince and Maggie send her away as punishment?

"Elaine?" Angela pounded on the door to the apartment above the gift shop, and then adjusted the baby she carried in her arms and knocked again. "Elaine, it's me, Angela."

Roused from her stupor by the attention-demanding pounding, Elaine rose to open the door. Ilene's friend, Angela, stood in the doorway, holding her blanket-wrapped new baby, born two weeks premature. Elsie, Angela's mother, had stopped by to gloat about it just last week.

"Angela, come in," Elaine said. Hearing the furnace kick on, she rushed to close the draft, nearly catching Angela's coat in the door. The high cost of heating fuel was making it tough for her to make ends meet.

"I wanted to show you little Daniel," Angela said as bouncy as ever, unwrapping her tiny bundle in the warm apartment. "Isn't he just gorgeous," she said, holding him out proudly. Elaine took the little bundle of life into her arms and gazed at the infant's carefree continence. Her face cracked into a smile.

"He's indeed gorgeous. Congratulations! He is perfect," she said, examining his tiny features.

"How's Ilene?" Angela asked, helping herself to a seat on the sofa.

"She's fine." Elaine said, following her. Handing Daniel back to Angela, she sat down beside her. Since there was nothing more she could offer concerning Ilene, she tried to steer the conversation back to the baby. "Your mother is awfully proud of her little grandson."

"Do you know where she is?" Angela prodded.

"Who, your mother, she's at home, isn't she?"

"Not my mother...Ilene...do you know where she is?" Before Elaine could fabricate an answer, Angela gasped and pointed.

"Oh, look, the painting!" she cried, pointing to the portrait of the crystal, shining brightly in the night, perched on a snow-covered spruce bough. The holographic crystal floated away from its two-dimensional background. Created by Rahlys long ago, the painting had inexplicable qualities. Fear gripped Elaine's throat, choking off words. How could she explain this to Angela? She should have taken the painting back down long ago.

"It's all right," Angela said, seeing the distress in Elaine's face. "Ilene told me about the unusual painting." Elaine didn't know if she should feel relief at that or not.

"She told you?" Elaine's voice quivered. The holographic crystal moved closer.

"Yes...and I know Ilene is not off to college. I just hoped you had some news of her." *How much did Angela know?* Elaine wondered. Could she become an ally?

"We can ask the hologram about Ilene," she said timidly.

"Really?"

"Yes, it has magical powers."

"That I want to see."

Muscling up her courage, Elaine focused her thoughts, directing the inquiry to the floating translucent crystal.

"Is Ilene all right?" Elaine asked.

Without hesitation, the crystal glowed into action, burning an answer in the air.

YES.

"Awesome!" Angela exclaimed.

The word sparkled clearly before them, and then faded.

"Where is she?" Elaine asked, causing a blazing fanfare as the crystal wrote out its answer.

ON THE DEVASTATED CONTINENT.

"Wow!" Angela cried, otherwise speechless, watching the sparkling message fade.

"Will Ilene return soon?" Elaine asked hopefully. The crystal didn't hesitate in answering.

UNKNOWN.

Elaine covered her face with her hands and cried. She knew the holographic crystal could not predict the future, but still she could not resist asking. As though the crystal felt responsible for her tears, it returned to the painting in seemingly self-reproach. Angela put a comforting arm around Elaine, who quickly regained control.

"You must not tell anyone about this," she told Angela, in dire seriousness.

"I won't. I promise."

"Not even your mother or your husband." Elaine didn't really know Angela's husband, Steve, but she could imagine how her mother, Elsie, would react to all this.

"I promise I won't breathe a word to anyone," Angela reassured her. "You're to let me know if you learn anything new?"

"Yes, of course."

"I really should be going. I told Mother I wouldn't be long. I think she has the rest of the day planned out for us." Angela bundled baby Daniel back up.

"Follow me down to the shop on the way out," Elaine said, grabbing a set of keys. The shop had been closed for weeks, but as the days continued to get longer and warmer with the approach of spring, she needed to start opening up again, at least on weekends, only she hadn't felt any desire to do so. Once inside the shop, Elaine picked out a knitted cap and sweater set for Daniel, wrapped it in tissue paper, put it in a bag, and gave it to Angela.

"Oh, thank you so much!" The two women hugged as best they could with Daniel between them, and Angela rushed out the door. After she was gone, Elaine mindlessly puttered around the shop for a while, feeling emotionally a little better. The warm human contact had done her good. "I think I will open the shop tomorrow," she said to herself, and got busy putting things in order.

———•———

"The first life forms I met were the musk-oxen," Caleeza said, looking down at the map of Alaska spread out on the table before them. "I spent the night with them."

"What do you mean you spent the night with them? I've heard these animals will team up to charge if they feel threatened," Maggie said.

"I communicated with the first male, and he let me sleep next to him for warmth."

"My word!" was all Maggie could say.

"So let's see, how did you get from musk-oxen to the upper Susitna Valley?" Vince asked. Standing at the table, the three of them leaned further over to better see the map.

"I followed a long road."

"The only long road that runs that far north is the Dalton Highway. It takes off from the Elliott Highway, seventy miles north of Fairbanks, and runs all the way to Prudhoe Bay on the North Slope."

"A man named Stanley gave me a ride in his big truck across high mountains."

"That must have been the Brooks Range," Vince surmised.

"Tell us more about Stanley," Maggie inserted.

"He shared his food and water with me. He wanted to share more, so I left."

"Oh...."

"I found a shelter made of trees...logs," Caleeza corrected herself, "and I stayed there during a snowfall. That's where I found boots and coat to help keep me warm."

"I think I can find some spare boots and a coat around here for you to use that will fit you better."

"So you must have eventually intercepted with the Elliott Highway," Vince said, trying to stick to the subject.

"Yes, I keep going south." Caleeza's English wasn't perfect, but it was improving by leaps and bounds. "I see...I saw...more people and more trucks. There was a store with hotdogs to eat. Then I took a ride in another truck. We came to a large village with lots of lights."

"Do you mean Fairbanks?"

"Maybe."

"Then I found the trail for the train and followed it."

"The Alaska Railroad runs all the way from Fairbanks to Seward," Vince said, tracing the route on the map for Caleeza with his finger.

"Passing right through the Susitna Valley," Maggie added. "So that is how you found us."

"I want to go home, but I don't know how to go back to my world. I wait for Sorceress Rahlys' help to return home," Melinda heard Caleeza say from the other room.

Vince and Maggie hadn't sent Melinda away as punishment as she had feared, but she received a severe reprimand for encouraging Leaf to teleport and for not telling them about Caleeza. Leaf was only reprimanded for leaving the yard without permission.

Caleeza wasn't sent away either. Vince and Maggie understood immediately her need for help, and allowed her to continue to stay at the schoolhouse cabin. With a desire to learn about family life on Earth, Caleeza visited every day. She soon became part of the family, taking meals with them, helping with laundry and in the kitchen, and tending to the increasing demands of the twins.

In fact, Caleeza's presence made life easier for Melinda. No longer Maggie's prime helper around the house, she had more time to devote to her own interests: art, music, botany, geology, and astronomy. Her side of the children's room was already cluttered with her artwork and specimens. Soon, the snow would melt, allowing her to collect more.

Caleeza enjoyed the immersion into family life. She did all she could to help with the huge volume of work entailed in raising a large family, consequently learning volumes about foods, tools, language, and customs...as well as child care and development. Maggie brought relief to Caleeza's loneliness. For Maggie, Caleeza's presence helped in filling the void left by Rahlys' absence.

Rock and Crystal were growing fast, seemingly getting stronger by the day, and were much more aware now of those around them. It was fun to try and make the twins laugh, especially together, and Leaf proved best at making the babies cackle up a storm. They liked being held in an upright position so they could look around while pushing their feet against the floor or against someone's soft, warm lap as though they were walking. When placed on their stomachs, the twins pushed themselves up with their strong arms and kicked their feet, sometimes making a little progress across a surface. They had to be watched all the time. Their little hands grasped anything within reach, and everything went in their mouths!

"Melinda, come, we're going to play a game," Leaf informed her as he burst into the room.

What kind of game?

"Monotony."

What? Do you mean Monopoly?

"Monopoly," he repeated after her.

You're not old enough to play Monopoly.

"Uh-huh, Mommy and Daddy and Caleeza said I could play."

Okay, I'm coming. Leaf ran out the room while Melinda put a final stroke on the painting she had been working on, dropping her paintbrush into a jar of water on her desk.

Maggie was already setting up the game, with Leaf getting in the way in an effort to help, when Melinda joined the family gathering at the large table. Crystal was sleeping at the moment; Vince stood nearby entertaining Rock by pretending to throw him up into the air. Rock cooed with delight. Melinda helped Maggie count out money while Caleeza struggled to understand the rules of the game, which involved concepts unfamiliar to her like "money" and "property."

"You use the money to buy property," Maggie explained. "Then you can charge rent."

The game lasted most of the afternoon, with Leaf and Caleeza ending up with all of the property. While they played, Caleeza told stories of her adventures on the Devastated Continent, describing the rifted valley, the great Crescent Mountains, and the foreboding ruins of the Temple of Tranquility.

"We were at the ruins when Cremyn went missing. For many rotations, the expedition sent out search parties looking for her. She was finally found cowering in a tiny tunnel of jumbled fallen stones, her body still alive, but her mind gone. Ollen, another member of our party, volunteered to escort Cremyn back to the beach to intercept Captain Setas. Then Traevus disappeared while crossing the central plains. We searched for him for a long time, but never found him. Eventually, we gave up and moved on. But most of the members of our expedition were lost in the Crystalline Landscape...including me."

"But you're not lost, my dear, you're here with us," Maggie consoled her.

"If your friends have entered the Crystalline Landscape, they may be in great danger," Caleeza said.

"What kind of danger?" Vince asked.

"Sarus says that the giant crystals store energy, creating powerful energy fields. These are triggered when someone stumbles across them, transporting the victim to someplace unknown, possibly even into the cold depths of empty space."

The festive mood was crushed. Rahlys, Theon, Ilene, Raven, Quaylyn, and Anthya were in grave danger.

"If you knew the place was dangerous, why did you enter?"

"We didn't know such a place existed until we came to it. At first, it didn't occur to us to blame the crystals when Caponya vanished. Others had disappeared during the course of our mission, long before we arrived at the Crystalline Landscape. It wasn't until Selyzar vanished suddenly that we made the connection. By that time, we had already ventured deeply into the Crystalline Landscape, and the slopes of Mt. Vatre remained tauntingly out of reach."

"So when did Sarus tell you about the crystals' powers?" Vince asked.

"Sarus communicates with me in my thoughts and dreams." She told Vince and Maggie about her contacts with Sarus in the Crystalline Landscape, and his promise to try and bring her home. "I've informed him of the new expedition approaching, and he's agreed to try and help them." Caleeza didn't say anything about Sarus' claim that his mode of existence had changed...for she didn't understand it herself.

"Are you sure you are making contact across the galaxy?" Vince asked. "Dreams can seem very real."

"I have regular dreams about him, too," Caleeza admitted quietly, "but the contacts are not dreams; I can tell the difference."

Chapter 19
The Crystalline Landscape

"Keep an eye out for these rogues," Anthya cautioned the group. "Remember, one of them may be able to draw energy from the elemental forces." By the light of a new dawn, they moved on, pushing deeper into the interior of the continent.

"What do you think happened to the lost expedition?" Rahlys asked Quaylyn, marching beside her, after some quiet reflection of her own. "We've only found one grave marker. It's not likely they were attacked by wild animals or eaten by cannibals." She recalled stories of Earth explorers long ago venturing into wild unknown territories, and the fate they sometimes met along the way.

"I don't know, but I sure would like to find out." Quaylyn's dedication to the mission had become calmly focused. "We have to keep looking."

Rahlys didn't mention her increasing desire to go home. "Do you ever think about returning to Earth?...for a visit," she added as an afterthought.

"More and more every day." Before Rahlys could ponder what Quaylyn meant by such a reply, Ilene called from behind.

"Rahlys, wait for me!" Zayla's demise left an odd number of hikers. With Anthya keeping Brakalar under guard up front, Theon and Rojaire discussing the fermentation of zan fruit, and Rhalys and Quaylyn paired off, Ilene had ended up the odd one out for this leg of the hike. After stopping for a time to examine a small outcrop of rocks and crystals seemingly erupting from the level plain, Ilene found herself lagging far behind the others and was now struggling to catch up. Rahlys and Quaylyn paused to wait for her.

The sky brightened, the heat of the day intensified, and Rahlys fell to day-dreaming as the three of them hiked together. She heard Quaylyn answering Ilene's questions about the Academy as background noise, while she envi-sioned a hundred different scenarios of Quaylyn returning with her to her log home in the Susitna valley...and Vince and Maggie's delight over seeing him again. She was still daydreaming of home when Anthya brought the group to a halt at the edge of a narrow rocky ravine with water edged by foliage. Looking down, Rahlys estimated a fifty-foot drop to the bottom. Raven swooped down to take a closer look, giving Rahlys a better perspective.

"Let's see if we can find a way down there," Anthya instructed.

"I can place us down there," Rahlys offered.

With their consent, Rahlys teleported the members of the expedition to the rocky streambed below. A small crystal-clear stream flowed across the rocks just inches from their feet. There were abundant edible plants growing in the moist shady margin along the ravine walls to add to their diet of ground nuts and zan fruit that had been collected from above. Following the stream for a ways, they came to a dry cove of higher ground, shaded by the wall of the ravine, and set up camp.

"We should be reaching the Crystalline Landscape in another rotation or two," Anthya informed them when they had all settled down.

"I wonder what it will look like," Ilene said dreamily, tucking escaped curls behind her ears. There were always escapees from the bundle of curls she tried to keep tied back in tight control.

Rojaire was the only one among them to have actually seen the Crystalline Landscape. Throughout the journey, Rahlys and Quaylyn had asked Rojaire numerous questions which he did his best to answer...as best he could without pain. "There are inexplicable forces at work in the Crystalline Landscape," he told them repeatedly, warning about vague dangers.

"The crystals generate boundless energy," Rojaire warned yet again. "We should really reconsider our intention of entering the Crystalline Landscape."

"But how do you know the crystals are dangerous?" Ilene asked.

Rojaire fidgeted uncomfortably. There was still one bit of information he was reluctant to share. Detecting Rojaire's unease, Anthya took a stab at the problem.

"Now would be a good time to tell us what you have been holding back," she told him.

Startled out of composure, Rojaire knew he would have no choice. How did she know he was holding something back, he wondered, or was she just taking a stab in the dark? Anthya was not only a warrior, but also a mentor trained by Zayla. Had she learned this technique of stealth attack from her?

Visiting the memories he kept locked away was still painful, even after all this time, but he knew it was time to reveal all.

"I made a trip to the Devastated Continent before coming here with the band," he began. "I wasn't alone. Kaylya..." saying her name out loud hurt more than he had imagined it would, and he came to a choking stop. Quietly, Rojaire took a deep breath. "Kaylya, the woman of my heart, came with me. We explored much of the southwest and interior portions of the continent together, eventually reaching the Crystalline Landscape." Rojaire paused, giving himself a little time to better compose himself. No one spoke while anxiously waiting for him to continue.

"We had never seen anything like it before; so beautiful, and huge! We also suspected the landscape may be dangerous, so we studied the area's outer edge for many rotations, looking for danger and finding none. Then we made a fatal decision: We ventured in among the crystals. We weren't aiming to reach Mt. Vatre; we just wanted to study the crystal field a little more in depth." Rojaire took a deep breath.

"As I've told you before, moving through the landscape is slow and difficult, even across short distances. Kaylya was studying a crystal formation of particular interest to her and asked to use a tool I carried to dislodge a specimen. I was a short distance away from her, but there were obstacles between us, although she was in my line of sight. So to expedite matters, I tossed the tool to her...but she missed the catch...and the tool disappeared," Rojaire was finding it harder and harder to speak, "...and she went after it," Rojaire's voice choked with grief, "...and then she was gone." There was a respectful pause while Rojaire regained control.

"What do you mean she was gone?" Anthya asked gently.

"One moment she was there and the next she was gone. She simply vanished. I never found her." His voice broke again with the last statement. Ilene gazed at him in silent astonishment.

Rojaire became lost in thoughts of the past as images flooded his mind of Kaylya, images of a happier time, with just the two of them conquering a continent. He saw Kaylya breezing around in a light blue shift, combing out her long golden-brown hair in the sparkling sunlight, washing off the sandy grim after a long trek. And he saw Kaylya standing in the Crystalline Landscape, the crystals glowing all around her.

"It's so beautiful," Kaylya said in her soft musical voice. The Crystalline Landscape was indeed an incredible sight to behold! They were the first living beings to ever see it, and the magnitude of their find was not lost to them.

"Rojaire." Was she calling his name? "Rojaire," Anthya called for the second time. Realizing the summons was from the present, Rojaire pulled himself from his reminiscing.

"What do you think happened to Kaylya?"

"I'm not sure, but she must have gone somewhere."

Speculation over Kaylya's disappearance from the Crystalline Landscape so long ago gave the expedition members new concerns to reflect on as Rahlys teleported them out of the small canyon for the next leg of the hike. The worst of the heat had passed with the blazing sun targeted on the western horizon. To everyone's surprise, storm clouds were moving in from the south. The land could sure use the rain, Rahlys noted, but she didn't want to get caught camping in a ravine during a rainstorm.

It was nightfall before the rainstorm hit. The increasingly desolate landscape offered nothing in the line of shelter to the weary travelers. Rahlys drew energy, forming a small protective domed shield around them against the wind and rain, just large enough for them to stretch out in and get some sleep.

The storm proved to be more huff than puff, the rainfall amounting to little more than a sprinkle. The storm passed quickly, unveiling the star-studded sky, and Rahlys released the shield.

"We're almost there," Quaylyn said, indicating a soft glow visible on the northern horizon. The glow in the sky looked like the reflection of urban lights; but Rahlys knew that instead of a metropolis, they were approaching the Crystalline Landscape.

"Aren't you afraid what we might find there?"

"Fear isn't helpful unless you are trying to flee."

The trek across the interior of the continent had been long and relatively uneventful, and now they were in sight of their goal. They headed out again in the coolness of early dawn, hoping to cover as much ground as possible before the heat of the day. The sun had climbed its way up above the horizon, when Theon stopped to stare at the ground.

"Tracks," he announced, pointing out a partial boot print to Ilene that the unrealized storm had failed to erase.

"Do you think it's from the lost expedition?" Ilene asked, with sparked interest. They hadn't seen another living soul outside their group since their journey began. She had almost forgotten there were suppose to be other people on the continent.

"I don't think so," Theon said, finding a second boot print in another patch of dry sandy soil nearby. "These prints were probably made by Rojaire's former buddies." Rojaire and Anthya caught up with them, and Theon showed them the prints.

"How long ago?" Anthya asked.

"At least a rotation, maybe two."

Quaylyn, Brakalar, and Rahlys reached the rest of the group, and Raven flew in to take a rest. "Do you know of a place where we will be able to take shelter during solar noon?" Quaylyn asked Rojaire, already anticipating the oncoming heat.

"Yes, over the last rise just before we reach the edge of the crystal field. It's not much, but we will have some shade."

"What about food and water?" Both were becoming increasing scarce.

"There are zan fruit bushes nearly to the edge of the crystals and a few edible plants closer to the hillside."

Many grueling hours later, with only a few brief periods of rest, the team finally climbed the last rise, the vista before them bringing the group to a standstill. A short distance away, the Crystalline Landscape stretched to infinity, glowing brilliantly under a glowing hot sun, competing with its brightness.

"Travel through the terrain is best on a cloudy day, or at night, preferably by Seaa's light," Rojaire said. "It can be blinding in bright sunlight. Even starlight provides enough brightness to travel by, especially since the crystals themselves generate some light."

An even more welcomed sight greeted them when they reached the bottom of the rise. A trickle of spring water flowed over a rocky streambed, undercutting the foot of the rise, providing a bit of cool shade under a slight overhang of stone. Everyone gratefully crawled out of the sun, on hands and knees, into whatever shady space they could find. Raven came in for a landing, finding a nook of his own. They quenched their thirst, ate, rested, and speculated about the Crystalline Landscape, visible in the near distance even from where they nestled. Gradually, the area of shade around them blossomed as the sun passed its zenith, giving them more room to move around.

It was obvious from the tracks the site had been recently occupied. "There are four of them. I can read four distinct sets of footprints," Theon informed them after close inspection.

"That's impossible. There are only three of them."

"Then they picked up another one somewhere," Theon insisted.

When the worse of the heat died down, the expedition made their way across the last stretch of land to the edge of the landscape of crystals. They were not here to enter at this time, only to look.

The crystals radiating in all directions along the leading edge of the outcrop reached knee to shoulder-height. Further in, the structures towered over them. Thick multi-faceted transparent crystals grew out of more of the same, all the way down as far as they could see. Like icebergs floating in frigid waters, the crystals were twice as large below the surface as they were above.

"I've never seen anything so beautiful before in my life," Ilene whispered to Rahlys in awe. The crystalline maze gleamed colorfully in the bright sunlight.

"Neither have I," Rahlys agreed just as softly.

Rojaire and Quaylyn watched as Ilene and Rahlys strolled away with Raven flying circles overhead. Then Anthya joined Theon, heading in the opposite direction. Brakalar stood a short distance away, his face void of expression or emotion.

"Amazing," Quaylyn said, gazing out over the incredible scene before them. "Imagine the amount of energy such a large mass of crystals might be able to generate!"

"That, I believe, is its danger," Rojaire agreed. After a moment of reflection, he turned to Quaylyn, "Do you think the Crystalline Landscape could generate enough energy to tweak time and space?"

"I don't know; I guess it's a possibility. How far in did you go before Kaylya disappeared?"

"It's hard to say, traveling through this stuff," Rojaire made a sweep with his hand indicating the gleaming terrain, "but see that taller pinnacle in the distance? I would estimate we made it in at least that far."

"Any shelter to be found in there?" Quaylyn asked.

"Some. There are places where you can work your way down under layers of crystal, blocking off the direct rays of the sun." Suddenly, Quaylyn voiced a new concern. "I was just thinking. The Crystalline Landscape generates a lot of energy. What do you suppose would happen if someone tried to draw energy in such an environment?" The more he thought about it, the more Quaylyn's heart constricted with fear over Rahlys' safety.

"You're probably right," Rojaire agreed. "It could be very dangerous for anyone capable of drawing energy from the elemental forces. The flow of energy could become overwhelming."

Quaylyn's concern turned to panic. "Quick, we must warn the others. I'll go and tell Rahlys; you catch up with Theon. Tell him not to draw energy for any reason. Explain the possible danger." They parted, hurrying off in opposite directions, leaving Brakalar standing alone staring across the landscape.

"We're all going to die," he murmured to himself, gazing blankly out into the distance. "If I have to go, I might as well take the chest and rod with me."

"You can't track anything through this," Tassyn grumbled as the sun started to set. After several rotations and no expedition, Stram lost patience again, and ordered a move into the Crystalline Landscape. They were supposed to be following the rest of Traevus' expedition, but crystal did not lend itself to tracking. The going was tough. They'd been fighting their way in for nearly a rotation, making frustratingly little progress. Only the dark smudge, what was left of Mt. Vatre in the center of the horizon, kept them from becoming totally disoriented.

During the peak of the sun's cycle, they funneled through nooks and crannies, taking refuge under layers of crystals, and slept. The rest of the time, they climbed, crawled, slithered, and squeezed over, under, and through the crystalline maze.

"They're in here somewhere," Stram insisted. "We'll find them." He crawled through two crossing crystals, pressing on with determination. Tassyn paused, watching Stram pull away, and Traevus, his hands no longer bond, made his way over to him.

"What do you say, Tassyn?" Traevus whispered, conspiratorially. "We could have Edty distract Stram...he wouldn't expect anything from Edty...while you and I take him by surprise, knock him out, and take the stone from him. Then we can leave this place...alive." Life was a valuable commodity. Tassyn had to admit it was a tempting offer.

"Over here! Look what I found," Edty called to the others. "Water!" he said, pointing downward. Water was another valuable commodity. The men made their way to where Edty stood and pointed. Beneath several layers of crystal, water flowed teasingly out of reach.

"I can take care of that!" Stram boasted. "Get back a ways! I'm going to blast a hole through this glass."

"What, you want to kill us all?" Tassyn warned with images of flying fragmented crystal propelled over great distances crossing his mind. "There would be glass flying everywhere."

"Tassyn's right. We don't want to be butchered by flying glass. Besides, that water is way down there."

Stram had half a mind to ignore their warnings and blast anyway when a loud unidentifiable squawk distracted him, drawing his undivided attention.

"Aaaarrrrrk! Aaaaarrrrk!"

"What in the name of Seaa's light is that?" Tassyn swore his mouth agape. "Aaaarrrrk! Aaaaarrrrk!"

Raven had taken it upon himself to explore the strange land of crystals ahead of the rest of the expedition. He wanted to know what Rahlys was getting into, not that she would heed any warnings. Spotting the men, he circled and landed on a crystal pinnacle to observe.

"It's a bird!" Traevus said, with astonishment. "Imagine...a bird!"

"Will it try to eat us?" Edty asked, his voice trembling. "It certainly is big."

"Not before I can blast it apart," Stram assured him, trying to hide his own fear.

"Where did it come from?" Tassyn asked, looking for more.

"You saw it came from the sky!" Stram shouted with unease. "Aaaaarrrrk! Aaaaarrrrk!" Raven cried out again, establishing his dominance. The Band of Rogues cowered under outcrops of crystal, seeking protection from the ferocious black predator with wings. Only Traevus remained out in the open, observing the flying creature with fascination.

Stram, Tassyn, Edty, and Traevus were not alone in their observation of Raven. Connected to the crystals, his access to their power unlimited, Sarus had become aware of the presence of the Band of Rouges as soon as they had entered the Crystalline Landscape and had been following their progress since.

There is the raven that Caleeza told me about; Anthya's expedition must be very near, Sarus reasoned. *But who are these other men and where had they found Traevus? They are not part of Anthya's expedition.*

Awareness over his domain had been an easy skill to master, compared to learning how to use the energy resources at hand to bring Caleeza home. That had proven very challenging, but Sarus was ready to try it, especially since a test subject had conveniently arrived. He needed to bring Caleeza home so she could warn the others of the danger; he just wanted some reassurance he could bring her back safely. Sarus decided to send the raven back to its own world first. If the bird arrived safely, he was ready to bring Caleeza home.

Traevus and the Band of Rogues kept their eyes targeted on the strange beast. Starting to feel like a coward for hiding while Traevus stood out in the open, Stram decided to take action.

"I'll get rid of it," he said, crawling out to join Traevus. At that moment, the raven spread its wide wings preparing to fly off, when it vanished before their eyes.

"Where did it go?" Edty cried. The men searched frantically around them, fearing a surprise attack from the strange creature. But the flying creature was nowhere to be found.

"I'm getting out of here," Tassyn decided on the spot and headed for the outer edge of the Crystalline Landscape. The others, equally spooked, followed without a word.

———————

Where's Raven? Rahlys wondered, searching the empty sky. He had flown off to scout ahead, what felt like hours ago, and still hadn't returned. She reached out mentally to find him, but couldn't detect his signature anywhere.

"Raven is missing," she announced to the group, busily packing up their personal belongings. Their water containers and harvest bags were full in preparation for departure. Today, they were venturing into the Crystalline Landscape.

"He will show up again," Ilene tried to reassure her. Quaylyn was not so certain. Had Raven triggered one of the crystals' energy fields? Soon, the expedition stood gathered at the edge of the softly glowing landscape.

"Before we enter, I want everyone to gather a pouch full of small stones," Anthya told the group standing ready to venture forth. "We will use these stones as a safety precaution. Always cast a pebble ahead of you before advancing. If the pebble lands, we will assume at least that distance is safe, but if the pebble disappears without touching the ground, do not advance."

Understanding how this may save their lives, the team set to work gathering pebbles. They were numerous and easy to find, and soon the expedition was once again ready to advance.

"We will make our way toward that taller pinnacle," Anthya said, giving them a focal point to steer toward. It was the same pinnacle of crystal Rojaire had pointed out to Quaylyn when asked how far he and Kaylya had gone into the Crystalline Landscape. "Make it that far and we will decide what we should do from there."

As they had been warned many times, the going was slow. The precaution of casting pebbles before them made the going even slower, but the resounding 'pings' made by tossed pebbles bouncing on solid crystal were reassuring. Rahlys was further impeded by her constant search for some sign of Raven, fervently watching for his appearance, while in her heart, dreading the worse.

As darkness descended, the crystals themselves lit the way. When they finally stopped to eat and rest, Raven still had not returned. Seeing how dejected Rahlys looked, Ilene momentarily placed a comforting arm around her shoulders, giving her a little hug, but said nothing.

By Seaa's light and the light from the crystals, they moved on, the crystalline pinnacle they navigated by still beckoning from a distance. Rahlys reached out mentally, time and time again, searching for Raven, but to no avail. Somehow she had to learn to accept that he was gone.

DANGER IMMINENT!

Rahlys gasped, pulling herself back to a quick halt. Terror gripped her heart, paralyzing her with fear. Because of her distraction over Raven, she had forgotten to toss another pebble before moving forward. Her heartbeat raced. Taking a deep breath to calm herself, she threw a pebble...only to see it vanish before her! Spotting Quaylyn only a few paces off to her right, she cried out to him.

"Quaylyn! The pebble...it vanished!"

"Okay, don't move." He could detect her distress, or was that his own heart pumping hard in fear of losing her? "You'll be all right," he said to calm her... or himself...he wasn't sure which.

He reached into his pouch for a pebble. "Here, catch!" he told her, tossing it her way. Rahlys made the catch. "Good," he said, smiling encouragingly, "now, make your way toward me."

Rahlys took a couple of tenuous steps over stubby crystals...and soon found herself in his comforting arms, Quaylyn having closed the distance quickly to reach her. "You're safe," he whispered, holding her close to him.

I am safe, Rahlys thought, *but Raven is still gone*. She allowed herself a moment of quiet release in his soothing embrace, before pulling away.

"Is everyone all right?" Anthya asked, making her way toward them.

"Oomph!"

Heads turned toward Theon who had just slipped, landing on the seat of his pants a short distance away. "Damn crystals!" Brakalar, standing next to Theon, reached down to give him a hand getting back up...or so everyone thought, including Theon. Catching him...and everyone else...completely off guard, Brakalar took advantage of Theon's compromised position wedged between crystals. In one fluid motion, Brakalar wrenched the pack Theon carried off his shoulder, and before anyone could respond, dove for the location where Rahlys' pebble had disappeared.

"Brakalar, no!" Anthya cried out, when she saw what was happening. It was too late. Brakalar, with the rune-covered chest containing the Rod of Destruction in his possession, vanished into oblivion.

"He's gone!" Ilene gasped.

"And he escaped with the rod," Theon added, still resting on his hind side. Ilene tossed a pebble his way, hitting him on the back, and then made her way toward him to help him up.

"Did he really escape with the rod, or did he destroy it along with himself?" Anthya asked, once Theon was again standing. No one knew the answer.

"Look! Someone's coming!" Ilene shouted, pointing in the direction the group had been headed. Rahlys counted four men making their way toward them.

"It must be the Band of Rogues," Rojaire guessed. As the men drew closer, he pointed out Stram, Tassyn, and Edty to Anthya. "I don't know the fourth person."

"I do," she said, watching the men approach. "It's Traevus, a member of the lost expedition."

"You mean we've actually found a member of the lost expedition?" Ilene asked, incredulously.

Upon seeing them, the Band of Rogues halted their frantic pace, coming to a stop. "Stay put," Stram ordered, working his way a few paces ahead of the others to take charge. Clutching the golden stone in one hand, he addressed the expedition.

"I am Stram, ruler of the Devastated Continent. State your business here."

"What did he say?" Rahlys whispered to Quaylyn, still standing beside her.

"Nothing good," he said, turning to her. "Listen, whatever happens, do not attempt to draw energy. I have a really bad feeling about this."

"All right I won't, or at least not until you tell me to."

Anthya took her time in replying, scrutinizing the group carefully. "By what authority do you claim to rule the Devastated Continent?"

"Councilor Anthya!" Traevus said, recognizing her voice, surprised to come across her...here...of all places!

"Quiet," Stram roared, turning toward Traevus, "you do not have permission to speak." With Traevus subdued, he turned back toward Anthya. "I am the highest authority and you, all of you, are my prisoners." Then, to Stram's surprise, his eyes rested on their old companion.

"Rojaire!" he exclaimed suddenly, spotting him among the group. "So you finally joined a real expedition." Rojaire didn't deign to answer.

"What makes you think you can take us as prisoners?" Anthya asked, drawing Stram's attention back to the business at hand.

"I have this," Stram said, extending his hand to show her the stone.

"You are going to need more than one stone," she said calmly. "I will show you what one stone can do," Stram answered threateningly.

Thinking he would send Anthya flying, Stram began to draw energy from the elemental forces around him. He focused mentally, aiming physically at his target. Almost immediately, he realized his mistake as an immense flood of unstoppable, surging hot energy swept through his body. Stram's eerie howls filled the air as swirls of searing energy twirled off the top of Stram's head, his eyes seared wide with shock, his burnt-out body beginning to glow.

"Get down!" Quaylyn shouted in warning, shielding Rahlys with his own body, as everyone scrambled for safety.

Boom!

Stram was consumed in a glittering, colorful explosion of light, the explosion reverberating through the crystals. The group watched enthralled as a shower of glittering fireworks momentarily arched through the sky.

When the air cleared, the group was pleased to discover that no one else had been hurt. With Stram's destruction, Traevus had been freed from the Band of Rogues and quickly joined the members of the expedition, while Tassyn and Edty stood by helplessly, their future undecided.

"Where are the others?" Anthya asked Traevus when they had regrouped.

"Cremyn lost her mind in the ruins of the Temple of Tranquility. Ollen escorted her back to the beach to intercept with Captain Setas."

"They never made it," Anthya informed him. "We found Cremyn's grave marker. There was no sign of Ollen. What about Sarus, Caleeza, Selyzar, and Caponya?" Anthya asked Traevus.

"In the Crystalline Landscape, I suppose. I was kidnapped by the Band of Rogues while we were crossing the central plains. Stram, the recently deceased leader of this pitiful band, got the notion in his head he would use his power to enslave the rest of the expedition, to build a monument to honor him...or something like that." Tassyn and Edty hung their heads in guilt.

"We had no choice," Tassyn explained. "Stram was in control."

The three men who had joined them did not speak English, so the interaction between Anthya, Traevus, Tassyn, and Edty was unintelligible to Rahlys and Ilene. Quaylyn explained what had transpired.

"Ask them if they've seen Raven," Rahlys requested. Quaylyn, knowing Rahlys was heartbroken over Raven's disappearance, posed the question as she telepathed images of her familiar. Her heart soared over their response.

Yes, they had seen Raven!

Chapter 20
Across the Galaxy

"Aaaaarrrk! Aaaaarrrk!"

Trees! Snow! Blue skies! Vince and Maggie's nest!

"Aaaaarrrk! Aaaaarrrk!" Raven squawked, elated to be home. But something was missing. Where's Rahlys? He reached out mentally searching for her signature...but she was nowhere to be found.

"Aaaaarrrk! Aaaaarrrk!" Raven cried in despair.

Raven's raucousness brought the whole Bradley family...with babies in arms, and Caleeza joining them...spilling out the door. "It's Raven!" Vince said, using his limited telepathic skills to confirm it.

Welcome back old friend. Where are the others?

"Aaaaarrrk!"

Raven telepathed images of Rahlys, Ilene, and Theon at the edge of a land of crystals under a pale golden sky. In addition to the pictures, they could also pick up on Raven's concern for Rahlys' safety, and his distress over the separation.

"How did you get back?" Vince asked vocally as well as telepathically.

Raven didn't know how he got back, but he tried to show what happened in telepathed images. They saw Raven flying over the magnificent landscape of crystals when he spotted four men down below. Wishing to better observe the men before reporting back to Rahlys, he landed on a tall octagonal crystalline pinnacle nearby. Vince and Maggie didn't recognize any of the faces in the images Raven shared, but Caleeza, also reading Raven's recollections, did.

"There's Traevus," she cried out. "He disappeared mysteriously while we were crossing the central plains."

In his distress over Rahlys, Raven had failed to notice the stranger among his friends, until she spoke. Responding to instinct, he flew up into a tree to put some distance between them.

Raven, this is Caleeza, a member of the lost expedition, Melinda informed him. *You need not be afraid.* Caleeza stepped forward on the hard packed snow.

Greetings, Raven, warrior of the sky, familiar of Sorceress Rahlys, Guardian of the Light. It is an honor to serve.

Having been duly honored and reassured, Raven responded to the group's urges for him to continue. In an effort to explain what happened next, Raven projected an image of himself perched on the monolithic crystal under a golden sky, followed by an image of himself standing on the snow in Vince and Maggie's yard, repeating the sequence a couple of times. One moment he was there, the next thing he knew, he was here.

"Sarus must have sent Raven home," Caleeza said, with renewed hope. "Raven could have perched near an energy field, but then what would be the odds he would arrive right here in your backyard? Only Sarus could have gotten it so right," she said with confidence.

* * *

After returning to the schoolhouse that evening, Caleeza decided to take care of one piece of unfinished business. Maggie had long ago found a spare pair of boots for Caleeza to wear, closer to her size, and a soft down jacket that didn't threaten to crackle to pieces when she put it on. She had also passed down to her numerous articles of clothing. It was time for her to return the items she had borrowed to the log cabin up north. She could simply send the clothing back without returning in person, but she wanted to see the little cabin that had sheltered her from the storm one more time.

Carrying the old clothing in her arms, Caleeza recalled the site in her mind, placing herself in the protective copse of trees where she had first spotted the shelter all those months ago. Winter still had a firm grip up here; the wind blew hard and cold. She huddled down in the copse of trees, searching for presence in the little log structure that stood so stoically against the ravages of nature and time.

After confirming the cabin still remained empty, Caleeza teleported herself inside. The small interior of the shelter was cold and dark. Forming a glow globe for light, she deposited the boots back under the counter and carefully folded the coat and other items, placing them back in the cardboard boxes.

Thank you, she said silently. Then, after a brief nostalgic look around, she teleported back to the little schoolhouse.

She tried to sleep, but after many sleepless hours in anticipation of Rahlys' imminent arrival, Caleeza gave up on sleep for the night. Sarus or Rahlys, eventually, one of them was bound to help her return home.

Caleeza! Sarus reached out to her. With the crystals at his disposal, he had no difficulty reaching across the galaxy, but it was easier for Caleeza to perceive him when she was sleeping than when she was awake.

Caleeza!

Sarus pierced her awareness.

Sarus?

Did the raven arrive safely?

Yes.

Then I can bring you home.

Without further warning, Caleeza felt the world around her dissolve away. It was finally happening; she was going home. Soon, she was standing barefooted among the glowing crystals wearing the pale blue cotton nightgown and dark blue robe Maggie had given her. Mt. Vatre rose darkly in the near distance. All her perceptions, from the sharp hardness of crystal under her feet to the cool dryness of the spring evening, told her it was real.

"Sarus?" Caleeza called timidly.

Caleeza, you must warn the others of the danger. I will tell you what to say.

"Sarus, where are you?" There was a moment of silence, and then suddenly Sarus appeared.

"I have generated an image of my former self to make it easier for you."

"Sarus, what has happened to you?"

How could he explain? He had lost his physical self, but had gained so much. And there was still so much to learn.

"I have become one with the crystals, and the crystals are connected with the universe...multi-universes! Caleeza, I have learned so much. Infinity is such a wondrous place!"

"Teach me...that I may also learn," Caleeza said, taking a step closer to the mere image of a man she had once loved. If what he claimed was true, then never again would they embrace. Never again would she feel his tenderly warm touch. Still, in her heart she loved him, what little of his human nature he had left. Did he still love her? Did he remember how to love? "Sarus, I love you; I want to stay with you. You need me. Without me, you will lose touch with your human self."

His mind overflowing with new wonders, Sarus gave little thought to the romantic relationship he and Caleeza once shared. Did he need companionship even in his new existence? Caleeza still professed undying love and a desire to be with him. But could he ask her to give up existence as she knows it...just to be with him?

Of course, the answer was no.

"That is a sacrifice I can't let you make. The Crystalline Landscape is unsafe for humans."

"But I would have you to protect me!" There was a long silence as she waited for him to express an emotion he was no longer subject to.

"I remember love."

Caleeza detected a hint of sadness, even loneliness in his words. Sarus had not become completely devoid of emotion after all...at least not yet.

"I will never let you forget love, Sarus...or sadness or joy. I will be your link to humanity. Send the others away to protect them, if that is your plan, but please...let me stay to serve." Again, there was a pause before he spoke.

"I will send those of Earth back to Earth," Sarus told her. "The others I will return to the Community of the High Council. It will take some time before another expedition can return here. You may stay until then."

———

The expedition of nine, with the loss of Zayla, Raven, and Brakalar, had been reduced to six, but the addition of Traevus, Tassyn, and Edty brought the number back up to nine. Anthya told the newcomers about the space-time warps the crystals formed and the danger of ending up somewhere unknown, or more likely, ending up in the void of outer space. She explained the use of the pebbles and how one such disaster had already been averted.

"What happens when we run out of pebbles?" Edty asked.

"Then we will come up with another plan," Anthya said. "If everyone is rested, we need to move on."

"You're going deeper in there?" Tassyn asked, amazed at this point that anyone would want to continue on.

"We still know nothing of the other four members of Traevus' expedition. Their goal was Mt. Vatre."

"You may still know nothing of them even after you reach Mt. Vatre... assuming these pebbles help you get there. If what you just said is true, those people are more than likely gone."

Unable to follow the discussion between Anthya and the three newcomers, Rahlys' thoughts turned back to Raven.

After a moment, Rahlys realized her eyes were closed. Had she nodded off standing up? She opened her eyes, but all she could see was a kaleidoscope of colored light flashing by. Suddenly, cold air engulfed her and she was standing in knee-deep snow.

A cold breeze ruffled bare birch branches and dark-green spruce boughs, helping them shake off their heavy burden of fresh spring snow, sending the snow load cascading down to the ground. Ilene wobbled beside her.

"Ilene, we're home!" Rahlys shouted and Ilene jerked to alertness.

"We're home," Ilene whispered, gazing around at the snowy woods and Rahlys' cabin glowing softly in dappled sunlight. "Where's my father?" Theon was not with them.

Rahlys reached out mentally searching for him, but it soon became clear he had not returned with them.

"He's not here," Rahlys confirmed, heating the air around them to cloak them in warmth, "but that doesn't mean he isn't safe." Then she thought of Raven. With a heavy heart, she sent out another feeler...finding his signature!

"Raven...he's here!" Rahlys shouted with delight. Raven felt her summons from his perch in his special tree above the bears' favorite fishing spot along the creek.

"Aaaaarrrk! Aaaaarrrk!"

He flew off, cawing raucously all the way to her. Upon arriving, Raven circled low over the two women, assuring himself they were really there, then landed on the snow-covered roof of Rahlys' still full woodshed.

"Aaaaarrrk! Aaaaarrrk!"

"Yes, I'm so glad to see you, too! I'm afraid I have nothing for you at the moment." But Raven didn't care. Having Rahlys back was better than any treat. Then Rahlys thought of Maggie, Vince, Melinda, and Leaf... .

Maggie! It's Rahlys. Ilene and I have made it back. It took Maggie a moment to absorb the news and respond.

Rahlys, where are you?

We are home. We're coming over! Rahlys teleported Ilene with her to Vince and Maggie's log home just a mile away as the raven flies, leaving Raven to follow on his own.

"Maggie! Vince! We're here!" Rahlys shouted from outside as they approached the door. They could already hear Raven's raucous approach in the distance. The door flew open with Maggie rushing out and Maggie and Rahlys shrieked into a joyful embrace.

Melinda appeared next, rushing up to Ilene to give her a hug. *Ilene, welcome back.*

"Melinda, it's so good to see you," Rahlys said, studying her carefully when Maggie finally let her go. "Looks like you've grown?" The frightened young girl she had rescued from Droclum's lair just a few years ago had become a young woman.

"Rahlys! Ilene!" Vince shouted, arriving on the scene. He gave them warm hugs.

"How long have we been gone?" Ilene asked. "What's today's date anyway?"

"It's April fifteenth; you made it home in time for breakup," Maggie said.

"You've been gone for eight months," Vince clarified. "Raven returned days ago, so we were hopeful you would soon follow. Where's Theon?"

"Still in the Crystalline Landscape, on the Devastated Continent, I fear," Ilene said. "How's my mother? Does anyone know?"

"She's fine," Maggie said. "Angela had a little boy, by the way."

"Oh, that's wonderful! What did she name him?"

"I'm sure Elsie told me, but I forgot. You'll have to ask her."

"Aaaaarrrrk! Aaaarrrrk!" Raven squawked, fast approaching.

"There's part of a muffin Leaf felt behind from breakfast on the counter," Maggie told Melinda. Melinda rushed in to fetch the half eaten muffin, returning just as Raven landed in the yard. She tossed it to him.

"Come on in," Vince said, holding the door open for them. An exchange of air in the house was always welcomed on a spring day.

"It's quiet in here," Rahlys said upon entering, "where is...." At that moment, Leaf bounded out of the children's room into the family room. Both women gasped. Eight months had made a big difference in the pint-sized wizard, transforming him from toddler to little boy.

"You remember Rahlys and Ilene," Maggie encouraged him.

"Rahlys and Ilene," Leaf said, pronouncing their names perfectly. Leaf wasn't sure if he remembered them or not, but allowed them to hug him. As though on cue, the twins woke up from their naps, a tentative cry coming from the bedroom.

"I hear a baby," Rahlys said, grinning with anticipation. She and Ilene followed Maggie into the bedroom where two six-month old babies with fiery red hair and emerald green eyes squirmed in their cribs.

"Father was right, it's twins!" Ilene gasped. The babies cooed with delight as Maggie opened the curtains to let in more light. Rock had already managed to flip over onto his stomach.

"Did you have a nice nap?" Maggie cooed back at them, picking up her little son. "Ready to get up and play?"

"Oh, Maggie, they're beautiful!" Rahlys said with some regret over not being here for their birth.

"What are their names?" Ilene asked. "This is Rock," Maggie said, handing him to her.

"Rock Bradley, what a fine name," Rahlys said taking him. "And this is...."

"Wait!" Rahlys said quickly. "Don't tell us; let us guess. Is the other one a girl?"

"Yes." Maggie picked up her little daughter; her tiny lips pursed, threatening to cry. She cuddled Crystal gently against her chest. "Wake up."

"Let's see, we have a Leaf and a Rock. We need a name for a girl. How about Star, or Creek, or Tree?"

"We don't know anyone by those names, do we?" Maggie whispered to the little girl nestling against her.

"It's your turn to guess," Rahlys said, turning to Ilene.

"Can it have more than one syllable?"

"Of course, girls are far more complex than boys," Maggie said.

"Leaf and Rock," Ilene said "...something to go with Rock...like Jewel, or Diamond...ahhhhh, I know what it is...Crystal! That's it, isn't it, Rock and Crystal!"

"What do you think of that, Crystal?" Maggie whispered in her ear, and Crystal finally erupted into wakeful tears.

The babies were changed and fed and the Bradley family and their guests gathered together in the family room, the afternoon turning into a celebration. Vince poured wine and offered to cook dinner, with Melinda volunteering to help, giving the ladies a chance to visit and play with the children. This in no way hindered Vince and Melinda from joining in the conversation, which they clearly heard from the kitchen, causing them to frequently emerge with a knife or spoon in hand to make a point.

"How's Quaylyn? Did you give him our letter?" Maggie asked.

"Yes, and I'm sure he would have replied given the chance," Rahlys said, explaining the circumstances of their departure.

"A member of your lost expedition was here," Vince informed them coming out to join the conversation. Ilene and Rahlys were stunned by the news.

"Who?" they asked in near unison.

"Her name is Caleeza. She stayed in the schoolhouse."

"I found her," Leaf spoke up, excited about all the company and wanting to be part of the action.

"You will want to use the firewood on the right side of your woodshed first, Rahlys. The wood on the left side has been replaced with green wood," Vince added quickly, returning to kitchen to stir his pot.

"Caleeza was second in command of the lost expedition," Ilene said, having memorized the names of those they had searched for.

"What was she doing here? And where is she now?" Rahlys added.

"We're not sure. Caleeza seemed to think she was in some kind of intermittent communication with another member of her expedition, Sarus, who was, supposedly, in the Crystalline Landscape," Maggie tried to explain. "She said Sarus was trying to bring her home. Then, a couple of days ago, she vanished without a word."

"Was this before or after Raven arrived?"

"Caleeza was here when Raven arrived. She recognized one of the men Raven saw before returning, another member of her expedition that had disappeared along the way. Did you find the rest of the lost expedition?" Maggie asked.

"We found only that one member of the lost expedition. He had been captured by the men Raven saw him with," Rahlys said. "We also found a grave marker."

"Dinner will be ready soon," Vince said, refilling the ladies' wine glasses as he and Melinda sat down to join them.

"I killed a wolf," Leaf told the visitors proudly, stunning the crowd to silence.

"What?" Rahlys asked cautiously. She knew Leaf had started to demonstrate uncanny abilities before she left to go on the mission. He had even teleported to her house. What was Leaf capable of now?

"He saved Maggie's life," Vince added calmly. Rahlys could tell the subject was not an easy one for Maggie and steered the conversation to the birth of the twins. Vince, Maggie, and Melinda described the trip through a snowstorm the night the babies were born and the wonderful home coming George had arranged.

After a fabulous dinner of long-missed foods, Ilene and Rahlys took turns telling of their adventures. Ilene described the Community of the High Council and the Devastated Continent...the birth land of her father...with great fervor. And Rahlys told the story of the Rod of Destruction; its discovery in the Sooty Caves, Zayla's death in the ruins of the Temple of Tranquility, and Brakalar's later demise in the Crystalline Landscape. Long after the children had been put to bed, the friends...friends glad to be together again... continued to laugh and tell stories until well into the morning.

—·—

Ilene was pleasantly surprised to find the gift shop opened and her mother serving a customer. The scene helped to dispel some of the images she had harbored in her mind of her mother alone and depressed. She waited outside out of sight until the customer left before entering. Her mother looked up right away.

"Hi, Mom! I'm home!" Ilene announced, coming toward her.

"Ilene!" Elaine shook with emotion. "Ilene!" she cried, rushing to her. Elaine had never expected to see her daughter again; that she was here seemed nothing short of a miracle. Ilene embraced her mother for a long time, soothing her tremors.

"All is okay, Mom! I'm home and I won't be leaving again for quite some time."

"Angela had her baby, a little boy she named Daniel," Elaine said, when emotions subsided enough for her to speak. "She brought him by to visit."

"That's wonderful, I can't wait to see him, and Angela, too."

"Did...Theon return with you?" Elaine asked, using his real name.

"No," Ilene said quietly, "he's still there." Ilene tried not to show her concern. "Have you kept the shop opened all winter?" she asked, focusing her attention on her mother, who seemed to have aged greatly while she was gone.

"No, the shop has been closed until this weekend," Elaine admitted.

"We have a lot of catching up to do, Mom. What do you say I help you close up the shop and we order a pizza," Ilene suggested.

Comfortably settled on the living room sofa, a half eaten pizza on the coffee table, Ilene patiently answered all of her mother's questions as she described her incredible adventures in vivid detail. Later that evening when mother and daughter were talked out, Ilene beckoned the holographic crystal from the painting still hanging on the wall. Ilene wanted to know what happened to Theon and the others after she and Rahlys returned to Earth. The glowing crystalline image darted across the room and spun around as though glad to be of service.

"Does Theon live?" Ilene asked, projecting her thoughts. She held her breath, fearful of the answer, as the ephemeral crystal blazed a sparkling path.

YES.

Ilene released an audible sigh of relief.

"Where is he?" she asked, now that she could breathe easier. The crystal zoomed about, blazing an answer across the room.

THEON IS HOME.

"Is he happy?" Ilene asked, a bit forlorn. It was a quick answer.

YES.

And with that, the crystal promptly returned to the painting.

———·———

Spring, a wonderful time of year! Trees leafing! New green shoots sprouting! *So why don't I feel as jubilant as I should,* Rahlys wondered? May sunshine streamed in through the window, begging her to smile. Rahlys glanced at the painting in progress resting on her easel. It was not of budding leaves and boreal forest, but of a land far away with golden skies, lavender soils, zan fruit bushes, and zaota trees.

Mostly, she thought of Quaylyn and his teasing glacial blue eyes, his dimpled smile, and that boyish charm that often made her laugh. He had been through so much, yet his true nature had been re-emerging as the emotional wounds healed. *A month has passed since the expedition, and still there is no news from Anthya,* Rahlys fretted. *Did the rest of the expedition make it safely out of the Crystalline Landscape?* she wondered.

"Aaaaarrrk!" Raven called, drawing her attention. Throwing on a light jacket, she grabbed her uneaten apple slices and waltzed out into the sunshine. It felt unexpectedly warm, she thought, as Raven came in for a landing beside her.

"Nice spring day we are having here, my fine-feathered friend. What brings you for a visit?" A vision of her hand holding apple slices formed in her head.

"Here you go. You deserve them," she said tossing the apple slices to him.

QUAYLYN APPROACHES.

The oracle's message resonated in her brain.

Quaylyn was coming! Suddenly, she felt flustered. How should she prepare? What should she do? Would he arrive in permanent or non-permanent physical time? Before she could give much thought to any of these considerations, Quaylyn appeared before her, casting a solid shadow in the bright sunlight.

"Aaaaarrrk!" Raven cried in startled greeting. Taking the last slice of apple with him, he flew up to the peak of the woodshed roof. Rahlys' heart fluttered as Quaylyn took a step toward her.

"Greetings, Sorceress Rahlys, Guardian of the Light...light of my heart. It is my honor to serve," Quaylyn greeted her, his dimpled smile lighting up blue eyes filled with love for her.

"Greetings, Warrior Quaylyn...warrior of my heart," she whispered softly to him. "It's a pleasure to be served."

"I have something for you," Quaylyn said, reaching into a large pouch that hung from his belt. He pulled out a much smaller one, made of woven zaota leaves, and handed it to her.

Rahlys opened the little pouch and poured the contents into her hand. She stared down at the star stone. It was accompanied by a note.

I promised I would give it back to you.

Theon

"How is Theon? Is he all right?"

"Theon is fine. He will probably outlive us all."

"What about the others? Did everyone make it back safely? Did you find the rest of the lost expedition?"

"Moments after you and Ilene vanished, the rest of us arrived at the Academy gardens, bringing an abrupt end to the expedition."

"So now the High Council has sent you to Earth on a new mission? What is your objective this time?"

"It's a mission of the heart...and the High Council is not involved." Quaylyn stepped closer, gently taking her hand.

Rahlys narrowed the gap between them, her heart pounding wildly, her vision blurred by tears. "Perhaps, you could tell me more about it."

"I intend to," Quaylyn said as their lips met, and Rahlys and Quaylyn fell into an urgent embrace.

"Aaaaarrrk!" Raven squawked in distaste and flew off over the leafing forest.